152

THE WAY TO ST. IVES

Other books by Sonia Gernes

THE MUTES OF SLEEPY EYE *(poems)*
BRIEF LIVES *(poems)*

THE
WAY
TO
ST. IVES

Sonia Gernes

CHARLES SCRIBNER'S SONS
New York

For my brother Norb

Copyright © 1982 Sonia Gernes

Library of Congress Cataloging in Publication Data

Gernes, Sonia.
  The way to St. Ives.

  I. Title. II. Title: Way to Saint Ives.
PS3557.E685W3   813'.54   82–636
ISBN 0–684–17492–8   AACR2

3 5 7 9 11 13 15 17 19 F/C 20 18 16 14 12 10 8 6 4 2

Printed in the United States of America.

As I was going to St. Ives,
I met a man with seven wives,
Each wife had seven sacks,
Each sack had seven cats,
Each cat had seven kits:
Kits, cats, sacks and wives,
How many were there going to St. Ives?
—English nursery rhyme

Chapter I

THE DAY AFTER THE FUNERAL WAS LIKE ANY OTHER DAY. ROSIE
Deane got up at six, chose a clean uniform from the closet,
washed her face, tied a headscarf on her head, and walked the
three blocks to 6:30 Mass. It was like any other day, she told
herself again on the way home, except that it was late September
and the air, even at seven, had that peculiar, lonesome, smoky
quality to it. It was a quality she had liked when she was a girl,
when she had walked the same three blocks from the Catholic
school, kicking leaves up to her knees and feeling lonesome and
smoky inside, like the women in *The Saturday Evening Post* seri-
als who suffered tragic losses before they found a second love.
She didn't like it anymore; she liked evenings at the end of
August sometimes, when a certain mellowness settled down on
the prairie, a certain golden light just before dusk when the farmers were done with chores. She would walk then to the edge of
the village of St. Ives on streets nobody had ever bothered to
name, and look out past the water tower to fields that glowed
under the subtle changes of light as they rolled westward to the
South Dakota border.

On the front porch, with her coffee cup in hand, she sat in the
rocker as she always sat until winter forced her to retreat to the
kitchen. It would be a day like any other day except that she was
drifting over some vast chasm. She felt apart from her body,
floating, like a bit of milkweed not quite let loose from the pod.
She held out her left hand and looked at her fingernails. The hand

was checked and mottled with shadow from the lattice on the east end of the porch where Mama's rambling rose was dead for the season. She hated that lattice, she realized; she hated the rambling rose, its spiny, tied-up branches, its puny blooms. She looked at the bars, the uneven grid the shadow made across her hand and across her lap. She remembered that when she was twenty, they had gone to see Aunt Nellie's cousin, who was a cloistered nun, and when the sun had come through the window behind them in the narrow visiting room, the grill had cast shadows like that on the nun's face, making a second, tighter grill. She had shrunk from it then, shrunk from the feeling that the shadow lay across her own life, and shrunk from the nun's language, which implied a greater poverty than even the nun intended. "We had a cold last week," the nun had said, "and runny eyes; but our body now feels better." She had talked of "our" prayerbook when she meant her own. She had even said, "We got a letter from *our* mother."

Are these "our" hands? the Rosie who seemed outside of Rosie wondered. Is this "our" body? Did she own this house now, she wondered? Did she own this body? Did she own the vast numbness and the strange anger that had swept through her in place of yesterday's grief?

Perhaps if she had been there—if she could have stood, as she had stood over Mama's bed, hearing the awful, rasping rattle of the final breaths, barely breathing herself until the last breath, like a slight issue of steam, disappeared into a time that was already gone—perhaps then her brother's death would seem real. But she had not been there; she had found Stumpy McNabb and Jim Hinely on the front steps when she returned from taking one of the nuns to the dentist in Worthington. It was Stumpy, with his short arm pulling at the beak of his cap, who told her: "Just keeled over, Rosie. Just made this noise, and when I turned around he was on the floor by that bin of hog concentrate. Grabbed his chest—maybe twice—and that was that. Nothin' I could do, Rosie; I'm real sorry. He was gone by the time I got across the floor." Jim Hinely, who was never quiet, just stood there, shifting on his feet, his fist socking rhythmically into the other palm. "Ambulance took him to Morton's, Rosie. We thought you'd want that," Stumpy said.

She did want that; it was the only funeral parlor in St. Ives. But Don Morton had guided her immediately through the door that connected the business with the family quarters, and Jeanette Morton had brought her coffee at the kitchen table, and she didn't see Jack at all. "Come tomorrow," they both said, "it will be better then."

When she finally saw Jack, he was a wax figure, like the flowers Mama had preserved in paraffin, and anything he might ever have felt was sealed either in or out. That was when the numbness began. It grew through the wake and the funeral; it grew with every pair of eyes that watched her for signs of grief, with every whispered "How's she taking it?" that came through the vacuum of Morton's upholstered room. Only at the burial, when the vastness of the prairie had reclaimed him, had opened and swallowed even her own vastness, did she begin to weep.

But the tears had gone again. They had disappeared among the casseroles and homemade cakes in the church cafeteria, where nearly half of St. Ives had gathered for the funeral lunch. She hadn't wanted to eat; she had thought she would be sick on the tuna-noodle hotdish that slid down the back of her throat. "Eat, girl; keep up your strength," Edna Mueller had said; but Rosie, who knew she was no girl, had slipped into the lavatory beside the furnace room and gagged over the open toilet seat. Nothing came, however, and she wiped her face with a paper towel and moved to open the door.

"What's she going to do?" a voice she couldn't quite recognize was saying.

"Listen, she's not poor," said Dora Heinkamp's voice. "There's that elevator, you know . . . and Rosie never did do much of anything."

"I know," the other woman said, "but she's all alone, poor thing. . . ."

"Well, it was bound to end this way," Dora said, "the way that mother kept her down. I don't think she ever even had a date."

"Well, she's done a lot for the church . . ." the first voice said, but Rosie closed the door again. She began to gag, but this time what rose like fluid in her throat was more anger than physical substance. "Poor thing . . ." "She never did do much of anything. . . ."

What about holding down a job? Wasn't that something? What about showing up here in the cafeteria at 7:30 every morning when Dora, who was supposed to be in charge, was sometimes late? What about those years she checked groceries in Riedemacher's store? She had always had a job, except for the three years after Mama's stroke when somebody had to be there to take care of her. What were they supposed to do—hire a nurse? And what about being president of the Rosary Society, and helping to organize the Homemaker's Group? And . . .

"Rosie, are you all right?" It was Edna Mueller's voice this time. Rosie swallowed and willed an impassive glaze over her face—over the anger, and the outrage of Jack's death, and the bewilderment—and went out to pick at a piece of apple-spice cake. The numbness had come back as she sat there on one of the old church pews that made benches against the wall, and it lasted through the night. This morning, all familiar things seemed different, and even her own body was strange.

"Poor thing," she mouthed as she pulled a wilted flower from the back of the trellis and crushed it in her hand. "She never even had a date." In the first place, that wasn't true; in the second place, there were reasons. She was Rosemary Agnes Deane, she recited to herself. She was forty-one years old. She lived and had always lived in St. Ives, Minnesota, population 1,817 according to the sign on the highway (Mama always said they counted the dogs). She lived in a square brick house, one of three brick houses in the town, three blocks from the Catholic church. Her grandfather had built this house, Mama always said, because he had enough sense to know those Germans would need another elevator for all that grain they were getting off this godforsaken flat land, all those soybeans, even if he was the only Irishman in town. And Jack was doing a fine job of running it even if he did have a little of his father's weakness for the pint, and Rosie—Rosie would stay with her as the good Lord in His mercy intended it. Rosie was a fine, healthy girl, a comfort and a consolation to her mother. And Maura Deane wasn't hauling her daughter off to Sioux Falls to some doctor just because she had a few little spells after her sick times started, when Doc Feltz was a good man, and the family, as everybody knew, had perfectly good blood. . . .

"Fits," Jack said, who was fourteen and had listened to Father McGraw talking to one of the nuns in the sacristy. "They think you got epileptic fits. He said if you ever started rolling on the floor in class to put a key in your mouth so you wouldn't bite your tongue off."

"I never had any fits!" Rosie said. "I just fainted a couple times. That's all. Mama said that's all. You heard her!"

"You stay with me," Mama had said. "I'll take care of you and you can take care of me. You keep yourself real clean, and stay away from anything nasty. You know what I mean, Rosie? You stay away from boys, and at night you keep your hands under the blankets but on top of the sheet. We'll get along just fine. You stay with me."

She was Rosie Deane, she told the self in the rocking chair, though she told it with a certain sorrow. It was September 29, 1967. She was forty-one years old, five-foot-five, and 139 pounds at her last checkup. She had been pretty when she was a girl—or almost pretty. Her skin was always too pale, and her nose a little too rounded. She still had thick, dark hair, though now a streak of gray ran across the left side like an odd planting. She was the daughter of John and Maura Deane, who had two children born in St. Ives, Minnesota, and one born before they moved here that had died. She made her First Communion at seven. She was twelve when she was confirmed. That year her periods had started and that was the year she had passed out in church, in the school cloakroom, getting the mail at the post office for the nuns. She still went to the post office every day. It was behind the post office that Michael Roekamp had kissed her when she was sixteen. It was an odd sensation—just pressure on the lips and the unfamiliar smell of a boy that close—but she had saved all the notes he sent in study hall. Then he got a job in Sioux Falls with a trucking firm, and his mother told Mama that spells of any kind get passed on in the blood, and Mama said it was just as well.

She was Rosie Deane, and the sun through the lattice made bars across her body all the way down to the point where her thighs entered the shadow. She put her finger through the center of each those squares. Mama's rose was dead for the year, and Mama was dead, and now Jack was dead. There was still beer in the refrigerator, and the cap that said "Supergro Feeds" was on the ledge above the sink, but Jack was dead. Yesterday they had buried him, and Rosie had cried, clinging to Aunt Nellie's arm as though her legs had been withered by an early, bitter frost. Today she was a woman sitting in a rocking chair, feeling pulled apart, like milkweed ready to float toward an undefined horizon. She was forty-one; she was alone, and part of her wanted to drift into a wide space of forgetfulness and sorrow, but in the other part, she could feel a hard pod of hurt. "Rosie never did do much of anything," she told the back of the trellis as she dumped out the dregs of her coffee. When she went into the house, she slammed the door.

Chapter II

ROSIE DIDN'T KNOW WHERE SHE WAS GOING THAT MORNING WHEN she changed from her uniform to a turquoise dress, but she knew she was going somewhere. She ought to go to work, of course —she had told Dora she would be in the cafeteria kitchen as usual, but Dora had managed without her before. Rosie clamped gold earrings in place and combed her hair slowly. Jack's death had dislocated everything, and even the face in the walnut mirror looked unfamiliar—a pale, pensive woman with a determined mouth and frightened eyes. She brushed a wave of hair up and back from her forehead to see if she could recognize herself. "Ought to get you one of them hairdos like Lila Hinely," Jack had said only a few weeks ago; ". . . could raise your own supply of wasps." Perhaps she *would* look better, younger, with more height to her hair—perhaps she should try rollers instead of pincurls—perhaps she should have someone besides Mildred Dorn cut her hair. . . .

The eyes in the mirror had a sadness that suddenly reproached her: it wasn't right to be concerned with looks when you ought to be in mourning. Perhaps it wasn't ever right. "Never mind," Mama would say when people said she was a pretty child. "She didn't make her bed today." It wasn't really right to wear a turquoise dress either, she realized, but some angry part of herself said, *What does it matter—who's going to look at a woman who never even had a date?* The color of the dress was good with her blue-gray eyes and dark hair.

Jim Hinely remarked on it when she filled the car with gas at the Standard station out on the highway. He was one of Jack's old friends, a small, wiry man who had a way of circling around a person the way a boxer does that always put Rosie on her guard. "Lookin' pretty spiffy, Rosie," he said. "Better watch out for the fellas now that you own all those elevator shares. . . ."

It hadn't occurred to her that she did. She had thought about the house, but not the elevator. Jack had looked after things like that since Pa died, as though property were something that directly passed from man to man. She frowned, trying to take it in. Hinely fumbled more than necessary with the gas cap.

"Course, you probably have business to take care of in Worthington," he said. "That's the hell of it, all that legal stuff has to be done right after a funeral when you just don't feel like crawlin' out of a hole." He paused. "Jack was a good fella," he said. "Good man. Did right well for himself."

He was waiting for comment, for information, and his words seemed bare and insufficient coming from someone she had known since childhood. "Yes," she said. "Thank you. How much for the gas?"

"Four bucks on the nose," Hinely said, and twisted his hands around a grease rag. "Yeah, you probably got a lot of business to get things straightened out. Seems that's the way it always is— spend half of what you get on the lawyers. . . ."

"Yes," Rosie said, "business." But his obvious interest annoyed her. "There's more to death than money," she wanted to say, and as soon as he handed her the change, she pulled away from the pump and deliberately headed southwest, away from lawyers and Worthington.

She had never driven to Sioux Falls before. She had been there, of course. After Mama's stroke, they took her to a specialist three times, but Jack always drove. He drove fast, and he never had time to stop at the new shopping centers that were going up in the early sixties. He would pull down the plain brown cap he wore instead of the gray ones that said "Supergro Feeds," hang his left elbow out the window, and say nothing the entire way except "Blasted bastard" when anybody tried to pass. He said it low enough so that Mama, who was partly deaf, couldn't hear. Rosie always sat in the back.

She had started sitting in front after Mama died. At first it was strange and she felt that she should make conversation, but all Jack would ever say was "Yeah? That so?" or "Beats me." She couldn't remember when he had become so silent. When they were children he had talked. He had told her when he stumbled on a still just beyond the bend in the creek where the biggest bullheads were, and he had told her how he and the Hinely boys roasted a streaked gopher over a fire they built along the creek and got Lester Monk to eat it by telling him it was squirrel. He had talked plenty the time she caught him smoking behind old lady Mueller's woodshed on the edge of town when he was in fourth grade and she was in first. Pa would have whipped him with his belt if she had told. He had sneaked her out of the house to watch the Monks' dog have puppies the summer she was nine and Mama had told her that Mrs. Kovatch, big as a cow in her sixth pregnancy, was just getting fat from eating too much poppyseed.

"See, Rosie, see!" he had said. "They just pop right out of the pussy!" Rosie wondered why he would say that about a dog. She leaned forward on the old horse manger with intense interest. From a hole below the dog's tail, but not the hole she knew about, a slick capsule of flesh was beginning to bulge. One of these capsules already wiggled and took animal shape beneath the rough towel of the bitch's tongue. Rosie held her breath as the bulge broke through the slightly bloody circle, grew longer as the bitch strained, and then dropped free.

"See, Rosie, someday you can pop babies out just like that," Jack said with a leering kind of smile that made her feel suddenly ashamed; the other boys were watching her. She had gone home then, quickly and on a lame excuse, gone home knowing it had been wrong to come, wrong for her even to have knowledge of such things. That must have been why Mama had said it was poppyseed in Mrs. Kovatch's stomach—because it was wrong to know.

Mama was opposed to certain kinds of knowledge that had to

do with bodies and barns. A year or two earlier, when Jack had been playing with his friends in the Hinelys' barn just beyond the edge of town, Rosie had been sent to fetch him. The barn had a ripe, fertile smell that drew her into the semidarkness. "Jack, you're supposed to come home," she said.

"Shit!" Lester Monk said, but not to her. "Look at that bugger!"

"Do another one," Jack said. As her eyes adjusted to the heavy light, she could see them standing around a yearling steer that was stanchioned in a row with three others. Jim had his hands on the steer's back.

"What are you doing?" Rosie said.

"Popping grubs," Jack said. "Go away."

"Mama said for you to come home," she said.

"Here's one," Lester Monk said, feeling along the top of the steer's rump.

"Let me do it," Jack said, and elbowed Lester away. "Here, Rosie, if you're gonna hang around anyway, feel that." He had his hand on the same spot Lester had been fingering. Rosie reached up and felt a lump about the size of a peanut under the steer's hide. "It's a grub," Jack said. "You know those flies that are always bothering cows—the ones they swish away with their tails? The buggers sting them in the ankles, see, and shoot their eggs right in there. Then the little buggers crawl all the way up under their skin and turn into grubs on their backs."

"You made that up," Rosie said. "You always make up stuff when you don't want me to know what you're doing."

"Yeah?" Jack said. "Watch this." He reached up with both hands and squeezed the lump as one would squeeze a giant pimple. Nothing happened. Then he squeezed again. A white streak shot out and bounced off Rosie's cheek. She screamed and jumped back, just missing the gutter, her hand to the awful contamination of her face. "See," Jack said. "Made it up, huh?"

"You hit me with that," Rosie screamed through her tears. "You hit my face!"

"Well, get out of the way," Jack said.

"Girls!" said Jim Hinely.

"Here it is," Jack said, nudging something on the floor with his toe. Rosie didn't want to look, but she couldn't help herself. On top of the manure-stained straw was something white that writhed slightly then curled into a plump circle. It was a pale, segmented grub.

The grubs in her dream were everywhere. They crawled across the toe of her new patent leather shoes; they were inside her bedroom slippers; and a whole strip of spiraling fly ribbon fell from a barn rafter and stuck to her back. The flies were stinging her. "I'll pop them," Jack said when the round lumps began to appear on her forearm. "I'll pop them." She stared as three lumps appeared, then four. She looked at her other arm, and the lumps were already there; under the skin she could see the plump segments writhing. She screamed and screamed.

"You'd think somebody was murdering you," Mama said, shaking her. "For goodness sake!"

She sat up shrieking about the barn and the worms wiggling. "Don't let them touch me," she sobbed, "don't let them!"

"What have you gotten into?" Mama said, shaking her harder. "What were you and those boys doing in that barn? What have you found out about?"

Rosie couldn't tell her. It wasn't just loyalty to Jack who would be punished, it was the sense that in barns you stumbled onto things you shouldn't know—things you couldn't tell about. "I was dreaming about worms," she said. "There were angle-worms in the manure pile, and I was dreaming they were all crawling over me." She never told anyone about the grub hitting her face, but for years she thought of it when Father McGraw gave sermons on death and hell and sins of the flesh. "Worms will crawl in and out the mouth and nostrils of those who have used their bodies to sin," he'd say, and Rosie would see welts rising on her arms.

She never told Jack about the dream, but they were still talking then. He was her chief source of knowledge for years. She couldn't remember when he had gotten silent. In high school he didn't talk much to her, but then he didn't talk much to any of the girls. He hung around with the Hinely boys and Jerry

Roekamp and Lester Monk who wrote things on his hands with a fountain pen and always looked at you sideways from under a forelock of greasy hair. They took to running around God-knows-where, as Mama said, in the Hinelys' old pickup, and sometimes she would wait up to get him to bed without too much noise so Mama wouldn't hear him stumble against the kitchen table and come out to smell his beery breath. She would say, "Jack, it's almost two. Where have you been?" and he would flop an arm heavily over her shoulder and say, "Never you mind, Toots. My sister is a real sweet girl."

He must have gotten silent sometime in those years after Pa died, when she was still in high school and had joined the sodality and the Legion of Mary, and had even wanted, for a while, to become a nun. By then Jack was running the elevator and had learned to come in quietly at night, but he still didn't talk. On Sundays he knelt in the very back pew at Mass, hunched up with his rear propped against the seat, and left as soon as it was communion time. By the time Mama died and Rosie got the job at the cafeteria, he was almost forty, and there wasn't much to say. Sometimes at supper he'd tell stories about some guy who'd tried to pull a fast one down at the feed store, or about Mary Roelling, the oldest Kovatch girl, who could lift fifty-pound sacks when she was eight months along. Or sometimes, when Rosie tried a new recipe from *The Ladies' Home Journal*, he'd say, "Jeez, what is this crap? The school kids wouldn't eat it, so you brought it home?"

And then one night at supper about a year ago, she'd said the dentist in Worthington was doing a root canal and she'd have to go every week. Jack said, "Have him pull it, for cripe's sake. I can't close down the store for a toothache."

"He already started it," Rosie said.

"Then go by yourself," Jack said. "Jesus Christ, you're almost forty years old. You'd think you could get a car a few feet down the highway."

"I don't have a license. . . ."

"Get one."

"I can't, Jack," she said, almost pleading with him to stop. She wished he wouldn't swear so much. She wished he would shave more than twice a week.

"Why the hell not?"

"Because I have . . . when I was a kid I had those. . . ." She struggled to make herself say it.

"Jesus!" Jack said. "How long since you've had a fit? Twenty years? Thirty?"

"I was thirteen," she said, "but sometimes I still get dizzy spells—sometimes when I'm scrubbing or weeding the garden, I stand up and everything around me starts to spin. . . ."

Jack groaned. "Christ," he said, "that means you're getting old. Did it ever occur to you that maybe you don't have it anymore? Maybe you never did? Jeez," he said, "ask that damn doctor sometime."

"But Mama always said . . . when I was dizzy, she'd say, 'Better go lay down quick, Rosie. . . .' "

"So what did Mama know?" he said, leaning close and breathing into her face. "What did Mama *want* to know? Mama took care of herself."

She backed away as though he were going to strike her. *So that's the way it is*, she thought. *That's the way it is.* Suddenly, all the years since she was twelve hung in the air in front of her, the way a sunflower droops over a fence—all the years she was in high school and had wanted to be a nun and had wanted to go out with Michael Roekamp—all the years of her twenties before Mama had the stroke, when she watched girls her own age bring babies past the counter where she checked groceries in Riede-macher's store. *So that's the way it is*, she thought. But it couldn't be true. Mama wouldn't lie. The nuns had excused her from gym class . . . it was taken for granted by everybody—*everybody*—even the men in town. The summer she was nineteen, Gene Thurly had parked on a field road, taking her home from a dance she had gone to with Jack. His mouth came down hard on hers, and his left hand grabbed her breast and squeezed it through her cotton dress. "Don't," she had struggled against him, "please don't. . . ."

"Jeez," he'd said, angry, as he started the car again. "Wouldn't think somebody with your condition could afford to be so fussy."

So he knew. Everybody knew. How could all of that have been a mistake? For a moment she thought she was losing her balance. Something was grinding in her head just as it did when she'd been bending over a garden row and got up too fast.

"Well," Jack said, "what are you staring at?"

"I'll think about it," she said. "I'll have to think about it; I'll see."

Dora taught her. Dora, who never drove further than Worthington herself and who tended to grab the wheel every time a car was coming, had somehow showed her how to shift and steer and told her that if you got the cop with a belly like a potato sack, you could pass the test without knowing how to parallel park.

And now it was September and she was driving to Sioux Falls. She didn't know why. She only knew that St. Ives circled around her the way Jim Hinely did when he wanted to know her financial affairs. Besides, there were things in Sioux Falls she might need now, stores she'd never seen, shopping centers Jack would never stop at. It was a world she'd felt excluded from for no good reason except that Jack was always in a hurry. There was no hurry now. The new stretch of Interstate 90 was open westward from the South Dakota border, and the car glided onto it like grease spreading in a pan.

Her mind drifted as fields of ripe corn fled past on either side. It was autumn now, but she saw herself standing on the porch on one of those days when you could smell spring in the air over the prairie even if you couldn't see it. She was standing there inhaling, feeling a surge of life or hope or whatever it was the thawing earth must feel. When had that happened? How old was she then? The memory eluded her and she couldn't bring it back. Something flickered instead—an old idea, a memory, a scene that played itself just beyond the corner of the eye. It was like the specks that floated across her vision when she was tired; if she tried to look at them, they darted away.

She tried to let scenes from the past replay themselves: Sunday dinner with Pa in his good clothes and Jack in a knitted vest with his hair slicked down, Mama bringing in the roast, and at the last minute putting the boiled potatoes through the ricer: hundreds of tiny potato worms emerged and dived for the dish. She had refused to eat them for nearly a year after the grub had hit her face.

She remembered one night sitting with Mama by lamplight. Jack and Pa were gone, and the radio was on. She remembered a little Rosie in pigtails looking through a photo album.

"Were you really thirty-four when you got married, Mama?" she said. That seemed an incredible age.

"I took care of my mother till she died," Mama said, "and never for one minute regretted it." She was darning socks with a light bulb for a darning egg.

"Weren't you afraid you'd be an old maid like Lise Keller?"

"I had my wits about me," Mama said. "Lise Keller wouldn't know it if a snake bit."

Rosie pondered the idea of a snake biting Lise Keller. She was a big-boned woman with a downy face. Little black hairs curled out above her lip and at the bottom of her chin. She always wore the kind of black-heeled oxfords that nuns and grandmothers wear, and her reddish hair was a giant chore-boy bush. Rosie pictured Lise talking in her loud nasal voice. The snake would slither up behind her, flick its tongue over her grandmother shoes, and sink its fangs into the back of her leg. Lise would twitch her heel a little and go on talking. "I'll never be an old maid like that," Rosie decided.

"Hand me that other sock," Mama said.

But Mama had almost been an old maid even if she never talked about it. Even the little Rosie knew. One summer they had stayed for a week with relatives in Fairmont while Pa went to a Rural Electric convention. It was late on a Sunday morning, and Mama had gone to visit a great-aunt at the nursing home. Cousin Alice was hogging all the toys, and Rosie had looked for her aunts to complain.

"Clyde Rainey was in church this morning," Aunt Mina was saying to Aunt Pet. Neither of them saw Rosie.

"I know. I wondered if Maura saw him."

"Don't see how she could help it. He came right down the center aisle and all."

"Oh well, it's been . . . what? Twenty years? And she's got a husband now."

"Yeah, and this one even made it to the church." They both laughed a little.

"Poor Maura," one of them said. "You've got to give her credit. She kept on trying."

"Oh, I never for a minute doubted she'd catch *somebody*," the other said. "Maura always was one to take care of herself."

Rosie slowed the car in traffic that was starting to clot. "Mama took care of *herself*," Jack was saying with his face close to hers. Rosie jerked her mind away and shook her head to clear it.

The skyline of Sioux Falls began to protrude from the horizon, and she panicked a little. Why had she come? What did she want? What could she hope to find here that she couldn't get in Worthington? There were no ready answers, and Rosie thought she ought to turn back; but she felt herself pull apart again, as she had on the porch in the shadow of the lattice, and she watched a calm woman inside herself grip the wheel as Jack would have done, and follow the signs into a shopping mall.

It was 9:30. The manager of the Penney's store was just unlocking the door, and Woolworth's hadn't opened. She headed for a drugstore and bought two paperback mysteries, one by Agatha Christie and one by Erle Stanley Gardner that she thought she had read years back in installments in *The Saturday Evening Post*. That didn't take long, so she went to Penney's for some support hose, but instead rode the escalator to the second floor. The clerk was wearing a pantsuit. The young girls in Worthington were wearing those, when they weren't in skirts above the knee.

"Pardon me," Rosie said. "Do you have any of those?"

"Those . . . ?" the clerk said.

"Those pants outfits," Rosie said. She bought one in burgundy with a tunic top and said she would wear it. The clerk said it was slimming. She bought a gold chain with a little pendant and wore that too. The clerk said it was the look for the year.

Before she left the dressing room for the final time, Rosie took the comb from her purse and back-combed the top of her hair as she had seen high school girls do it in the far corners of the lunch room—"ratting" they call it. Dora's daughter did it all the time, though Dora didn't approve. Rosie's hair didn't come out quite the way she intended it, but it made her look a little taller, younger, less like a dumpy old maid, she thought with a certain bitterness. It somehow called attention to the roundness of her eyes.

She spent a long time in a card shop. She picked up some "Thank you for the sympathy" cards, and then browsed through the other racks. The shop had a small room off to the side full of plants, plump candles, baskets, and objects made of wood. It seemed a place where one ought to be silent—to think long thoughts as one did in a grove along the creek, or to stand and watch how the sun changed the color of the leaves. She watched a candle flame flicker through a large brandy snifter covered with chips of purple glass and finally picked out a thick candle that smelled of vanilla. "In case the lights go out during a thunderstorm," she told herself, and had an instant vision of Mama lighting blessed candles in the front room, and sprinkling holy water all over the house.

The Walgreen Drug no longer had a lunch counter, and Rosie found herself instead in a dimly lit room where a hostess in a very short skirt, her hair piled into one of the tortured hairdos Jack deplored, led her to a soft booth with black vinyl upholstery and candles in red bowls covered with a kind of plastic mesh.

"Would you care for a cocktail before your lunch?" the waitress was asking her. Rosie glanced around. What were people drinking in those short, squat glasses full of ice at this time of day? Beer? A shot of brandy? Highballs? "Here, Rosie, have a snort," Jack would say when the weather was too bad for him to take the pickup down to Swedes's place.

"No, thank you," she said, feeling a flush starting at the back of her neck. "I'll have the hamburger special. No—" she remembered it was Friday; she didn't feel right about eating meat even if the Pope said it was no longer a sin— "I'll have the shrimp."

She had that strange feeling of pulling in two again as she waited for the order to come, the feeling of vast numbness. Here she was, Rosie Deane, who should have eaten at the lunch counter at Walgreen Drug (except that there wasn't one anymore), and whose brother had had a heart attack only five days before, and here was a woman in a burgundy pantsuit who didn't care that the shrimp cost $2.98, and who calmly began to play with the mesh on the glassed candles, fingering the little squares, stretching them into different shapes.

A heavyset man with bloodshot eyes was coming out of the men's room. His path took him past Rosie's booth and he frankly eyed her up and down. She looked away, but her hand moved to straighten the gold chain. When he was past, her hand moved up to smooth her hair.

The sun seemed too bright when she stepped back out onto the sidewalk at the far end of the mall. "Let us save your soul for you," said the sign in the shoe repair shop; "let us save your sole." "Fresh apple tarts," said the bakery sign. She stopped in front of still pictures of a beautiful woman tucked with furs into a sleigh. "Return Engagement," she read diagonally across the poster. The man in the picture had a moustache and languid brown eyes— eyes with that liquid, pleading quality of children who are afraid to cry. The letters on the marquee said *Doctor Zhivago*, a familiar name—the book had caused a big stir in Russia, and Charlie Chaplin's daughter was in the movie. It hadn't played in St. Ives, of course. The Chateau was open only on weekends and played old Disney films.

Rosie didn't know the Legion of Decency rating, but those ratings seemed looser now anyway; the last couple of years, the priest didn't even make them stand up in church and take the Legion of Decency pledge. One of the nuns, Sister Carol Ann, who taught release-time religion classes to the kids who went to public school, had seen the movie somewhere about a year ago, so it ought to be safe. She gave the girl her money and went in.

The theatre was new and semicircular, but the seats still had the heavy red plush of an old-fashioned theatre. It was appropriate, she thought. There was something warm and secret about a theatre, warm and intimate. The darkness that revealed human joy and grief and terror on the screen also hid the human beings in the theatre—all the hands dipping into popcorn boxes, groping for combs or coins or whatever they'd lost, all the lovers kissing silently in the back row. It was right that the darkness should be warm and lined with red.

The scenes that came on the screen were more white than red at first: a blonde girl walking through the snow, then Charlie Chaplin's daughter swathed in furs, and a train breathing steam into the frosty air in a way that made it alive, like a theatre, like a dragon with a great icy breath. Rosie stepped back through time into frozen Russia. She had always become the people she saw on the screen, enduring their trials and receiving the final passionate but chaste embrace. She and Lois Roekamp had seen most of Doris Day's movies in the late forties and early fifties. Lois was about her age and not married either. But then Richard had come along, and Lois had married, and Rosie wasn't quite brave enough to go by herself. Jack said movies were a waste of cash after they got TV; he hadn't seen anything since *Ma and Pa Kettle Go to New York*.

The scenes on the screen were changing to red now—to red and to purple. The blonde girl was with a gross man—not obese, but coarse, unclean somehow, oozing grease. Once in a dark theatre, she remembered, a man had put his hand on her knee and started to move it up her thigh. She had jumped up, of course; she had told Lois they had to sit someplace else, and she had never seen the man's face, but the shape of his head as she had turned to him in amazement had been like that: gross, coarse. She imagined that he looked like this—like Rod Steiger playing the coarse man. It was just an act, she reminded herself, but his eyes were on the blonde girl, and she shivered with having seen eyes like that before. The man and the girl were dancing in a room that was red, all red, but the beauty was turning seedy and sour. Then they were meeting in a small room and the girl's red dress showed half her bosom. Rosie was afraid.

She tried to concentrate on the man's face, on the trapped innocence of the girl. Then the scene changed and he was forcing her into a bed; she fought him, fought for her virginity, but then relaxed, and it was obvious what was happening. *Don't think about it*, Rosie told herself. *This doesn't concern you.* She looked at the man's eyes again, and suddenly she was not watching the screen. She was watching a reel unwinding in her own head. She was fourteen then, and Pa was still alive, and they were in the old Ford going to the State Fair in St. Paul. It was a long way; they had left at 5:00 A.M. and now they were stopped for gas in some little town. She couldn't remember the name of the town, but the attendant was cleaning the windshield, and they were all watching it like some kind of performance or display, and Mama was saying, "Well, I don't know about you, but Rosie and I won't want to spend the whole blessed day on Machinery Hill." She could remember it that clearly: Mama wearing a blue-sprigged cotton dress and herself watching the boy who emerged from behind the gas pump. He was about her age, and his eyes and mouth held a kind of grin that was shamed and cocky and challenging. His hands were a little way below his waist and holding something.

My God! Rosie thought. *My God, it's his thing!* But she didn't move. She didn't take her eyes away. He wagged it up and down at her roguishly, like a broken tail, like a fat, pale sausage that had gone a little limp. *My God!* Rosie thought, and turned her head sharply when Jack began to stir.

". . . would rather go to the 4-H building, wouldn't we, Rosie?" her mother was saying. "You could meet us there." Her father was putting the car in gear. "Rosie," her mother turned around but her face showed that everything was in place, "you want to see the 4-H building, don't you?"

That was how it had been. That was how men's eyes looked when they were aroused. That was how a rapist must look. She watched the fat man on the screen. Was his thing pale like that boy's? He had fat thighs. Was it swollen and fat like his thighs?

She jerked herself back to the screen. There were soldiers now; there seemed to be something about socialists. "You can't let your mind dwell on those things," she told herself. "You can't allow that kind of thoughts." She tried to pay attention to a young man who was thin and wore wire-rimmed glasses (he was the girl's fiancé), but the face of the boy in the filling station kept nudging in between. "When bad thoughts tempt you," the nun had said in seventh grade, "put something good in their place. Think of the Blessed Mother, or think of ice cream if you have to, but move your mind away. Even thoughts that lead to impure thoughts can be occasions of sin." She moved her mind back to the screen and the thin young man, but only part of it obeyed. "Ice cream is really silly," the other Rosie was saying, "and pictures of the Blessed Mother never stay." The blonde girl on the screen was confessing to the socialist fiancé now; earlier she had gone to confession to a priest in strange, ornate robes, without even a screen to shield her. *She had to think about her sin in order to confess it*, Rosie thought. *Is that another sin?* Does the priest think about it? Does he take courses in the seminary to know which kind of thoughts are which kind of sins?

When she was very young, she had impure thoughts without realizing it; and then, of course, it wasn't a sin. When she was young—twelve, maybe—she had dreamed all the time of getting married, and she could still remember how the dream had gone: how he would propose to her, and how she would answer, and the flowers she would carry down the aisle, and the shape of the veil. And then they would go on a honeymoon—to Lake Shetek, maybe, or all the way to the Black Hills, and in the hotel room they would both get undressed—they would have to—and slide between the sheets. Then he would start to kiss her, and press his body all over against hers, and then he would press his body all the way into her, and she would have a baby, because that was the way it worked. Jack had told her the year before that that was the way it worked. She would lie there in bed on summer nights when it was still a little too light to sleep and look at the rows of fading rosebuds going up the wallpaper, and think that this was how it would be. She would caress her body sometimes, as he would caress it, and feel the wonder of it all run through her being in a kind of ecstasy, and hug herself for joy. Then she was confirmed and Mama gave her a prayerbook for a confirmation gift. In the back was "An Adult's Examination of Conscience." Then she knew that what she had been doing was wrong.

Time was passing on the screen. The man with the cocker-spaniel eyes who was playing Dr. Zhivago had fallen in love with the blonde girl, though both were married. They were living together, sleeping together in a country house of some kind, an absurd mansion with onion-shaped turrets out of a fairy tale or a strange, elaborate dream. Everything was white; everything was snow and ice and frosty panes of glass that they could clear with their breaths. Everything was pure. Rosie was well acquainted with snow, with blizzards that would roll across the plain from South Dakota. She had stood at the upstairs window and watched as fans of frost had gradually encroached and become a solid furry white. She had scraped into it with her fingernails, had scraped hearts and initials, and secret messages, standing there in her flannel nightgown—messages that the lover she dreamed of would find. But it had never been like this: in the midst of her whiteness, there had never been a bed of tangled fur and sheets. *That* belonged to a hot, steamy setting, to coarse people who committed adultery. Here, in Russia, in the snow, in a country house that came out of a dream, everything was pure.

She thought about it on the drive home. "Pure, conjugal love," the priest said in the wedding ceremony, and Rosie had always imagined a chaste embrace, a wife greeting her husband after a day's absence, or a couple at home in the evening in the lamplight (he would be reading *The Farm Journal*, perhaps, and she would be knitting a baby sweater), and he would reach over and begin to stroke the hair at the base of her neck. It was more than that, of course; it was sex, it was conceiving children, but she had always stopped her mind before it played out images of tangled bodies in the dark, of a man's breath that might smell of ciga-rettes or whiskey mingled with your hair, of nakedness. . . . *Did people really do it naked*, she wondered? Or was that just in exotic movies that had nothing to do with places like St. Ives? Pa had worn his shorts to bed, she knew, and in winter his long underwear. Jack, she guessed, had done the same. And the women she knew all wore pajamas or nightgowns—you could see them hanging on the line on washday. Did they take them off when they got in bed?

She jerked her mind back. What was the matter with her? These were things adolescents thought about, not grown women. She hadn't thought about things like this for years. She fixed her attention on the landscape as the highway wove on in gentle undulations; as soon as she passed one small town, she could see the water tower of the next. The corn in the great square fields had turned brown—no, it was more of a soft, golden beige that implied ripeness and harvest. She liked harvest; she liked to see the corn pickers go down the rows, wrestle the rustling stalks into their geared grip, and send the golden ears spouting back into the wagon. There was a sense of ripeness and fruitfulness about it all; she liked that as she had liked, when a child, to take the red wagon back into the garden on the edge of town and load up the fat orange pumpkins, hugging them to herself as she hoisted them off the ground. Had her parents ever gone to bed naked? Did people on their honeymoon? Did they begin to wear clothes after the children came? "Stop that!" she told herself. "You can't think about things like that!" But if you were getting married, she knew, you would *have* to think about it. You would have to decide what you were going to do. But how would you know what he expected? Would you ask him? Would you discuss it? Would you confess your ignorance to a married friend? Or would you just know? Would you just figure a man knew by instinct (or maybe by previous experience) what to do? That he would take off whatever clothes he needed or wanted to take off? That he would know what to do first?

"Stop that!" she told herself sternly again. "But if you were getting married, you'd need to think about a lot of things," the other Rosie said. "You'd need to think whether or not you'd get your period on the wedding night . . . you'd need to worry about spots on the mattress and stains. . . ." "Stop it!" she told the separate self who rode with her in the same car, the same body. "You aren't getting married! You aren't ever getting married at all!"

Chapter III

IT WAS AFTER SIX WHEN ROSIE PULLED THE CAR BACK INTO THE drive. Dora Heinkamp had been loading groceries into her trunk when Rosie drove past the Jack Sprat store, and Dora pulled her car into the drive immediately behind Rosie's now. She was shorter than Rosie, but heavier. With each of three pregnancies she had put on a few pounds that never came off. She did not simply get larger, as most women did, or grow thick hips and a big stomach that looked solid and firm. She bulged out like a balloon that has been constricted in places and left to expand in others. It was as though certain bands of skin had simply refused to stretch. She prefaced most of what she said with "Now, listen . . ." and somehow it added to her weight. Dora was out of her car before Rosie was, and came hustling up.

"Listen, I called to check, because you said you were coming to work today," she began in a hurry. Dora was always in a hurry. There was never enough time to find out or to tell all the information that concerned her. "Afraid a toilet might flush she didn't know about," Jack used to say. Dora grew up near Pipestone, but Rosie had gotten to know her well the year they were on the Decency Committee for the Catholic Women's League and went to every drugstore in Nobles and Murray counties to ask the proprietor to take *Playboy* and other dirty magazines off the rack. Dora was very persuasive. After Mama died, the pastor offered Rosie the job as Dora's assistant.

"You know, I told you you didn't have to come in," Dora

hurried on, "but you said you were coming anyway, and when there was no answer on the phone, I got the fish sticks in and came right over to check. . . ." She looked at Rosie brightly, cocking her head to one side like a plump chicken.

"Thank you," Rosie said. "That was nice of you."

"Now, listen, I wouldn't have thought a thing of it, if you hadn't specifically said you were coming in," Dora said. "And when I came over and rapped on both doors, and then I saw that the car was gone. . . ." She eyed the car now, expectantly.

"I had to go out of town," Rosie said, hoping that would be enough. She couldn't say she had gone shopping the day after the funeral; she couldn't say she had gone to a show.

"Business, I suppose," Dora said. "You must have gotten a call late last night?"

"I just had to take care of some things," Rosie said. Dora was eyeing the pantsuit.

"That's new, isn't it?" she said. "At least, *I've* never seen it."

"Well, you know how cold it gets," Rosie said. Her voice sounded lame, and she regretted the impulse that had made her buy it.

"Got your business straightened out, I s'pose?" Dora said. "When Jerry's father died, we had to go four times. 'Course, he was the executor. . . ." She let her voice trail off and Rosie said nothing. "Well," Dora said. "I s'pose I should be getting supper started. There's that chivaree tonight, but I wanted to make sure everything was all right. Wouldn't want you to think nobody was looking out for you."

"What chivaree?" Rosie said.

"Oh you know. Johnny and Mary Kay Mueller. She's the second-oldest Hines girl from up by Wilmont. They moved in a trailer on the home place last week when they got back from their honeymoon," Dora said. "The gang's going up at 8:30, so I'd better get some supper on."

"Are you going right out, or are people meeting someplace first?" Rosie asked. She hadn't heard much about chivarees lately. She had gone to a few with Jack or Lois when Mama was still well, but she hadn't even thought of them for years.

"They're meeting at the Shoemacher place just down the road," Dora said. "It should be good and dark by then. Why?" Dora turned back with a sharp pivot. "You aren't going?"

"I might," Rosie said. She was surprised to hear herself say it, but a stubborn anger had come flaring back in the face of Dora's questioning, and within it movie reels were turning. "I've got to find some place to wear my new pantsuit." She laughed a little feebly.

"But," Dora said, "people don't usually. . . ." She stopped to consolidate her confusion, looking Rosie up and down. "Of course, *I* wouldn't like to sit in that empty house alone, either," she said. "It won't be so bad once you get used to it, but it's too bad nobody around here thought to invite you the first night or so after all the excitement died down." She paused. "Listen, I'll tell Jerry," she said, "he's pretty good about that kind of thing, and we can just stop about a quarter past eight. . . ."

Dora plumped like a hen when she was pleased with things. Rosie could see her segregating two or three women at the chivaree and confiding in a low tone: "Poor thing! You know it would never occur to most people to think how awful it must be to sit there in that empty house . . . I mean, she's not a widow or anything, but it amounts to the same thing! And Jerry said, 'Well, heck, she can just come along with us.' And I said, 'Listen, what if people do think it's awful soon . . . I mean, I know how I'd feel, and we can just tell them we brought her along with us. . . .' "

"I can take Jack's car," Rosie said. She wasn't sure she wanted to spend the evening with Dora.

"No, no!" Dora said. "Jerry wouldn't hear of it. Not that I expect anybody to say anything, but it would just be better all around if you came with us." She backed into her car's open door. "Now, listen, we'll pick you up at quarter past eight," she called as she put the car into reverse.

Rosie felt both the anger and the vastness dissipate as the Hein-kamp car pulled quietly into a farmyard huddled with other cars and groups of people suppressing their laughter as though hoarding it for a future show. She was riding in the back seat again, and Dora was making motherly sounds. She must have been no more than seven or eight when her parents had taken her to a chivaree for Aunt Nellie and Uncle Gus, and her mother had made the same kind of maternal fussing. She had squeezed herself into the corner of the back seat, she remembered, her legs sticking straight out in front of her, and Jack was hunched in the other corner. Between them were all the large pans in the house: a tin dishpan, an old kettle usually used for boiling corn, a big blue enamel pan with conspicuous chips, and the largest of the cast-iron skillets. Big metal spoons were sticking out of the enamel pan, and a cowbell was nestled inside. It was all very mysterious, she remembered. They had circled the house silently —like Indians, she had thought—like Indians about to attack a cowboy camp. Ben Geil with the big stomach had given the signal, and she had beat on the enamel pan with the big mixing spoon as though her soul depended on it. The adults had changed into other creatures, boisterous, rowdy, forgetting to frown. There was Mama, ringing the cowbell with both hands, and Pa, whacking the iron skillet and whooping until someone handed him two potlids that he banged together as though leading a parade.

"Come on out, we know you're in there!" someone had yelled.

"Aw, they're busy!" another voice came out of the dark. "Whatcha doin' in there? Whatcha doin' in there in the dark?" Rosie imagined they had been asleep, and that was the joke: to wake them up, to wake them up with a great racket.

"Come on out!" a woman's voice yelled. "We know you weren't sleeping!"

Then the porch light went on, and a few seconds later, Nellie and Gus had appeared. They both looked a little embarrassed; he had his arm around her waist, and she seemed to be trying to hide under his shoulder. But they were both laughing. They had been asleep and everybody had banged pans and kettles to wake them up because they were newlyweds, and that was the joke. Then the crowd had streamed into the house, and a couple of men had gone to the basement with Gus and appeared with a keg of beer. Then a case of pop appeared—orange and grape and strawberry —and Nellie got some bowls out of the cupboard, bowls she had gotten at her shower, and a big sack of peanuts salted in the shell and some Cracker Jacks for the kids. They seemed to be ready for a party, though it had all been a surprise. Rosie had curled up in the corner of the new secondhand sofa with her bottle of grape soda. There weren't any straws, and she knew she was getting a purple moustache, but she didn't care. This was a strange new world that appeared late at night and she was part of it. The teasing murmur of adult voices floated over her. There were occasional taunting calls back and forth between the huddles of women and the men with their feet on the rungs of the chairs. She was still clutching the Cracker Jack box when she fell asleep.

Thirty years later, she was still sitting in the back seat with the pots and pans, she reflected a little ruefully. She had brought the old corn kettle, or one that had somehow replaced it over the years. It was sitting beside Dora's largest stainless-steel kettle with the copper bottom, and some sort of klaxon that Jerry had brought from his hardware store—a contraption that was supposed to make squawking noises when you swung it around.

"Listen, we might as well stay in the car," Dora said; "looks like the gang's just about here." She settled more firmly on the front seat, but Jerry got out, and Rosie felt a childish desire to join him, to be part of the snickering excitement of the little groups. Two more cars pulled into the drive, and a slow procession started. One by one the cars left the yard and turned down the gravel road, headlights off, radios silenced.

It was absurd to feel so excited, Rosie told herself. This was just neighbors carrying out an old custom, just ordinary people performing the last of the wedding rites. Perhaps it was the crisp, smoky quality of the night air that made her feel she was on an adventure. She remembered a Homecoming Weekend bonfire in Worthington—she had been allowed to go when she was a senior —and how a snaky line had wound around and around the fire in the dark. Perhaps her feeling came from the fact that they were sneaking, under cover of night, to make a surprise attack on lovers who would be in bed, who would be caught. . . . Of course not; that was absurd. Who went to bed before ten o'clock?

The car pulled silently off the road and into an alfalfa field about a hundred yards from the farmhouse. The newlyweds' trailer was further back. "Shhh!" Dora said, as they stepped from the car, and Rosie passed the pans up. "Don't slam the door!" Rosie had no intention of slamming the door. She watched the other people moving toward the house, the hardware they were clutching making strange, clumsy silhouettes. She recognized most of them: Stumpy McNabb with a washboard under the shorter of his arms, the Riedemacher sons, Mary Roelling who was pregnant again, several of the Farnholzes, assorted faces and figures she recognized from church or from her years in Riedemacher's store.

They were spreading out now around the trailer. It wasn't dark, as Aunt Nellie's house had been. A light was on in what appeared to be the living room, and the TV was going. She heard a woman's voice giggle, and several others said, "Shhh!" She looked in the direction of the voices. There were Jim Hinely and Lila, his bleached-blonde wife who looked her age anyway, and a man with them who looked familiar. It was the milkman from school lunch, the man from Mellomilk in Luverne who brought the half-pint cartons every Monday, Wednesday, and Friday. He was new on the route this fall, and his name was Ray something. "Ray" was embroidered on his uniform in red. He seemed to be a pleasant man, but Rosie had never really talked to him; Dora handled all the delivery men.

Someone blew a toy police whistle and the din began. Rosie banged on her pan, Jerry whirled the awful-sounding klaxon, and Dora, who had dropped her spoon when the whistle blew, was yelling, "Listen, wait a minute!" to nobody in particular as she felt around in the grass. The lights in the trailer went out.

Rosie felt a queer sensation. There was no light at all now, except for the stars and one rather wan yard light. She stopped banging on her kettle and took a pace back from the din. She felt alone, strange, wrapped up in a sleeve of darkness. The figures around her seemed ragged, pagan, like natives in *National Geographic* doing some sort of dance. The circle began to close in and she half expected there to be spears and masks and something slung from a pole. Someone began making catcalls and two or three voices took it up.

"Hey, watcha doin' in there?" someone yelled. "Want us to come in and find out?"

"Come on out," another voice took up the melody, "just as soon as you get some clothes on!"

"How about some music for lovers?" Jerry yelled, and swung the klaxon around. He was joined by Stumpy, who ran thimble-covered fingers up and down his washboard. The level of the din rose again, but still the newlyweds did not appear.

"Well, hell, are we gonna have to go in and get 'em?" Jim Hinely said.

"Don't try sneaking out the back," a woman's voice was shrill. "We got you covered!"

"I didn't know them tin-can things had back doors!" old Ben Geil shouted to a chorus of guffaws.

Finally, a yellow bug-light went on above the trailer door, and the newlyweds appeared. Johnny was barefoot in bib overalls that were several sizes too big. He had a ragged straw hat on his head, a corncob pipe in his mouth, and carried an old kerosene lantern which he held aloft in a mock effort to peer into the crowd. Mary Kay was wearing her wedding gown, but had a bright apron over the top of it, an old curtain on her head, outsize freckles painted on her face, and a drooping sunflower for a bouquet. When she grinned, one tooth had been blacked out. The crowd hooted with approval and then quieted down.

Johnny was peering out over the lantern. "Vat dem fellers vant, d'ya s'pose?" he said in a bad imitation of the old German accent. Mary Kay had the giggles by this time and covered her mouth with the hand holding the sunflower. It made her sneeze. "Ya s'pose we should invite 'em in, Katie?" Johnny said to his bride.

Rosie felt perplexed and a little disappointed; this wasn't the way it was supposed to be. There were assigned roles here, and Johnny and Mary Kay weren't playing theirs. They were supposed to be embarrassed, blushing, and a little shy, as though they *had* been caught in lovemaking.

"Aw, somebody told!" Ben Geil said, low and a little disgusted.

"Well, you have to hand it to 'em," Jerry said. "They had it all planned out."

"Listen," Dora said. She was gathering up the pots and pans. "Kids these days know everything before they're old enough to button their own pants. . . . I told my Ellen the other day, 'There's no use wrapping presents if you already know what's in the box.' "

Rosie looked back toward the trailer. The lights were on, soft squares of yellowness, and Johnny was handing out folding chairs while one or two fellows came up and thumped him on the back. The keg materialized and was propped up on hay bales in the semidarkness like some kind of idol or sacred pig.

Rosie was a little in awe of the young bride all evening. The girl had changed the wedding dress for a plaid shirt and jeans, but she still wore the curtain on her head as she circulated with bowls of potato chips and caramel corn, answering the women's questions and tossing back retorts to the men. She couldn't be more then twenty, Rosie knew, and there she was, taking the ribbing without a single blush. Rosie had felt strange and insecure ever since the bold bride and groom came out. She shouldn't have come, a day after the funeral; it wasn't right. People were noticing her in the new pantsuit that was too dressy for the occasion, even for someone not in mourning—but it was more than that: *she* would have blushed. . . .

"What the hell, Rosie, you drinkin' pop?" a voice boomed in her ear. Jerry Heinkamp grabbed the can out of her hand and stuffed in a paper cup of beer. She was grateful for his gruffness. She had been afraid people would be too nice to her—would make her aware that an aura of death still surrounded her, though all she felt was the numb sense that something important was gone. When Mary Kay came by again, she offered to help pass the chips.

"Rosie," Jim Hinely said. "I tell you! You're looking better every time I see you! Isn't she?" he demanded of his wife and the new milkman from Luverne. "This morning she was all dolled up and off to see the lawyers. Better watch it! One of those geezers is liable to get the hots for you!" He poked his elbow into the milkman's forearm. The milkman laughed as was expected of him, but Jim's wife didn't look amused. She was drinking Coke, and Jim wasn't. He was leaning a little to one side, and his shoulder was starting to list. Rosie felt him take his boxer's stance.

"You know Ray Bowen here, don't you, Rosie?" Jim boomed. "He hauls for Mellomilk."

"We've met," Rosie said, extending her hand. "He delivers milk for the school lunch. Rosie Deane," she said.

"Good to see you again, Rosie," Ray said. He had hazel eyes with rather large pupils that looked at her keenly through his glasses. They were the kind of eyes that you expected to laugh. He was probably about forty-five, she decided, not handsome, but a solid-looking man. His handshake was firm but not lingering. She liked that. There was an honesty about it.

"Well, hell," Jim was saying, "Ray here is single! We don't need no lawyers! Huh, Ray?" He poked his elbow into the other's arm again. "Ray's what? A widower?"

Ray looked embarrassed. "Yes," he said softly, poking some loose hay with his shoe.

"Rosie here just came into the chips," Jim said.

"Shut up!" his wife said. "She don't need no help from you."

"Well, hell!" Jim said. "Two nice people ought to get together. Then we can all come to another chivaree, huh, Rosie?"

"You're drunk," his wife said.

Rosie could feel her neck getting red splotches of embarrassment. She looked at Ray Bowen, expecting him to be embarrassed too, but he was watching her with bright-eyed interest. Like a squirrel, she thought. Squirrels always had those bright, intelligent eyes. But his body had more the firm square build of a friendly dog. She became aware of the small pit of silence in the general din.

"Excuse me," she said. "I'm supposed to be passing these."

Rosie offered the potato chips to one more cluster of men and then edged back toward the trailer. Dora, she figured, must have gone inside. The kitchen and what she could see of the living room were surprisingly large. The kitchen was paneled, and a formica table was built out from one wall. "Their trailer is real nice," she said to Edna Mueller, who was ripping open more potato chips, her stomach balanced against the small built-in sink.

"Well, I think so," Edna said, "but you're supposed to call it a 'mobile home.' That's what Johnny says. Go look around. Mary Kay don't care."

Dora was sitting on the couch that took up most of a living-room wall, across from Mary Roelling and another woman Rosie didn't know. Dora's voice was pitched higher than usual, but was just as fast.

"A wiener!" she was saying. "What do you mean, a wiener?"

"Well, it was one of her cousins from over by Wilmont," Mary said, "found out where the suitcases were hid."

"Where?" the other woman wanted to know.

"I don't know," Mary said. "In the fruit cellar or someplace."

"Should of known better than that," Dora snorted. "Listen, when Marty got married, we locked hers in the trunk of our car."

"Anyway," Mary said, "he didn't have any pajamas in his, so they sewed his shorts together—little tiny stitches like quilting— so he'd have to rip it out the next morning in the motel. . . ."

"I thought they usually did stuff to the car," the other woman said. "Didn't they do anything to the car?"

"Well, shoe polish and that kind of thing," Mary said. "I don't know, maybe a few tin cans. Anyway, they took Mary Kay's pajamas—she had some real cute light blue lacy ones—and sewed the sleeves shut, and all the buttons shut down the front, and across the bottom too, I think. And then they took the bottoms and sewed the legs shut, and sewed a wiener right in the front inside!" Mary looked pleased with her story.

"A wiener!" Dora said, the pitch of her voice raised from the beer. "That's awful!" She tried to sound indignant, but she was giggling. "A wiener! I never heard of such a thing!" She rolled her head back against the couch and caught Rosie's eye as she stood in the doorway. A look of caution came over her face. No one said anything.

"Excuse me," Rosie said. "Edna said I should look around." She headed past the couch and into the tiny hallway that led to a room filled with a dresser and a double bed. There was a bathroom on one side of the hall, and a door that went outside at the end of the other.

"Well, that's mean! I just don't think that's right!" the woman in the living room was saying as Rosie stepped out into the grassy night. There was no one on this side of the trailer, and the only light came from the windows of the little living room. She heard male voices breaking into laughter at the end of a joke.

The picture hung before her vividly in the dark: dainty blue pajama bottoms, and a wiener, redder than usual, or maybe very pale, the skin beginning to dry and wrinkle, hanging there obscenely. She shouldn't think about it; it was going to bring back all the thoughts the movie had aroused, but she couldn't make the picture go away. Blue pajama bottoms hung in the air, and now they blended with a boy sticking out from behind a blue and white gas pump, and now with a blonde girl and a man with liquid eyes in a white house, in a white winter, blowing with white breaths on the window frost, and sleeping in white sheets that somehow were still pure. She couldn't figure it out. Perhaps she had drunk too much beer. It had been years since thoughts like these had crowded in upon her, and now, in one day, all the barriers she had carefully constructed of religion and will and long endurance had come tumbling down, and she could make no sense of it. She couldn't figure out the impure and the pure, the chaste and the obscene, what it was all right to imagine when you were twenty and married and never blushed, and what wasn't all right when you were forty-one and not. She didn't feel like moving back into the half-circle of hay bales and light where the pig-shaped keg presided. She didn't want anyone else to talk to her. She wanted to go home.

Chapter IV

WHEN SHE WOKE UP, SHE KNEW SHE HAD SLEPT TOO LONG. SHE HAD a vague headache, and something else was wrong. She rolled onto her back to think what it was. Jack was dead, and she was suspended in a kind of numbness, but it was more than that. It was Saturday. She knew that wasn't good, and she tried to remember why. It meant that there wasn't any job to go to, for one thing— any kids to cook for. There wasn't even Jack to cook for anymore. She rolled over and stuffed her face deeper into the pillow and tried to sleep. It wasn't any use. It was Saturday and that meant a silent, empty house all day. It also meant confessions in the afternoon.

She winced as though she had bitten down on a rotten tooth. Her mind was back in the darkened theatre. A fat man was looming over a blonde girl, and somewhere in a filling station a boy was standing behind a pump sticking out his thing, and she could feel her flesh stiffen. "A wiener," Mary was saying, "a wiener!"

She shook her head to clear it. "No," she said, almost aloud. "No, I won't think of that." She could feel shame rise from her stomach. But how was she to know if her thoughts had been a willful act, she explained to the consciousness that always judged her; she hadn't really willed those images that moved in and out of each other. She had thought the movie would be about history, about the Russians, maybe about concentration camps. *Full consent of the will*—she had memorized in the catechism in third grade; you couldn't commit a mortal sin unless there was full consent of the will. Had she consented to all those thoughts that made her body stir, those pictures that floated in front of her as though on a screen—or had they just come? Had she tried hard enough to get rid of them? She wasn't sure—she was never sure of things like this. That was why confession was so difficult.

Rosie rolled until her face was completely immersed in the pillow. Where was the self who had been with her yesterday? Where was the split-off part who calmly and without wincing had driven the car, had met the eyes of the men at the chivaree? *Sister Carol Ann saw that movie.* She grasped at the thought, trying to recall the other Rosie. Sister Carol Ann said it was well done. She said the photography was excellent. She probably saw it with another nun . . . all the other nuns probably saw it . . . no, that wasn't true. No one else had ever mentioned it in the lunch-room conversations. . . .

It wasn't working; the other part of her refused to come back. Sister Carol Ann probably closed her eyes at the rough parts, Rosie thought, but the shame rising from her stomach was less acute.

She tried not to think about it as she got up and took an old housedress from the closet. Confessions didn't even start until three o'clock. She counted up; it was only three weeks since she had gone. She used to go every other week, but the young priest, who always unnerved her because he asked questions like, "What do *you* think your penance should be?" had said that for someone with her sins, once a month ought to be enough. She'd been a little offended at that, but relieved. Something always turned over in her stomach when she went into the church on Saturday afternoons, even in the old days when Father McGraw, a little deaf near the end of his twenty years at St. Ives, used to assign a decade of the rosary no matter what you did. Then he always said, "If Our Lady showed the flames of hell to innocent children at Fatima, how much worse will it be for us. Make a good act of contrition for your sins."

Once, when she was in high school, she had gone to confession to a Jesuit who was preaching the yearly Forty-Hours Devotion.

He was a young man, but rather gruff, and Rosie told him she had accidentally let the host touch her teeth when she went to communion. She knew it wasn't a serious offense, but the nuns had always said it should only touch your tongue. "That's no sin," the priest said. "Don't waste my time being scrupulous. What else?" She looked up "scrupulous" when she got home: "conscientious even in small matters, not neglectful of details, (over)attentive to small points of conscience." None of that seemed so bad—not bad enough to deserve a reprimand in the confessional. She was hurt and confused. Scrupulosity was just one more thing to worry about.

As she washed her face and combed her hair, Rosie tried to focus on Father McGraw and those endless early confessions of skipped night prayers and uncharitable thoughts and anger at her mother and occasional lies. She tried to remember when she was a child and had emerged from the box feeling spotless and white, her soul a pure new garment, but already she could feel the familiar tightness of fear moving down her intestine toward her groin. Only once had she been eager to go, and that was before she was old enough to reach the age of reason. "I could go to confession too," she had volunteered one afternoon when she was six and Jack was almost nine. He had made his First Communion the year before, and Rosie longed to be one of the initiate. "I could go with you," she said. "I can say all the Commandments."

"No, you can't," Jack had said. "You mess everything up."

"Bet I can," Rosie said, and started reciting.

"You skipped one," Jack said. "You skipped 'covet thy neighbor's wife,' and besides, it's not 'dultery,' it's *a*dultery."

"Doesn't make any difference," Rosie said. "I know what it is."

"What?" Jack said. "What do you know that it is?"

"It's sassing back to adults," Rosie said. "It's what you do all the time, and you're gonna get it!"

"Jeez, what a dope!" Jack said. "You don't know your head from a hole in the ground!" He slapped his knee and tried to laugh like a grown-up. "Adultery is bad, secret things about your body," he said. "Everybody knows that."

[38]

Rosie eyed him somewhat belligerently and stuck the end of one pigtail in her mouth. "Huh!" she said, turning away. "You don't know neither."

"Jimmy Schultz committed adultery," Jack said, knowing it would make her turn. "Jimmy Schultz did it." Jimmy was in third grade.

"What did he do?" Rosie wanted to know. "What did Jimmy Schultz do?"

"He peed in old man Breen's mailbox," Jack said. "Old man Breen wouldn't let him trap gophers on his land, even after the bounty went up, so he got his brother to kneel down in the road, and he stood on his back, and he peed in the mailbox." Rosie was impressed. "Served the old coot right," Jack said. "He don't need the bounty from them gophers."

"Did he tell it?" Rosie said. "Did he tell the priest he committed adultery?"

"You'd like to know, wouldn't you?" Jack said.

It was no use. The innocence of those days was of no use even if she could laugh about it. She had ceased to be innocent; she had become an adolescent, and then an adult, and she had entered the world of sin . . . *in thought word and deed, through my fault, through my fault, through my most grievous fault*, the little altar boys bowed to the floor at Mass, and chanted without taking a breath.

Rosie let the rhythm of the Confiteor chant run through her head, but she tried to change the words: she had things to do today, she said as she pulled the covers tight on the bed, things to do, things and things to do. The mail hadn't been opened for three days, and there were sure to be bills to be paid. Except for leftover funeral casseroles, she hadn't much food. Stumpy McNabb had said he'd stay on at the elevator, but "arrangements would have to be made." What did that mean—"arrangements?" Would they hire a new manager? Would Stumpy take over and hire a new man to do his work? "Listen," Dora had said, "you have to dispose of his things, you know, Rosie. It's absolutely the worst part—going through the closets and all those pockets and never knowing what you'll run up against. Best to do it while you're still numb. Best to get it over with. Thanksgiving clothing drive is coming up."

She could do that. She could go to the Jack Sprat store that used to be Riedemacher's and get a few boxes; Jack never did have many clothes. Or she could go through the stack of envelopes left at the funeral parlor and see if there were any more Mass cards and take them over to the priests' house. She rejected that thought immediately; it was too close to the ones she was fending off. She could see young Father Griffin, his big, freckled hand leaning against the rectory door. "Ah Rosie," he'd say, "you keep us in business," and then he'd put down the envelopes and say, "Time to hit the confessional." Or the new pastor would be at the door, Father Schwartz, whose eyes were cautious and curious like a cat's. "Is that all you wanted, Rosie?" he'd say.

She got the boxes from the grocery store and dawdled over Jack's closet most of the day. She packed the shirts, keeping out a couple that would be good to wear for painting or in the garden, and she packed the socks, and the big, square linen handkerchiefs that had gotten dingy over the years, despite the trouble she had taken to keep them bleached. She took out some of the trousers, and his winter coat and ran her hands over the material, but put them back. She was afraid, and she didn't know why. It was as though those dark garments with their tangled arms and legs would somehow pull her into the tangle—as though there was a secret life in all those dark, limp limbs. And then there were pockets: "You never know what you'll run up against," Dora said. She didn't want to put her hands into the dark, secret places of Jack's life; she didn't like dark, secret places. The theatre with its red plush seats flashed into her mind—anonymous people thinking secret thoughts in the dark—the red velvet curtain of the confessional with its whispering, whispering. "I have sinned in thought," she would have to say. She pushed the trousers back into the closet and shut the door. The room was stuffy; rooms get stuffy fast in September when the sun still has a lot of life. She opened both windows and breathed in the brisk air. Already there were afternoon shadows lying sideways against the house, stretching their darkness toward her. Shoes. She would pack shoes. It didn't take long. In addition to the pair he was buried in, Jack had only two more.

It was after 3:30 when she got to the church. There was no point in being the first in line—no point in sitting right there in the pew where the priest would walk by when he came in. The little red light was on above the young priest's confessional. She chose a pew on the other side of the church and began automatically the Act of Contrition: "Oh my God, I am heartily sorry for having offended thee. . . ." *How did that little light go on?* she wondered. It must be attached to a switch under the seat the priest sat on, because the little white lights above the boxes went on when a penitent knelt down on the kneeler. One of those lights was going out now, and a farm woman Rosie barely knew emerged. Her tow-headed son replaced her. *He must be in fifth grade*, Rosie thought, *in Sister Mary Walter's room.* What if a little kid wasn't heavy enough to trip the switch and somebody walked in on him? What if the light in the priest's box got stuck, and he got called on a sick call, and you went in and recited all your sins and there was nobody there? Would you have to do it all over? Would you have to come back again? She imagined herself kneeling there, the white light burning outside, whispering her sins to a secret box of darkness. "I have sinned in thought," she would say. The only way to be safe was to tell it. "I was impure."

Movement in the front of the church caught her eye: a nun vacuuming the sanctuary. The nuns always vacuumed the sanctuary; it was too holy a spot for anyone else. Nuns were exempt from ordinary temptation; they didn't have impure thoughts. But Sister Carol Ann had seen that movie. Sister Carol Ann. *She must have closed her eyes at the bad parts*, Rosie thought. She must not have sinned in thought. Mrs. Goering was herding her two youngest daughters into line. The littler one was giggling about something, and her mother cuffed her softly on the side of the head. There was no one else in the pews now. Everyone else was in line. There were five people in line, and the young priest was slower than Father Schwartz, so it would be a while. But three of them were children, and children almost always went fast. The young priest was slower because he asked questions, Rosie remembered and then tried to forget. What would he ask her? What *could* he ask? He was over six feet and weighed too much. He was relatively thin below the waist, but had a large chest and shoulders that always hunched forward a little. He had played football in college, Dora said, but some of that muscle had turned to fat. He drank. No, that wasn't true. Dora's husband said he had a snootful half the time, but that wasn't true. He ate lunch with the school kids or the rest of the faculty since the housekeeper quit, and never once had he been drunk. Sometimes there was a faint vinegary smell, but that could be left from the wine at Mass. It *probably* was left from the wine at Mass. Maybe, in fact, it was something in his clothes.

There were only three people in line now; he was going fast. She would have to get up soon. She could sit here until everybody was finished, but then the young priest might come out of the box. He might say, "Sorry, Rosie, I didn't know you were here," and go back in the box again. Then he would know; there wouldn't be the secret darkness of anonymity in the box. It would be like confessing to his face. Or perhaps she could just leave when the last person went in—pretend she had just been making a visit and slip out the side door. Then tomorrow she would come to Mass, and everybody would be watching her because Rosie Deane went to a chivaree the day after her brother got put in the ground, and when communion came, she would have to stay in the pew because she was in sin.

The nun in the sanctuary had turned the vacuum off. Rosie got up and got in line. Mrs. Goering and the older girl were ahead of her. She had a good view of the windows on the other side of the church. They were of angels, silly-looking teen-age angels in long robes of pale orange and baby blue and pink. Some carried harps and some trumpets but none of them looked like they were capable of playing a thing. What would such foolish creatures know about carrying out God's justice? "Insipid," Sister Carol Ann had said about them once. What would they know about being impure?

She heard the soft scrape of a little wooden door being pushed back, and was aware that the low whispering had, for a moment, ceased. The little Goering girl pushed back the heavy red velvet curtain and stepped into the dark box on the priest's right. *I must prepare*, Rosie thought. *I must examine my conscience.* "Bless me Father, for I have sinned," she would say. "It has been three weeks since my last confession. I missed night prayers once, was inattentive during daily Mass two or three times, and I gossiped about my neighbors. I lied to a salesman, and I was impatient with my brother before his death. . . ." No, she couldn't say that. "I was impatient with a member of my family. . . ." That didn't sound right either; Jack was dead. The wooden slide scraped back again, and the one on the other side opened. The little Goering girl came out and her mother replaced her. Rosie moved two steps closer to the confessional. *What would the little girl tell?* she wondered. What would the mother? She remembered watching her own mother in the confession line, a scarf tied beneath her chin, her old coat half-buttoned, and a black rosary in her hand. What did she confess? Did she have things hidden, like all those hidden pockets in Jack's dark winter clothes? Did she think secret thoughts while poking in all the dark closets? Did she think secret thoughts in her big walnut bed? Wood scraped softly on wood again, and Debbie Goering came out. It was Rosie's turn to go in.

She pulled the heavy curtain aside and knelt on the thinly padded kneeler. It seemed to sink down only a little. Was that enough to trigger the switch for the little light? She folded her hands on the ledge below the square of black cloth. She could hear soft female whispering. There were a few old ladies in the parish who talked so loud she had to plug her ears so she wouldn't listen. She always plugged her ears. The female voice ceased and a male one took up the whispering. Now there were traded whispers back and forth. She couldn't hear any words. She didn't want to hear. The whispers were not nearly as loud as the sound of her heart. She tried to go back over her list, but it wouldn't come; she had forgotten it all. "I never rehearse," Dora had said once. "I just go in and say it."

"I rehearse," Rosie said. "In case I get nervous." *I* rehearse! I *rehearse*! She wanted to scream it, to scream it at Dora, and then she heard one sound of wood on wood and then another.

"Go ahead," the young priest said.

Back in the pew, she tried to sort it out. She felt relieved; she had told her sin; she had made a good confession. But mixed with the relief was a new kind of apprehension. Confession was supposed to be like a formula, a set of rules like a math problem, and the answer always came out the same. She had gone in, that was the first thing; she had told her sin; the priest had said, "I absolve you in the name of the Father and the Son and the Holy Spirit"; but here she was in the pew with no real penance and without the tidy feeling of groceries listed and purchased and stacked away. In one sense, this was easier than the old way. Father Griffin had not chided her; he had not brought up Our Lady of Fatima or the flames of hell, but somehow it didn't feel right.

"Bless me, Father, for I have sinned," Rosie had said. "It is three weeks since my last confession."

There was a pause then. No one said anything. Rosie could feel the racing of her heart.

"I was inattentive at Mass," she said, a little too fast. "I gossiped. I was impatient with my brother." She had forgotten to tell how many times.

There was another pause. Surely the priest would say something! Surely he would cut in with some pious words about how we must never fail to try to love Our Lord more each day, but he was silent; he sat waiting.

"I went to a movie I shouldn't . . . I shouldn't have gone to," she said. She took a breath but it caught in her throat. "I had impure thoughts." She said it so softly there was hardly voice mixed with the breath, but she had said it. She had told her sin. Now she could hear about our Lord's Passion and how His Blood had washed away the most vile of our sins, and then she would be finished and she could go.

"What movie did you see, Rosie?" the young priest asked calmly. *Priests*

Even now, as she remembered it, she was stunned, amazed. This was the most secret of secret places, behind a red velvet curtain, whispering to a voice that came through a grid in the dark. At that moment, her astonishment was greater than her shame. "You aren't supposed to know who I am!" she had hissed.

There was a low chuckle on the other side of the black square and Rosie became aware that she could see the outline of a head behind the cloth-covered grid. "I know who a lot of people are," the voice said, rather amused. "I just can't tell anyone what they said." There was a short silence. "Does that upset you?"

"No," Rosie said, but she realized even as she said it that it wasn't true. "I just thought it was all supposed to be secret. So people wouldn't have to worry if they met you on the street. . . ."

"People don't have to worry if they meet me on the street," he said. "Most of the stuff I hear isn't interesting enough to be worth remembering. Besides, that's not even the point. We're all sinners, Rosie. We need to forgive each other. So you went to a blue movie? Why should I bother to remember that? I've done worse things."

Rosie's mind leaped to imagine what he might have done—to that faint smell of wine in his clothes, but she stopped herself cold. "It wasn't a blue movie," she said. "It was *Doctor Zhivago.*"

"And that gave you impure thoughts?" he said. There was a tinge of disbelief in his voice. Rosie said nothing. "Ah, yeah," he said after a moment. "I wouldn't worry about it, Rosie. To have thoughts about sex is a natural thing. We're all sexual creatures; we were made that way. . . ." His voice slowed down as though he realized he was starting to sound like a speech.

"Ah, look," he said. "I don't want to keep you here all day. I just wouldn't worry about it too much if you find that thoughts about sex or the body run through your mind occasionally. That means you're still alive and healthy. If that bothers you, maybe sometime you can talk to somebody. Okay?"

"Okay," Rosie said. She didn't know what else to say.

"Is there anything else?" the young priest said.

"You didn't give me a penance," Rosie said.

"Okaaay," he said with a sort of sigh. "Let's see. How about if you plan something to be good to Rosie this week? Something nice for yourself, since you've been through some pretty rough days lately. Maybe find a way of meeting people who will fill up some of the space that Jack left—make one new friend. Do you think you can do something like that?"

She said five Hail Marys anyway. That was usually the minimal penance, and it seemed the least she could do. "I wouldn't worry about it, Rosie," he had said. "It means you're alive and healthy."

"A married woman can think about her husband all day," Sister Marisa had said in sophomore year during girls' homeroom, "but an unmarried woman must never think about a man in that way. Even thoughts that lead to such thoughts are sinful." The sun went under a cloud and the little spots of color on the pews disappeared. "I wouldn't worry about it." That was the advice she had been given in the confessional. That was God speaking in her life. But the penance? Do something nice for Rosie? She'd already bought a pantsuit. And how could she make new friends when she already knew everybody in town? She heard the dull thud of the wooden slide and realized, as a lone penitent emerged, that both white lights were out now; the priest would be leaving soon. She pulled her cardigan closer in anticipation of a September breeze and slipped out through the side door. She didn't want to face the young priest, whether her sins were interesting or not.

Chapter V

"WELL, IT'S ABOUT TIME!" DORA SAID WHEN THEY HEARD THE clatter of milk carton racks coming down the steps to the cafeteria. The clatter was accompanied by female giggles, and two sophomores in colored stockings and very short skirts burst through the door.

"We're helping the milkman!" Cheryl Hinely announced, entering the room rump first as she hung onto the dolly. Her hair was bleached almost as light as her mother's, and she wore it in a long straight style modeled after the Beatles fans in *Life* magazine. Doris Lean, who hung on the other side, had identical hair in dark brown that completely covered her eyebrows.

"He said he was late, so we're giving him a hand," Doris said, turning to the milkman with her coyest smile. The milkman looked a little embarrassed.

"Ah, I had a flat over by Lismore," he said. "That's what held me up. And I got ambushed by these two in the parking lot."

"Listen, why aren't you two in school?" Dora came from the kitchen to demand. She was holding the sloppy joe ladle in one hand and catching the drips with the other.

"McIvers threw us out of study hall," Cheryl said proudly.

"What for?" Dora said. The milkman had skirted behind the girls and begun to stack the racks of cartons next to the lunch trays.

"Ooo—let us help you!" Doris said.

"Never mind!" Dora stopped her with a sturdy arm. "Why did you get thrown out of study hall?"

"We were just playing cards," Cheryl said. "We play cards all the time. Study hall is sooo boring." She rolled her eyes and Doris began to giggle.

"You play cards in study hall?" Rosie said. There were some things she didn't understand.

"Did Mrs. McIvers tell you to come down here?" Dora continued.

"She sent us to Father Schwartz, but Mickey Runkle said . . ."

"What does Mickey Runkle have to do with this?"

"Well," Doris said, flipping her long hair first over one shoulder and then over the other with a self-conscious gesture, "that's why we got kicked out. We always play cards across the aisle—real quiet like—but today Mickey and Gil Simons turned their chairs around to play with us, and Runkle started bidding out loud." Both girls found that amusing.

Rosie knew the Runkle kid. He was a big, blond senior who usually needed a shave and was sullen and surly. He was nineteen but still in school. "Too smart to quit," Jack said; "they'd send his ass to Vietnam." Rosie used to feel sorry for Marion Runkle years ago when she brought her children into Riedemacher's store. She seemed to be always pregnant, always pulling a kid off a display, always hiding at the end of an aisle to count the contents of her change purse. One time Mickey slipped a Hershey bar into his back pocket, and Rosie told his mother. Mickey, who was eight or nine, had stared at her with such a betrayed, accusing look that she felt guilty for days.

"And did you go to Father Schwartz?" Dora asked.

"Mickey didn't," Doris Lean said. "He went to take a whiz." Cheryl doubled over with giggling. "We did though," Doris added. "We're such good girls! Father said, 'Well, go have lunch, and keep out of her hair from now on.'" She imitated the pastor's cocked head and slightly nasal tone. "He was playing with his printing press."

Father Schwartz spent most of his time playing with his printing press, Rosie knew, or at least it seemed so. He was a small, quick man with dark hair that was balding back from what had been a widow's peak. He wore glasses that were gray plastic on top and gold on the bottom over a rather arched nose. Dora said he looked like a Jew. He had set up a printing press in the basement of the rectory, "so we don't have to buy all those Sunday bulletins," but he was now doing two- and three-color printings. In addition to the bulletins, he did raffle tickets, programs for the school plays, auction handbills, rather shaky wedding announcements, and was lately doing stationery and cards. Rosie had gotten some as a present at the end of the term last spring. The cards said things like "Be groovy, not greedy," or "I am a human being. Do not fold, spindle, or mutilate," or "What if they gave a war and nobody came?" He even did cocktail napkins. He was officially administrator of the school, and the nuns often sent over discipline problems, but he wasn't very strict. "Aw, give the kids a little leeway," he said one day when he came to the cafeteria for an early lunch. "Those nuns are all neurotic, especially since they shortened their skirts." Then he showed Rosie his new calling cards that were printed to look just like engraving.

"Want us to help you with the second load?" Cheryl said to the milkman. He had finished stacking the first rack of half-pint cartons and was wheeling the dolly out.

"No thanks," he said. He caught Rosie's eye and gave her a puzzled shrug. When he returned, bumping the dolly down the steps, the oldest Roelling boy was with him. Jack used to call him "Alfalfa." "Why not?" he said. "His mother calls him 'Timothy.'" Rosie thought it was cruel. The boy had been born partially deaf and wore two hearing aids with cords that seemed to tie him down to a battery stalk on his chest. He was very bright but undersized for a seventh grader, and when he couldn't understand, his eyes would fill with tears. He looked a little tearful now.

"Ister hed I could have unch early," he said in a voice that was full of h's and timidness. "I have a octer appoinmen."

"Sure," Rosie said. There was something about this child that made her want to mother him. "I'll fix you right up." She took a plate and went back to the stove.

"You want green beans?" she called, turning just as Mickey Runkle and his sidekick, Gil Simons, came through the door.

"Hey, Timmy-baby," Runkle said, coming up to the serving counter. "You aren't supposed to eat lunch early. Don't they teach you no manners in grade school?" The two girls started giggling as Runkle plucked the blue feed-store cap off the little boy's head. "Hey, Simons, catch!" he said. Timmy Roelling grabbed for the cap, but Runkle pushed his arm down and sent the cap spinning.

"Hive it to me!" Timmy said. His eyes were starting to fill. If he ignored them and went on with his lunch, the cap would eventually come back unharmed, Rosie knew, but Timmy couldn't seem to learn that. "Hive it to me!" he said again, his voice getting shrill.

"Give him the cap," she said quietly. Simons eyed her steadily, as though trying to decide the weight of her authority; then his face moved into a strange half-grin. He tossed the cap up to Mickey Runkle, who twirled it on the end of his finger high above his head. Timmy began jumping for it; he was crying now.

"Say 'please,' Timmy-baby," Runkle said, backing away.

"Give him the cap!" Rosie said, this time sharply. "And stop tormenting him!"

"Aw, Timmy should learn some manners, Rosie. Say 'pretty please,' Timmy," he said again.

"The lady said to give him the cap," Ray Bowen said. Rosie had forgotten him, but his voice burst through so firmly that even Runkle was startled. Bowen was standing with both hands on the top rack of cartons; his forearms and his back were tensed. Rosie saw the two of them face off, each taking the other's measure. They were about equal in height, and for a moment, she thought there might be a fight. "And get the hell out of here until it's time for you to eat," Bowen said, his eyes never flickering.

Runkle slid the cap down, but his eyes never left the milkman's face. "Here you are, sweetheart," he said, not looking at Timmy. "Keep your head nice and warm." He turned and ran his eyes over Rosie as he and Simons left the room. "Bitch," he said, just loud enough for her to hear.

The first graders were coming in then, their little voices swooping down like locusts. Dora was at the steam table, and before Rosie quite recovered, she found herself dishing sloppy joes to a three-foot-tall line that twisted and walked backwards, and bent over to pull up knee socks. When she looked again, the milkman was gone.

It was 2:30 when Rosie gave the last wipe to the steam table and headed for Worthington to see Williard Schreck. Schreck was a lawyer. He had been a lawyer for as long as any of the present generation could remember, and he practiced out of a two-room office over Landy's funeral parlor, which he filled with the smoke of very thin cigars. "Wouldn't want you girls to smell the stiffs," he had said to Dora once when she told him the cigars were foul. He lived on the edge of town and raised mink in a little poleshed. He had been gap-toothed until about five years ago, and Rosie could never get used to the smooth, pearly flow of his dentures. "Hell, Schreck is goin' to choke one a these days," Jack said when he first saw the upper plate. "Ain't used to having to open his mouth to spit."

Schreck pursed his mouth so the teeth didn't show as Rosie sat before him that afternoon in a room lit only with slanting October light. "Hmmm," he said, "not too bad. Not too bad." He was surveying the will and the contents of the safe-deposit box spread out before him. "Seems that house has been in your name ever since your Ma died, and you got close to a half interest in that elevator, and a couple, three thousand worth of blue chips. Course, all this has to go through probate...."

"What kind of blue chips?" Rosie said. She had paid no attention to the stock market until Mama got sick and she had to quit her job at Riedemacher's. She was bothered by money as soon as she realized that she had none—none except the $200 she had salted away from her weekly checks, and the three war bonds about to come due. Jack gave her money for groceries, and Mama could still sign checks for the few things they charged around town, but she had nothing of her own. She had started noticing the stock reports that came on the radio after the hog market report, and one day she saw a letter from United Mutual Investment Company on Dora's dining room table when she went to borrow vases to decorate the altars for May crowning. "I've got these war bonds that came due last winter," she said, "but they pay so little I'm tempted just to cash them in."

It was all the opening Dora needed. "Listen," she said, "my brother-in-law—Muriel's husband, the one with the limp from over by Pipestone—he's selling mutual funds. . . ." Rosie listened, but she was wary. She still remembered the time Dora talked her into having a party to sell Stanley Home Products and the only premium she earned was a toilet brush. But she went over the next week when Muriel's husband came around, drank coffee with him and Dora, and signed on for $20 a month. "I don't know what the family would think of this," she said as she was leaving. "I'd be obliged if you didn't mention this to Jack."

After that she watched the mail and carefully extracted the statements before she gave the mail to Mama. When Jack was out, she sat at the old rolltop desk in the room Pa used for an office, and added up how much she had gained and how much she might expect. It was like a game, like a secret fingering of gold coins in the dark, and she guarded it as she might have done a secret vice. After Mama died, Jack took over the family affairs and pushed aside her questions, but there were wages again, and every month she invested a small amount.

"Ah, the usual," Schreck said, in response to her question about blue chip stocks. "A little AT&T, a little General Motors. Problem is you got to liquidate some of this to pay the inheritance tax."

"What are you recommending?" Rosie said. She didn't like the idea of selling good stock.

"Well, seeing as that elevator has been in the family since your grandpa . . . 'course, you may not even plan to stay in St. Ives. . . ."

"I'm not going anywhere," Rosie said. "Where would I go?"

"Well, you might . . ." Schreck said. "Way I look at it, Rosie, you're sort of like a widow—you know, you're on your own now, and you can run the show. . . ." He leaned forward across the desk and his upper plate gleamed. "You won't find a widow to admit it," he said confidentially, "but some of 'em find out they kind of like the deal—you know, take the dough and run the whole circus yourself . . ." His mouth closed into a sly smile. "Less of a nuisance too, some of 'em think . . . if you know what I mean." He leaned back and put his hands behind his head.

Rosie was embarrassed. She was not a widow and they both knew it. "But what should I sell?" she said.

"Well, why don't you let me take care of that?" Schreck said, leaning over his cigar drawer. "No reason you should worry about it."

"I'm not worried," Rosie said. "I just want to know what you're going to do."

"Well, I don't know yet, little lady," Williard Schreck said, as though speaking to a forward child, "but you got a lot of paper here. My opinion is, a woman ought to have some cash on hand, some chicken feed to spend when she gets the notion. . . ." He slowed and his eyes narrowed. "You got some big plans?"

"No," Rosie said. She felt rebuked, put in her place, but her plans or lack of them were none of Schreck's business. And he needn't think she was too stupid to handle stock.

"Well, then, there's the elevator," Schreck said above the smoke of the cigar he was trying to light. "You don't own more than half anyway. . . ."

"But would that give someone else a chance for controlling interest?" she said.

Schreck looked at her with new respect. "Got this figured pretty good, haven't you?" he said. "Tell you what, why don't I get together a list of your options, and you can come back Thursday. Meantime, you can get Stumpy to show you the books."

"Fine," Rosie said. "Thank you." She headed for the door feeling amazed at herself, and a little frightened. She could understand columns of figures easily enough, but she really had no idea what would be the best course to take. She was not about to tell Schreck that, however. Her small but secret hoard of mutual funds had been her main source of pleasure these last years, and she was not about to let some mink-farming lawyer take that pleasure away.

It wasn't until Wednesday, when the milkman came again, that Rosie had a chance to thank him for Monday's rescue. She was emptying the day's tin cans into the trash bin in the parking lot, thinking of his boldness in rebuking Mickey Runkle, of Mickey's impudence. . . .

A half-scene from the month before flicked through her mind: Cheryl Hinely throwing her weight to one hip as she pushed her tray through the cafeteria line, the hip jutting out enough to tilt the miniskirt, the eyes flicking over Mickey Runkle who was just behind her in the line. But it was not Mickey, it was Gil Simons with the pimply face and furtive look whose eyes were hungrily on her.

"Want a bite?" Cheryl held out an apple coyly toward the boys.

Mickey Runkle grabbed the fruit and sank his teeth into it, while Gil Simons said, "I'll take any bites I can get."

Cheryl's face changed; a cold sheet dropped down over her expression. "I bet you would." She took the apple back from Runkle and moved forward with her tray. An arrow of pain flashed across Simons' face, Rosie remembered, before he lowered his head and hid his eyes behind the flopping forelock of his hair.

The milk truck from Luverne pulled in, and Rosie waited until the milkman jumped down to tell him she was grateful for his help on Monday.

"Don't thank *me*," Ray Bowen said. "I know I shouldn't have butted in, but that hoodlum made me mad. I wanted to boot his little ass!" He flushed slightly. "Excuse my French."

"That's okay," Rosie said. Jack's language had been worse.

"You really like that little deaf kid, don't you?" Ray said, changing the subject.

"Yes." Rosie smiled. "I do. I don't know what it is, but he seems so helpless. . . . Do you have children?"

He shook his head and put the lid down on the trash bin for

her. "Nope," he said. He looked a little uneasy. "They just never came, and it's probably just as well now. They'd be hard for me to raise alone."

There was a silence as Ray loaded the dolly. Rosie didn't know whether she should stay or walk across the parking lot ahead of him. Either seemed awkward. "Well, anyway, thank you again for coming to my rescue the other day," she said to say something. The rattle of the dolly made conversation unnecessary then, and Rosie was relieved. She relaxed and found herself noting the warmth of the autumn sun on her arms as she walked across the parking lot beside him.

Chapter VI

ROSIE BEAT ON THE KETTLE FOR ALL SHE WAS WORTH. "FASTER," Dora kept saying, "beat faster. We've got to keep them inside." They were circling the trailer, and all the lights were out. "Faster, Rosie," Dora urged, "faster." She stomped her feet as she pounded with the spoon. The entire circle was stomping its feet, circling around and around in a kind of frenzy. We can't let them out, Rosie knew, we can't let them out. Ahead of her Dora wore a hat with a feather that stood straight up like an Indian's. Across the circle, Jim Hinely wore a large Sioux headdress. The feathers were a pinkish color and jiggled as he stomped up and down. "Beat faster," Dora said, and Rosie could hear bells in the cacophony of sound. The figures jolted up and down. Some wore fur and bells on their ankles; the bells jingled, and they stomped and stomped. A feather fell from Jim's headdress. Rosie stopped to pick it up, but it wasn't a feather, it was a wiener. Suddenly the headlights of a car caught her, blinded her, and she stood paralyzed like a small animal in the road. She stood in the glare holding the wiener and the bells rang. All the other noises stopped, and the bells rang and rang.

It's the alarm, Rosie thought. *No, it's the phone. Dear God, it's the phone.*

She caught her foot in her nightgown as she stumbled out of bed and down the stairs to what had been Mama's bedroom. It was Monday. She was late for work. Dora was calling. "Listen, do you have any idea what time it is?" Dora would say.

"Hello," Rosie said. "Hello?"

Dora said something about a truck, but that didn't make sense.

"What?" Rosie said again, but it wasn't Dora's voice. It was a man's voice and he was talking very softly, or else he was very far away. "What did you say?"

"I'm going to fuck you," the voice said. "I'm going to come over there and fuck your sweet little ass."

Rosie dropped the phone. It hit the baseboard with a crack, and bounced to the floor. The cord coiled upward like the tendril of a creeping vine. For a moment she thought feet were still stomping, but it was her heart. "I'm going to fuck you," the voice had said. "I'm going to come over there . . ." She backed to an old straight-backed chair against the wall and sat down. The receiver still dangled from its tendril like a kind of evil fruit. *Jack*, she thought. *Jack can put it back on the hook.* But Jack was dead. Jack couldn't be wakened. There was no one else in the house. "Bong," went the clock on the old oak buffet. "Bong, bong." It was 3:00 A.M.

I should call Stan Kemp, Rosie thought. Stan Kemp was the village cop. He drove an old green Chevy with a red light on the top. There wasn't much to do besides ring the curfew bell and break up fights after the basketball games, so he worked a few mornings a week at the elevator, and drank beer most of the afternoon. *I should call Stan*, Rosie thought; but what could she say? She couldn't say, "A man called and said, 'I'm going to fuck you.'" She couldn't say, "A man called and says he wants to come over here." Rosie looked at the phone still dangling to the floor. She would have to pick it up to call; she would have to touch it. She left the phone where it was, walked from the room and headed for the stairs.

But what if he comes? Rosie went to the kitchen door and tested it. Most people in St. Ives never locked their doors. "Hell," Jim Hinely used to say, "I got nothin' anybody'd want, and the only time they'd take Lila was if it was awful dark!" The kitchen door was locked. "I got a young girl in the house," Mama used to say, "and that highway keeps going all night long."

The front door was locked too. Rosie took a big old-fashioned key and stuck it in the lock. That way you couldn't stick a key in from the other side. She had read that once in a magazine. The windows had locks too. She couldn't remember ever locking them, and the old metal half-circles turned hard, but she locked every one—even the windows in the dining room that had become Mama's bedroom where the phone still lolled on its twisting stem. She realized as she looked at it that something was different now. Mama was dead and Jack was dead and the windows were locked. The clock ticked off the seconds into separate spaces where anything could hide. This was a new kind of fear.

"Rosie got an obscene phone call," Dora announced when they had both put down their lunch trays at the table where the second shift of faculty was eating. It was 12:30 and only a few high school students remained, lounging in a far corner of the lunchroom.

"Here? In St. Ives?" the young priest said, swallowing the cornbread in his mouth. He looked amused. "I didn't know anybody had that much gumption."

"Well, Father!" Dora said.

"When?" Mrs. McIvers said. "About a week ago? I got one too!" Everyone at the table turned to her. Mary McIvers was small and pretty with oversized glasses. She hadn't been teaching long.

"No, this was just last night," Dora responded.

"About three in the morning," Rosie added for accuracy, but she was sorry they were discussing this. It made her feel like she did waiting in the doctor's inner office—like an object somehow aware of its flesh. She had told Dora only because she kept forgetting how many eggs she put in the cake mix, and where she was in the tray count. She thought if she told someone, she could get it out of her mind.

"The St. Ives Caller!" Father Griffin said, buttering another square of cornbread. He was obviously still amused.

"Well, it isn't funny!" Sister Grace leaned down the table, her tucked and pleated bosom just missing the macaroni and cheese on her tray. She taught typing and shorthand and was one of the nuns who still wore the full long habit. Most of the others had changed over the summer to mid-calf skirts and veils that showed an inch of hair in front. "Some pervert called the convent a couple of weeks ago," she said, "and that's about as low as you can get!"

"When?" Sister Carol Ann demanded. She was one of the younger nuns, twenty-six or twenty-seven, a tall, slender woman with Scandinavian good looks. She suffered from hay fever and the slight redness around the eyes and nose gave her a wistful look.

"The first week of school," Sister Grace said with the air of someone with privileged knowledge. "Sister Geraldine didn't see any sense in upsetting the younger Sisters." Sister Geraldine was the superior.

"Sister Geraldine wouldn't know those words," Sister Carol Ann said half under her breath.

"That's not so!" Sister Grace said. "He wanted to know what color panties the Sisters wore!"

Father Griffin and Sister Carol Ann looked at each other in amazement and burst into laughter. Mary McIvers giggled. Rosie found herself wanting to laugh with them, though it was dreadful to say such a thing to a nun.

"Is that what he asked you?" the priest said to Rosie.

"It certainly is not!" Dora said. "He threatened her. He used barnyard language about you-know-what!"

"Mine was a threat too," Mary McIvers said. "A rape threat. In no uncertain terms. Glenn was out of town last week, and I was scared to death."

"That's a different story," the priest said. His face had sobered, and his eyes focused on Rosie. "What did this guy say to you?"

"He said he was going to come over and . . . he said he was going to rape me, I guess," she said, but the words still stung in her ear: *I'm going to fuck your sweet little ass.*

"He seems to know who he's calling," Sister Carol Ann said. "He wouldn't ask about the Sisters' panties if he were just picking random numbers."

"Well, he wouldn't be picking random numbers, anyway," Sister Grace said, as though teaching a class. "Sister Geraldine says most obscene callers know their victims. She says that's a proven statistic, just like rape."

"Did it sound like anybody you'd recognize!" Dora wanted to know. "Anything peculiar about the voice? You could start listening to all the men. . . ."

"Now, just a minute," the priest said. "You can't just go around suspecting people. Voices are too much alike."

"I told Sister Geraldine to call the police," Sister Grace said. "I told her if it happens again, to call the police, and I don't mean Stan Kemp either. I told her to get right on the phone to the sheriff. You should call the sheriff too, Rosie."

"It wouldn't do much good now," Rosie said. She realized she had been stirring her macaroni and cheese, but hadn't tasted it. "And it probably won't happen again."

"Let's hope not," the young priest said. He looked as if he were going to say something else, but the dull sound of the five-minute bell came from across the school yard.

"Some days I think I'd rather hear a pervert than that bell," Mary McIvers sighed, and everybody laughed. "Well, onward and upward!" She picked up her tray and the others followed. Rosie was left under Dora's gaze.

"Listen, Rosie," she said, reaching across and taking hold of the edge of her tray. "Who do you think it could be?"

In one way or another, the obscene caller appeared at the lunch table almost every day that week. Dora and all the older nuns had stories of what happens to people in big cities where perverts lurk behind every tree.

"I always tell my girls they don't know how lucky they are to live here," Dora said.

"You said it," Sister Grace said. "That's what I tell the girls in my homeroom: 'Be grateful the good Lord put you where He did!' " She waited as Sister Carol Ann, the last of the younger faculty to leave the table, moved out of earshot. "You know why we're getting those calls," she said, averting her head just slightly toward the younger nun. "This never happened before we got into all *that* nonsense."

Dora turned quickly to look at Carol Ann's departing back. "What?" she said. "Oh—you mean the skirts?"

"Well, it stands to reason," Sister Grace said. "If you're going to dress like a secular, you'll act like a secular. . . . And whose fault is it if men get ideas?"

"But a person who makes obscene calls . . ." Rosie began.

Sister Grace shifted her head to focus Rosie in the bottom half of her bifocals. "Now, I'm not saying it has anything to do with you," she said. "You only took them to that fashion show because Sister Geraldine asked you to."

It was true. Rosie had been dubious last spring when Sisters Carol Ann and Gaelynn had squeezed, giggling, into the front seat of her car to go to the "Change-Your-Habits Fashion Show," as they had called it.

"It's all nonsense," Sister Geraldine had said when she asked Rosie to drive them. "Nothing will come of it. But they got the material from their families, so what could I do?"

The story, as Rosie pieced it together from Sister Geraldine and the two who were so obviously pleased with themselves in the front seat of her car, was that some cardinal in Europe had written a book about nuns in the modern world, which said habits should be more practical. "This is really the dress of a European peasant in the twelfth or fourteenth century," Sister Gaelynn said. It was a phrase she seemed proud of. She ran her hand over the linen wimple that covered all of her neck and left a slight red ridge where it cut into her chin. "And if we dressed like the common poor people back then, we should dress like them now," she said with certitude. Rosie had a flash of nuns in faded print dresses or in overalls, looking a little like Marion Runkle.

The Sisters of Mary Mediatrix had always worn an ample black habit, pleated down the front, a large stiff collar, a linen wimple around their heads, and a stiff linen band that held the veil. All that was due to be modernized. "It's just a concession to a few

[61]

agitators," Sister Geraldine said. "Just a handful who want it." And Rosie found herself driving two of this handful to the motherhouse on a bright spring Saturday to model the habits they had designed.

"Mine's blue," Sister Gaelynn volunteered. She coached the cheerleaders, and Rosie sometimes had the feeling she'd still like to be one. "They didn't say they had to be black."

"Will you wear these veils?" Rosie asked.

"Oh, no!" they said at once.

"I made a short veil that fits on a headband," Carol Ann said. "It shows about an inch of hair in front."

"And I don't think we need a veil at all," Gaelynn said. "Common poor people don't wear veils." She pulled a pin somewhere on the back of her head, lifted up the back of the veil and ducked out of the whole contraption as though it were a helmet. She had a head of shining brown curls with just a touch of auburn. Rosie was so astonished she almost swerved into the other lane. There was something unsettling about having a nun sitting beside her with her head exposed—it was like seeing someone bathe.

"Carol Ann thinks the veil is still a symbol," Gaelynn announced. "She's more conservative."

"No, I'm not," Carol Ann said, as though it were a damaging charge, "I'm more realistic. I don't think you're going to get away with it." Her face took on the impatient, wistful look it sometimes had. She was a slender woman with that lithe, natural grace that inspires unconscious envy in other women. Lately, however, the wistful expression appeared more often, but maybe it was just the hay fever getting worse.

Rosie went shopping during the "fashion show." It took place somewhere in a cloistered part of the motherhouse she was not allowed to enter. When she came back at three o'clock, as arranged, the portress-nun looked her up and down disapprovingly, but ushered her to a parlor of stiffly carved chairs. There was nothing to read except a *Lives of the Saints* on a low shelf of a side table, and nothing on the white walls except a crucifix and a worn tapestry that appeared to be peasants harvesting sheaves of grain. She waited alone for over an hour. Now and then she heard soft bell tones that seemed to be a kind of signal: one-two-one, or three-one-four, or two-two-three. She imagined they called the nuns to prayer, or to perform some kind of penance. She listened carefully after each bell code, but she could hear nothing except soft footfalls or occasional distant voices. The nuns who taught in St. Ives weren't so mysterious; they bought groceries at the Jack Sprat, and sometimes got impatient with the children, and gave blood for the Red Cross in the public school gym, lying on the table in their habits with a bare arm spread out like the underside of a dark wing. But here in the motherhouse, even nuns who had taught in St. Ives seemed to have all the intrigue and clandestine secrets of her childhood. Jack had brought home amazing stories one summer when he was about twelve and had taken to hanging around with Protestants.

"See, they have this tunnel that goes from the convent to the rectory," he said, "and at night they all sneak back and forth. And there are all sorts of rooms down below the basement—that's where they shave their heads to keep the young ones from running away—they shave them every night—and. . . ."

"I don't believe that," Rosie said. Sister Theresa was young, and one day on the playground when the wind caught her veil, Rosie had gotten a glimpse of straight, dark hair. And she didn't believe that Sister Casmir, who was so old even her eyebrows were white, went through any tunnel at night.

"Well, it's true," Jack said. "Maybe not here, because the nuns we get are mostly ugly, but in places like New York and Europe. And in the middle of the tunnel, they've got a well where they drown the babies. . . ."

"What babies?"

"The ones the nuns and priests have. That's where they get all those little babies people adopt out of the Catholic orphanages. Where'd you think they came from?"

Rosie thought with astonishment of Sister Casmir or Sister Theresa drowning a baby. It was quite a revelation, but there was still something about it that didn't make sense. "How can the babies be in the orphanage if they get drowned?" she said.

Jack looked perplexed, but only for a moment. "Well," he said, "I suppose the ones that can swim they let live."

Mama got wind of the story somehow, but she was less upset than Rosie would have expected. "That's the kind of lies you get from Protestants," she said. "What do you expect from people who don't have a true religion?"

Rosie heard another soft bell call in the motherhouse, and suddenly the two young nuns were with her, looking disappointed, but full of laughter. They told her about it on the way home.

"Well," Gaelynn said, "we didn't win."

"I wonder if anybody won," Carol Ann said a little sourly. "Mother Demetria got up at the end looking slightly purple and thanked us all for our participation and said"—she switched to a higher, pinched-mouth tone—" 'I wish to assure the Sisters that whatever decision eventuates, it will be made with the utmost regard for propriety and religious modesty.' "

"Well, that leaves out Gleason," Gaelynn said. They both laughed. "Terri Gleason came in a little green suit that she borrowed from a dress shop, and it had a mini-skirt," Gaelynn explained. "She stood up there with her knees hanging out and said she would have let it down, but it was on loan. And boy, did she flunk the genuflect test!"

"We had to walk across the stage in the auditorium one by one, and sit in a straight chair, and come to the edge of the stage and genuflect," Carol Ann said. "Was that a sight! Half the nuns almost fell over, they were so nervous that Mother D. might catch a glimpse of their thighs." They both giggled. "But who would have thought forty people would show up?" Carol Ann marveled.

"Not Mother Demetria, that's for sure," Gaelynn said. "But just wait, she'll pick one of the dumpy ones."

"Like Sister Prudencia's?" Carol Ann said. "With fourteen tucks across the front for bosom modesty?" Then she turned serious. "You know, she almost has to. I mean, there's already such a split." She turned to Rosie: "Most of the old nuns are really opposed to this—and some of the younger. Some of the old ones have been in the order so long they never wore a short skirt—not even before they entered. It's a hard thing," she concluded. "Old Sister Margaret—she must be about ninety—grabbed my arm as I was going to the auditorium and said, 'Aren't you ashamed, exposed like that? What would the blessed Mother think?'"

"She'd think blue was prettier," Gaelynn sighed, and they all were silent.

"I'm sorry we were late," Carol Ann said after a while.

"It's okay," Rosie said. "I just sat there trying to figure out if all those bells were some kind of code."

"The call bells? They are. If one of the sisters has a phone call or a visitor, they just ring her number. It saves a lot of steps."

"Oh," Rosie said. She was disappointed.

Rosie was glad no one brought up the obscene call the day the milkman was late again, and Dora told him he might as well stay for lunch. When Rosie got to the table, he was sitting across from Sister Carol Ann, who was picking gloomily through a kidney-bean-and-ground-beef casserole.

"Are kidney beans supposed to be protein?" she asked.

"Why?" Rosie said.

"Well, no offense," the young nun said, "but there's so little meat in here you could have eaten it on Friday even before they changed the rules."

"Sorry," Rosie said, but her feelings were a little hurt. "Government surplus was big on kidney beans this month."

"Think of the starving children in China," Sister Gaelynn volunteered.

"Or Africa," Mary McIvers said. "All those little kids with the big bellies and empty bowls . . ."

"All right, you guys!" Sister Carol Ann held up her hand to stop the teasing. "I think it's very nutritious, and very good, and I'd be delighted to have it again tomorrow."

"What a martyr!" Sister Gaelynn said. "I'll bet in grade school, you were one of those kids who wanted to be a missionary and get stoned to death!"

"Well," Sister Carol Ann said, "as a matter of fact, I spent most of third grade drawing pictures of the lions that ate the Christians."

Rosie had never drawn lion pictures, but she could still see the big *Lives of the Saints* on the shelf under Mama's sewing basket in the parlor. About half of the saints in it got fed to the lions; most of the rest were tortured by Indians or savage Moors. As a child, she always worried about what she would do if tortured. She could see it yet: a young Rosie suspended over a pot of boiling oil. "Do you renounce your faith?" her tormentor would ask. Or worse: a grinning pagan would be pulling her fingernails out one by one. "No! No!" she could hear herself screaming, and then: "Stop! Stop! I'll say I don't believe! I'll say anything!"

Everyone at the table was laughing. "You look so serious, Rosie," Sister Carol Ann was saying. "We won't let the lions get you. I think they only eat cheerful Christians, anyway."

Rosie was confused. "I don't think I could be a martyr," she said, her voice very sad. "I used to worry about it when I was a little girl. If they tortured me, I'm still afraid I'd chicken out."

"Can't you see Rosie as a martyr," Sister Gaelynn giggled, "willingly letting the heathen toss her into a boiling vat of government surplus soup?" They all laughed again, and Rosie forced herself to smile. She could feel the milkman watching her.

She wished they wouldn't joke about it. Of course, she knew she wouldn't be boiled in oil, but what if there were real situations in which you had to choose. . . . What if, for instance, someone tried to rape you and had a knife? What if he said he'd kill you unless you let him do it? What if someone broke into your house . . .

The five-minute bell rang, masking something Sister Gaelynn was saying. "Leave your trays," Rosie said. "I'll clear them."

It was at least ten minutes before she took the baskets of discarded milk cartons and napkins up to the trash bin in the parking lot, but Ray Bowen was still fiddling with something on the back of his truck. He strolled over and lifted the lid on the bin for her. "You know," he said in a voice she recognized as deliberately casual, "I worried about that kind of thing when I was a lot older than you were. Not about martyrs—but I got drafted just before the end of the war. I worried about Japanese prison camps, and what I'd do if they tortured me. I worried about it my whole senior year."

Rosie looked up at him. He had the alert eyes of a squirrel, she thought again, but they were very kind. Jack would never have been so gentle, nor would Pa. "Thank you," she said. "Thank you for telling me." And then, to hide her confusion, she dumped the baskets so fast a few cartons missed and went tumbling to the ground. The milkman stooped and tossed them into the bin.

"Well, have a nice afternoon," she said. It sounded banal and stupid; a high school girl could have done better, but there was nothing else to say. She grabbed the baskets and started across the parking lot, holding herself to keep from running.

Chapter VII

THE PEASANT BLOUSE WAS CUT LOWER THAN ANYTHING ELSE ROSIE owned. There was no real cleavage, but the skin revealed a gentle undulation in the structure beneath it, the way the prairie sometimes revealed a slight draw or dip in its surface by a gentle undulation of the wheat. Last year, she had raised the neckline by means of a safety pin that bunched together some material in the back. This year, she decided that that was awkward and uncomfortable; the blouse would have to do as it was.

Rosie was excited despite herself as she buttoned the tight black vest and tied on the tiny apron. It was the only costume she had ever had; and though she didn't really look like a Bavarian *Frau*, it was close enough for the St. Ives Oktoberfest.

The Oktoberfest had started as an ice cream social at the Catholic church when she was a very little girl. A bake sale was added, then a quilt raffle and a booth of home-canned goods, and gradually it moved to a weekend in mid-October and picked up a carnival atmosphere. The American Legion set up a beer garden, the Lutherans added booths, high school bands from towns big enough to have them began to play—somehow, it had become the Oktoberfest. "Damn Germans just want an excuse to play their kraut songs," Jack said; but he always worked one of the kegs in the beer garden, and he always came home singing and drunk.

Rosie had felt strangely disappointed after the Oktoberfest the last few years. It was a little like Christmas—you never got over your childhood expectation that some exciting surprise was sure to arrive, and once you were grown, nothing ever did. It would be another year of pies for the bake sale, of buying raffle tickets from every kid in the neighborhood, of shivering over the bratwurst and sauerkraut as the afternoon turned cold, of helping friendly drunks count their change. . . . There would even be the same people working in the lunch stand: Dora, Lila Hinely, Gina Pratt . . . and then Ray Bowen.

Father Griffin had stopped her three days ago on her way out of Mass: "You and Dora are running the lunch stand at Oktoberfest, aren't you?" Rosie nodded. "Well, that fellow who hauls the milk was asking me about the fest and volunteered to help. I thought we'd put him in the food stand." He paused. "You know him, don't you?"

"Well, he hauls the milk . . ." Rosie said.

"Good," the priest said. "He can lift the pop canisters and do the heavy stuff." The priest's lips formed a slight smile. "Be good to him," he said.

She was excited, Rosie told herself, not about the Oktoberfest, but because it was one of those perfect days that October can produce in Minnesota, when the cold seems to stay its hand like an indulgent parent, and the sky stretches out forever. There was a sense of ripeness everywhere, Rosie thought as she walked toward the church. On days like this she used to dream that she was in a covered wagon, rolling westward through an endless meadow of late, golden grass. She would wear a sunbonnet, and her husband would be beside her steering the oxen, his eyes squinting into the future they would make together. Sometimes in the dream, she would be big with child, or sometimes a toddler would be sitting on her knee.

Rosie laughed at herself as she looked down at her German costume. There were no sunbonnets on the prairie anymore, and she would never have a child. Instead of a line of covered wagons, she could see crepe paper streamers looped over the two-by-fours that framed the booths in the parking lot. People were beginning to gather beneath them, and Jim Hinely had already established himself behind the bingo cage and was testing the microphone: "Under the B: 15," he called, "I: 19, and under the O: my friend Rosie!"

She flushed and laughed and ducked inside the booth, where Dora, who was in charge of the second shift, had come to see that things were set up properly. Dora was counting out change, letting each coin drop with a deliberate clink; she had the ruffled look of an agitated cluck-hen. "Hello," she said curtly to Rosie and went on counting. *There's been trouble already*, Rosie thought; not everyone took kindly to Dora's bossing. Lila Hinely, with a purple mum in her hair and a blouse cut much lower than Rosie's, was making the coffee with extraordinary concentration, and Gina Pratt, an eager young woman whose husband was principal of the public school, was breaking the buns apart, her small face gathered in a nervous frown. Only Sister Carol Ann rolled napkins around silverware with a deliberate serenity.

"Dora," the young nun was saying, in a tone one might use with an unreasonable child, "it's no reflection on you. These are adult people. They can choose their own lives."

"Yes," Dora said, her plump hand quivering, "and disgrace everybody else."

Rosie looked from one to the other. Lila continued to fuss with the coffee pot, and Gina was putting the buns back in the plastic wrappers with elaborate care.

"I asked Dora if she was related to the Charlotte Heinkamp whose picture was in this morning's paper—the one who married the priest," the young nun said. "I didn't mean to embarrass her."

"It's all right; it's all right." Dora snapped shut the cash box. "It's already out there for all the world to see." She whipped a newspaper from underneath her purse and handed it to Rosie. "PRIEST MARRIES FORMER HOUSEKEEPER," the page-three headline said.

Bright paperback covers in a Sioux Falls drugstore flashed through Rosie's mind. "Would his passion for Irina be stronger than his priestly vows?" one said above the drawing of a half-naked woman and a priest who looked like a movie star. "He was a spoiled priest, and she was untouched innocence," said another. The newsprint photo Dora gave her was of an ordinary middle-aged man in a sport shirt and a plump woman with bouffant hair and glasses. They looked as if they had been married for years. "Ex-priest Fritz Mathis and his wife, the former Charlotte Heinkamp," the caption said. Rosie had a vague memory of Charlotte as a girl. She had stayed in St. Ives with her aunt and uncle all of one summer—a plain, self-effacing girl with a slight stutter. She was Jerry Heinkamp's first cousin.

"How could he do that?" Dora was demanding. "There's no excuse for Charlotte—though she always was a goose—but how could *he* do that? Say Mass one day and run off with a woman the next? Hear somebody's confession and then turn right around and do worse himself!" Dora got short of breath when she was excited, and she was almost wheezing now.

"Two priests from Detroit got married last year," Lila volunteered, moving in close. "I read it in the paper. I think they were Jesuits."

"He could probably do it because he had to," Sister Carol Ann said. "It sounds like he's gone through a lot, and he probably decided this was the only way he could . . ."

". . . and drag everybody else through the mud with him," Dora said. She was clutching the cash box against her breast like a lost child.

Rosie looked from one to the other, saying nothing. It was amazing to think of a priest you actually knew getting married; it was like thinking of your mother as an adulteress. It was shocking, but in some part of her brain, she felt a surge of gladness she didn't understand. "I've done worse things than that," the young priest had said to her in confession. . . .

"He says he's just following his conscience," Gina said shyly.

"Listen, it must be nice to have a conscience that lets you walk off on your responsibilities . . ." Dora began, but Rosie's eyes were flicking down the column of newsprint:

I came to the conclusion that celibacy is not necessary for the service of God or even for the ministry—that I serve an incarnate God who is present in the sufferings and needs of those around me, and that I can best meet those needs when I am a whole and growing person. For me, that means the freedom to give and receive love . . .

"Well, you could just about see it coming," Rosie heard Dora's voice continue. "First they change the Mass to English, and then they tear up the church and turn the altar around, and then the nuns stop wearing habits. . . ." She looked Carol Ann's short black dress up and down. "And the next thing you know, the priests and their housekeepers are running off!"

"Society is changing too," Gina Pratt said softly. Dora turned her head and stared at her; she was in no mood for contradictions from someone who'd lived in St. Ives less than two years.

"Why can't priests get married?" Carol Ann said. "Ministers seem to manage."

"Well!" Dora said, taking a large spoon and plunging it into the vat of hot potato salad. "I'm sure I'd like to go to confession to a married man!"

"Why not?" Ray Bowen said in a teasing tone. None of them had seen him come up and stand with his elbows on the plank counter.

Dora glared at him, then stirred the potato salad with great energy, her breath coming in little puffs. "Some people talk in their sleep, you know!" she said. She made a final thrust into the potato salad, grabbed her purse, and stalked off. Both Ray and Sister Carol Ann looked as if they wanted very much to laugh.

Customers began coming then, and Rosie found herself making change at the cash box. Business was brisk, and Ray Bowen hummed next to her as he worked the pop machine. The numbers Rosie rang up jingled in and out of numbers that came from the bingo game. "B: 13," the loudspeaker would call, and Rosie would ring up seventy-nine cents. The numbers jingled in and out of Ray's humming and images of the smiling priest and his plump smiling wife, in and out of Dora's stricken anger. . . . Maybe Dora was right; maybe things were better before. At least, you knew where you stood then. Maybe it was better when things were more secret—when the priest hunched over a secret sacrament, and nuns hid their hair, and you never got called by name in the confessional. She spotted Father Griffin across the parking lot, the sun glinting off his straight, sandy hair. He was wearing the light blue sweatshirt again, and when he saw her looking at him he raised a glass of beer in salute and almost spilled it. Rosie laughed in spite of herself. He was such a hearty young man, so much the soft heart beneath the rough surface of his freckled face, and he meant so well. She thought of how he had explained some of the liturgical changes to the older ladies at her circle meeting, teasing them as he did so. "Of course the priest should face the people at Mass. Mildred"—he had singled out a widow in her sixties—"how would you like it if I invited you to one of my glorious spaghetti dinners and then turned around and ate it facing the wall?" Mildred Lewis had flushed with the pleasure of being noticed, and Rosie had gone home so convinced she even tried to explain the Kiss of Peace to Jack.

"Spreads germs," he said.

"Well, I didn't say anybody was going to kiss you," Rosie said. "You turn to the people on either side of you, and shake their hands and say, 'Peace be with you.'"

"And then what do you do," Jack said; "*do si do* and *alamande left?*"

"Oh, honestly!" Rosie said. "You never want to learn anything! Father Griffin says there's no point in going to church to mumble prayers to God, if you aren't going to love your neighbor, and Sister Carol Ann said our goal at Mass should be to grow, and that we grow by performing acts of love."

"Said that, huh?" Jack said. One side of his mouth slipped into a grin. "Somebody's gonna get a tit in the wringer yet."

When their shift was over, Gina filled plates for Rosie and Ray and herself. They sat on the slat folding chairs at one of the long tables. "Good bread, good meat, good God, let's eat!" Ray said. He picked up the bratwurst sandwich with both hands and bit into it with great energy. Rosie was about to do the same when she noticed that Gina Pratt's hands were trembling.

"You okay?" she said.

"I'm fine," Gina said, but she raised her coffee cup halfway to her mouth, and it started spilling.

Ray reached over to cover her hand with both of his and lowered the cup gently. "You're not okay," he said. "Do you feel sick?"

"No," Gina said. "I'm fine really. I'm just . . . a little weaker than usual." She kept her eyes down over the coffee cup. "We were on our feet a long time. . . ."

She's pregnant, Rosie thought, though she had no idea how she knew. She glanced down at Gina's slim body. There was no evidence of a pregnancy, but there was no evidence that she had already borne three daughters either.

"I'm fine," Gina said again, but she didn't sound convincing.

Maybe she doesn't want to be pregnant, Rosie thought; maybe she hoped it wouldn't happen. She remembered when her friend Lois was expecting her fifth in six years. "I just wish Richard would understand that I . . ." she said, and then she burst into tears.

Contraception was the one thing that had been covered explicitly in the unit on marriage in Rosie's high school religion class. "Contraceptive devices are intrinsically evil," Father McGraw had said. "A gun or a knife may be used to kill someone, but they're not intrinsically evil because they have other uses. A birth control device has no other use." That was all she remembered from the unit on marriage—that and the fact that if you had a miscarriage, you should baptize it. But now the Pope had appointed a commission to reexamine the issue of birth control; she had read about it in *The Diocesean Messenger*. She had never really understood why birth control was wrong; but still, there was something unsettling in the fact that sins could change—it made the past seem not quite worth it. "Those folks frying in hell for eating meat on Friday," Jack said last year when the rule changed, "they must be really pissed."

Rosie felt Ray Bowen looking at her, and realized that they had all been silent. She flushed a little and began talking about the size of the crowd until she noticed Marion Runkle heading toward them, carrying a sewing-booth doll whose crocheted skirt hid a roll of toilet paper. The doll's blonde hair was only loosely glued to its head, and it looked like Marion herself: hair that was never quite combed, that seemed ready to float away in dry, dull wisps, like so much cottonwood.

"Well, I s'pose you heard," Marion said in her usual slow speech as she seated herself. "Mickey spent the night in jail." Her arms fell loosely on the table and she still had not looked at any of them. There was a confused silence, which Marion seemed not to notice. "My girl wants to join the Air Force," she said, as though it connected. "Says she wants to travel." She turned the doll upside down to see how its legs were fastened to the toilet paper tube.

"Is your girl out of high school?" Gina Pratt asked politely.

"Graduates in June. Same as Mickey. I wish he wouldn't drink so much," she concluded, righting the doll and smoothing the skirt down with large-knuckled fingers. "That priest got 'em out this morning—him and that Simons boy—but now I s'pose they have to go to court." She sighed, her voice emotionless. "Don't know what good it does; that priest drinks too." She sighed again and petted the doll on its loose hair. Then, with no acknowledgment of their presence, she got up and left the table.

"That woman's incredible," Gina said. "She sits down, announces that her son's in jail, and then walks away and leaves us to imagine the charges."

"Probably drunk driving or disorderly conduct," Ray said. He paused. "*Does* the priest drink too much?"

"Oh, he may have a beer or two once in a while," Rosie said. Her eyes followed Ray's across the parking lot. Father Griffin was on the edge of a small crowd near the stacked-up bingo cards talking to Sister Carol Ann, laughing and gesturing widely. Just as he pointed toward something with the hand holding the beer cup, someone with a food tray bumped him from behind. He stumbled foward, unbalanced, and the beer slopped down Carol Ann's black dress. She could see his mouth apologize, and his hand brush the beer away. He brushed in clumsy but firm sweeps, down her shoulder and over her right breast.

"Who'd like to play bingo?" Rosie said, standing up rapidly.

Gina excused herself to check on the little girls, but Ray helped Rosie with her chair and insisted on paying for the bingo cards.

Jim Hinely joined them, his face flushed from the sun and the beer he'd been drinking "to keep his throat limber." Rosie found herself resenting him. He talked almost continuously, demanded both of their attentions, and kept winking or poking one of them. "Why, when I saw you over there with all them women," he nudged his elbow into Ray's ribs, "I said to myself: Now, there's a man knows his ass from his elbow." Ray said nothing, and Jim turned to Rosie: "He taken you out yet?"

"Watch your card," Ray told him. "You just missed a number."

When Jim finally won a twenty-dollar jackpot, it was time for Rosie to help with the cleaning up. Jim took Ray to the beer garden, and Rosie went home alone. After the clicks and hums and voices of the afternoon, the quiet seemed to seep through her, and she moved restlessly about the house, stopping to pick dead leaves off a plant, picking up a magazine only to put it down, thinking she might have stayed longer. She had expected to spend the evening settling the accounts on the food booth and paying the bills, but Dora had waved her off. "I'll give you a ring when I get it counted," she said. She was still in a sulky humor, and that was that.

She must have counted the money very slowly, Rosie thought, because it was almost ten when the phone rang. "Well, how much did we clear?" Rosie said as she picked it up.

There was silence for a moment, and then, "Are you alone?" a low voice said. Rosie felt her heart stop, and then she slammed the receiver onto the phone. She tried to reason with herself as she sat in the rocking chair, aware that a pulse was beating in her neck. Maybe this wasn't the same person. Maybe it was a wrong number. She couldn't even be sure the voice was a man's this time. Maybe someone wanted to tell her something confidential and needed to know if she was alone. The phone was ringing again, and Rosie counted seven rings, determined not to answer. At last she gave in. "Hello?" she said cautiously.

"Well, where were you?" Dora said. "In the basement?" She didn't wait for an answer. "Two hundred forty-seven dollars and thirty-six cents," she said. "That's pretty good. That's better than last year, but of course we got more of the stuff donated."

Rosie agreed that it was pretty good. She agreed that the weather had been perfect, and that some of the pies were a little underdone, and that people shouldn't bring children to public events if they didn't intend to watch them. Before she had a chance to say anything else, Dora hung up. Rosie locked the doors and windows; she had locked them every night since the first call almost two weeks ago, though no one in St. Ives locked anything. Unless he broke through the glass, there was no way the caller could get in. Still, that wouldn't prevent the phone from mingling with her dreams. To lock even that out, she lifted the phone off the hook before she went upstairs.

Chapter VIII

AS THE WEEKS OF AUTUMN SLID PAST HER, ROSIE KNEW THAT Sundays were the worst. Her grief for Jack had never been the kind of pain that is a wrench tightening around the throat, and her initial sense of numbness gave way not to hurt, but to a vastness—a sense that all that grassland prairie had been depopulated, all buildings demolished, and she was alone in brown fields that rolled into wasteland forever. It was like standing at a window for hours in a season of drought and watching bits of cottonwood blow. She was fine most of the time; she kept busy. She watched TV most evenings—or played cards with Dora, or went to Luverne to the grocery store—but suppertime was hard, when one place set at the table looked more like a decoration than a meal; and Sundays were the worst. After she had gone to Mass and read the Sunday *Tribune* from Sioux Falls, the rest of the day stretched out in tiny segments, each of them a gulley she must cross. It seemed that the empty prairie pushed inside her then, crowded her ribs, and sped up the beating of her heart. She never heard the clock when things were going well. But now, on Sunday afternoons, it would sit on the shelf in the front room and click off the segments that remained of the day, ticking just a little faster than her heart.

When she was a very small child, it had been like that sometimes. She would have her dolls propped up in the living room, ready to have their tea or go "visiting," or she would be halfway through a page in the coloring book when she would notice that there was no sound from the kitchen, no footsteps creaking slightly on the floorboards upstairs. First she would sit very still, and then she would go to the cellar stairs and listen, and then she would begin to hear the ticking of the clock. The whole house would fill with those measured sounds, as though some terrible creature were waiting in every room. "Mama!" she would call, and if there was no answer, she would race to the safety of the out-of-doors. "Mama!" And there Mama would be, picking the raspberries on the back fence, or hanging out the wash, or down the block talking to Mrs. Gideon. "Rosie, here I am," she would call, and the sound of the clock would stop again.

There was no one to answer now, no one to call, and Rosie would look for a magazine, or turn on the TV. One Sunday she had walked out along the road past the Protestant cemetery; another time, she had gone for a drive, taking the back roads southeast toward Worthington through fields of ripened corn; but now it was early November, and the sky was a cold, spitting gray.

She wandered upstairs, picked a few dead leaves off the impatiens plants that she, like Mama, always brought in for the winter and kept in front of the window at the end of the hall. The door to Jack's room was partly open, and she could see the boxes she had started packing over a month ago. She would have to finish the job sometime, she knew; Jack's clothes would not go away by themselves.

The trousers packed easily. She found in the pockets three handkerchiefs, a loose key, and $1.86 in change. She buttoned and folded the two suit jackets. The pockets of one were empty, and the other, oddly enough, contained an unused ticket to the Fablieux Theatre in Sioux Falls. She went to the closet and took out the only overcoat Jack had ever owned. She remembered when he had gotten it: "Oh Jack, you'll look so handsome," she'd said. He was nineteen then, and she had pictured him in it, a young wife on his arm, a baby's blanket leaving just a trace of pastel lint on his shoulder. She pulled a thick wad from the pocket. It was one of those tiny red *Mission* magazines edited by Bishop Fulton Sheen, and an envelope, like a church envelope, pictured a starving child holding out a bowl. "What did he want with this?" she said to no one in particular. The envelope had his name and address printed in pencil in the appropriate blanks, and opened to reveal a twenty dollar bill.

"I'll be darned," she thought, smiling to herself. "I didn't know he had it in him." Of course, she would never have thought Jack ungenerous, it was just that he made such awful remarks about anybody who asked for money, especially if they were foreigners.

"You think the little gooks'll wear those?" he said last spring when she was helping to pack clothes for an orphanage in Vietnam. "What if they can't work buttons?"

Another time, at the supper table, he said, "You know, I heard today there used to be a Chinese laundryman in St. Ives." (Rosie doubted that this was true.) "Him and his wife had a baby, and instead of those slanty eyes, it had eyes like regular people. They named it 'What Went Wong.'" And then he laughed until he choked on his coffee.

Rosie turned over the envelope in her hands. In small print at the bottom, it said, "Thank you for your monthly contribution to feed the hungry." She wondered how many months this had gone on, how many years Jack had been a secret donor. "Bunch of bunk!" was what Jack had said to feeding the hungry when she was in high school. "Are those nuns still selling pagan babies?" he said. "When I was a little kid, Rudy Theiler got to name all the pagan babies our class bought because he gave the most money. Can you imagine all those little pagans named Rudolph? Half of 'em are probably girls."

He said that in her junior year, when the nun from the Medical Mission came to collect money after the Masses on Mission Sunday. On Monday, the nun talked to all the high school girls. "Well, babies really don't get abandoned in our region," she said. "But there's a lot of malnutrition, and we're trying to get an inoculation program going to curb some of the disease."

After that, Rosie paid more attention to the vocation ads in *St. Anthony's Messenger* and *Sacred Heart Journal*. "Come Follow Me," some of them said above the picture of an African toddler with enormous eyes and a distended belly. Or: "Could This Be

You?" above the picture of a nun in white surrounded by six or seven seminaked natives. They were all grinning. Rosie pictured a thatched clinic surrounded by palm trees. She was a young nun who would emerge at sunset, weary and lonely for her own people, but aching mostly with the fact that there was not more that she could give. Every ad had a coupon at the bottom: "Please send me information on how I can serve. . . ." Late in her junior year, Rosie sent one in.

The next day she panicked. She usually picked up the mail at the post office after school, but what if Jack or Mama, walking to the store, got there first? Jack would snort, and Mama would say, "Well, there's certainly no need to go so far away. We have poor people too, you know." Rosie began to sneak down to the post office on her lunch hour; Leona Metzger usually had the mail put up by then. The day it came, she felt as if she was carrying an explosive. The thick brown envelope seemed to bulge out of every notebook, and there was no place private enough to open it. In the study hall, it had gone crashing to the floor.

Mama was peeling potatoes at the sink when Rosie came in from school, and she kept her back turned. "We get any mail today?"

"Oh yeah," Rosie said. Something told her she had better make this accurate. "Some of us went for a walk at noon, and I picked it up. The phone bill came." She fished it out of her notebook and laid it on the table.

"Anything else?" Mama said. There was a funny quality to her voice.

"Oh," Rosie laughed deliberately, "I got an envelope of stuff from some missionaries. I guess they don't get enough money from grown-ups, so they're starting to send stuff to high school kids."

"That's nice," Mama said. She still hadn't turned from the sink. There was a pause, and then she said, "I met Leona in the variety store this afternoon. She said, 'Well, I didn't know your Rosie was going to be a nun. She got a package today from Mary-knoll.'"

Rosie said nothing, and Mama went on: "I said, 'Well, it's news to me, and I bet it's news to Rosie. Won't *they* be surprised when they find out they're trying to sign up a girl with fits!' "

The words stung through her again, standing there in a chilly bedroom on a November day when more than twenty years had slid away. *That was cruel!* she thought. "That was a cruel thing to say!" But Mama had not been a cruel person. Mama was a little old-fashioned at times, or set in her ways, but not cruel. If Mama had been trying to knock foolish notions out of her head, it must have been for her own good. "Let him learn," she had said the time Jack spent all his prize money from the fair on a device to develop instant biceps that he found in the back of a comic book. "Let him waste the money—it'll do him good." Rosie began to fold in the lids of the cardboard box with more energy than necessary. She tied them shut with pieces of twine she found in one of the drawers.

"Sometimes, what seems like cruelty is really kindness," she told herself, but Jack's face was there as she closed the lid on his overcoat. He was leaning his face close to hers and saying, "So what did Mama know? What did Mama really want to know? Mama took care of herself."

An enormous, bitter surge came up from inside her and caught at her windpipe. She made a sound that wasn't a cough and wasn't a laugh. Her hands fumbled on the knot she was tying and she let go of it. She went to the window, put her hand on the crossbar, and began slowly pulling one finger over the pane. The burning in her throat continued, and she raised and opened her mouth, almost like a turkey hen waiting for rain.

So she might have been a nun. She might have gone to a novitiate in upstate New York and prayed through the novitiate years in grottoes lit with sunlight, and silent, peaceful corridors, and groves of apple trees. She might have gone to Africa and borne the heat, and watched the zebras run, and caressed a sick baby's soft, black skin—or to China, and have learned to bow and nod, and live in a hut with bamboo shades. Or she might have married Michael Roekamp. . . .

But she might not, told herself when the surging began to subside. She might have applied and gone for the physical, and discovered that what Mama thought was true. . . . And what did Jack know, anyway? She could have had it at the time. Sometimes symptoms just disappear after a while; sometimes they just go away over the years.

She turned from the window and picked up one more empty box. Jack's work clothes were the last thing she had to pack. She opened the drawer and pulled out the gray wash pants and the gray shirts that said "Supergro" over the pocket. She pulled out the new ones he had never worn. She ran her fingers gently over the cloth as she put them, one by one, into the box. Tears were falling lightly on the gray pants and the overalls, and she made no attempt to stop them. Jack was gone and she missed him. She missed him at the supper table, and in front of the TV, and she missed the way he always said what was on his mind. She missed him more than she had missed Mama. "I hate her," she said, not knowing where it came from and knowing it was wrong. "I hate her; I hate the old bitch." And then her hands rose to try to cover the sobs that wouldn't stop.

Rosie sat for a long time in the front room in the rocking chair that she had brought in just last week from the porch. The boxes of Jack's clothing were all neatly tied and stacked close to the front door. Tomorrow she would begin taking them to the church basement for the clothing drive. They would go in the storeroom at the other end from the kitchen, and they were labeled carefully so that when the women sorted, they wouldn't even need to open the boxes. She thought about these things as she waited for the rain, as she rocked and rocked. Sometimes a dog barked, or a car door slammed, and once she heard children's voices in the street. She didn't know what time it was, and it didn't matter; when it got too dark to see, she would turn on the light and go to the kitchen for something to eat.

She didn't expect anyone to knock. In fact, she froze and thought she had imagined it, until it came again. Then she checked her dress, and checked her face for puffy stains, and turned on the porch light. Ray Bowen was standing at the door.

He looked a little sheepish. "I hope I'm not disturbing you," he said.

"Oh, no," Rosie said.

"I was just driving around—you know, on Sundays there's not much to do—and I happened to see your car in front of the house. . . ."

"Oh, I wasn't doing much of anything," Rosie said.

"I shouldn't impose myself like this," he said, peering around her into the dark front room. Rosie quickly flicked the light switch, and stood back to motion him in. "I was just driving around, like I said, and I had these two tickets to the Knights of Columbus bingo game—it's over in Worthington—but I kind of figured I wouldn't use them, and then I saw your car, and I thought . . . well, Rosie likes bingo. . . ."

"Oh," she said. Was this an invitation? Could this man be asking her out? She tried a neutral statement. "Jack used to buy those. Jack used to get K. C. tickets from somebody at the elevator."

"I got these from a fella runs the cafe down in Worthington. He's a fourth-degree knight." He paused. "Well, would you like to go?"

"Well, I . . ." Rosie looked around. There was no one to ask or even tell. "Sure," she said. "It's for a good cause. Why not? Sure, I'll go." She could hardly believe she had said it.

Ray looked at his watch, said he'd pick her up at half past seven, and ducked through the doorway. He turned back once to smile, and was gone.

My God, what have I done? she thought as she stared at the door and could hear his car door close and the engine start. Here it was, a cold November Sunday, and she had sprinkled Jack's clothes with some leftover tears, and had sat in the rocking chair and thought about how most of life was past—most of what counted, at any rate. . . . And now she had a date. She was partly glad and partly frightened, but someone inside her was smiling. "Oh, I had a busy weekend," she could casually say tomorrow morning. "I got all of Jack's things packed for the clothing drive, and Sunday night I had a date."

She went into the kitchen and opened a can of chicken noodle soup, but knew she couldn't eat it. She made herself a cup of coffee, took a package of chocolate chips from the cupboard and ate a handful of those instead. She took the coffee cup upstairs with her, and traded her house dress for the burgundy pantsuit, and sat down on the vanity bench to comb her hair. She wished it were shorter, or longer perhaps. She shouldn't have let Mildred Dorn give her that permanent.

Rosie carefully touched her face with powder, drew on the lipstick, then took from a drawer a little compact of blue eye shadow. She had never worn it. Mama had scorned women who wore eye shadow. "Look like chickens that got coccidiosis," Mama said. "Look like chickens with that blue ring they get around the eyes before they die."

Rosie dipped the little sponge brush into the silky blue and spread it above her eye. No. Too much. She *did* look like a sick chicken. She wiped it off with a Kleenex, and fished a pair of gold earrings from the drawer. The woman who looked back from the mirror was not pretty, but there was a beauty about her in the soft light. The curve of her cheek was nice, and there was a sincere, smiling look about the eyes. Even the gray streak in the hair could look distinguished if she held her head just right. Rosie watched the woman pick up the little eye-shadow brush, and, more gingerly than before, spread and blend it above her eyes.

"It had been a lonely afternoon, and now she was kissing a man she had never met before," said the large print above the lead story in one of the magazines. As she waited, Rosie looked at a misty illustration of a couple in rapturous embrace. The woman, in a long gown, seemed to be floating, but you could tell by the tension in the man's arm that he was straining her toward him. She, Rosie, had had a lonely afternoon, and soon she would be . . . she slapped the magazine shut and stopped the rocking chair with a jolt. What was Ray Bowen expecting? What kind of woman was he used to? After all, he wasn't a kid—and neither was she. "Old enough to know better," Mama used to say about anyone over thirty. "No fool like an old fool." Rosie felt apprehension steam in her throat. They would go to the bingo game and sit at crowded tables with other people, and the worst he could do was rub against her leg; but what about after? She remembered Gene Thurly, his rough hand grabbing her breast, his mouth pressing down, the sound of her own voice: "Please, please don't. . . ." What if Ray Bowen pulled off on some back road, or said he ran out of gas? And what if she pushed him away, and he responded with scorn and never asked her again: "You really *are* a prissy old maid, aren't you? I'd heard as much. . . ."

She wouldn't go. That would settle it. Why should she face either guilt or humiliation? After all, he had just come bursting in here without warning, without being invited—and she had been so startled she said yes. She said yes out of politeness. But she didn't have to go. She could meet him at the door, her body sagging a little, and say, "I'm so sorry, I have a terrible headache. It must be the way the weather is changing." That would do it. And she *was* getting a headache. She went to the mirror and decided her eyes looked droopy. She lowered her shoulders too—she had a tendency to hunch—and it made her whole body relax.

She was off guard when the knock came. Ray was more hand-some than she remembered. "It stopped raining," he said, holding his hand palm upward. "Maybe it will bring us luck." He smiled, but seemed nervous, and there was a little sadness caught in the corners of his eyes. "I'm really glad you could come," he said quickly. "Sundays can get so damn long. . . ." His eyes took in the pantsuit and the color in her face. "You look really nice," he said.

"Oh," she said. "Thank you. I have a little headache——"

The smile vanished. "You aren't sick, are you?"

"Oh, no," she said. "It's nothing. No. I'll be fine." Long years of politeness suddenly betrayed her. Before she knew it, she had handed him her raincoat in a gesture so natural she was sure some other person was doing it. Some other person slid her arms into the sleeves, picked up her purse, smiled back at the man with bright, squirrel eyes, and walked with him through the door.

Chapter IX

"WELL, GUESS WHO HAD A DATE LAST NIGHT!" DORA SAID AS ROSIE hung up her coat and reached for her checkered apron.

"News travels fast," Rosie said. She hadn't expected Dora to know quite this soon; she had thought it would be midmorning before the topic came up. "Oh, I wasn't home last night," she had imagined herself saying. "I had a date."

"Not that I'm surprised or anything," Dora said, trying to take the curiosity out of her voice. "It was obvious he'd taken a shine to you."

Rosie busied herself checking the menu and getting gallon cans of peas out of the storeroom.

"You win anything?" Dora asked.

"Three dollars. Your cousin's kid from Lismore got the fifty-dollar jackpot."

"So I heard," Dora said. Her family apparently made very late or very early phone calls. "The bingo probably got out too late for you to stop anywhere. . . ."

"Oh, we had coffee," Rosie said. She went back to the store-room for the last can of peas and grinned at the rows of government surplus labels. Dora was dying to know. Dora, who regarded her own life as the model of decent success and cheerful propriety, was hanging on the droplets of information Rosie was giving. It was almost cruel to keep her in suspense. Besides, she really wanted to tell her. Dora seemed to approve of Ray, and she didn't approve of all that many people. "It was a nice evening," she volunteered as she returned to the kitchen and ran through a quick synopsis.

And it had been a nice evening, Rosie thought as she cleaned celery and prepared carrot sticks. They had both been nervous and awkward getting into the car and driving off. They had yelled a few obvious remarks about the weather over a blaring radio before it occurred to Ray to turn it down.

"Sorry 'bout that," he said. "I'm usually in here alone, and it keeps me company."

"It's okay," Rosie said. She wished she could think of something clever.

"Are you chilly or anything?" He started fiddling with the heater. "I got the car cleaned out, but I didn't think about adjusting this stuff."

"I'm fine," Rosie said. "Really." His obvious nervousness and her wish to put him at ease were calming her.

"I guess I might as well confess," Ray said. "I haven't been out—with a woman, I mean—for ages. You probably aren't used to such shabby treatment."

"I don't get out much either," Rosie said. "I used to go to bingo with Jack sometimes, but he never held the door or got my coat."

They both laughed a little. "Jack was an interesting fella," Ray said. "I used to see him sometimes at The Anchor. He ever tell you any of his jokes?"

"Sometimes. The ones he thought I was old enough to hear." They both laughed again. It was becoming easier. Ray repeated Jack's story about the city slicker who went coon hunting, and Rosie told the one about the Chinese laundryman, and soon they were in Worthington.

Walking into the Knights of Columbus hall, Rosie found herself standing a little straighter; she was "with" someone; she was part of a couple; she was a regular unit in society, and not some extra appendage, not some lopsided fruit that had been mistakenly grafted to the vine. She fell back half a step to ally herself more closely with Ray. It hadn't occurred to her to expect this rare and subtle pleasure. Not that anyone was looking at her, of course, but if a woman's eyes should meet hers, she wouldn't have to face a vague, unstated pity, an awkwardness of manner that said, "I don't want you to feel bad, but you've upset the balance of things. You really are irregular, you know." She wouldn't have to watch women unconsciously move closer to their husbands, or take their escorts' arms in a way that said, "See, I have someone. See, I belong."

Ray put his hand lightly on her back to move her through the rows of tables and folding chairs. "How's this?" he said, and seated her at a table across from a woman who was sifting through a cottage-cheese carton full of little red disks she had brought to cover the numbers. "You look like quite a professional," Ray said to the woman as he reached down the table for two big handfuls of the usual shelled corn.

The rest had been easy. They had to listen too hard to the caller to make much conversation, but there was bantering back and forth at the tables, even among strangers, and great teasing the time Ray sneezed suddenly and blew most of the corn off his card. Rosie forgot about her fears until the bingo was over, and Ray was again opening the car door.

"How about some coffee?" he said as he slid into the other side. "Or would you rather have a beer?"

"Coffee's fine," Rosie said. It would probably keep her awake all night, but she didn't want to go into a tavern. She didn't want to see the strange blue sheen that men's faces took in the light of a neon beer sign—the strange blue hint of a growing beard. . . . "They'll get you drunk," Mama had warned after Marion Runkle's sister had a baby out of wedlock. "Men are like that. That's what happened to Evelyn—and it happened with a married man!"

The cafe wasn't crowded, and the coffee was strong and hot. Ray was surprisingly easy to talk to; his whole face seemed to smile when she tried to be amusing, and his eyes approved of everything she said.

"So you've lived in St. Ives all your life," he said.

"Yeah," she said. "Long enough to know every cat and dog, and every litter of pups. You weren't always from Luverne, were you?"

"Nope. Just since the middle of summer. I've been in Illinois for a long time. But I grew up over by Le Sueur."

"What did you do in Illinois?"

"Worked for a division of Mellomilk," he said. "Same thing I do here." He twisted his coffee cup all the way around and breathed a little uneasily. Rosie thought perhaps her question brought back painful memories of his wife's death, but then he looked up and grinned. "You should be able to tell I'm a native," he said. "Otherwise, I'd have said I grew up *near* Le Sueur. When you were in school, did the teachers ever get on you for stuff like that?"

"Yes," Rosie laughed. "But I still say it. I go *over by* Aunt Nellie's place or *over by* Luverne."

They both laughed. "I had to write: 'My name is Ray Bowen. I live *near* Le Sueur' three hundred times on the blackboard once —though I think it was connected to some other crime." He was smiling into his coffee as though the memory floated there.

And so the evening went. They took out bits and pieces of their childhoods and dressed them up or left them plain, and found that the colors had become more refined and gentler, the sharp edges had been weathered away. Rosie was still telling about how Jack and his friends roasted the streaked gopher when they pulled up before her door.

This was the worst part, Rosie knew, as Ray came around the car to her door—the saying good night. Would he kiss her? Would she let him? Would there be a slight scuffle in front of her door? At least he hadn't parked and tried to paw her as Gene Thurly did so many years ago. But would they both stand there, not knowing what the other expected, shifting feet and shuffling? She always read the "Advice to Teens" column that a priest wrote in *The Diocesan Messenger*, and the column by Loretta Young. Last week, one or the other of them had advised a girl to pray aloud with her date for a safe and chaste evening as soon as they got in the car. The column also advised sticking your hand out for a quick handshake before the man had time to kiss you, or mentioning, as he brought you up the walk, that a parent usually waited just inside the door.

"Got your keys?" Ray said. He touched her lightly on the arm.

"Oh, I didn't lock it," Rosie said. "I mean I forgot . . . but then, most people here don't lock their doors at all." She could see him frowning.

"That's not a good idea," he said. "Even in a town this small. Too many kooks around. You're all alone, you know."

Rosie knew. She knew very well. But she really couldn't say: I would have locked it except I was too worried about everything else. . . . "Okay," she said, "next time I will."

"Speaking of next time," Ray said—he was smiling now— "there's a benefit card party for the hospital next Saturday. Would you like to go?"

"Well . . . sure. That'd be okay." Her voice was a little uneven.

"Look, Rosie . . ." He put his hand on her arm again. Her spine stiffened, but there was no graceful way to back away. "I'm not trying to put a rush on you or anything. I'm really not looking for a romance—I'm not in a place where I can take that on yet. It's just that . . . well, it gets lonesome sometimes. I thought that since you were alone too, maybe we could be friends. That's all."

Rosie didn't understand why her jaw and chest seemed to make a sudden dip, though she knew they hadn't really moved. *This was good news*, she reminded herself. "I'd like that," she said. She wouldn't have to worry if they were "just friends." "I'd like that," she said again.

"So I'll pick you up at seven-thirty next Saturday, okay?" When she nodded, he gave her arm a squeeze and turned down the walk. Halfway to the car, he paused. "And lock your door," he said.

There were little red disks all over Rosie's dream. Little red disks and numbers lined up in boxes, and handfuls of shelled corn. She was packing Jack's overcoat, and found a pocketful of corn. He was sending it to the starving children in China, she knew, and she saw that shiny red disks had replaced all the buttons on the coat. "Ring-O," called the man who was announcing the numbers. "Ringgg-O, Ringgg-O," and then she knew that the phone was ringing.

The door was locked; that was her first thought as she stumbled down the hall. "Hello," she said. "Hello?"

It was the muffled voice again. "I've been thinking of your nice, naked body," the voice said. "I know you're there alone. . . ."

Rosie slammed the phone down. She stomped up the stairs to bed and snatched the covers back. "Some sicko!" she said, as she rolled on her side. Her eyes stayed open. She was really more angry than she was afraid this time. Some part of her brain was being the other Rosie—the one who processed thoughts and information calmly—but she refused to look at what it was processing. She willed her eyes to close. She lay there for a long time, stubbornly fighting whatever her brain was adding up. When she fell asleep, her jaw was still clenched.

Chapter X

THE NIGHT OF THE CARD PARTY, IT SNOWED. A FEW FLAKES HAD begun to filter through the grayness of late afternoon, and Rosie was glad. November can be so still that any movement is a relief, she thought; it was like watching a dying relative breathe in and out, then finally seeing the eyelids flutter. Snow in November meant a certain change in the air, a certain excitement. She was glad for the card party too; she would sleep in until the late Mass tomorrow, and Sunday would not seem so long. She made a little pot roast for supper with carrots and browned potatoes. When she took it from the freezer, she pictured herself calling Ray on the phone: "I thawed it by mistake," she would say, "and it's way too much for one person . . . and I thought since you were coming anyway . . ." She got his number from information in the middle of the morning. Twice during the day she started to dial but convinced herself that this would be a bad time to call: he would be eating—or he would be out. The third time, she even let the phone ring once and then hung up. "He wouldn't want to come on such short notice," she said. As usual, she ate alone.

Ray was not pleased about the snow. "Awful damn early," he said. He seemed more tense than last time, more distant.

Rosie laughed. "This is Minnesota," she said. "You used to live here, remember?" For her own part, she was relaxed. The first date had shown her there was nothing to fear from this man, this "friend," and to ride through the night with him seemed an adventure. She liked driving into flakes that swirled and parted, as if to escape the windshield, and then surrendered to it. She liked even the slight feeling of danger about driving in the snow—a chance of breakdown, perhaps, or of being stranded. Alone, Rosie would have set her jaw, gripped the wheel, and felt her stomach harden. But she wasn't alone. There was a man beside her.

They played 500 at the card party, the winners of each game advancing from table to table and changing partners, so that there was always a new foursome. Aunt Nellie was there, and kept casting furious looks in her direction, but Rosie won as often as the older woman did and kept several tables ahead. Once when she looked across the room, she saw that Aunt Nellie was playing with Ray, her eyes on him more intently than on the cards. When their game ended, the old woman took a route past Rosie's table on her way to the ladies' room.

"Where did you meet him?" she hissed.

"At work."

"He's not from here."

"He is now," Rosie picked up a deck and began to shuffle.

"What do you know about his people?" the old woman demanded.

Rosie looked up from the cards and smiled. "Nothing at all," she said.

And it was true. She didn't really. They had talked about snowstorms they remembered, and grade schools and funny things that had happened when they were young. She asked once about his family, but there wasn't much to learn. His older sister had died of polio at nineteen, and the younger one was married to a career army man and lived in Germany. They had four children, and were worried that Vic would be sent to Vietnam. No one was left in Le Sueur—his parents had sold the farm and lived in Arizona for some years before they died. There were some cousins around Le Sueur, but they could pass each other unnoticed on the street.

One Friday, Ray had forgotten to pick up a stack of empty milk cases and stopped for them late in the afternoon when Rosie was cleaning up. Dora poured him a cup of coffee, and the three of them sat down.

"Jerry has relatives over by Le Sueur," Dora volunteered suddenly. "Did you know any Heideggers?"

Ray shook his head. "Can't say I did."

"Well, they actually live closer to St. Peter," Dora said. "Was your wife from . . ."

Ray shook his head quickly. "From Illinois," he said.

"Oh," Dora said. There was a silence, and Ray cupped his hands around the coffee cup. "Did she . . ."

"She had a brain tumor," Ray said. "The first time they opened her up, they thought they got it all, but then they had to go in again . . . and. . . ." He paused. When he was nervous, he had a funny way of snapping his jaw so the teeth made a series of sharp little clicks.

"That's what happened to that Roelling girl," Dora said, "the one that married that Kirschner from up by Walnut Grove. . . . They said inside of her head looked just like cottage cheese. . . ."

Rosie saw Ray wince. "How about more coffee?" she said, getting up. "It's nippy out. The radio said we're in for snow."

It was nippy coming home from the card party too, but Rosie's sense of warmth lasted even as she got ready for bed. She was almost undressed when she remembered the altar-boy surplices. She had washed all of them that afternoon, but half of them were still in the washer, and the others were in a now-cold dryer load. "Blast it!" she thought. "There's nothing over there for the 6:30 Mass tomorrow." In her debate about calling Ray to share the pot roast, she had completely forgotten them. She pulled her dress back on, retrieved two medium-sized garments from the dryer, and ran the iron over them hurriedly. "Whatever kid serves the early Mass tomorrow," she muttered, "these are going to fit."

There was no one in the street when she went out. She felt a little thrill along the edges of her backbone, and she wasn't sure if it was fear or cold; she had never gone walking this late. There was a peculiar, awesome silence in the streets—the kind that comes only after evening snow. Everything was muted, hushed, less angular; yet everything seemed to be more intensely itself, as though somehow lit from within. Her feet made the first tracks in the white path that pointed toward the spire of the church, and she was reluctant to disturb such serenity.

A very dim light shone through the nearest church window as she used her key to the sacristy. *Vigil lights*, she thought. She felt her way up the three steps, tripping on one, and flipped the switch that turned on a single low bulb at that end of the sacristy. Some cupboard doors were open, and a bottle that didn't look like altar wine was sitting open on the table. The high school girls forgot to clean up again, she thought as she opened the surplice cupboard. Then she heard the floorboards squeak.

"Drop it!" a male voice yelled, and a huge shape burst out of the vestment closet. "Drop whatever you've got!"

Rosie screamed and dropped the surplices. The shape was Father Griffin.

"Rosie," he said accusingly, "why are you robbing the church?"

The smell on his breath reached her even before he moved far enough into the light so that she could see his eyes. A wisp of hair stood up in back like a rooster comb, and something like tomato juice was spilled down the front of the sweatshirt he was wearing under his black suit coat. She moved instinctively to the light panel and flicked two switches. The priest blinked and stepped back. She could see the whole sacristy clearly now; the bottle on the table was Jack Daniels.

"I'm not robbing the church," she said. "I brought some clean surplices for tomorrow's Mass." She had forgotten the surplices; they were on the floor in a heap.

"Well, you know," he said. He swayed and backed up to lean one elbow on the counter. "You know, you sure fooled me. I came to shovel the walks," he said illogically. "I thought, 'Got to get the walks shoveled,' you know, and then I heard somebody coming in to rob the church. . . ." His eyes took in the bottle on the table. "And I had a little drink to keep me warm."

"You had more than *one* little drink," she said. She should have been afraid: it was late, they were alone, and this large stumbling man was the priest who knew her sins, but her pulse was returning to normal. She had been here before; she was sixteen again, and her brother had just come stumbling in.

"Let's make you some coffee," she said.

"Un-unh." He shook his head like a child. "I know you, Rosie. You work too hard. You aren't gonna wait on me."

"I want some too," she said. "I'll make it for myself."

"Do you know how to work my stove?" His eyes were cagey now.

"No," she said truthfully, but remembered the cafeteria just downstairs. "I know how to work my stove though. Come on." She moved to take his arm and he didn't object. "We're going downstairs where we have lunch every day," she said. "We'll make it a little party." She flicked out all but the little light on the end. Moonlight was coming in through the latticed windows now, and the weight on her shoulder was an old, familiar one as they made their way across the sacristy, stepping through softly elongated squares of light.

Rosie put water in the big enamel pot they used for lunch and set it on the gas; there was nothing smaller. Father Griffin had lifted his head and was staring across the tables at the opposite wall. He looked amused, sitting there, but his eyes were still frightened and sad.

"You give a real nice party, Rosie," he said. "This is real nice. You even decorated the bulletin board."

"I'm making you coffee," she said. "Black coffee."

"You know, Rosie," the priest was saying, "I gave a party tonight—that's why we're all here. . . . I gave a party, and I invited all the priests within thirty miles—all except the real old farts, you know . . ."

"Now, father . . ." Rosie said.

"I gave a party, you know, 'cause the pastor was gone for the night—but he drinks too, you know—just doesn't like crowds. And I gave a party . . ." He had lost his train of thought.

"You gave a party and invited all the priests. . . ."

"You got it, Rosie. I sent out real nice invitations, and told 'em . . . I said I was gonna cook spaghetti myself, and maybe we could talk about how to implement the new changes in the liturgy. . . . Implementation, you know, that's real important, Rosie." He leaned across the table toward the kitchen. "Real important. And not one of those bastards came."

"Maybe you got the dates mixed up." It was all she could think of to say.

"Nope. No dates. Schneider, you know, from Luverne, he calls and says he's got two wakes. Buggers dyin' all over the place. And I says, 'Come after,' but he didn't come. And Malloy from Pipestone says it's too far in the snow. Seven invitations, Rosie, and you know, not one of the bastards came."

His eyes were filled and he was staring at his hands. Rosie could think of nothing to say.

"I even invited the happiness boys," he said morosely.

"Happiness boys?"

"Yup. All those boys who want a parish where the money just rolls in, you know, and they can play golf three days a week. . . ."

The coffee was done and she poured him a large mug.

"You know, Rosie," he said, "you know, in my first parish the pastor said to me . . . I was trying to get somebody decent on the welfare board . . . and he said, 'Hell, you take all that stuff too seriously. Sit down and have a drink.' That's what he said, 'Sit down and have a drink.' And I said, 'If they cut that budget, two social workers get the axe.' And you know what he said, Rosie? 'Sit down and have a drink.' It was happy hour, you know. You always gotta be happy between five and six o'clock."

He was staring into the coffee. "Drink it," Rosie said. "Drink the coffee."

He took a large swallow. "Hot," he said. "And you know what, Rosie?" He leaned across the table confidentially. "That spring one of the little kids we had in CCD class? Her old man beat her almost to death." His eyes filled again. "Cutest little kid you ever saw and her old man damn near killed her."

"Drink the coffee," Rosie said.

"And all those little kids at Halloween, you know?" He put down the mug halfway to his mouth. "The Lutherans and the Methodists and all our little kids from CCD? We were gonna have 'em all collect for UNICEF, and the pastor says, 'Nobody from my school's messin' with that Commie stuff.' That's what he said, you know. 'You take this stuff too seriously.' "

"Maybe you did take it too seriously," Rosie said. She didn't think she should be hearing this.

"Yeah," he said, drinking more rapidly now. "So they packed me up and shipped me west. That's what happens, you know. You mouth off to the bishop—or mess with a woman—or take things too seriously, and you get shipped to the west of the diocese. Out to the boondocks." He laughed. "The happiness boys out here are really pissed."

"You got sent out here as a punishment?" Rosie said.

"No-oo," he said as though that were a silly idea. "Gotta do worse than that, Rosie. You know why I got sent out here?" His eyes narrowed and fixed on her. " 'Cause I taught the kids in high school religion class that evolution is possible. That's what I did, Rosie. I told 'em . . . I told 'em science and faith can be reconciled and that some of the stories in Genesis are metaphorical. Did you know that, Rosie?" He leaned over the table again.

Rosie said nothing. She tried to remember what "metaphorical" meant.

"Say, Rosie," he said, "how did we get talking about this?"

"You were telling me about your party," she said.

"Oh, yeah, I was telling you about the most popular guy in the diocese." He squared his shoulders and worked his mouth into an ironic smile, but the sadness around the eyes didn't change.

"I'm sorry," she said. He seemed to be sobering up enough to accept that. "I'm really sorry."

"It's okay, Rosie," he said. "A man who's got Jesus shouldn't need people too." His voice was ironic again. "Right?" he said. "Isn't that what they taught you?"

"I don't know," Rosie said. "I guess so." There was a long silence.

"I can't do it, Rosie." He was weeping openly now. "I can't be alone all the time. Maybe having someone is wrong, but I just can't go on being alone like this." His head was down on his tightly fisted hands. She couldn't see his face, but she could see tears hitting the back of his hands and making a bright trail until they disappeared into a watchband or cuff. If this priest had been a woman, she could have put her arms around him, pulled his head to her breast, saying, "It's okay . . . it's okay." Now there was nothing to do. She listened to the strangling sounds he was making—an awful effort to hold back, to pull all that wetness back into the throat.

"How old are you?" she demanded suddenly.

The abruptness of the question startled him. "Thirty," he said. "Almost thirty-one." His face was smeared and spotted, and the freckles had nearly vanished into the red.

"That's too young," she said. "Maybe priests who've lived their whole lives can just need God, but you haven't gotten there yet." She didn't know why she had said that. She wasn't quite sure what it meant, but it seemed to be the right thing. His face softened a little and the lines of pain relaxed.

"Thanks, Rosie." He reached across the table and put his hand over hers on the coffee cup. "Thank you."

The gesture touched her, as though she had done something magnificent, but through her pleasure came the thought that this was a priest's hand warming hers. She panicked for an instant— what did this mean?—but then the hand had gone away, and he was pulling out a slightly soiled handkerchief and blowing his nose.

"I'm really sorry about this . . ." he started. "I don't usually do things like this; I don't want you to think . . ."

"Please!" she said. "It's okay. Really. I'll rinse the cups out. You go home and get some sleep." She could hear the gentleness in her own voice. She had never heard just that tone before, and it pleased her—it was how she'd always wanted to sound.

"You're a good woman, Rosie," he said. "You're a good friend." They were both silent as she rinsed the cups and put the coffee pot away. "I'll walk you home safe," he said.

"I think. . . . Thank you, but it might look better if you didn't. . . ." She stopped.

He laughed. "They might suspect me, Rosie, but never you!

Okay," he said, "but I'll come out and watch to make sure you get there."

He pushed open the door, and they went up the stairs and into the cold. He was standing straight now, trying to look dignified. The street was deserted. "Good night, Rose," he said and put out his hand.

She shook it. "Good night," she said.

There was something unreal about walking home in the early morning hours through snow that was still marred only by her own tracks. She felt again that she was somehow detached from her own body, floating across the surface of the snow as milkweed would float on the surface of the creek. All of the night's events had happened to someone else—perhaps to the woman who pulled her coat closer and moved her feet one after the other, but not to the Rosie who floated above the snow. She wondered how long the priest stood there watching, but she didn't turn to see. When she got to her door, she looked back down the three blocks. The spire of the church stood out clearly, but the rest was dark shadow, a mass that would engulf any individual. She turned her key and went into the house.

She was past sleep. The weariness she had felt when she ironed the surplices had long ago faded. The strangeness of the night would have kept her awake if the coffee had not. She pulled the rocker from the front room into the little-used sun porch, but turned on no lights. *How strange*, she thought, as she traced a bit of streetlight that came in the window and caught her knee. She had been afraid of priests since she was a little girl—their knowledge, their holiness, their threats of hell. You feared them because they knew your sins and the secrets of your soul. And you knew nothing of theirs—you did not touch a priest as you did not touch a chalice or a ciborium.

She held her breath as Father Griffin's hand closed again on hers around the coffee cup. "Thanks, Rosie," he said. "Thank you." Not once during that night had she thought of her confession, or her shame at facing him. Not once had she feared him. She felt again the warmth of his hand, a man's hand, but this time she did not pull away from the memory.

The whole evening began to replay itself: Ray, the card party, the sense of his closeness as they hurtled through the snow. And then the surplices, the priest lurching across the sacristy. . . .

"Oh, dear God!" she said aloud and stopped the rocking chair. "The sacristy!" The surplices were still in the heap where they had fallen, the cupboard doors open or ajar; the bottle of Jack Daniels was perched, plain as a setting hen, on the countertop. The servers were likely to be there earlier than the priest was—if he made it to the early Mass at all. "I hear he had a snootful again the other night," she could hear Dora say.

Once more her feet moved over the silent snow. The sacristy was as she had pictured it. She shook out the surplices, closed all the cupboard doors, put the whiskey in a paper sack and took it home. It was strange that she should have walked off without remembering the bottle, but then, the whole evening had been strange. *Two men*, she thought. *I've never really known any men but Jack, and tonight there were two of them.* But even that thought was strange, she realized. She had never really thought of a priest as a man before.

Chapter XI

RAY WAS GONE FOR A WEEK. HIS FACE, WHEN HE DELIVERED THE milk on the Wednesday before, looked a little strained, Rosie thought, but he said he was feeling fine. "Another guy will be taking the route next week," he said. "I've got to take a business trip." That sounded a little pretentious for a milkman, and he added hurriedly, "I still own a little property in Illinois, and I've got to take care of some complications—you know, taxes and stuff." He was stacking the racks of milk cartons and his back was turned. "So I'll be back on my route a week from Friday," he said as he straightened up and turned.

Rosie was disappointed. She made herself smile and say, "Have a nice trip," as he backed out the door with the empty racks in more of a hurry than usual, but she found herself frowning the rest of the morning. It was a silly reaction, she told herself. He was, after all, just a friend, and there was no reason to think that she would have seen him this weekend anyway—he hadn't asked her—maybe he would never ask her again—but an unreasonable heaviness settled itself in her head, and the weight of it was pulling at her lips and cheeks with an old, remembered gravity.

There was another problem. Thanksgiving was coming. She didn't want to go to Aunt Nellie's and submit to a day of questions and endless advice, and she didn't want to spend the day alone. Last year, she had invited the relatives from Luverne because Jack refused to go to Aunt Nellie's and eat in the same room as "that goddam canary." They were reminded of this lapse through the entire meal.

"Pootie is sensitive," Aunt Nellie said. "He knows. He knows when people stop coming by the house. . . . He knows what happens when you get old."

"Pass the spuds," Jack said.

The only Thanksgiving that was worse in her memory took place during the depression when Aunt Mina came into a minor windfall of some sort and brought Cousin Alice out on the train. There was no turkey that year, Rosie remembered, but Pa had gotten a young goose from old Mrs. Geil in exchange for chopping wood. Mama roasted it in the cook-stove with some acorn squash, and the rich, dark smell was everywhere.

"I get the wishbone," Rosie said when the carving started. "You promised, it's my turn."

"Maybe Cousin Alice wants the wishbone," Mama said.

"Let Rosie have it," Aunt Mina said. "Alice can pull if she wants to." Rosie was glad. Jack always won when they pulled the wishbone, but Alice was younger than Rosie and skinny. It would never snap on her side.

"All right, let Alice pull," Mama said when they were ready to clear the plates. Rosie carefully wiped the grease off the wishbone with her napkin, and Alice took a rather limp hold.

"First you wish," Rosie told her and closed her eyes. There was no question of what she would wish for. Christmas was coming, and she wished with all her young fervor for the nurse's kit in the Sears Roebuck catalog on page 129.

"All right—pull!" Mama said. Rosie opened her eyes just in time to see Alice slide her index finger up behind the narrowest part of her half of the wishbone and bring her hand down and her elbow up fast. The bone snapped about an inch from Rosie's fingers.

"She cheated!" Rosie said. "She put her fingers way up there! You're only supposed to hang on to the end! She cheated!"

"Rosie!" Mama said. "Alice is company!"

"I did *not* cheat," Alice said.

"But she cheated," Rosie said. "It's not fair."

"Rosie!" Mama said. "Do you want dessert or don't you?" Dessert was Apple Betty in a time when any dessert was rare. Rosie stayed at the table and ate it, but the apples were sour and the oatmeal caught in her throat.

The rest of the day was worse. Alice and Jack played running games and whispered secrets they wouldn't share. Alice, of course, was allowed to play with the paper dolls Rosie had cut from an old catalog and pasted on some cardboard Pa brought home from the store. Alice left them where the puppy had easy access. By the time Rosie finished wiping dishes and found them, all three were tattered and the head and left arm of one were completely gone.

She spent the evening in a dark corner of the dining room while Jack and Alice played Chinese checkers in the living room with the adults. She was almost asleep, clutching the mangled paper dolls, when she heard someone behind her. Pa scooped her up and sat with her in the dark window seat. He brushed the hair back from her eyes. "What was it you were wishing for so hard?" he said. Rosie turned her face to his rough flannel shirt and cried.

Rosie didn't want to be with relatives this year. She had thought first of inviting Ray for dinner, but that would never do. Holidays insinuated something; they implied a relationship, or a future relationship, or at least a distinct hope for a relationship on the part of the one inviting. You couldn't invite someone to Thanksgiving dinner who was just looking for a bingo partner and happened to know you were around. But perhaps if she gave a party. . . . She pictured herself in a sleek black dress, dispensing drinks and witty remarks while rivulets of laughter flowed around her.

She would invite the two youngest nuns, Sister Carol Ann and Sister Gaelynn—they never went home for the holidays—she would invite Tom and Gina Pratt and their three little girls (they were from Omaha), and whichever priest stayed in town. She would roast a turkey, make pumpkin pies with a pecan topping, and use Mama's recipe for giblet dressing. She would serve whiskey sours and use a cheese puff recipe from *The Ladies' Home Journal* for hors d'oeuvres.

But now there was no way of inviting Ray. School let out at noon next Wednesday, so there would be no hot lunch, and no milk delivery, and Ray would not be back before then. Maybe he wouldn't be back at all. Maybe the trip was just a bluff—an excuse to cover the fact that he had asked to have his route transferred—that he wanted to end whatever their relationship had been. The trip could have come up suddenly, she knew, but he hadn't asked to see her again. . . .

Rosie pondered it when the substitute milkman arrived on Friday. "You're new," she said, out of Dora's earshot. "Is this your route now?"

"Naw," he said, chewing gum. "Bowen went to Indiana or one a' them places. He'll be back." The new milkman was about twenty with curly hair that needed to be cut, and a jacket with a cigarette pocket on the sleeve. He came late and dawdled over the job until the high school girls started to come in.

Father Griffin solved the problem. At least he gave her an excuse not to spend Thanksgiving sipping sweet wine in the fly trap of Aunt Nellie's parlor. "What are you doing for Thanksgiving, Rosie?" he said, coming through the cafeteria line just as she was ready to close it. He had never referred to last Sunday night. Rosie had been afraid of embarrassing apologies, of a sense that she knew far too much for him to be comfortable in her presence, but like her confession, it seemed never to have occurred.

"I was thinking of having a party," she said. "I thought I might invite the Pratts, and Sister Carol Ann and Gaelynn, and whichever priest stayed in town. . . ."

"Aw—" he said—"you're stealing my guest list—you can't do that! Besides, I'm a good cook, and Schwartz will be at his sister's."

"I already bought a turkey," she said. "They were on special in Luverne last week."

He paused for a moment, looking at his macaroni and cheese

with an exaggerated frown. "Okay," he said. "I'll make you a deal. You can have the party if I can come help cook. I'll make my sweet-potato casserole, and mince pie . . . and I'll bring the wine. How's that?"

"That's fine." She laughed. "I was going to make pumpkin pie . . ."

"Both!" he said. "We need both. And I'll do all the dishes."

"Oh, no. You don't have to." She couldn't imagine a priest at her dishpan.

He shrugged. "I'm better at that than cooking, to tell the truth . . . and besides, I owe my mother-confessor something." He gave her a quick and slightly sheepish smile and walked away with his tray.

Rosie had never shared her kitchen with anyone other than Mama, and apprehension ticked around her like a timer until Father Griffin arrived at three. He presented two mince-meat pies that looked surprisingly good, two half-gallons of wine, a sack of sweet potatoes, butter, marshmallows, and a portable radio. "I thought you might not have FM," he explained. He accepted one of her half-aprons, demanded a knife, rolled up the sleeves of his sweater, and set to work on the sweet potatoes. He was deft and neat with the knife, and Rosie relaxed as she cut celery sticks to fill with cream cheese and tried to make radish roses. The smell of turkey and hot pies pervaded. The priest sang "Puff, the Magic Dragon" along with the radio, and launched into tales of the year his father died, his mother went out to work, and he, the oldest of eight, was supposed to learn to cook. "My mother should have had the girls first," he said. "Poor planning."

Rosie watched him through the open kitchen door as she took the silver and wine glasses from the buffet and gave them a quick polish at the dining-room table. He had poured himself a glass of wine from one of the half-gallon jugs, sipping it as he worked. His body, as he moved from the sink to the table, had the loose solidity of a happy body. "That's the way we should be," she thought, "houses full of cinnamon and light, and no one alone. . . ."

The priest moved to the doorway and held out the casserole, white miniature marshallows like a lumpy batting across the top. "Enough for ten?" he said.

"Nine," Rosie said, the light and warmth suddenly diminished. "Nine, and that's plenty."

"Who's not coming?" the priest said. "Two nuns and Ray and five Pratts . . . you invited Ray, didn't you?"

"I was going to," Rosie said, "but he went out of town."

"But he's back," the priest said. "I saw him in Luverne last night at the liquor store."

"Oh," Rosie said. "But he wasn't on the route Monday and that's the last time I could have invited him. . . ."

"Well, call him up," the priest said, turning back to the kitchen and putting the casserole carefully into the oven beside the turkey. He returned to the doorway. "He has a phone, doesn't he?"

"I guess so," Rosie said, polishing hard on a knife handle. "He called me once." He had called her twice, in fact, and she knew he had a phone because she had gotten the number from information and found that it stuck in her head as firmly as her own.

"Well?" the priest said.

Rosie got up and pulled the phone book from a drawer in the buffet; it was a slim book and covered the whole county. "He's probably gone somewhere by now," she said, handing it to the priest, "but why don't you try anyway?" She hoped she sounded casual.

The priest sat down with the phone book, but he didn't open it. He looked at her steadily across the table. "Why didn't you call him, Rosie? Don't you want him to come?"

Rosie kept her eyes on the silverware. She felt as if she was back in the confessional again, obliged to answer questions, and obliged to tell the truth. "Well, he went out of town," she said again, "and he acted a little strange about it, and I thought . . . well, maybe he doesn't want to see me anymore—he didn't invite *me* for Thanksgiving. . . ." She blurted it out in a tone that sounded more hurt than she had expected. She raised her eyes to the priest's, but his expression hadn't changed.

"There's one way to find out," he said and pushed the phone book toward her.

"I can't," she said, knowing that he wouldn't understand. "I can't just call a man like that. You call. It's your party too."

The priest's face relaxed into a smile. "Rosie, Rosie," he said. "You block your own path just like the rest of us." He opened the phone book, ran his finger down the page, then called information and dialed the seven digits. "Here," he said, putting the receiver in her hand. "I dialed, you talk." He strode quickly to the kitchen.

Rosie thrust the phone out after him, but he didn't turn. He pulled the kitchen door shut, winking at her as he did so. The phone was ringing on the other end.

"Hello," Ray's voice said, rather dully.

"Hello," she heard her own voice saying. "Hello, this is Rosie. Father Griffin and I are having . . . we're cooking a Thanksgiving dinner, and he just told me you were back in town. I know it's awfully late, but could you come? Provided you don't have other plans, of course . . . we'll eat at 5:30 or 6:00."

"Sure," the voice sounded brighter and not really embarrassed. "I was just . . . ah, I got back too late to make any plans, and I thought I'd just go to a restaurant . . . but a home-cooked meal sounds a lot nicer."

The nuns arrived at 4:30. "What a great old place," Sister Carol Ann said, peering around a little enviously. She was wearing her veil farther back than usual, and her blonde hair seemed to have waves on the side rather than sweeping straight back. Rosie noticed that her fingernails, though unpolished, were shiny and filed to a point. "Dress like a secular, and you'll act like a secular," Sister Grace had said, but Carol Ann never seemed to act improperly. She was roaming around the living room now, examining old pieces of furniture and bric-a-brac, a half-smile on her face. "Look at all this oak woodwork," she exclaimed. "If this were mine, I'd fix up that little sunroom in bright colors—yellow, maybe—with a thick rug and loose-weave curtains. I'd put in some plants and make it a private sanctuary. . . . Of course, it's nice as it is," she hastened to add, "it's just that I always dream about being able to decorate places. . . ."

The Pratts were there promptly at five. "This is for you," said Lisa, who had just turned six. "We made it." It was a large cranberry-colored candle that was only a little crooked on top and had a wreath of spruce twigs around the bottom.

"We stole those from the cemetery," Karla volunteered. Karla was five. Rosie kissed them both and led Jill, the three-year-old, into the kitchen to get the cranberry juice she had poured into wine glasses for them.

"How come all your stuff is so old?" Jill said, as she surveyed Rosie's furniture.

"Jill!" her mother said, but Rosie laughed.

"It *is* old," she said, feeling a glow that was not simply wine. "I guess I've never thought much about it."

But some things are new, Rosie thought as she passed the celery filled with cream cheese and the little cheese puffs. *Here are the nuns, out of the cloister and drinking wine like any other guest, and here's a priest washing his own dishes, and here am I, a hostess who even at the last minute can call up men. . . .*

The doorbell rang, and there was Ray, looking happy, with a box of Fanny Farmer's in his hand.

Chapter XII

FATHER GRIFFIN OPENED THE RECTORY DOOR AND WAVED THEM inside, holding the door with his foot. He had a phone receiver at his ear, and the cord was writhing out of the nearest parlor office. "Un-huh," he was saying. "Un-huh." He put a hand over the receiver when he had closed the door. "Phil!" he yelled toward the stairs, "Carol Ann and Rosie to see you." In a moment, the pastor was coming down.

Father Schwartz was a small, thin man—too thin perhaps. He seemed always in motion, never at rest. Rosie had the feeling those dark, alert eyes never slept. She was glad he had not been her confessor after her trip to Sioux Falls. He would not have been unkind, she knew, but she had a feeling those eyes remembered everything. Father Schwartz swept into a mock bow as he reached the bottom step. "Well," he said, "and to what do I owe this visit?"

"I brought that Conception Abbey catalog you wanted," Sister Carol Ann said, holding out a bright rectangle, "and Rosie is already playing Santa Claus."

"It's fruitcake," Rosie said, holding out a foil-wrapped loaf, "and it needs to age a bit." It was only the second Saturday in December, but she found herself wanting to feel festive, to give gifts. She had just delivered two loaves to the convent.

The priest accepted both offerings politely and balanced them on the square newel post at the bottom of the stairs. "Come see what I'm doing," he said, and headed for the basement.

Rosie had been in the rectory basement years ago, but not recently. It was poured concrete like hers, but well painted and partitioned into several rooms. Odd combinations of clerical and household items shared wall space in the large open area at the bottom of the stairs: four cardboard cartons of old Latin hymnals leaned against the washer and dryer, and neatly stacked boxes of church envelopes perched on the same shelves as jars of home-canned fruits and vegetables, obviously donations from parishioners.

Father Schwartz led them to a room that opened off to the left. Paneling had been installed on the walls, and the floor had a coarse carpet, though the ceiling studs and duct work were undisguised. The room was fastidiously neat compared to the general disarray of the basement. Two metal cabinets held paper supplies and square cans of ink and fluid. A narrow table along one wall was obviously set up for cutting and folding, and in the center of the room, squatting like a mechanical toad on a low platform, was a small printing press. The pastor looked pleased with himself.

"So this is your playroom," Sister Carol Ann said.

"My *workroom*," he corrected her. He explained the features of the press, flicked a switch, and ran a stiff piece of deckle-edged paper through it. "See," he said proudly. The paper displayed a yellow circle that was flattened on the bottom and surrounded by some small yellow dots and lines. It said:

Providence   rise

                                    morning sun!

"That's very nice," Rosie said. She wondered why he didn't space the words evenly.

"Now, you understand, this is just the first run," Father Schwartz said. "The red run will fill in the flowers and make these letters orange, and then I'll do a black run to get in the stems and leaves and print the rest of the quote: 'Providence will rise before the morning sun.'" He took the card from Rosie and added it to a stack like it on the cutting table, lining up the edges precisely.

"So, what are you girls up to?" he said. "Plotting a little get-away with friends or something?" He was fussing more than was necessary with the stack of papers. Upstairs, the phone was ringing again.

"Where would we get away to?" Sister Carol Ann said. "The Sioux City stockyards—like the seniors do on skip-day?"

"Oh, I don't know," he said; "people your age seem to find plenty to do." They eyed each other steadily. Something was going on that Rosie didn't understand. She turned her head toward the sound of heavy feet on the basement stairs. "Rosie?" Father Griffin was calling.

"Thank God!" he said, appearing in the doorway. "I need you right away—both of you. Tom Pratt's on the phone. Gina's hemorrhaging and the kids are in the house alone."

"My God!" Carol Ann said as they turned the corner. "That's the hearse!" The sleek, gray vehicle swung around them and turned toward the highway.

"No, it isn't," Rosie said. "When the curtains are open, it's the ambulance. It's the only one we've got." She slammed the car into "park," and they both jumped out in front of a three-bedroom ranch-style house that was one of the newest in St. Ives.

The door of the house was ajar, and Rosie felt warmth oozing out. Lisa, the six-year-old, was standing in the doorway with one hand reached up to the knob, and the other twisted into her sweater. Her corduroy pants were on backwards so that the patch pockets stuck out over her stomach; her thin face was very white.

"Jill's crying," she announced. "I'm not crying because I'm in charge. Daddy said I was in charge till somebody got here."

Jill was indeed crying, as was Karla, the five-year-old. They were in separate rooms, as though their grief were too great to be shared. Rosie unwrapped Jill from the dining room drapes in which she had wound herself and carried her back into the living room. The child had dark, straight hair, and at three and a half was just lengthening out of roundness. Rosie could feel the tiny chest heaving against her own and a wetness warming her neck. Carol Ann was moving the coffee table with her free arm and pulling Karla from underneath it. The five of them sank back into the sofa in a heap. For a very long moment, the only sound was that of even sobbing. Jill's small shoulder blades rippled beneath Rosie's hand; the face which snuggled into her neck was incredibly soft. Something in her own chest swelled, as though she had been breathing too deeply. She thought, and then felt guilty for thinking, that she never wanted this weeping to stop; she never wanted this moment to be over.

Jill stirred, as though the realization of her grief had overcome her once more, and began to sob so hard it caught in her throat and choked her. Her head went back, and her eyes were ringed with fright above the oval of her mouth as she gasped to breathe.

"Shake her!" Carol Ann said. "Hit her on the back!"

Rosie thumped the child's back, trying to gauge her force. "Breathe," she said, "breathe!" Jill gasped, choked once, and gasped again and began a great wail. The other two had stopped crying and were watching her coldly.

"You hit my sister," Lisa said, standing up. "You hit her!"

"Your sister was choking," Carol Ann said, turning the child's face toward her. "Rosie didn't *hit* her. She just gave her a thump to get her breathing again. See, now she's all right."

"Is she going to bleed?" Karla wanted to know.

"Of course not," Carol Ann said.

"Is she going to die?"

"No, she's not going to die."

"Mommy bleeded." Karla was very matter-of-fact.

"She did not," Lisa said. "She did not, and you don't have to tell!"

"Mommy bleeded in the bathroom. She fell down and she didn't wake up, and blood was coming out. . . ."

"Shut up!" Lisa said and struck at her. "Shut up! You don't have to tell!" She jerked away from Carol Ann and ran around the divider into the corner of the dining room.

She's ashamed, Rosie thought. She's terrified, but she's trying to protect her mother from some kind of shame. In a flash, she saw herself at—at what age was she? Five? Seven? She was staring at the blood on a homemade menstrual pad Mama had accidentally left in the bathroom. She was afraid of it; it meant Mama was sick. Maybe it meant Mama would die; but there was something secret about the sickness, something shameful you couldn't talk about. She knew it was shameful from closed doors and closed cupboards and questions that never got answered but made her feel guilty that she had asked. She pushed the pad behind the hamper where Jack wouldn't find it, and she said nothing. The next day, the pad was gone.

"Lisa," Rosie said, stooping to her height and stroking her back, "it's all right. We already know your mama was bleeding. Your daddy told us." She didn't know where the words were coming from, but they sounded right. "Your daddy called Father Griffin when we were at his house. It means your mama is hurt inside, but it's nothing to be ashamed of—it's nobody's fault. They took your mama to a hospital, and they're going to put more blood in her and fix her up inside so she's all well again and can come home to you. So, it's okay. It's okay that Karla told us. Do you believe that?"

The little girl said nothing, but turned and buried her face in Rosie's shoulder.

The rest of the afternoon was like a dream, a kaleidoscope in which everything shifted, changed, made different patterns. Rosie kept trying to fix something in place: an emotion, a scene, a stance they took toward one another, but always her attention was drawn to something else and when she looked back everything was changed. She would be comforting a child who seemed a soft, weighted bag of sorrow draped across her neck, would put the child down to let out the Pratts' scratching terrier and would return to a quarrel over the ownership of a box of popsicle sticks. She would turn from Jill's defiant pout to catch a glimpse of Carol Ann, her face alive with a tender animation Rosie had never seen. She would listen to a long description of the dog's habits from Lisa, only to have Karla announce: "Know what? Jill had worms. But she didn't go to the hospital. She had to eat big orange pills. . . ."

"Huh-uh!" A strong denial from Jill herself. "Lellow pills. I had lellow pills."

"I think we need an activity," Carol Ann said. "Why don't we color? I like to color a lot, don't you?"

"No," said Lisa and Karla together. "I think it's dumb," Karla added. Jill went to the window and wrapped herself in the drape.

"She had to go potty," Karla said.

"How do you know?"

"She always has to go," Karla said. "That's why she sucks her thumb."

Carol Ann unwound the little girl from the drape and led her to the bathroom, but Lisa, arms outspread, blocked the door. "You can't go in there," she said.

"Why not?"

"Because you can't!" she said hotly. "You aren't supposed to see our bathroom."

"If Jill needs to go, we have to get into the bathroom," Carol Ann said reasonably, and began to pry the small arm from the doorjamb. Lisa let go, but ran shrieking to the davenport and flung herself on it. "I told you!" she sobbed. "I told you!"

Carol Ann began to push back the door, but reversed the motion midway through it and pulled the door shut. "Let's wait just a little," she said to Jill. "You can hold it just a little, can't you?" Her eyes appealed to Rosie as she said, "How about some cookies? I bet none of you know where Mommy keeps the cookies, do you?"

The bathroom was a mess. Towels lay in a soft heap underneath a broken towel rod, their fringed edges soaking like a wick in a partly dried pool of blood that was smeared from the toilet past the sink. The roll of toilet paper was partly unwound, and a bloody wad of it floated in the toilet. Pink streaks went straight down through the unstirred water, and a dark clot had settled on the bottom near the trap. The wastebasket was overturned, and a plastic water glass and two combs were on the floor near the rug. Rosie flushed the toilet and threw a towel over the blood that had not yet hardened. She found a sponge in the cabinet under the sink, and began to wipe the floor. *She tried to catch herself on the towel rack as she was going down,* Rosie thought but she couldn't make herself focus on Gina; she kept seeing a small hand on the doorknob, and round, solemn eyes looking at the woman lying in her own blood on the floor. Something about the scene resonated in her own memory, as though it was her own self, small and lost and innocent, that she was seeing, but she couldn't make the scene come clearer. When she emerged from the bathroom, the young priest was coming up the walk.

"Your mommy's okay," he assured the three who were suddenly silent and frozen into cringing positions. "The doctors in Worthington are taking real good care of her, but she's going to have to stay in the hospital for a while. And she loves you very much." He motioned Rosie and Carol Ann outside to the steps where frost was inching up the cement. "They don't know for sure," he said. "It might be a tubal pregnancy. They're doing surgery right now, but she's lost a lot of blood." He pulled out a big linen handkerchief and blew his nose. "You two better plan to stay the night," he said. "I doubt Tom will make it home."

The children were full of questions then. She tried to explain to Lisa what a hospital was, and assured Jill that "a while" would be over before Christmas. To give herself some air, as much as to divert the children's attention, she suggested that they drive to her house to get some oatmeal-raisin cookies out of her freezer. "I hate raisins," Karla said, but all three insisted on going along. Carol Ann stayed to answer the phone.

"There wasn't time," Carol Ann was saying into the receiver when the children burst ahead of Rosie through their door. "There wasn't time to call or come home. You can't leave children as small as these alone in a house. Yes. I was going to call as soon as things got settled down." There was a pause, and Carol Ann closed her eyes as she listened. The skin around her eyes had that thin, transparent look that Irish women sometimes have, a faint blueness that hints of veins close to the skin. It had the same vulnerability as a baby's open, pulsing skull. "Yes," the young nun said, "he told us the same thing. He wants Rosie and me to stay overnight." Carol Ann paused again, but her face took on its impatient look. "I know all that, but it doesn't make any sense.

These are real people in a real situation. . . . Why not? . . . Why not? . . . What difference does it make?" She had turned so that Rosie could see only her back, but her voice was rising, getting sharper. "I don't think this is the same thing. . . . Yes, I know that . . . but . . ." The voice dropped in a kind of despair. "Yes . . . yes, I'll be home by five o'clock. . . . I don't need a ride—I can walk."

Carol Ann hung up the phone very slowly and sank into the upholstered rocker near it. The impatience had given way to a kind of bleakness that made her look old. "Sister Geraldine wants me home for Office and dinner," she said. She was silent for a moment, and Rosie was afraid she might begin to cry, but she put out her hand toward Jill. "You were going to show me how your Tinkertoys work," she said.

She told Rosie about it as they searched through the cupboards for supper ingredients. "Sister Geraldine thinks it's a great concession for me to be here at all," she said. "And, if you go by the book, it is. 'A Sister may, in the company of another Sister or Sisters, make brief visits to private homes of parishioners who are ill or in spiritual need,'" she quoted. "And that's the new, 'liberal' interpretation."

"You came for Thanskgiving," Rosie said.

"Yes," Carol Ann smiled ruefully, "but we had to make a big case for being alone over the holidays as 'spiritual need,' and I don't think Sister Geraldine knew you'd have other guests. And then," she added, "we got in trouble for staying until after nine o'clock." Her voice had an edge of bitterness that Rosie had not heard before. "I can't stay overnight because that's another rule; and besides," her voice shifted into sarcasm, "it might give scandal to the community."

Rosie didn't understand. "What would be scandalous about staying . . . oh!" she said. "Well, I'm here too, so that's really kind of silly."

"A lot of things are silly," the young nun said. "Having to give all your letters to the superior to be sealed and stamped is silly, and not being able to ride alone in a car with your own father is silly, and being told that we must remain 'detached' from the people we serve because 'human affection might impede our spiritual growth' is the silliest of all!" She looked down at her clumsy nurse's watch on its black leather band. "I have to leave in fifteen minutes," she said. "I was reminded not to be late for community prayers."

The house was quiet after Carol Ann left. Jill had fallen asleep on the couch; Karla was backed against a kitchen cupboard, hugging a somewhat unwilling dog and sucking her thumb; and Lisa was making a precise and elaborate game out of setting the table, narrating her movements to herself as she did so. Rosie remembered that she and Ray were going to see a movie that evening.

"Hey!" he said when he heard her situation on the phone. "I'm a real pro at bedtime stories. And the kids will remember me from Thanksgiving."

He got there in time for supper. There was tuna casserole and coleslaw, a tube of biscuits, and strawberry ice cream. Ray seated the little girls with great, but clumsy, ceremony, his big hands more careful than necessary of their tiny limbs. He was being hearty and merry for their sake, but the effort didn't seem forced.

"Look," he said to Jill who had been awakened and was red-cheeked and glowering at them through a haze of tangled hair, "I bet I can eat all the casserole on my plate faster than you can!"

"So what?" Jill said and continued to glower as she twisted a finger round and round through a strand of her hair. "You're fatter."

Rosie laughed, and suddenly all three children laughed with her. "She always says stuff like that when she's mad," Karla volunteered. It was the first laughter of the afternoon.

The couch was too short for Rosie and she slept badly. After Ray left, she had searched the cupboards and found two extra blankets and a pillowcase to put over the latch-hook pillow. At first she was afraid to sleep—afraid she would not hear the children if they cried or called—and then her back began to ache.

"Why don't you sleep in the bed if Tom's not coming home?" Ray had said, but she couldn't do that. She couldn't wake to have

Tom find her there, clothed or not. She had lain on the couch listening for the breathing of the children at first. "Sometimes, when they're very small, you think they aren't breathing, and you panic," Gina had said at Thanksgiving. "Then you touch them, and they jump and start to squall . . . children make you conscious of death," she'd said.

Rosie got up and tiptoed into the bedrooms where Lisa and Karla were both sprawled diagonally across their double bed, and Jill, in her youth-bed, clutched a shredded blanket to her mouth. Rosie tugged very lightly at the blanket and the grip tightened. "She's breathing, all right," she said to herself.

She thought of Ray when she lay down again. He had given the three of them piggy-back rides all around the house and up and down the basement stairs for nearly an hour. Then he told them an elaborate story of a puppy that fell and broke its leg when it stepped into a gopher hole. "Poor puppy had to go to the hospital and have his leg in traction," he said.

Rosie was a little jealous of the way the children took to him. She could never have invented a story like that, never have captured the children's attention the way Ray had almost immediately snared and held it. She envied him his charm, his easy affection, the blithe way he was able to move through the world. Still, it was a shame he never had children, Rosie thought as she watched his profile, surrounded by three softer profiles under the lamp. He was such a natural father, his body so comfortable, his arms so at ease as he gathered them in.

"You know," he said when the children were finally asleep, "I used to have this dream all the time—not when I was sleeping, but a daydream—of teaching a kid to fly a kite. The kid was always about four or five years old, and sometimes it was a little girl, or a boy and girl both—and we'd run and run, and the kite would catch and sail—just perfect, you know, just the right height—and I'd be so proud; and the kid would fly it all by himself, and then, when we were getting tired, he'd trip and drop the string, and the kite would go off with the tail bobbing until it was like a little bird, and then a speck, and then just clouds. And the little kid would cry and cry, and I'd hold him and say, 'It's all right. It's all right. . . .' "

Ray stopped. He made a "humph" sound through his nose as though embarrassed by the silliness of what he had just said.

"Did you want children?" she said softly.

"Yeah," Ray said. "I guess I thought it was automatic." He grinned a little sadly. "Some things aren't meant to be, are they?"

A sharp cry came from the bedroom and Rosie jerked up. She had been dreaming. Yes? No? She had been halfway into dream. She hurried to the bedroom. Jill was on her back now; she had let go of the blanket, but she was still sound asleep.

Rosie gave up trying. Her back wouldn't permit her to sleep, and she was afraid of where thoughts of Ray and children might lead her. She watched the patterns that lights of an occasional car made on the drapes, and she studied the configuration on an end table: a lamp, an ashtray, and a doll that was bent forward, its head on its feet. Sometimes, shadows seemed to slip past, dim figures from the future or the past, but it wasn't until the low voices in the kitchen became distinct that she knew she had slept.

". . . seems so unreal," Tom was saying. It was still night, and Rosie could hear the faint clink of a cup or glass. "She looked like wax when they brought her out with that tube in her nose. I thought for a minute she was dead."

Father Griffin's voice said something about "How long?"

"I don't know," Tom said. "I don't even care, as long as she comes out all right. Her mother is flying into Sioux Falls tomorrow afternoon to take care of the kids—if Rosie can stay that long."

"I'm sure she can," the priest said. There was a long silence, and again the cups or glasses clinked against a surface.

"I feel so rotten," Tom said. "It's really my fault."

"Tom, it's not. . . ."

"Yes, it is," Tom's voice got louder. "The doctor in Omaha told her not to get pregnant again. She wanted . . . oh, hell, she wanted a diaphragm, but I said we'd manage. . . ."

"Tom," the priest said.

"She almost died," Tom said, as though it were news. "I knew it was risky. She could die yet. . . ."

"She won't die, Tom. We won't let her." Again there was a pause.

"Are they going to change it?"

"Change . . . you mean the thing about birth control?"

"Yes," Tom said.

There was a space as though the priest were nodding his head. "They almost have to," he said. "There's just too much that can't be ignored anymore." There was the sound of something being put in the sink. "I'm gonna shove off before we wake Rosie up," the priest said. "And you get some sleep."

"I think I'll go back to the hospital," Tom said. "I just needed to see the little girls. . . ."

"No, you won't," the priest said. "That's stupid. You've got to stay in some kind of shape. Just get in bed and set the alarm for six."

Another piece of dishware was put into the sink. "Hey, listen, Jim, thanks for staying there with me."

"It's okay," the priest said. "Call me if there's any change . . . and get some sleep, huh?"

Rosie closed her eyes and feigned sleep in preparation for the swinging door from the kitchen to open, but instead she heard the back door scrape against the sill and the young priest's footsteps, sharp against the brittle cement, as he stepped into the lean and frosty night.

Chapter XIII

IT WAS JUST AFTER CHRISTMAS THAT RAY KISSED HER. BY THEN, IT was becoming natural to be with him. They'd gone to movies in Worthington, to a home basketball game in St. Ives, and had pizza one night after grocery shopping in Luverne. He'd gone with her to see Gina Pratt, her skin paler and more delicate than her bed jacket, in the Worthington hospital, and he'd arrived at her door, the Saturday before Christmas, with an armful of toys. "Help me wrap these," he said. "They're for Gina's kids."

He never talked about his trip to Illinois, except to say that things were "leveled out again," and Rosie didn't ask. Sometimes, she felt that there was a layer of happiness around her like a cushion—like the padding that kept someone in a bumper car from really feeling the crash. She sensed that it wasn't a solid cushion—it was more like a balloon or an inner tube that one ought not to prick. She didn't feel any need, in fact, to go poking around, and that was part of the happiness; she didn't need to examine everything any more. She did bold things that almost astonished her: in October and November, she had gone to confession to Father Schwartz when it was time to go, but this month, she had gone back to Father Griffin, and she started out by telling him her name. She went to movies without checking the Legion of Decency ratings; she got a college-bound book list from the high school English teacher and started to read real novels again, after years of *Readers Digest Condensed Books* that Aunt Nellie passed on. One night she sat up till three finishing *The Great Gatsby*, amazed and absorbed by the frenetic Long

Island life. She liked best the scene in which Gatsby displays his beautiful shirts for Daisy, and that weekend she went out and bought a quilted satin robe that she didn't need at all.

She no longer worried about whether Ray would kiss her; they were just good friends, and it had become obvious that he would not. Sometimes, however, she wanted to touch him. She would look over at him as they were driving, the headlights picking up stray snowflakes in the dark, and she would want to touch his face, to soften the stern profile that sometimes almost frightened her when he was driving and lost in thought. Or they would be sitting in a cafe, and she would notice how clean his hand was, how neatly his fingernails were trimmed, and she would want to reach out and cover that hand with hers. Sometimes, starting home, she shivered against the cold upholstery of the car, and her body itself seemed to form an image of his arm coming around to pull her against him. But he would look over and smile and fiddle with the dashboard and say, "The heat should be up soon." When they were in crowds, sometimes he touched her. He would put his hand on her arm to draw her out of the way of teen-agers who hurtled toward them on the sidewalk, their long bangs half blocking their sight; or he would touch the small of her back to nudge her forward when they were waiting in a movie line. Sometimes impure thoughts still plagued her, and sometimes Ray drifted into them, but they tended to float away without much effort on her part to dispel them; and, after two more late-night episodes, the obscene phone calls had stopped.

Christmas was less of a problem than she had anticipated. She had dinner and spent the afternoon with Aunt Nellie's family (there was no way to refuse). They gave her a three-pound box of chocolate cherries, and she gave them a subscription to *National Geographic*. Ray was never mentioned.

Rosie worried a little about how he would spend the day, but he said he enjoyed the luxury of a day to sleep, and they could spend the evening together at a good movie. They spent Christmas Eve together as well. Ray took her to dinner at a place in Sioux Falls that had live lobsters in a little glass tank. After dinner, he took from his pocket a slender, unwrapped box. "To my dear friend Rosie" said the little card. Inside the cotton batting was a delicate silver chain holding a silver scallop shell.

Rosie hadn't known what to do about a present. She didn't want Ray to feel awkward if he hadn't gotten her anything, but she didn't want to be empty-handed if he had. That meant it had to be a present small enough to fit into her purse. She settled on a smooth leather belt with an *R* on the buckle, and wrapped it in bold, red foil.

The day after Christmas, the fog set in. It had been a mild, dry winter, but there was something unnatural about a whiteness in dead December that wasn't snow; it muted everything. The familiar was gone. The sky, rather than the ground, was colorless, and objects faded into it and emerged again as if by some sleight-of-hand. The world beyond the sunroom windows was an intense blank full of imagined or remembered outlines, and sometimes she caught herself fearing that nothing at all was there.

Rosie had little to do in the days between Christmas and New Year's; school would not reconvene until January 8. She spent an afternoon with Gina, who was home but fragile, and the little girls, who had an excess of new toys. One day, she took cookies to the rest home, but there seemed to be tins of cookies everywhere, their frosting hardening, their edges getting soft. "I wish it wouldn't all come at once," the nurse sighed; "it's this way every year." Rosie was sorry she had come, and instead of heading home, she walked out along the road to the Protestant cemetery. Once, a car came toward her, the lights merely undefined circles in the haze. *Like the eyes of a chick embryo*, she thought for some reason; and then suddenly the car, which seemed so far away, was there and gone.

Even in the cemetery, distance was out of kilter. Frost crystals were beginning to form on the blue spruce trees, making the lower branches look like something dipped in sugar, but the top branches were fuzzy, and the reflecting sky was gone. The rows of stones lost color and shape and became only a slight change in the density of air. Rosie remembered some of these people—some of the names that solidified as she approached each stone. She couldn't call them to mind clearly, however. Her memories lacked color, lacked shape. She used to come here as a girl, she knew, used to bring books here in the long, languid days of summer. Perhaps it was during the years she wanted to be a writer, to weave tales of romance in vague misty settings with words that sounded like grasses moving. The mood of those old, watery dreams was on her now, but precise memories evaded her, and when she tried to step closer to them, the air closed in and they too were only a different density that she wanted and could not know.

She was afraid walking back. She was in a world where the usual physical laws no longer governed, where a tree or a post could be anywhere. If a car came from behind her, she would not be able to see the lights, and it was very unlikely the driver would see her. She walked most of the way in the ditch. The dead grass and weeds crunched as she walked, and the ground was uneven. About her, crystals were beginning to form on the smallest of weeds, and she plucked something that had once been a cockleburr. Even in the thick light, it glistened as she turned it. Tiny slivers and spurs of ice had attached themselves to every surface; the thin stem was plump in its frosty sheath, and the remaining burrs flared out like oriental bells. Rosie wished for the sun to turn the burrs into a thousand mirrors, but the sun, she knew, would melt the bells. She held the cockleburr until the warmth of her hand made the crystals soften; then, because she could not both keep and preserve it, she let it fall.

The phone was ringing when she entered the house. It clanged like an alarm in air not cushioned by the fog. The voice on the other end was Ray's: "Want to go to Mankato tomorrow?" he said. "The boss needs some parts. I could pick you up at quarter to eight."

It was after ten when they reached Mankato. Ray had had to take it slow in low-lying areas, and Rosie was tired from peering into the fog. She was glad to be inside a department store while Ray went to some kind of supply house, and glad to let coffee and hot soup steam her face when they met in a little restaurant at noon.

Ray didn't seem to mind the fog; his energy kept bursting over into questions: Was Aunt Nellie her father or mother's sister? Had her parents lived here all their lives? Where had she gone on vacations when she was a kid? What had she wanted to be? (Ray had wanted to be a cowboy, and then a spy, and then an aviator). "Why did you stay home after high school," he said; "why didn't you go after one of your dreams?"

She blanched a little at that, but told him the truth: the spells at twelve, the suspected epilepsy, Mama's warnings—and then years that had gone by as air goes by a closed-up box. "It must not have occurred to me that I could leave . . . that I could change things," she heard herself saying. "There was always Mama to be taken care of, and then there was Jack. . . ."

The fog was lighter when they started back. Where it had been barely possible to see the other lane before, you could now see frosted fences along the edges of the road. Rosie gasped when the road curved suddenly outside of Trimont: three weeping willows were bowed down under a weight of frost crystals, frozen into a rhythm that flowed like water down a small cataract or wind through an open hand. Ray slowed the car. "It's so beautiful!" Rosie said. "I've never seen anything so beautiful!" Then the willow trees blended with the fog.

"You stick with me, kid," Ray said in an imitation of James Cagney. "You ain't seen nothin' yet!" He told her about little geysers in Yellowstone that had that same frothy quality, and mountain streams in Washington that were melted from glaciers and had a grayish tinge until the water hit rocks and exploded into foam. "I was stationed at Bremerton at the end of the war," he said. "When I got out I saw a lot of the West."

Ray pulled off Highway 60 somewhere near Heron Lake. "This should be gorgeous if I can find it," he said, and turned down a gravel road. The road went straight, as all roads in western Minnesota do, crossing at one-mile intersections. Ray chose one of these, and suddenly trees appeared—a twisting corridor of shadowy froth that merged with the fog in the distance. It was a creek, Rosie knew, or a small river. Trees did not grow of themselves on the great plains except on the banks of a stream. All other trees were in groves, planted by homesteaders who staked their claims with windbreaks. It seemed a good idea, the planting of trees. Sometimes when she was in open country, Rosie felt those squared-off groves were the only thing that kept the sky from pressing down.

But now it seemed the sky had fallen. They stepped from the car and moved through ground-level clouds to reach the creek. Ray held down the fence so Rosie could cross—in an unreal world, in the middle of a cloud, there seemed to be no such thing as trespass. Her mind told her this was a usual creek, a lazy meandering of shallow water that would be flecked with cottonwood fuzz in the summer, and harbored bullheads in its deepest pockets, but her senses denied this. It was a white river, forever fixed in its crystal form, forever moving in a dark, mysterious liquidity past that foamy break in the ice. It was a dream of purity, where the tops of the tallest, white-twigged cottonwoods merged with the cloud, and the scrub-brush that preferred closeness to earth glistened, each twig distinct, silverplated, each broken tendril an important part. It was more beautiful than the weeping willows, more beautiful than any painting she had ever seen.

They said nothing for a while, conscious, it seemed, of every intake of breath. "I feel I'm in a dream," Rosie said.

"Maybe you are," Ray said, and she knew what he meant. There was a sadness in all this beauty, the same sense she had had with the cockleburr—only in a dream would this survive the slightest wind. . . .

Ray stepped around to face her. "You're very beautiful," he said. His hand came up and cupped the edge of her cheek.

No one had ever said that to her, and she knew in daylight it wasn't true, but they were floating in a cloud, and she realized, as though it were important, that they were the only color in a landscape where everything was white. "Thank you," she said.

His hand began to stroke her face, her neck, and his hand was so familiar she wondered when she had wandered into this cloud before. Perhaps when she was young and had stood at the upstairs window, tracing the fans of frost on the pane and engraving secret initials with her fingernail; perhaps in a story, a half-waking fantasy. Ray's eyes were large behind his glasses, brown and unwavering. She heard herself say, "I love you," just before his lips came gently down.

She knew it was a dream because there was no awkwardness. She had wondered how lovers in the movies knew which way each would tilt the head, how their arms never clashed on the way to a first embrace. She had been sure her own clumsiness would ruin the moment if it ever came, that there would be the minor collisions that accompanied doorways in a comedy routine. But her cheek was against Ray's now; her arms had slid around him of their own accord, and his hands held her firmly, one on her back, one at the base of her neck. She could feel his breath against her throat; it was warm and steamy—a red breath—but everything else was white, everything was pure. They had traveled to a zone where nothing quite touched the earth; and when Ray's mouth circled her cheek and came down again, moist and moving this time, she only slipped more deeply into the obscuring white, into the grounded sky.

When they walked, at last, back to the car, Rosie feared the dream was ending, that Ray would never again speak, never again touch her, that they would ride off separately from a place that had never been.

"You cold?" he said as he started the engine. She shook her head. They were far apart down the gravel road, but when they were back on the highway once more, Ray's arm reached out as it had so often in her fantasies, and she slid inside it, her face against his shoulder, her nose and mouth against the corduroy of his clothes. They were in the cloud still, and it rode with them all the way home.

Rosie awoke knowing only that something was different. *The fog is gone*, she thought. It was not yet fully light, but when she went to the window, distinct shapes had reappeared, and there was a yellow, waking window on almost every house on the street. The steeple of the church was a dark shaft against a lesser darkness. When she remembered the creek and Ray's kisses, she thought at first that she was not yet fully awake, or that she was remembering a fantasy that had swirled around her in the days of fog. As she dressed, the memory came clearer.

She savored how he had held the fence for her, how his eyes, which were hazel-brown and keen even in the haze, had come closer, closer, and how her own eyes had shifted to his lips, as though by prearrangement, before his lips came down. She wondered again at the ease of it all, hugging herself now in the chilly bedroom, as a shiver went through her back. All the warmth—the bulk of his body that was heavy and solid, all the strength of those arms. . . . Then he was kissing her again, and this time it was not just the gentle pressure of lips touching. His mouth had opened around hers, pulling her in. His lips were wet, and her head was locked in the crook of his elbow, so that she could not move back from the waves that went through her as she felt his tongue, and there was nowhere for the waves to go but down, down. . . .

Rosie shook her head to clear it and moved resolutely from the window. She was cold; the room was cold; even her hands were getting gooseflesh—but a fire was burning low in her body, and sudden guilt flashed through her. She should not have let him do it; she should not have let him kiss her that way. Their first kiss had been proper, had been chaste, but this was something different. This was red, was scarlet, was the way men kissed who had slicked-back hair and moustaches, and women who had smoldering eyes and black dresses slit deeply into the breast. She was ashamed; she felt something red-orange rise up through her chest. Why had Ray done this? He was a good man—a good Catholic—why had he behaved like this? But yesterday she had not felt this way. She had not blamed him; she had not been so aware of her lower body as he was kissing her—she had only registered the strange and urgent sensation of his mouth.

Was it possible? Could she be more sexually involved now, in retrospect, then she had been in his arms along the icy creek? She tried to remember the creek to cool down her body, her cheeks, but the water that flowed beneath the gap in the ice seemed dark and treacherous. How badly had she sinned? Was it a mortal sin to let a man kiss you like that when it happened so fast—when it felt more strange than wrong at the time?

She wanted Ray there; she wanted to say: "Did you intend it to be like that? Did it just happen? Does it mean you love me? Was it a sin, Ray? Is that how you kissed your wife?" She tried to summon his presence, to have him beside her in her mind as she had so often of late, but the picture wouldn't form. She wanted to hear his voice, the voice that was always so calm, so sure, the voice that could tease her out of her fears, that could say, "Hey! You're doin' okay, lady!" when she tried to bowl for the first time in almost fifteen years.

Perhaps he would call her today. Perhaps he too was feeling guilty and amazed. Perhaps he was worried about how she was feeling on this morning—or perhaps he was back at the moment when his hand began to stroke her cheek. Rosie cupped her own hand along her jawline and was amazed at the softness of her face. Perhaps he had no compunction at all about what had happened—perhaps he had planned it, had deliberately chosen that frozen spot—a man who had been married was used to things, after all. . . . Perhaps he would come and lock her head in the bend of his arm and try to kiss her like that again. . . .

Rosie realized that she was dressed but still barefoot, and that she had stopped in the middle of making the bed and began to brush her hair. She tried to gather herself together, to be rational. "You've got good sense, Rosie," Ray had said the night she stayed with Gina's girls. "You can handle this."

She made herself sit down and put on the shoes. She finished making the bed. She would drive to Worthington late this afternoon to a church where none of the priests knew her and in the darkness of the confessional, she would say: "I let a man kiss me in a way I shouldn't have." That would take care of it, whether or not it was a sin.

And Ray would call today. Even if he wasn't worried about her, even if he didn't mention yesterday, he would call and she could tell something of how he felt from the sound of his voice. He would call and they would plan something for tomorrow night, which was New Year's Eve.

Rosie went downstairs and put water on for tea, but found herself sitting in an old chair in the front sunroom, staring at the street. When the teakettle began to scream, she was sure it was the phone.

Chapter XIV

"THAT PRIEST WAS DRUNK AGAIN," MARION RUNKLE SAID, HER HAND on the sleeve of Rosie's coat in the beverage aisle of the Super-Valu in Luverne. She had appeared suddenly in an old maroon storm coat and a green wool scarf that had slipped back far enough to let her hair come drifting out. "Mickey seen it," she said, eyeing the rows of Coke and ginger ale. "Him and that Simons kid seen the priest run his car right off the road over by Adrian." There was no emotion in her voice, only a bland certainty. She wheeled her cart down past the pretzels. "I guess he's over in Memorial," she said, just before she rounded the display of Hamm's and disappeared.

"What?" Rosie said. "Who is?" She wheeled her cart down two aisles, nearly sideswiping a pregnant woman, before she caught up with Marion unloading at the checkout stand. "Who's in Memorial?" she demanded. "Father Griffin?"

"Well, that's what they said." Marion directed her attention to the rack of cigarettes in front of her. "He better be careful though. My girl says those flowers people send eat up all your oxygen."

"Is he hurt?"

Marion looked at her for the first time with a kind of amazed surmise. "Well, why would he go to the hospital?" she said.

Rosie drove too fast on the roads to Worthington. "Slow down," she told herself; "you'll be in Memorial too." There were slippery patches on the highway; snow had begun again three days after the fog left, and the wind had turned cold. You didn't have to be drunk to slide off the road; that much she knew. All you had to do was hit a patch of ice the wrong way and the car would glide to a ditch on its own.

It must have happened last night, she reasoned—Friday. School had been in session all week, and Father Griffin was at lunch every day. Except for a leak in the steam table, she had been glad when school started again. After days in the fog of her empty house, she took pleasure in stirring a vat of chili, in watching a gallon of slippery kidney beans go sliding into the thick, red broth. The younger children were still full of Christmas; you could tell the new stocking caps by the way little girls held their heads, or new boots by the exaggerated shuffling. It was good to be surrounded by sounds again.

She had been nervous on Monday morning when it was time for the milk delivery. She had heard nothing from Ray since that afternoon by the creek, but he bumped through the door as usual, followed by a young man with a red, wind-chapped face and Scandinavian features. "This is Tommy Olson," Ray announced. "He's our new sub, and he's learning all the routes." Tommy bobbed his head at them and said nothing. "See you," Ray had waved when they left. On Wednesday, the scene repeated itself without the introduction; and on Friday, Tommy came by himself.

She didn't understand Ray's silence. It had only added to the general emptiness. Sister Carol Ann and Sister Gaelynn had both gone to make a retreat after Christmas, and the Pratts were at Gina's relatives in Omaha. She had needed Ray then, if only to tell him she didn't understand what had happened among the crystal trees by the creek, if only to say that sometimes she was still swept by the ease and wonder of it all, and sometimes by the guilt. She would understand if he blamed her, if he had somehow lost respect—after all, he had just wanted to be friends—but she could explain that she was sometimes two people, that the real one would never have allowed that kiss. . . . *And besides*, she thought, giving the accelerator of her Chevy an extra nudge, *he was the one who started it.*

She was nearing Adrian now; it was twelve more miles to Worthington. Across the prairie, she could see three elevators with their dull, galvanized towers. "The sky is that color all winter," she thought. "The sky is the same color as the pillars that keep it off the ground." Ahead, she could see the place where the new TV booster was going up. It was a bright, rigid tower, but it didn't hold the sky as the elevators did; it pierced it—it made things more dangerous, she thought, as though coaxing something down.

Ray said once that they would get two more stations when the tower was completed. If so, it might be worth it. She had spent New Year's Eve watching a fuzzy Guy Lombardo, and New Year's Day seeing the Rose Bowl parade through an intermittent haze of static snow. When the parade was over, she had paged through old magazines for want of anything better to do. There was an ad for Hawaii in last month's *National Geographic*. It said, "Aloha means welcome," and a girl in a grass skirt was lowering a flower wreath over a smiling man's head. Below the ad was a coupon for a free seven-page booklet that reminded Rosie of her high school missionary coupons. She cut it out with the kitchen shears. She then cut out coupons for information on a tour of Greece, a mountain lodge in West Virginia, and a boat trip along the Alaska shore. She got another stack of old magazines from the basement and cut until she had seventeen coupons for places as varied as the world itself. She didn't know why she was doing this, but it seemed to be a kind of protest against Ray's silence, against the fact that he sometimes disappeared. She could disappear also if she wanted to. She got out the stamps left over from her Christmas cards, walked to the box in front of the post office, and dumped the coupons in.

It was late afternoon when she got to the hospital. The young priest was propped up in a single room painted that green color called "robin's egg blue"; Sister Carol Ann was sitting with one hip on the edge of his hospital bed.

"Hey, look who's here!" the priest grinned, but his voice was weak. He had one black eye, a patch on his forehead, and bad scrapes along his right cheek. His right arm was in a sling.

"What happened?" Rosie said. "Marion Runkle told me your car ran off the road." She had automatically put out her hand and he took it with his left one and held it.

"Thanks to her darling boy," Carol Ann said and moved to a chair.

"Just wanted a winter vacation," he said, "like everybody else." He started to shift his shoulder and winced. Rosie looked at him more closely. He looked worse than she had thought at first, more in pain, more vulnerable. He was pale, even though his bare neck and hairy left arm were ruddy against the hospital gown, and she was frightened. "What happened?" she said again.

"Oh, Runkle and his sidekick got into a little trouble. . . ."

"They stole a car," Carol Ann put in.

"They *borrowed* it. That's their version. It was sitting by the edge of a side road, and they decided they'd like to try it out, so they jumped the starter. Probably would have gotten away with it, but they ran a red light."

Rosie's mind flicked back to the woman in the grocery store: "That priest was drunk again," she'd said. "Was it your car they took?" Rosie asked.

"No, no. Some farmer near Worthington. The cops called me because I bailed them out the last time, I guess. Runkle wouldn't give them his old man's number—he's over eighteen anyway . . . and I hit a patch of ice on the way home and lost control. The kids were right behind me. . . ." He tried to move his shoulder again; the pain was obvious. "Could one of you get me some coffee?"

"I can," Rosie said, "I know where there's a vending machine." She began to dig in her purse for change as she left the room.

"Are you in pain?" she heard Carol Ann say in the soft tone Rosie had heard her use with little Karla. She glanced back to see the young nun bending over the bed, her hand on the priest's pillow.

Rosie tried to carry three paper cups, but it was slow going, and hot coffee kept spilling on her hands. Finally she gave it up and abandoned one on a window sill. When she got to the room, Carol Ann was back in the orange chair, and Ray was standing by the bed. They were telling "accident stories," laughing with the slightly forced goodwill of the sickroom. Rosie tried to laugh with them.

A nurse scowled her way into the room. "I'm sorry," she said, her voice like a robot. "Only two visitors allowed at a time. One of you will have to leave."

"I'll go," Ray volunteered.

"You just got here," Rosie said. She reached for her coat. "I'll stop by the next week, Father, if you're still here. . . ."

At the elevator, listening to the rumble of the vertical tracks, she realized that she had been glad for the escape; some part of her didn't want to face whatever Ray's silence might mean. He was plainly not avoiding the rest of them—it was only her that he didn't want to see.

"Looks kind of tough, doesn't he?" Ray's voice said behind her.

"Yes," Rosie said, but she didn't turn. "We shouldn't have made him laugh so much." The elevator stopped and an orderly got out with an empty wheelchair. Ray entered behind her, and they both stared up as the little red numbers lighted one by one. When the door opened, they crossed the lobby in silence. "Say something," Rosie pleaded with herself, but her throat refused to form words. At the front steps, she turned toward the parking lot, but Ray took her elbow.

"You never got any of that coffee," he said. "Could I buy you some?"

The cafe next to the hospital was one of the oldest in town. It still had dark varnished booths with no upholstery, and was lined with a series of cardboard Coca-Cola signs.

"How have you been?" Ray said, looking hard at the menu.

"Fine," she said. "I've been fine." What else could she say— I've been unhappy? I've spent two weeks listening to the clock tick? Then she heard her voice saying, "I had a nice, quiet New Year's at home."

"Yeah," he said. "Yeah. I did too." His voice was embarrassed, and she wished she hadn't said it. Now he might say nothing more.

"I slept most of New Year's Day," he said. "I watched TV at Sweeney's till late the night before."

"Is Sweeney a friend?"

"No." He was embarrassed again. "It's a bar."

A teen-age waitress appeared, poured coffee, and stood with one hip jutting out to take their order. When she had gone again, there was silence. Ray was swirling the coffee around in his cup, coming close to spilling it. Rosie thought of Jack, of the way he sat at the kitchen table staring into his coffee, staring away her ideas, her questions, her simplest thoughts. Men were like that, she guessed.

"It's all right," she said. "You don't owe me anything."

"I should have called you, Rosie," he said. "There's no excuse." She was aware of his hands on the cup, of their strength, of the soft brown hair that went up to the first knuckle on each finger, of their gentleness.

"I owe you the decency of being courteous," he said, and took a swallow of the coffee. He still had not really looked at her. "I owe you a lot more than that. . . ." His voice caught on something. "I owe you a lot," he said again.

Something she couldn't identify rushed through her throat and up behind her eyes. "It's just that when you didn't call, I didn't know what I'd done." The thing behind her eyes became liquid, and she lowered her head quickly.

His hand reached out and covered hers on the countertop. "Rosie," he said.

"It's just that I've been so lonely. . . ." Her voice sounded like a child's, but she couldn't help it. She wanted his hand to stay on top of hers.

"I'm sorry," he said. His thumb was stroking the side of her palm. "I'm sorry."

"I just wish I understood what happened," she said. It was as hard now to keep the words back as it had been to force them out a moment ago. "I thought when we came home from Mankato that day, that we were close—that you really wanted to be close to me. What happened by the creek—I don't know, maybe I was a different person then—maybe I ought to feel guilty . . .

and I do—but I didn't think it was all my fault—I didn't think you'd lose respect. . . ."

"Rosie, Rosie . . ." He was shaking her palm and reaching for the other hand. "That's not it. That's not it at all. I never want you to think that." His face was concerned now, and almost a little amused. "You're the best person I know," he said. He was holding both of her hands tightly and looking straight into her eyes. "You did nothing you should feel guilty about. Ever." He looked down again at the coffee cup. "That day by the creek was one of the most beautiful days I've ever known. It's just that . . ."

"It's just what?"

He let go of her hands, and then took the right one back again. "It's just that . . . that I don't have my life under control right now. I can't take on any more. I promised myself that we'd be friends—just friends—and then out there in the fog . . . I lost my head, I guess . . . the way I really feel came through. I love you, Rosie, you must know that." He raised his head to look at her and then lowered it again. He spoke more slowly: "You are kind and gentle and beautiful, and your whole soul is right on top. Most of us have buried ours, Rosie." There were tears in his eyes now, and she didn't understand. "Most of us have put ours away where it's not so likely to get hurt."

The waitress came and put hamburger platters down in front of them. Rosie took a napkin from the metal holder and unfolded it demurely in her lap. She really didn't care what Ray was saying. He had said "I love you, Rosie"; she could live on that for years. He loved her—but was he saying he didn't want to love her? She looked at him again, confused, but he was smiling.

"Do you think we could be friends again?" he said. "One of these days, I'll get myself together—but in the meantime, do you think we could be friends?"

She nodded, and could see him visibly relax, but she was aware of her own tension. She had begun her confession and he had interrupted her. "Do you think what happened . . . what we did down by the creek . . ." She wanted to say, "Was it a sin?" but that sounded stupid, almost silly. She kept her eyes on the hamburger plate. "I'm not sure if that was wrong," she said finally.

There was a little silence. His hand began to stroke hers with great gentleness. "Hasn't anybody ever kissed you like that?" he said.

"No," she said. Something far back in her mind said she ought to be embarrassed at forty-one—to feel stupid and ashamed—but she listened instead to the tenderness in his voice. He was saying he was sorry if he had caused her distress, had caused her worry or guilt, but he couldn't be really sorry if he had given her joy. His thumb was caressing her hand again. Above all, he said, he thought she was beautiful, he thought she would always be innocent.

Their hamburgers were cold and they laughed about it. Ray aimed the catsup at his french fries, and a great glob shot all over the plate. They had just agreed to a movie on Sunday night—as friends, as very good friends—when a shadow fell over her shoulder.

"Hey, you two," Jim Hinely said, "A guy can't even get your attention to see if you'll share a booth—they're full up around here." He slid uninvited into Ray's side of the booth. "You look thick as ticks on a dog. Makin' big plans?"

Rosie eyed him evenly. "We were just talking about what kind of flowers to send sick friends," she said.

Chapter XV

"WERE YOU PLANNING TO GO TO SIOUX FALLS ANY OF THESE Saturdays?" Sister Carol Ann said one noon in February. She had come through the cafeteria line just as Rosie was closing it down; Dora was already at the table. "I mean, just to shop . . . ?" she added.

"No," Rosie said. "Not really." She handed Carol Ann her plate. The young nun's eyes and nose had that red-rimmed, allergic look, though it was too early for the spring allergy season. "Why?" Rosie said. "Did you want something?"

"No," Carol Ann said, "no, I just thought you might be going. . . ." She pushed her tray down past the milk cartons, picked it up, and sat with it at the crowded end of the faculty table where Rosie could not join her.

It was strange. Sister Geraldine always made the request if one of the nuns needed Rosie for transportation. Otherwise, two of them would borrow one of the priests' cars. The nuns went everywhere in pairs, even walking in St. Ives—it reminded Rosie of salt and peppers—but none of them had ever requested to go alone before. . . . If it were Sister Gaelynn, Rosie might have suspected something, but Carol Ann, for all her modernness, seemed careful to stay within the rules.

Still, if the snow didn't get worse, a trip to Sioux Falls might be fun, Rosie decided as she finished washing the pots and pans. She could take Carol Ann for whatever she needed, go back to the little shop that seemed like a secret garden, and pick up some spring dress material.

She crossed the parking lot to the new addition of the school as soon as she finished cleaning up. It was a squat, square, cement-block building that reminded Rosie of the sod dugouts of the early settlers; its plainness made her feel a little forlorn, as she imagined pioneer wives had felt, denned like small animals in the prairie itself.

Carol Ann was not in her classroom. Four sophomore girls, their long hair hiding their faces, were hunched around one of the front student desks. "Is Sister Carol Ann here?" Rosie asked.

"Doesn't look like it, does it?" Joni Heinkamp said. She was Dora's youngest daughter, a blonde whose breasts and hips were too developed for her age and made her look at once very young and middle-aged. One of the other girls giggled.

"Do you know where she is?" Rosie could feel her jaw tighten. "Nope."

"What are you doing in her room anyway?" It was a quarter to three, and school didn't get out until three-fifteen.

"It was empty," Doris Lean said. She cocked her head in a challenging attitude that she must have learned from Mickey Runkle.

"It's our free period," Joni said. "It used to be called 'study hall.' " They all giggled.

"Well, tell her I was here," Rosie said. She wasn't about to argue with smart-mouthed kids. "No," she decided, "I'll leave a note."

"Suit yourself," Joni said, and the four bent over whatever they were doing as Rosie took a pencil from a flowered mug on the desk.

"Ask it who's going to be the next president," Cheryl Hinely said.

Rosie looked up. Two of the girls were sitting knee to knee, facing each other, with a rectangular game board balanced between them. They had their fingertips on some sort of little tripod that began to move around the board. "*R*," one of them said.

"It's going to be a republican," Joni said.

"O," the Hinely girl announced, her long bleached hair swinging down toward the board. "No, it's going to be Rockefeller."

"Well, now you made it stop!" Doris Lean complained. She and Joni had the board on their knees, and the little tripod had stopped moving. "Why don't you just shut up until it's done!"

"Maybe it will go again if you concentrate," the fourth girl, Mary Jane Keller, said softly. She had been very shy as a child, Rosie remembered; she had lisped then and still had a tentative, wistful look.

Rosie had finished her note and was about to say, "What *is* that thing?" when her eye caught the top of a cardboard box on the floor. In bold letters it said: "Ouiji Board." Oh-eye-ji, Rosie puzzled, Oh-ee-gee. And then it clicked: wee-gee board. She had never seen one, but she had heard of them; they were in the same class as fortune tellers, seances, voodoo dolls, and other forms of witchcraft—all sins against the second commandment, her childhood nuns had warned, all works of the devil. "Is that a ouiji board?" she demanded, and without waiting for an answer, said, "You can't play around with that thing!"

"Looks like we are," Doris said. "Let's ask it something personal."

"How many kids will I have?" Cheryl Hinely wanted to know. The two at the board repeated the question.

"You can't bring that in here!" Rosie said. "This is a Catholic school." Mary Jane and the Hinely girl looked at her as though that were a stupid statement. Both of them had bangs so long they had to tilt their heads to look up, and it gave an added arrogance.

"Seven," Joni announced. "It went right to seven."

"Jesus," the Hinely girl said. "I'm not having seven kids."

"How old will I be when I die?" Mary Jane volunteered shyly.

"Where did you get that thing, anyway?" Rosie demanded again.

"My ma gave it to me for Christmas," Doris said, and bent over the board. "How old will Mary Jane be when she dies?" In spite of herself, Rosie stood still and watched the tripod move. "One—eight. You'll be eighteen," Doris said. Mary Jane turned pale.

"That's three years from now," Joni said. They were all suddenly quiet.

"Now see what you've done," Rosie said. "She's scared to death. You shouldn't be playing with that thing." They looked at Rosie and then at Mary Jane.

"Oh, she doesn't believe it," Doris said. "It's just a game. . . ." They looked at Mary Jane again, and she managed a weak smile.

"Ask it about somebody else," the Hinely girl said. "Ask it about McIvers."

"No," Doris said. "Carol Ann. It's her room."

"Okay," Joni said. "Will Sister Carol Ann be back next year?" The tripod moved to *H*, skittered across the numbers, then settled on "No."

"No?" Joni said. "Where is she going?" The tripod circled the board, hesitated, then began to spell: "*M . . . A . . . R . . .*" Again, it hesitated and stopped at the edge of the board.

"Marshall," Doris decided. "She's going to Marshall."

"Wait," Joni said. "It's going to move again." The tripod circled the board. "*R . . . I . . . E . . . D.*" Then it stopped.

"Ried?" Doris said, puzzled. "Mar-reed?"

"Married," Cheryl Hinely announced. "She's going to get married!"

"Carol Ann's getting married!" Joni exulted. Rosie could see that they were all delighted. This was juicier than they had hoped.

"Who's she going to marry?" Mary Jane said. Even she was back in the game. Joni and the Hinely girl were both giggling. Doris put the question, but the tripod just sat on the board.

"What is the name of the bridegroom?" Doris intoned with mock solemnity. This time the tripod began to circle: "*J . . . I . . . G . . .*" and then it stopped.

"Jig what?" Joni demanded. "What kind of name is Jig?"

"Maybe it's initials," Doris said, "or a nickname—it's kind of a neat nickname."

"Let's ask Carol Ann if she knows anybody named Jig," Cheryl Hinely giggled.

"Ask it if I'll get married," Mary Jane said, a little color coming back into her face, "or have children."

There was a barely perceptible moment of hesitation, and then Rosie broke in. "You shouldn't be playing with that thing," she said. "You're asking for trouble."

"Let's ask it who Rosie is going to marry," Joni said with a triumphant expression. "Let's see what it says."

"I don't need information from a thing like that," Rosie said. She folded the note to Carol Ann and put it down, though a part of her wanted to stay.

"Who will Rosie marry?" Joni asked, louder than necessary as Rosie left the room.

She strode down the hall swiftly, but couldn't get past the water fountain. She stooped and turned the bubbler handle but stood without drinking. As her eyes revolved, she caught a pair of eyes watching her from across the hall: Gil Simons at a library table. Embarrassed, she moved her mouth directly over the stream of water, still not really drinking, but listening for the "Ooo-ooo" and the swift laughter that inevitably came from the room she had left.

Rosie told Ray about it the next evening on the way home. "Funny things have been happening," she said.

"What funny things?"

"Well, remember when I kept getting those phone calls last fall? Last night I got another one."

"What did he say?" Ray said.

"It wasn't quite as bad this time. It was about ten-thirty, and I was just ready to get in bed. He said . . . he started talking about parts of my body, but I hung up." Suddenly, she didn't want to talk about it, she didn't want to be telling Ray.

"Did it scare you?" Ray asked.

"Of course, it scared me!" She was irritated at his calmness. He should be alarmed, protective, concerned about her safety and the filth she was hearing.

"Well, I wouldn't pay too much attention," Ray said. "It's just somebody getting his kicks."

Rosie didn't answer. They were pulling off the highway into St. Ives, and she sat in silence as they passed the dark feed store, and the Jack Sprat that used to be Riedemacher's, and the three-story bulk of the old Sloan Hotel. The church steeple rose at the end of the street like an awl punched upward. It was snowing a little—hard compact kernels that bounced on the windshield like rice.

Ray pulled up in front of her house. "What other 'funny things' have happened?" he said.

"Oh, just the school kids," she said. "They're running wild over there. Today they were messing around with a ouiji board."

"Yeah?" he sounded interested. "Some of those little guys bring it in the lunchroom?"

"No," Rosie said. "It was Dora's daughter and some of the other girls. Carol Ann wanted to see me . . ." And in spite of herself, Rosie found the whole story spilling out.

"What do you think?" she said. "It's none of my business, but I had to say something . . . and I must have sounded like the witch herself. . . ."

"Not a chance," he said, leaning over and flicking his forefinger across the very tip of her nose. "We had one of those things when we were kids—my cousins did. I waited till they were in bed one night and took it apart—I was sure it must work with magnets, but the damn thing was just some sort of plastic or celluloid with felt tips."

"Weren't you nervous fooling with it?"

"I don't think so. I was a Methodist until I got married, so I didn't have nuns to warn me about such things. I think I put it in the same class as Catholic superstitions—like St. Christopher medals, or candles in front of statues, or those little felt things Catholic kids wore over their shoulders on two strings."

"Scapulars," Rosie said. She wanted to add that those weren't superstitions, but Ray went on.

"I think you're right though," he said, "about fooling with it. My cousin was engaged to a guy in the navy—this was toward the end of World War II—and he was stationed in San Diego, so one night, right before I got inducted, we asked it, 'Is Florence going to get married?' and it said, 'No.' Florence got really nervous, but the rest of us all laughed and said that proved it didn't work. About a month later, some machinery slipped, and her boyfriend got killed. My aunt burned up the ouiji board in the cookstove, but I don't think Florence ever forgave us."

"She thought it was your fault?"

"No, not really, I guess. But it's sort of like that girl dying at eighteen. If you think something will happen, maybe it will," Ray said. "People will believe just about anything. Maybe that's where the evil comes in."

Rosie thought about it for a moment. Would Ray kiss her if she thought he would? Would they ever be anything but "friends"? "Then how *does* it work if there aren't any magnets?"

He shrugged, then wrung his face into a grotesque contortion. "The spirit world, my dear," he said in a falsetto, ". . . the power of suggestion . . ." He laughed and relaxed his face. "Who knows? Want me to get you one?"

"No," she said. It still wasn't funny. "I'd rather decide things for myself, thank you."

"Okay," Ray said. "Can you decide about the Knights of Columbus dance tomorrow night?"

She felt herself smile, and then his arms were around her. His kiss was very warm, but still and brief.

It took Carol Ann over a week to answer Rosie's note. When she came through the lunch line, she was always surrounded by children pulling at her black skirt or was in the middle of telling Mary McIvers something very earnestly. Rosie began to suspect that the sophomores had torn up the note. The next Tuesday, however, the young nun looked up from her tray and said softly, "I could come over after dinner tonight to talk about Sioux Falls."

Carol Ann looked flushed when Rosie opened the door at seven to let her in. There was a kind of overexcitement about her eyes, a certain fey energy that made Rosie think she was about to take off and dance or levitate. "What a nice old house," she said again, running her hand over the oak post that was part of the doorway into the dining room and fingering the key to the china closet. "I wish I had some antiques . . . they sold most of my grandma's stuff when I was in the novitiate. Nobody thought it was worth anything."

Rosie never thought of Mama's old furniture as antique—it was simply there. She motioned Carol Ann to sit down in one of the rocking chairs. "We could leave about nine on Saturday," Rosie said. "Is that too early?"

"No," Carol Ann said. "Nine's fine." She was looking around the room as though something she feared was hiding there. "Nine's fine," she said again, running her finger through the carving on the arm of the chair.

Rosie waited. It was her turn to speak, but there was something about the silence that reminded her of being in the confession line. "Is . . ." she started.

"I ought to tell you why I'm going," Carol Ann said, almost at the same time. "I need to get some things . . . some clothes. . . ."

"Okay," Rosie said. She realized she was holding her breath.

"I'm getting a new job—I mean I'm applying for one . . . in the Twin Cities . . ." Carol Ann glanced up at Rosie and then stood and went to the corner whatnot shelf. She took down a pair of old glass bookends molded in the form of scotty dogs and began caressing them. "I'm leaving the convent," she said very quietly.

At first Rosie thought she had heard incorrectly. The Nieman girl had come home from being a postulant, and Mrs. Redder's niece had quit when she was a novice; but Carol Ann was a professed nun. She wore a ring, and that meant she had made final vows, promised her life forever. Rosie's mind flicked back to the newspaper clipping about the married priest. . . .

"I made the decision a couple months ago . . ." Carol Ann was saying, her attention fixed on the way her fingers moved on the glass bookend. Her voice was coming out in little tremors. "I haven't been at peace for a long time, and . . . well, I think I have to do this. . . ."

"Why?" Rosie said. It sounded cold and analytical, but she couldn't take it back.

"It's hard for me to explain," Carol Ann said, not looking up. "It's all so complex . . . I teach these little kids, and I think, 'this could be my child,' and . . . oh, I don't know. . . ." There was a crack in the edge of her voice, and tears began spilling over. "It's just that nothing makes sense anymore. . . ." She turned her back, and Rosie could see small ripples of emotion travel through her shoulders.

"I'm sorry . . ." Rosie said.

Carol Ann shook her head and turned around. She pulled a large handkerchief from her habit pocket and blew her nose. "*I'm* sorry," she said. "I shouldn't be laying all this on you." She blew her nose again, shook her head as though she were tossing back hair and tried to smile. "I've tried, Rosie," she said. "I've really tried. . . ."

"I'm sure you have," Rosie said. She wanted the nun to stop crying.

"Someone said to me last fall, 'What do you do as a nun—what things that are really important to you—that you couldn't do if you weren't in the convent?' And I thought and I thought, Rosie, and I couldn't come up with a thing. Not a single thing. I could still teach, and pray, and try to be a witness, and care for people. . . ."

"And that's why you want to leave?" Rosie was a little incredulous.

"No," Carol Ann shook her head again. "I want . . . oh, I don't know—I want to be an ordinary person, I guess. I want to be free—to get up in the morning and *decide* what I'm going to do—to have a job that's mine, and that I can walk away from on weekends, and a place that I can fix up and decorate to be my own. . . ." She turned herself all the way around as if to survey how Rosie had decorated hers, and then sat down on the hassock. "I don't know," she said again. "I want to do simple things—like write as many letters as I want without permission—on any color stationery—and get my mail unopened. I want to choose my own friends. . . ." She looked up at Rosie and then down again at her hands clasped around her knees. "I want to be with people who aren't all nuns—with the people I really want to be with—men and women both—and not have to feel that it's somehow wrong, not have to feel like I'm sneaking. . . ."

"You want to get married," Rosie said, a little dryly.

"Yes," she said. "I want to come home at night to someone's arms; I want . . ." She hesitated. "I want sex, I guess; it's as plain as that . . . but not really. . . ." She lifted her head suddenly and looked at Rosie. "You know what I want?" Rosie shook her head, and the young woman continued, musing. "I want . . . well, when I was a little girl, we lived in an old house where the heat came up through registers in the floor—you know the kind I mean?" Rosie nodded. "And my sister and I had the room right above my folks. Some nights I used to lie there and listen to them talk. They had a special tone they used in bed—quiet and tender and sort of teasing. I don't think I ever heard that tone otherwise. . . . They would talk about ordinary things—about what happened that day, or about something funny one of us said—that's why I used to listen, to see what they'd say about me—but always in that tone . . . always so that everything sounded like soft laughter. . . .

"My parents were pretty prudish the rest of the time," Carol Ann went on, her face relaxing. "Sex wasn't discussed much. The daytime view I got was that sex was perhaps a necessary fact of life, but a pretty unsavory one—something you associate with tattoos or girlie shows. . . . But then there was my parents' nighttime tone—a tone that said everything could fit within it, everything was all right. I used to fall asleep inside that tone, all warm and comforted. . . ." Her voice tapered off. "That's what I want, I guess—to share that with someone." She sat up straight again. "Does that make any sense?"

Rosie nodded. "It makes a lot of sense," she said.

Carol Ann put the glass dogs back on the shelf. "The dispensation should come through by the end of the term," she said. "Mother Demetria made me promise not to tell the other Sisters—I guess they don't want the contagion spreading," she added a little ruefully. "My family's not too happy, but they'll accept it. I got permission to go to St. Paul over Easter to apply for jobs . . . but I can't apply for anything in this." She spread out her calf-length black skirt and attempted a smile. "That's where Sioux Falls comes in." The tears were gone now, and she was looking at Rosie closely. "You haven't said much. This hurts, doesn't it?"

"Yes," Rosie said quietly. "I guess I want people to stay what they are."

"I'm sorry," Carol Ann said. "I think I would have left earlier except that a lot of people were counting on me to stay what I was. . . ." She laughed a somewhat embarrassed laugh. "That sounds pretty egotistical, doesn't it? I seem to think the world will change if I do something that's not quite by the book —that the sky will come tumbling down. . . ." She walked to the window and looked out at the darkened street that ran through St. Ives.

And maybe it will come tumbling down, Rosie thought. She felt a sense of loss, of betrayal, of secret wrongdoing in what the nun had told her. If priests got married, if nuns did not keep their vows, then nothing was steady; none of the things they taught you could be counted on. All the rules that had kept her world solid began to shudder, and Rosie wanted to clutch at what she felt was slipping away. She had a crazy vision of a nun in a kind of medieval dungeon being divested of her habit in an awful, silent ceremony. The nun stood shivering in sackcloth and bright, shorn hair while a small circle of nuns stripped the habit from her by torchlight. The superior nun opened a door with heavy iron rings, and outside shone the blueness of a winter night. The superior motioned toward the empty cold, and the woman in sackcloth slipped out, wrapped only in her shame. The heavy door closed. . . .

". . . and I'll be here at nine on Saturday," Carol Ann was saying. She had turned from the window. "If that's still all right?"

"Sure," Rosie said, making herself smile. "Fine." What else was there to say?

Rosie went over it again and again as she heated leftover casserole for supper, read the Worthington paper, and finished a baby layette she was making for the Mission Storehouse project. She laid it out in her mind as in a diagram: there was nothing wrong with taking someone shopping; it was a favor, a humane thing to do. There was nothing wrong with the act of buying clothes; she was not transporting them to any evil—but still, it wasn't right. The clothes were for a woman losing her vocation, and she, Rosie, was aiding in that. She pictured candles flickering against stone walls, and women gliding down halls as silently as water-fowl. . . . But if the mother superior knew Carol Ann was leaving, and if the dispensation came from Rome . . . Rosie couldn't sort it out.

She replayed the scene in her living room twice while she hemmed the baby clothes. "You want to get married," she heard herself saying. "Yes. Yes, I do." She pictured Carol Ann in a wedding gown, then serving dinner to a husband, then holding a baby gently against her breast. She saw a man's arm around the young nun's waist, a small, desirous smile forming on his lips. He was a big man with sandy hair that was just beginning to thin. . . .

Jig! Rosie thought. "*J-I-G!*" She couldn't allow the thought to move to the center of her brain, couldn't allow the complete picture to form. She put down the half-hemmed smock, went aimlessly to the window, aimlessly straightened the doily on the back of the rocker. Then her mind cleared, and she headed for the basement stairs.

She always saved the diocesan newspaper. She didn't know why—Mama had always saved them to check on things like Ember Days. After a couple of years, she threw them out. She rummaged now through last year's stack: September . . . July . . . and then the issue for the middle of June. That was when priests were transferred from one parish to another. The bare bulb gave just enough light to glint off the rows of fruit jars, and she moved directly beneath it. His name was third in the list. "Rev. James D. Griffin," it said. "Assigned to St. Ives Parish, St. Ives, Minnesota, effective June 15."

"Daniel?" she wondered. David? Donald? It didn't matter. His name wasn't Jig.

"How's this for a 'getaway dress'?" Carol Ann pulled a dark blue linen sheath from the rack. It had three-quarter sleeves and hung cleanly from a white yoke that was hand-stitched in blue. "It's tailored enough for interviews," she said, "and it would do for both fall and spring." She held the dress against the black nun's coat she had tried to disguise by tucking a pale scarf into the neckline. The coat hung about ten inches below the dress and drew attention to the black oxfords and the thick tan hose that gathered in opaque little folds on her ankles. "Service-weight," Carol Ann had sniffed. "They get them by the gross at the motherhouse just like they get the black ones. I'll have to get some real nylons, some decent shoes, some makeup, a slip that's not black, and maybe some earrings, don't you think? I don't want to look 'nunny.' "

Carol Ann's excitement was contagious, and Rosie had felt reassured since Wednesday when Sister Geraldine laid a grave hand on her arm: "I appreciate this 'service' you're doing for us this weekend," she said; "God knows we can't just let her go shopping in Worthington . . . and I know you'll be discreet. . . ." Carol Ann seemed interested in discretion too. She had left her veil on until they reached the freeway, then plucked a comb from a black purse with two sturdy handles—the kind Mama always carried—and ran it through her hair. The hair had obviously been set, but not well. There were distinct ridges where each roller had been, and straight ends stuck out on the bottom. It reminded Rosie of her own first attempts to use rollers last fall.

"How long have you been in the convent?" she had asked, and when Carol Ann flushed, regretted the question.

"Eight years," she said, "almost nine . . . I'll practice setting my hair before I go for interviews."

Rosie couldn't help thinking that the young woman looked

"nunny" now, the smart cut of the blue dress held against all her excess material. She saw a salesclerk eyeing them—a thin woman with rhinestones in the corners of her black glass frames. "Try it on," Rosie said to Carol Ann.

The woman with the rhinestone eyes moved closer. "Did you want to try the dress, Sister?" she said.

Carol Ann made a swift move to replace the dress on the rack, dropped it, and dropped her purse as she bent to retrieve it. "No, no," she said hurriedly. "I was just thinking it would look nice on my sister. She's graduating this year. From college," She grabbed Rosie's arm, and they were out on the sidewalk.

"You can tell, can't you?" Carol Ann said. "I look like a nun. What am I going to do?"

"The shoes," Rosie said. "Get the shoes first. With those shoes —at your age—you're either a nun or you've had polio. Or get a different coat."

"I can't afford a coat," Carol Ann said. "They didn't give me much money."

"How much?"

"Fifteen dollars. And somebody else—a friend—gave me ten."

"They only gave you fifteen dollars?" Rosie said.

"Well, all Sister Geraldine agreed to was a dress, and she hasn't shopped in years, and—well, let's face it, she's not exactly thrilled."

"But, fifteen dollars . . ."

"We only get paid a hundred a month," Carol Ann said softly, "and quite a bit of that goes to the motherhouse . . ."

"Of course," Rosie said. "Of course you do. I forgot." Her mind was ticking rapidly. "We'd better get the shoes at Penney's," she said.

They found a pair of simple black pumps with stacked wooden heels on a sale rack for $9.99, marked down from $13. "Wear them," Rosie said, "and try this scarf instead." She pulled a new paisley print in blues and greens from her pocket. "And let's leave that purse in the car." She steered Carol Ann past the jewelry counter on the way out. "What kind of earrings do you think would go with my pantsuit?" she said loudly for the clerk to hear. "You know—something that *you* would wear if you were picking them."

Carol Ann held up several pairs against Rosie's ears. "I think these," she said. They were small gold hoops designed to look as though the ears were pierced.

Rosie paid for the earrings, and watched while Carol Ann adjusted them to her ears in the car. Rosie was beginning to enjoy this—the purchases, the transformation, and the feeling of being slightly devious. She always felt a little guilty when she spent money on herself, as though all the clothes at home in her closet spoke with Mama's voice: "Why do you need something different?" they said. "We already clothe you; we already know who you are."

In Stevenson's Carol Ann found an olive green knit sheath on the clearance rack. It had a straight, unbuttoned jacket and little bands of white and yellow knit around the neck, the jacket front, and the ends of the sleeves. It was $38, marked down to $19.

"That's four dollars more than I have," Carol Ann said, as she caressed the material, "but it would be so nice for interviews, and I could wear it without the jacket when it was warmer . . . or as a jumper with a blouse. . . ."

"Get it," Rosie said. "I'll loan you twenty dollars till you get a job."

This time the saleslady said, "That would be nice on you, Miss; it's an excellent buy."

With Carol Ann's remaining $15, they got two pairs of nylons, a white slip, a blusher-lipstick combination, and a small tube of mascara. Rosie added a pale yellow blouse as a gift. "I have three-fifty left," Carol Ann said in amazement.

"How about some spring material for a skirt that will go with that blouse?" Rosie said. "I'll sew it up for you. You can put a temporary hem in the coat when you're in the Cities, and I'll loan you a better purse. That should just about get you through."

When the bags and boxes were safely stored in the closet of Jack's old room and Carol Ann had gone home, Rosie wandered to the dining room and back again in the bluish light that winter had laid across everything. It would be dark soon. She stopped at the end table, at the corner cabinet with the china teacups, at the windows in the little sunroom that overlooked the street, as though somewhere she could find a name for what she was feeling. There was an enormous emptiness in her suddenly, an enormous sadness of prolonged winter. Carol Ann's life was changing; there was a future before her—excitement had replaced the wistful expression in her eyes. Rosie looked around a room in which nothing much had changed in twenty years, and she felt suddenly old. She wanted to give in to the feeling—to sadness, to sleep, to dullness, but in the midst of the sadness, something was alive; something said, "Trust me. Things can change." She looked at the living room with Mama's braided palms from Palm Sunday stuck behind all the pictures, and Mama's throw rugs over the carpet, and Mama's doilies on the back and arms of all the chairs. She walked to the window at the end of the room and looked at the last of the prairie's light. "Men don't like fussiness," she said. By the time the old streetlight came on, Rosie had gathered the palms into a pile for burning and had rolled up both the rugs.

Chapter XVI

"It's hot out," Michael Fleck announced as he elbowed another first-grader aside to be the first in the lunch line. He was sweaty from running and carried his jacket, mittens still dangling from the little suspenders that hooked them to the ends of the sleeves.

"It's not hot!" said the little Goering girl who had also been running. "It's all brown. It's all yucky and brown and it makes you *feel* hot." She looked at the plate Rosie had just lowered to Michael's tray. "I don't want that!" Her voice got shrill. "I hate cottage cheese!"

"Try it," Rosie said. "Eat just a little." She scanned the forty first graders who had burst into the lunch room with a greater explosion than was usual even for a Friday. Sister Immaculata was separating the participants in a small fight at the back of the line, and a shouting match seemed to be erupting between three girls in the middle.

The nun looked weary as she slid her tray past the steam table. "A bunch of little barometers," she said, "I knew we were in for something even before the sky started to turn."

"In for what?" Rosie said. "A blizzard?" It was March 29, and such a thing was quite possible. She remembered a terrible storm on Easter the year Pa died, but this had been a strange, mild winter, and March was dry—no snow to speak of, no rain, and the fields had gradually become bare and brown again as the ragged hem of snow crept backwards.

"I don't know," the nun said. "I'd say a thunderstorm or a cyclone, but it's awfully early in the season."

Dora put the stainless steel cover back on the mixed vegetables. "I'm going up to see what's brewing," she said. "Hold the second grade back a minute." Rosie looked toward the two high basement windows along the east wall; the bottom branches of an old lilac bush seemed to be moving a little, but it wasn't dark, and the thin strip of sky she could see through the lilac twigs looked blue.

"Heck of a thing!" Dora said as she burst through the door just ahead of the second grade. "Looks like a duststorm."

"Are we having that stuff again?" a second grader demanded.

Rosie remembered dust storms, but they belonged to that hazy area of childhood when events outside the family remain on the periphery. She could see herself in a feed-sack dress and an itchy gray coat Mama had made from an old suit jacket of Pa's (it would have been in the worst of the depression), coming in with grit in her eyes and crying. She could see Jack going off to school with a handkerchief tied over his face—"Stick 'em up, Rosie," he had said, "Hand over that piece of bubblegum," and she was frightened by his strangeness. She remembered Pa, home in the middle of the afternoon, his foot up on the cook-stove. "That's three more wiped out," he said, staring at the embers in the fire-box. "It may shut us down, Maura, it may shut us down. . . ."

When the last of the high school students had gone through line more quietly than usual—each grade had been successively more quiet, as though the barometer were swinging from one edge to the other—Rosie grabbed her coat and slipped up the stairs. It was not as windy as she had expected, and the sky to the northeast was still a grayish blue . . . but there was a strange light on everything, a light somewhat sulfurous, like the glow that fastens down just before a thunderstorm, but different, more diffuse, grimmer. She stood facing the northwest as she had faced endless storms coming across the prairie from the Dakotas, until she realized that the darkness came from her left. To the south-west, above the road that led to Kanaranze Creek, the sky was a brown wall. It was as though a moving partition of dirt, like a piece of stage scenery, hovered there, a tangible barrier that might or might not move in. She shivered, though it was not really cold. From her childhood, she remembered grit in the mouth, dirt drifted like snow in the ditches, but she didn't remember what she was feeling now—this sense of excitement combined with doom.

"Listen, it's all that fall plowing," Dora said as they were cleaning up. "It's all that winter wheat. If they just let the land alone over winter, this wouldn't happen." She wrung out a dishcloth with plump hands and forearms, nipped in at the wrist. None of Dora's family were farmers; her husband ran the hardware store. "Just like the depression," she said. "All that topsoil blown right in the ditch. And here goes another inch. Gone with the wind—ha!"

Rosie didn't know if she was right or not. Jack would know. Jack made fun of the county agent from the State Extension Service because he was young and wore dress shoes even in the fields, but whenever there was anything to do with the land— with things like nitrogen replacement or soil erosion—Jack listened. Jack would know why this was happening. Rosie felt a sudden rush of grief that she thought had passed months ago. Dora had opinions, as she had opinions about everything, but Jack would have known, and Pa would have known, and maybe even Mama would have known. They were all here when the dust storms came before . . . they were all around her then. . . .

Rosie shook her head to clear it. There was no reason to let a simple storm affect her like this. Jack was dead and she was doing just fine without him. She watched Dora, who was wiping off the steam table she had wiped off only minutes before. "Barometers," she said to herself.

Rosie tied a headscarf over her hair before leaving the cafeteria, turned up the collar on her coat, and walked the seven blocks to the post office. It wasn't so bad. The air was gritty, and the wind at her back pushed her into little running steps now and then, but there was no use being melodramatic. The post office was full, and old Ben Geil was deep into a story about a calf that got buried by drifts of dirt in the thirties. Rosie turned toward home, *The Ladies' Home Journal* and the electric bill under her arm, and found she was walking into something brown and substantial. The wind, which had been a jostling hand at her back on the way down, was now a muscular enemy she must push against. She squinted and turned her head to the side, taking short breaths, pushing up the gradual slope of the street; but her eyes were already grainy, and when she instinctively began to breathe through her mouth, she tasted the texture of dirt. She turned her back to the wind again, managed to force the bill and the magazine into her coat pocket, and pulled a handkerchief from her purse. With one hand she clamped it over her nose and mouth, and with the other she tried to shield her eyes. She was cold, colder than when she began walking; the temperature had dropped. *Jack*, she thought again, as though he could rescue her. *Jack would know what's causing this.*

Back in the house, the air was clean, but stiller, deader than it had been before. "Listen, there'll be dust all over everything," Dora had predicted, "you can't keep it out," but there was no evidence of dust yet. This was a tight house, square brick with a sun-porch across the front, half enclosed and half open. She stood in the enclosed half now, with its three walls of windows. Mama had used the room mostly for storage, had hung old draperies over the French doors, and stored her rug rags in brown grocery bags. It had stayed like that until the night Carol Ann had put her green dress in Jack's closet and she, Rosie, had taken Mama's rugs and braided palms out of the parlor. Later that evening, Rosie took the old grayish-pink draperies off the French doors and threw them in the trash bin. She moved a half-braided rug and two sacks of rag strips to the attic. She sorted out the stacks of old papers and magazines and stacked the *National Geographics* neatly on one end of the bookshelf; the others she took to the barrel next to the alley that she used as an incinerator.

When she stepped back to survey the room, she found herself suddenly nervous, as though she had disturbed something—some established order—as though she had opened something sealed. She stood there for a long moment, quieting the hands that wanted to replace the old draperies on the doors, to fetch back the discarded copies of *Farm Journal*. "This is the way it is now," she said low but aloud, as though that "other" Rosie who sometimes appeared were saying it. She took down the limp curtains that had hung in panels across the windows since the summer she was twelve and dumped them in a pile on the kitchen floor. The seven windows in the little room were bare, black rectangles that at one time might have frightened her. Then she went to bed.

The next Saturday she went to Worthington and got creamy white paint to cover the brownish rose of the walls, loose-woven gold curtains that would let in the light, and a bright print in orange, gold, and brown to cover the back and seat of one of the chairs. The other chair was overstuffed and hopeless, so she moved it to the attic and pushed her favorite rocker over into its place. Ray helped her pick out a carpet remnant that was orange with flecks of gold, and they installed it one Sunday afternoon, laughing at the way one edge always curled up as soon as they turned their backs.

She surveyed the room now in the brown cloud of the dust storm. The seat of the chair was re-covered, but the back wasn't, and the cushion in the rocker was still a faded gray with large pale pink blossoms. She had meant to work on them tonight, perhaps to finish them, but even when she flicked on the lamp, the light in the room was brown, was thick. She couldn't work here. She tuned the television to a variety show, but didn't watch it, started to write a letter to Aunt Pet, but went to the kitchen for some cheese and Ritz crackers, and never returned.

She wandered upstairs to her room at the back of the house, to the little room next to it that Pa had used as an office when he was alive, to the room where Jack had slept every night of his life. She sat on Jack's bed and picked at the old quilt in a Turkey Run pattern. Some of the pieces—those in a brown print with tiny white flowers—were disintegrating. The fibers were simply coming apart. Why did she miss Jack now, six months after his death, when she had gotten through the winter, through the holidays, and the long siege of January and February without him? His smell was all around her: the musk of ground cattle feed tinged with an odor of alcohol. "I can't be alone all the time," she could hear the young priest say in a thick, liquored voice as she stared at the stretched skin on the knuckles of his fists, "I can't be alone like this."

She wasn't alone, she reminded herself. She had friends. She had Dora and Gina Spratt, and some of the nuns, and all the ladies in her circle at church, and she had Ray. They were going to dinner tomorrow night, and maybe to a movie afterwards. She was with him at least once every weekend, sometimes twice. She would probably be with him tonight except that he had other plans. "Some of the guys from work are playing cards," he said. "I would have said 'no,' but it's at the boss's house. . . ." Ray needed friends too, she reminded herself. He needed men to play cards with. . . .

Ray needed friends—that was perfectly logical. She wouldn't want it any other way; she wouldn't want to be anything other than his good friend, as he had said so often. She wouldn't want what had happened among the crystal trees along the creek when his mouth had moved her mouth open, and her whole body had become something other than her own. As long as they were just friends, she didn't have to deal with that; didn't have to feel guilty; didn't have to go to confession. . . . And though he held her hand now in movies and when they were driving, and his kisses were longer, and he pulled her body closer to his, he had never kissed her like that again.

Their friendship was good; it was what she wanted, she told herself. She was used to an empty house; she was used to eating alone, and waking alone in the night—and she liked her privacy, she said firmly to herself as she sat in the brown light that was deepening now, sat on her dead brother's bed, and ran her fingers over the squares in the quilt where the fibers no longer held, and the tears that she was determined to ignore fell on other, brighter squares. . . .

"I must do something," Rosie said to herself the next morning as she sat with her coffee in the sunroom, her oak rocker turned away from the street, away from the dust, away from the panes of moving brown air. She put her head back against the up-holstered headrest and closed her eyes. "Keep busy," that was what Sister Mercedes had said to her when she had individual conferences with each of the senior girls before they left for their senior retreat. "It's important for all of us not to give the devil a chance to slip in, but it's even more important for some-one like you who has a special cross to bear. . . ."

"Why?" Rosie had thought at the time. "Does she think idle-ness brings on fits?" She figured out years later that it was about sex again—it seemed most everything was. A girl with fits was not likely to marry; a girl not likely to marry would have a lifetime of temptations to resist. . . .

By the end of the afternoon, she had "done something." She had cleaned the house, baked a batch of oatmeal-raisin cookies, and finished up the letter to Aunt Pet. She had sewed the remain-ing cushion cover for the sunporch, paid the electric bill, and had gone in the car for the mail. Mostly, she had filled up the day; she had kept moving from a sense that if she stopped, she would sink through her life as through a strange daylight dream.

Only the mail provided a small release from the restlessness, from the constant awareness of the moving brown air. She spread it out on the dining room table after she had shaken the dust from her coat. There was a copy of *The Diocesan Messenger*, a notice that Jack's subscription to *Farm Journal* would run out in a month, a "boxholder" coupon for a new detergent, and a letter from the lawyer in Worthington. "Dear Miss Deane," it said, "I am forwarding a check from the estate of the late John Deane for an amount which includes proceeds in excess of taxes from the sale of stock which we undertook on your behalf and at your request. . . ." Rosie smiled at the formal language. Old Schreck wasn't so formal in his two-room office above Landy's funeral parlor, his hair slipping off the combed-over bald spot, his upper plate gleaming. "This is what I want you to sell," she had said when she returned in October. "This and this." Schreck had pulled a pair of glasses from his top drawer. "I talked to Stumpy," she continued, "and to Mr. Douer at the bank . . ."

Schreck had adjusted his glasses and looked down at the list. "You sure about this?" he said. "This doesn't leave you much interest in the elevator—but then, it's your ballgame. . . ."

Everything was settled now, according to the letter. The remaining stock was in her name, and she was holding a check for $2,041.57. It was more than she had expected. She put the check in the second drawer of the buffet with her other important papers; she would deposit it on Monday. The drawer was fuller than it used to be; she moved over a stack of Jack's memorial cards and found below them two fat envelopes held together with a rubber band. "The travel folders," she thought. They had come throughout January and February from the coupons she sent in. Perhaps she could go on a real vacation this summer. . . . She could cash the check on Monday and instead of putting it in the bank, she could put it into traveler's checks. . . . Perhaps she would go to Hawaii where "summertime means off-season rates," and where the air would be cooler than on the heated prairie. She could picture herself strolling in the early evening at the very edge of the tide in one of those big, floppy dresses. The scent of something oriental, like jasmine, would be everywhere, and she would have a flower in her hair. "How about something cool to drink?" Ray would say, and they would be sitting in a little outdoor cafe sipping frothy, exotic juice out of whole pineapple shells as the moon came up, and a man in a Hawaiian shirt would play the ukelele and sing like Arthur Godfrey. . . .

What was she thinking of? Rosie dropped the brochure back on the table, and bundled the envelopes together with the rubber band. She couldn't go to Hawaii with Ray—not if they were just "friends." And what fun would it be to go alone? She put the travel folders back in the drawer, and the scent of jasmine faded.

The dust that poured relentlessly past the house seemed to pour inside now, to cover her, to catch in her throat. She felt angry—but at what?—at whom? It wasn't Ray's fault that she had come into a little money . . . that men and women who were "just friends" couldn't travel together. . . . She shoved the drawer shut with her knee but it stuck, and she had to pull it open and shove it closed again. When it stuck a second time, she almost swore—swore as Jack would have done—but her anger was turning to sadness. The little rectangles of color and excitement were all put away; around her, the rectangles of her windows were the color of porous stone.

"Where's your sense of adventure?" Ray said that evening when Rosie wondered aloud if they should drive all the way to Worthington in dust that continued flowing. "This is historic, Rosie. You can tell your grandchildren about the great dust storm of '68." He was prowling around her living and dining rooms with as much energy as the wind.

"What grandchildren?" Rosie wanted to say, "And why should I be concerned with history?" She didn't care about what was coming in the future. She wanted *now* to be safe, secure, to have protecting arms around her. Ray had given her a hug when he came in the door, and then let go. He was restless, excitable, anxious to be off. "What'd you do all day?" he said, pacing through her rooms as though looking for evidence. It was obvious he wanted to tease, to be carefree, to race like a child chasing the neighborhood dog, but Rosie couldn't bring herself to run with him. His eyes were laughing, his glance bouncing off the surfaces of the room, off her own still sadness.

Why do moods always have to be so different? she wondered. Why couldn't the storm have affected them alike? There was no way she could ease her unreasoning grief by telling him of it, no way she could reach him with the angry sadness she didn't understand, no way she could absorb his gaiety. She watched him pick a wax pear from the bowl on the buffet, toss it into the air, and catch it with one hand. "Ready?" he said.

"You must have won big," she said to him in the car. Her voice sounded nagging and unpleasant, but she couldn't seem to control it. "Either that or you like dust storms. How much did you make?"

"You disapprove or something?" He glanced over sharply. "I wasn't exactly betting the home place, you know."

"No," she said a little too defensively. "No, I know you

wouldn't bet too much. Maybe I'm just jealous that men always have such fun at poker and women are always left out. . . ."

"Oh, come on," he said. "Women have things like bridge clubs."

"I know." She didn't want to argue, but nothing she said seemed to come out right. "Maybe it's just this dust," she tried again. "It makes me sad or frightened or something . . . and I can't figure out why you're so happy about it. . . ." The last phrase sounded petulant despite her efforts.

"I'm not happy about it," he said. "Anybody connected with farming knows it's going to cost . . . and I won $9.35, if you really want to know." There was a small pause. "It's just . . . well, it's something different—it's something that hasn't happened for thirty years. . . ."

She looked at his profile against the sheen of the car window as he lapsed into silence. He was not smiling now, and there was something stern, stubborn about the thickness of the shoulders, the muscles of the neck. She looked for the wayward locks at the back of his head that always made her want to reach out and smooth them down, the way one smooths the hair of a child, but he was wearing a cap—the tweed, flat-billed kind that golfers or Englishmen wear—and his hair was flattened in back. She could see through the edge of one of his glasses, and the chrome bar at the side of the windshield was wavy and distorted. The lights of a car were coming toward them. *Who is he?* she thought. *What am I doing riding through the night with a man I know so little about?*

They rode in silence for a moment after the car had passed, and when Ray turned, the edge was gone from his voice. "It's really not so bad out," he said, obviously wanting to make peace. "Visibility is a lot better than it was in that fog."

"I know," she said. "I don't know why it's made me edgy. There's really nothing to be afraid of. . . ."

The movies playing in Worthington were *Torn Curtain* and *The Killing of Sister George*. Rosie had wanted to see *Torn Curtain* because Julie Andrews was in it, but the movie made her frightened and sad all over again, and Julie Andrews, who usually seemed so innocent, was a little risqué. Only a handful of people huddled in the lobby waiting for the second show.

"Havin' a good time, Rosie?" a young male voice said, and Rosie made out Mickey Runkle leaning against a poster of Gina Lollobrigida with her breasts bulging out. Gil Simons was slouched on the other side of the poster, in an old denim jacket that looked as if it had been worn in the barn.

"Or maybe you guys just come to sit in the back row," Mickey added, his grin widening. Rosie felt Ray stiffen beside her.

"Ignore them," Ray said under his breath. "Just keep walking." There was fury in his voice, and he pushed her forward a little too roughly. She caught one more glimpse of Gil Simons: his face too was covered with an insolent grin, but his eyes were a hard, smooth surface watching. . . . "Bye, Rosie," he said softly.

"Little bastards!" Ray sputtered out on the sidewalk, loosening his grip on her arm. "If I'd been alone, I'd of nailed those kids."

"Oh," Rosie said. "They weren't really doing anything. . . ."

"No, but they were thinking it," Ray said darkly and gripped her arm again. His happy mood had dissipated into the gritty night. Perhaps it was her fault; perhaps her mood had infected him. . . .

They stopped at a cafe downtown for pie and coffee, and then rode home mostly in silence. They tried to talk about the movie, but neither of them had liked it, and there was little to say. The headlights kept picking up ridges of dirt like snowdrifts that rose from the ditches and fingered the road. "This is bad for the farmers," Rosie had said; but all Ray said was "Yeah . . ."

When the door was locked and the sound of Ray's car had died into the air, Rosie wandered through the house, picking up a magazine here, a cup and saucer there, leaving lights on in all the rooms behind her. She wasn't tired; it was only 10:30, and she didn't want to sleep. She wanted to be clean, to wash away the grit and discontent of the last thirty-six hours, but she also wanted light: she was tired of moving, day and night, through a troubled brownness. She poured a double dose of bubble bath into the tub and turned on the hot water. She brought a novel Gina Pratt had lent her and put it on the old piano stool Mama.

always kept next to the tub. *To Kill a Mockingbird* was about a little girl and her brother in the South. Rosie ran twice as much water as usual, and leaned back in the tub the way she saw women do in the ads. To read a novel in the bathtub seemed a luxurious, almost forbidden thing. It had an aura of wealth and leisure about it—an aura of being sleek and pampered. . . .

In practice, it didn't work. Her hands were wet in the first place. When she reached out and pulled on a towel, it fell into the tub. Even with dry hands, there was no place to rest the book. She stuck one knee up out of the water, but couldn't risk using it to balance a book that belonged to someone else. She held the novel straight out in front of her, but after six or seven pages, her arms were tiring, and her back began to cramp. She gave it up, put the book on the old piano stool, and sank down into the water. Even this was a luxury she seldom indulged in, but the glamorous, sensuous edge was taken off.

She read late that night, curled in a rocking chair in the little room that used to be Pa's office—at least she could indulge herself to that degree. Scout and her brother, romping through an Alabama childhood, became as real, as visual as her own memories sometimes were. She could see Jack at seven, at ten. "See, Rosie, see . . ." he would say and lead her to the shed where the Monks' dog was having puppies, slimy little capsules of flesh that squeezed out of a hole below the tail. But she ran through summer evenings in the South now, ran with Scout and Jem, and hid from Bo who was a combination of all the bogeys she and Jack had ever conjured up. She was hiding with them when the phone rang. The old electric clock above the desk said a quarter to two.

She didn't know why she answered it. No one decent called at this hour. Ray should have been safely home hours ago, and except for Aunt Nellie, there was no one who was likely to call after midnight even in the event of a death.

"If we were sitting together in the dark," the voice said, muffled, but still clear, "I could run my hand up under your skirt and stick it right up your cunt. . . ."

"Who is this?" Rosie shouted, surprised at herself, her anger rising faster than fear. "Why are you calling me?"

The caller was surprised too. There was a little breathy start, as though he were going to speak and then silence.

"Who are you?" Rosie demanded. "Say something."

"A friend . . ." the voice said enigmatically, and then rang off.

Rosie stood with the receiver in her hand, looking at it as a strange, found object. The caller had never hung up on her before. She wasn't sure what she was feeling, but it was different this time: fear, anger, a sense of outrage, but also a sense that the voice was familiar; there was a clue she must follow, a demanding desire to know.

She walked up the stairs slowly. She was trembling slightly, tremors of fright, rage, tremors of the same kind of doomed anticipation she had felt when she saw the wall of dirt approaching over the prairie. Knowledge was heavy, she remembered; it didn't always set you free. She picked up the novel again, but didn't bother to make herself comfortable in the rocker. She couldn't read any more tonight. She couldn't lose herself, except perhaps in sleep. She turned out the light in Pa's office, and in her own room she lit only the lamp that sat on the bedside table. She realized with a kind of relief that the phone calls no longer held the horror of the first one, that they had worn her down. By sheer exposure, the edge of terror had been removed, despite her pumping heart. Whoever was calling was unlikely to harm her; he was most likely an ordinary person except for some dark, sudden ravine in his mind—some pit of sickness as unexpected as a sudden cliff on the plains.

Rosie went to the closet to hang up her bathrobe. She had gotten more clothes since fall, but had not yet thrown the others away, had not yet even moved them to a different closet. They hung there now, faint-smelling limbs, pale and dark, that tangled into one another. They reminded her of something she couldn't name. She stood in the doorway, one hand bracing against each side of the jamb, and looked at them. She was very tired; it was very late. Pale limbs floated before her: a woman in a car wreck near Currie; Vietnamese civilians in the news on TV. She remembered her own long legs in those adolescent summers when she sneaked out to the deserted cemetery and pulled her skirt all the way up to tan her thighs. A boy in the gas station had thick thighs, and something pale and limp was hanging out—a man in a theatre, his hand moving up her leg—Ray's hands, the small brown hairs up to the first knuckle—theatre seats in the dark. . . .

Her body went rigid, and her heart gave an enormous squeeze, as though it had turned over within her. "If we were sitting together in the dark . . ." the voice had said. "If we were sitting together in the dark, I could run my hand up under your skirt. . . ."

"Oh, my God!" Rosie said. Ray, who desired her . . . Ray, who had kissed as though all of his body yearned to come inside of hers . . . Ray, who that very night had sat with her in the dark. . . .

She couldn't finish the thought. Her mind panicked, darted to the clothes, to the polka-dot dress she told Carol Ann she would give her, to Scout, who lived in the South and didn't have a mother, and whose real name was Jean Louise. . . .

There were red dots in front of her . . . red dots on the polka-dot dress that should have been black—that she knew were black. Red dots, that were little plastic chips, floating in a dream of bingo games, and at the end of the dream the phone was ringing, ringing, and at the end of the ringing there was something she hadn't allowed her mind to know. . . .

She knew it now. She knew it with all the clarity of the buttons on the coat sleeve that hung directly in front of her. "I know you're there alone," said the voice that came out of the red-dotted dream; and the other voice—Ray's—speaking just hours before: "You're here all alone, you know. . . ."

Rosie felt sick. Her stomach heaved itself into her throat and she gagged in reflex. Everything was in waves now: her mind, the undulating lines of the clothes, the floor. She ran to the bathroom, flipped back the toilet seat, and doubled over it, one arm clutching her midsection, and gagged and gagged, but nothing came. She wiped her mouth with a piece of toilet paper and sat, in the dark, on the edge of the old claw-foot tub.

The first call had come in September, after the chivaree. Before she met Ray, before he moved to Luverne from wherever he came from, there had been no calls. The next one came the night of the Oktoberfest—she had spent the bulk of the day with him. Then there was the bingo game with the red-chipped dream, then the night in January, when she hadn't seen him for a week (except in the cafeteria), but nevertheless. . . . And then tonight. . . .

Rosie got up from the bathtub and pulled her robe tighter. She started to go downstairs for a cup of tea—for something comforting, but she couldn't go; it was too close to the phone. She couldn't go into her own room either, to the open closet door where her garments hung like limp but stubborn witnesses that wouldn't go away. She went instead to Pa's old office, to the rocker where she pulled her knees to her chin and rocked and rocked to console herself.

Of course, Ray didn't make the phone calls. That was a dream, an illusion, a fantasy rising out of a mind that was too tired, too upset. . . . Of course, she was upset. The dust storm had sanded at the end of her nerves for nearly two days, and she and Ray had quibbled tonight, and she had gotten an obscene call. . . . Anybody who got obscene phone calls had a right to be upset. Anybody. When you were upset, you thought strange things—you jumped to conclusions—you put pieces of a puzzle together and mashed the edges to fit. . . .

Ray was the sanest person she knew. He responded well in emergencies, and he had a good sense of humor; he liked children —he was good with them. He was a perfectly healthy, sane person . . . except perhaps for a dark ravine. . . . Rosie shook her head. No. The voice didn't sound like Ray's. Even muffled, it didn't sound like him. Even if he put a handkerchief over the phone . . . but then, she had never heard a voice through a handkerchief. She pulled up a corner of her robe and talked through it. "Hello," she said. "Hello." She couldn't tell. It sounded the same to her, only a little rubbery. Perhaps there was some way she could find out, could tell. . . . If it weren't almost Easter, she could give a Mardi Gras party and make everybody wear masks. She could give Ray a mask that had cloth over the mouth—she could give all the men masks that had cloth over the mouths—one for Jerry Heinkamp, one for Jim Hinely, one for Tom Pratt and for Father Griffin. . . .

"Now wait a minute," the young priest had said at the lunch table. "You can't just go around suspecting people. Voices are too much alike." Rosie stopped rocking. She felt an enormous surge of guilt. Ray was her friend, her best friend. Ray was someone she loved, and she was ready to suspect him. . . . She was ready to convict him of dark, diseased ravines in the soul, of being corrupt, sick. She was ready to convict him when she had no proof. "Circumstantial evidence," that's what Perry Mason always said when he defended his clients. "Circumstantial evidence . . ."

It was a terrible thing, it was sinful, to think malicious things about someone. Even if that person was your best friend, it was still a sin. It was calumny or rash judgment, or one of those sins against the eighth commandment. Maybe it was as terrible to think that of someone as it was to make the obscene phone calls. Maybe it was worse. . . .

No, it wasn't worse. At least, not if you didn't tell anybody . . . if you didn't let it harm him. But maybe making obscene calls wasn't so bad either. . . . It wasn't like rape—it wasn't like murder or beating somebody up or robbery . . . even the police weren't very interested. And maybe he didn't make the calls to anybody but her. Maybe . . . because he was a widower, remember, and men have terrible urges . . . maybe he didn't want to force himself on her, didn't even want to try to convince her, because he knew she'd feel guilty . . . and maybe this was his way of releasing it. Maybe all he needed was a wife again. If they were married, and she gave herself to him whenever he wanted (and however he wanted—because she knew there were dark and different ways of sex) maybe that was all he needed. Maybe he would never make another call again. Maybe he could just whisper to her in the dark of their bedroom. Maybe if she offered herself to him now. . . .

Rosie stopped. It was a mortal sin, what she was thinking of . . . but if it would save him. . . . No, it was more than that. It was an assumption that he was guilty, and that was sinful too. She got up from the rocker. She was too tired to think any more, too tired to put any more pieces together. The luminous hands on her

Little Ben pointed to four o'clock when she walked into the bedroom. She slipped the robe from her body in the dark and let it fall to the floor. When she slept, she dreamed of blue chips— blue translucent chips at a poker game, and Ray was selling them. You could use them in payphones as you would use a dime or a slug. Rosie knew that, but did Ray know it? Did Ray know what they were worth? She clutched her money tighter and said, "I won't bet, but I want to play."

When she woke, she had a headache, and she sat up in clear, merciless light. The wind was down; the dust storm was over.

Chapter XVII

FOR WEEKS, IT SEEMED TO ROSIE THAT SHE WAS LISTENING—LISTENing to Ray, listening to the older students as they came for lunch, to Jim Hinely and Stumpy McNabb—listening to every male of her acquaintance. On Monday, she listened to Ray tease Dora about her new hairdo; she listened to the voices of the two priests as they carried across the lunchroom above the younger and more feminine voices. She listened to the teller in the Worthington bank saying, "You want *all* this in traveler's checks?" and counting out the $2,000 as though such an amount pained him. She counted it again when she got home—twice—fingering the supple but crisp texture of the substitute money, listening to its sound.

She listened to all the male voices at the Pratts' party on Saturday night, but by then she was tired, and the voices began to blend together. "The kids want you to come and stay again," Tom Pratt said. "Rosie, you and I have got to have another party," said the young priest. "Nice dress, Rosie," a voice said. "Let me fill that . . . haven't seen you for a while . . . did you hear about . . ."

"Rosie, come look at Gina's new bedroom curtains," a female voice said, and it was Carol Ann. She was in her usual short black habit, but somehow she was making it look jauntier these days, and her eyes no longer had that wistful look. Rosie wondered how she had gotten permission to come alone.

"I've got an interview," Carol Ann said, closing the door behind her. "Two of them, actually, but the one I really want is a seventh grade in a mixed neighborhood: some black, some white, and quite a few Chicanos."

"Congratulations!" Rosie said. "In Minneapolis?"

"St. Paul," Carol Ann said, and gave Rosie a sudden hug. "I'm so happy," she said. "And the salary is around seven thousand, so you'll get your money back before you know it."

Rosie laughed. "I'm not worried," she said. "What about summer clothes? How about another trip to Sioux Falls?"

"Well . . . maybe . . ." Carol Ann said. "But only if you let me pay everything back . . . And there's another favor. . . ."

"Speak," Rosie said. "I'll see what I can do."

"I need a key for the cafeteria kitchen," the young nun said, and began an elaborate explanation about long distance calls, job interviews, and the impossibility of using the convent phone, which was right in the middle of a hallway where everyone could hear.

"Why don't you just use *my* phone?" Rosie said.

"Well, I would, but if somebody like Sister Grace saw me visiting you twice in one day, it would look a little fishy," Carol Ann said. She was sitting on the bed and began to bite nervously at a hangnail. "Anybody seeing me go in the side door of the church wouldn't know I was going downstairs. . . ."

"But the phone bill goes to the rectory, and the priests will——"

"I know," said Carol Ann. "I thought of that." She examined her nails closely. "I told Father Griffin about my plans—I had to start telling a few people—and he said he'd cover the bill, but he's never had a key to that door. He could get one, of course, but I'm afraid Phil—Father Schwartz—might ask questions." She looked at Rosie expectantly. "Of course, if you don't think you ought to. . . ."

"No problem," Rosie said and tried to make light of it. "I'll get a duplicate, and if anyone starts stealing powdered eggs, we'll know it's you." Still, it would have been simpler to use her phone, and she began to suspect that Carol Ann was enjoying the intrigue for its own sake.

There was little intrigue in the rest of St. Ives, it seemed. "What a dull month," Father Griffin was saying with mock seriousness back in the living room. "Only one funeral, no accidents, no teen-agers pregnant, no kids in jail . . ." He looked over at Rosie. "No more obscene phone calls, I hope. . . ."

"Well," she said, "not many . . ."

"You're still getting those?" He leaned forward. "Since when?"

"Not often," Rosie said. "And I just hang up." She didn't want to talk about this, and yet she wanted to watch the faces in the room. She glanced from the priest to Ray but found both pairs of eyes meeting hers and glanced away again. "They don't scare me so much anymore," she said. "It's mainly just a nuisance."

"Well, but . . ." the priest said, "if it's been going on this long, they ought to be able to put a tracer or something on your phone. . . ." He and Tom Pratt began to discuss what was legal and possible on a rural exchange, and Rosie gratefully withdrew. Ray was not looking at her now; he was scowling with a kind of concentrated energy, his eyes following the conversation that went back and forth between the two men. He looked concerned; but if he was really agitated, he was keeping it under control. She watched for small tics, grimaces, shifts of the eye that might betray tension, but his expression remained the same.

On the way home, Ray took her hand as usual, but said little. It was late, and he was either tired or still distracted. He slipped his arm around her waist as they walked from the car to her door, and on the porch he kissed her. He took her face in both his hands for a moment, and seemed to study it in the darkness. "You're very special," he said. "You know that?"

She nodded. "You're very special too," she said.

He kissed her again. "I'd better go," he said, but one hand stayed on her cheek. "You're still locking that door, aren't you?"

"Yes, I'm locking the door," she said.

"Good," he said, touched the tip of her nose, and departed.

As the weeks went by, Rosie found herself still listening, but more often it was to her own mind than to external voices. There were two voices within her, sometimes more, and they wondered and dreamed and argued back and forth like a commenting chorus. The idea that Ray was the obscene caller faded as time went on and no more calls came. It had been a silly idea, one of those waking dreams that almost convinces the dreamer of its truth, the sensible Rosie argued; it had come out of the murky cloud of the dust storm. But there was still a mystery about him, another voice countered. Right after Easter, he had gone to Illinois again, to a little town called Paxton. . . . But there was nothing alarming about that, was there? He had given her an explanation: "Got to see if the old house is still standing," he had said. "You never know about tenants. Got to get the thing sold one of these days."

Sometimes, the inner voices (or perhaps they were urges) pulled her in so many directions that she felt worn out. She longed to see more of Ray—she was confident of her trust in him—but if that were true, why did she arrange so often to have others present? Why, for instance, had she gotten tickets for the high school play with Gina and Tom, or given a party on a Saturday night she and Ray might have spent alone, or arranged to meet him for dinner with Carol Ann on their way back from Sioux Falls? Could it be that, after all, she still suspected him?

The first warm weekend of May, she had the flu. It was the stomach and dizzy-headache variety that had been making the rounds of the school children, and it began with a violent onslaught of vomiting that settled into days of aching listlessness. Ray had called when he heard the forecasts for temperatures up to 65° and wanted to take her fishing. Instead, she had stared at a bowl of Campbell's chicken soup, tried to convince herself to eat it, and looked at the Worthington paper. There were two full pages of engagement pictures. Everyone was getting married in June, it seemed, and she couldn't even catch a fish. What made it worse was that she had gone to school with some of these girls' mothers.

By the time she dragged herself back to the lunchroom on Tuesday, it had turned cool again, and had rained overnight, but spring was full-blown. The crocuses along the side of the church were splayed out as though hot steam had caught them; tulips were open, and Dora's plum tree was in bloom. "The world's getting hotter," Dora said. "It's those Chinese and Russians testing all those bombs." Rosie didn't know about climatic changes, but she felt she had missed something by spending three days in bed. As always, life seemed to manage its significant changes without her.

"Ray and I might go to Lake Shetek on Sunday," Rosie said to Carol Ann as she put up the hem on the nun's new flowered skirt that evening. "He said he'd call before he goes to poker tonight."

"I wish I were going," the young nun said, standing rather stiffly on a dining room chair. "It's my favorite place out here."

"You've been there?" Rosie said. She had seen nuns demurely picnicking with parents in the town park, but Lake Shetek, the largest in southwestern Minnesota, seemed too public, too secular. . . .

Carol Ann sighed. "Another of my crimes, I guess," she said. "The people who were supposed to deliver Gaelynn and me here last fall came by way of an afternoon at Lake Shetek. Gaelynn had it all arranged before she told me." She shifted her feet to the left so that Rosie could remeasure a spot on the hem. "They taught us to water ski, and it was glorious," she said, laughing a little, "but we paid a price. A sunburn feels twice as bad when you have to hide it under black serge."

"Well, that takes care of the front," Rosie muttered through the pins in her mouth. She straightened up and stepped back to view the effect before she continued pinning. The skirt was well above the young nun's knee, which was where she wanted it, but Rosie couldn't help wishing it were a bit longer. She was about to ask if Carol Ann wanted to check the length in a mirror, when the phone interrupted. It wasn't Ray, as she expected; it was Dora saying that old Mrs. Geil, who lived across from the church, had seen a light in the cafeteria kitchen about ten o'clock last night. Did Rosie know anything about it?

"Do I know anything about a light in the cafeteria about ten last night?" Rosie repeated for Carol Ann's benefit. The young nun looked frightened and confused for a moment, then quickly began to pantomime dialing the phone. Rosie nodded to her. "No, I don't," she said. "Oh, wait a minute. Father Schwartz said something about printing some paper napkins for the graduation brunch. Maybe he went down to get a few to practice on." It was a lame explanation, but it seemed to work. Dora rang off, and Carol Ann checked the skirt as Rosie held a mirror on the floor. She was just threading a needle when the phone rang once again. "This time it's got to be Ray." Rosie laughed.

"The forecast is for a hot weekend," familiar muffled tones said. "A good time to ram it up your hot little . . ." Rosie held the phone away from her ear and turned a stricken look to Carol Ann.

"Dora?" the young nun mouthed, afraid that their excuse for the lighted basement had not, after all, been accepted. Rosie shook her head but could say nothing. She held out the phone as one would hold a recently bloodied weapon. Carol Ann took it, put it to her ear, and listened for a moment. Her mouth came open, and she screamed, "What? Who is this? Get off the phone!" and slammed the receiver back in its cradle. "Bastard," she said.

"I'm sorry," Rosie said. She didn't know what impulse had caused her to hand the phone to Carol Ann. "I'm sorry; that was dumb . . . I should have just hung up."

"Bastard!" Carol Ann said again. She threw herself down on a dining room chair but sat forward quickly as the pins in the hem began to stick her. "Is this the same one?"

"The same guy as before? Yes," Rosie said, and suddenly realized that she had a witness—she had someone else who had heard and could perhaps identify the caller. "Did you . . ." She started to ask if Carol Ann had recognized the voice, but stopped, her heart beating fast.

"I heard enough," Carol Ann said. "He's obviously some sicko." They looked at each other blankly. "I didn't recognize him, if that's what you mean, but he sounded sort of familiar. . . . In fact, I'm almost sure I've heard that voice before. . . ."

"Well, I've heard it before," Rosie said, affecting a jocular tone. "On the phone—and it always says just about the same thing." They both laughed a little.

"Women are so helpless in this kind of thing," Carol Ann said. "I mean, what do you do?"

Now that the topic had become general, Rosie breathed more easily. She began sewing the hem in Carol Ann's skirt, forgetting about the length, and then asked Carol Ann to help her go through her own spring wardrobe. She honestly wanted the advice—she had gotten used to shorter A-line skirts, and most of her dresses looked dumpy—but she also wanted the companionship. She wanted someone to fill the space, to keep the lonesome clock from ticking.

Chapter XVIII

SUNDAY WAS, AS RAY HAD PREDICTED, ONE OF THOSE DAYS WHEN everything is the perfect color. The sun seemed to shine not on but through the translucent green of tender leaves and the fragile white and pink of apple trees that filled an occasional farmyard with blossoms. Barbed wire, strung between the silvered roughness of old fence posts, formed shaggy melodic scales against the flat fields. Here and there, birds perched like scattered notes. It was a perfect morning, Rosie thought as they rode toward Lake Shetek. She looked at Ray in his plaid, short-sleeved shirt, sunglasses hiding his eyes, his jaw relaxed in anticipation. He turned his head toward her and smiled.

He had called yesterday morning. "Jeez," he said, "you must be the most popular girl in town. I tried for half an hour to call you last night, and the phone was busy. . . ." She tried to explain, but his voice waved her off. "That's okay, that's okay. Never mind," he said. "Just remember to bring your bathing suit."

Rosie hadn't worn a bathing suit since her early twenties. Carol Ann had burst into laughter when she reluctantly pulled it out Friday night, the polka-dot bow drooping over a shirred bustline. "This must have been a Betty Grable special," the young nun said, grabbing it and waltzing around the room, "but Betty never had so many folds of cloth." She tugged at the front panel that covered the abdomen. The rubberizing of whatever sort had hardened and made a slight crunching sound as Carol Ann stretched it out. The material, unable to spring back, hung like a fist-sized frontal tumor. They both laughed. "I think I ruined it," Carol Ann said, "but just imagine what would have happened if the whole thing gave way in the water."

So she was wearing a new bathing suit under her blouse and slacks. She could smell the cold fried chicken in the picnic basket —that and potato salad, a jello ring, and a carrot cake. Ray brought beer and a portable radio. "Let's go to early Mass and get a good start," he'd said. "We're supposed to be back at the Pratts' by seven-thirty." So here they were, driving together under a generous sun, not needing to talk, and happy.

"All set?" Ray said as he pulled into a dirt parking lot. He was as eager to be off and running as he had been the night of the dust storm, but this time she was with him. They walked to the largest beach, but several families were already established there with dogs that swam into the water to fetch sticks, gangly teen-agers, and a quantity of racing children. "Let's keep going," Ray said.

They wandered along a shore that sometimes spread into little sandy beaches and sometimes dropped sharply into the water. Birds were loud around them. Eventually, they spread the old Indian-weave blanket on a stretch of sand that sloped down from a small cliff washed out by the waves. The beach extended for a hundred yards to the west, narrowing to a point where a willow tree, its new leaves more yellow than green, bent into the water. It was quiet here; the more populated beach was out of sight and the yells of the children reached them only as murmurs. They had passed an older couple fishing from the little cliff. The man and woman looked almost the same in old overalls and flannel shirts with sleeves rolled up, their bodies equally stocky. The woman had nodded to their greeting, her straw hat rocking slightly.

"Any luck?" Ray asked.

The man's face was hidden by the bill on his cap, and he didn't turn his head. "Couple a' chubbs," he said. "Nothin' worth spittin' about."

The couple was out of earshot now, but well within visual range, grown into the bank like colorful stumps. They seemed to be silent totems watching over the waves of the lake, and it gave

Rosie a sense of comfort. She began unpacking the lunch, laying out paper plates and old silverware, opening the Tupperware containers. "Oh, not yet," Ray said, "though maybe a swallow or two of beer wouldn't hurt." He was stripping off his shoes and socks and starting to unbutton his shirt. "First you swim, *then* you eat."

"It's too cold," Rosie said. "That water must be freezing."

"No-o," he said in the loud, teasing tone he used when he wished to cajole her. "No, you've just got to get yourself wet and then you don't feel a thing." He was standing up now and unbuckling his belt. Rosie averted her eyes and concentrated on putting the lid back on a container. She was embarrassed to just sit there and watch him, and ashamed at her embarrassment. From the corner of her eye, she saw Ray fold his pants and toss them on the corner of the blanket. He was wearing navy blue trunks with a white drawstring at the waist and looked trimmer, more muscular than she might have expected. His chest and legs were covered with curly brown hair. She fumbled for a beer and the opener she had brought. "You wanted a swallow . . ." she said.

He took it from her and grinned. "So you're just going to sit there and let the water go to waste," he said.

"Later," she promised. "Later . . . but I really can't swim."

"I'll let you know where it starts to get deep," he said, and handed her the beer. He took a running start and plunged into the lake, but the water splashed only to his knees. "You're right. It's a little on the chilly side," she heard him say as he strode outward for several yards, then flopped his entire body into the lake. He came up grinning. "See," he called, "doesn't hurt a bit." Then he did a clowning imitation of frozen drowning. He paddled a bit further, righted himself, and announced, "I'm still touching," then swam again.

Rosie, for the first time, really looked at the lake surrounding him. It was the same light but deep blue as the sky—like the center of a morning glory, and the breeze made little ripples and dimples in the surface. She had thought Lake Shetek was as big as the ocean when she had first seen it at seven or eight. The far shore was visible, but it was more a shaggy green line than a horizon. Several motorboats were drifting languidly with their motors off and immobile fishermen hunched over invisible lines in their bows. On the eastern shore, a sailboat, a rarity in these waters, floated away like a receding mirage. All that was visible of Ray was his head, a seal's head, a dog's, floating. She felt an influx of peace, of relaxation, as though life really had come, in some primordial time, from the waters; as though some of that steady, primeval force was flowing through her now.

She unbuttoned her blouse slowly, letting the breeze flick across her shoulders like a cool, feminine hand before she dropped the blouse to the blanket, and began to unstrap her sandals. The new bathing suit looked greener than ever to eyes adjusted to the blue of the lake and sky, but it was a pleasant green. She was loath to unbutton the slacks and slide them from beneath her, shy about exposing her naked legs, but it was better now than when Ray returned. She moved her hands as surely and slowly as the little waves, the slacks slid off, and the sun settled in to protect her from the newness of the air. To her right, she saw the fisherwoman on the bank snap her line from the water. On the end of it a small and silver fish glinted and flicked its tail.

Ray swam toward her then and walked from the water, little rivulets twining down his legs. She could see gooseflesh on his legs and arms, and he shivered slightly but refused to admit that he was cold. He was famished, he said. The chicken was still crisp and the potato salad creamy; the jello was a little melted on the edge, but the fruit in it was good, and the beer tasted better than she ever remembered it tasting.

Ray wasn't cold long. The sun had taken all the chill from the air by the time they had finished eating, and together with the small lapping of the waves, the warmth spread through them. "Oh, too much, too much," Ray said, rubbing his stomach. "You're too good a cook, Rosie." She smiled; she had eaten too much also, and the beer was making her sleepy. She watched Ray snag his trousers from the edge of the blanket with his foot, roll them up, and ease them under his head for a pillow. "Can't swim after lunch, so might as well sleep," he said, grinning at her. He adjusted his sunglasses over his eyes and folded his hands on his stomach. Rosie glanced up at the silent fishers who seemed not to have moved in the hour they had been there. She reached for her own trousers, rolled them into a pillow, and stretched out on her stomach parallel to Ray, the picnic basket between them.

She didn't intend to sleep; she never slept in the daytime; but a fly was landing on her foot, and as she twitched it off, she had a sense that time had been passing. The fly persisted, and when she opened her eyes and rolled over, the fly was Ray, one finger tickling the ball of her foot. "Come on, Sleeping Beauty," he said, "you haven't gotten wet yet."

She sat up and blinked. "I really can't swim," she said, "really . . ."

"Last one in's a rotten egg," Ray chanted, sprang up and sped toward the water.

"No fair," Rosie called, "you got a head start," but she was running too, and before she knew it, was thigh-deep in water. She stopped there. The water was cold, and the feel of it on her thighs was a strange sensation. She didn't want to go further, didn't want to thrust the warm core of her body into the penetrating cold.

"Come on," Ray said, and held out his hand, "you aren't even wet yet."

"No," Rosie said. "It's cold." She ducked to avoid the splash she saw him heaving toward her. The drops were cold fingernails drumming her back, but she was laughing, and she splashed him back. She felt like a child again—like a pale and somewhat sickly child who has not played in a long time but has watched and remembers. She could feel herself get stronger as she played, less wistful. Ray backed deeper into the water, forcing her forward if her splashes were to reach him, but she stopped short of allowing the water to touch her crotch.

"Come on," Ray said, trying to grab her hand, but she backed away and splashed him again. He shrugged good naturedly. "Well," he said, "I'm for total immersion," and holding his nose, he sank out of sight.

Rosie stirred the water with her hand. It was still cold, but it no longer felt quite as frigid. *The surrounding air must be in the high seventies by now*, she thought. Then something grabbed her ankles. She felt her feet leave the sand, her body fold like a chair, and in a single piercing instant, before she had time to yell, the cold water sucked her in.

She came up splashing and choking, her feet once again on the bottom, the water nearly up to her waist. "Darn you! Why did you do that?" she wanted to say, but she could only sputter.

"You okay?" Ray said, his hand on her back. "I shouldn't have done that; I'm sorry." His voice was sincere, but he was laughing. Rosie splashed a double-handful directly into his face. "So the war's still on," he said, and heaved water at her. She shrieked this time, retreated in the direction of the willow tree, but tried to keep up her end of the battle. Ray was by far the better splasher, his hands methodical as a waterwheel, and Rosie took a blast head-on as she reached deep into the water with both hands and tumbled backward into the lake. When she came streaming to the surface again, they stood waist-deep in the water in an unde-clared truce, laughing, panting for breath.

"Can you swim at all?" Ray said after a minute. "Can you float?" He moved toward her and extended his arms below the surface of the water, palms up. "Come here. I'll teach you. Just lay back across my arms."

"No," Rosie said. "I'll sink."

"You won't sink," he said. "I'll hold you. And what if you do? You'll get wet, that's all."

She moved toward him hesitantly. "Turn around," he said, and a strong arm swept under her buttocks, tipping her back into the water until another arm caught her under the neck. She gasped and clutched at him. "Relax," he said. "Let your arms and legs dangle." His arm slid up to the small of her back, and the other arm eased under her shoulders.

"I'm going under," she said, straining upward.

"No, you're not," he said. "Just relax."

She let her limbs dangle. She wasn't relaxed, but as she lay there she sensed a pleasant security in the warm arms that formed a truss against the water.

"Okay, arch your back," he said. "That's right. Remember that the water's going to hold you. Now let your head go—your neck's all tense. Most of your head will go below the water, but your face won't—you can still breathe."

She tried to do what he told her, tried to trust him, but her body felt at once exhilarated and unnatural, stiff.

"Now pretend you're sleeping on the beach," he said. "Take a deep breath and let it out very slowly. Lean back on the water; it's supporting you—it's going to hold you." As she slowly exhaled, she could feel Ray withdraw his arms. For an instant, the water was a soft, secure cushion, and then, as she doubted that fluid could hold, she began to sink. She tensed her body forward and plummeted, seat first.

Ray grabbed her arm and pulled her up. "Almost!" he said. His eyes were a rich color against his browning skin as the two of them stood dripping together. "Try again," he said, and she obeyed. This time she trusted his arms, felt, instead of a darkness pulling her down, the combination of flesh and water holding her up. "Don't be afraid of a little water in your face," Ray said. "You're neck's still too stiff." She arched her back as he told her to, and this time stayed afloat for more than a second until a slight wave nudged her and she again descended.

"Once more," Ray said. This time he instructed her to lie back on the water with only his hand under her back to support her. It was marvelous. Her body was buoyant, and the firm cushion of water let her lounge into it as into a mattress of sponge. She felt herself smile; she felt the sun shine on her face. Then Ray withdrew his hand, and the mattress faltered. She felt herself struggle, but tried not to strain, tried to keep her back arched, her head low, to relax. She managed to stay afloat for ten or fifteen seconds. "You're getting it," Ray said, "you just need to practice a little. Try it on your own." But Rosie was suddenly tired. She headed for more shallow water, but turned to watch Ray's bold strokes carry him out in the direction of the single sailboat.

"How about a beer?" he said when he finally joined her on the blanket. He finished one in silence, gazing happily toward the lake, and began another while Rosie finished hers. Suddenly he was looking at her, frowning. He slipped his sunglasses down and looked more intently.

"What's the matter?"

"You're really burnt. Or at least, you're getting there." He put the beer down. "I should have thought. Your skin is a lot fairer than mine."

"I don't feel burnt," Rosie said. She wiggled her shoulders back and forth.

Ray moved over and put his hand flat against her back. "Your skin's pretty hot," he said. "Did you bring anything?"

"Like lotion? No."

He stood up and looked around. The sun was low enough to have produced a patch of shade outward from the willow tree. "Put your shirt back on," he said, "and let's move the blanket over there." He was still frowning when the blanket was relocated, closer to the water, partly in sun, partly in the willow shade. "That tackle shop back on the other road has a sort of general-store counter," he said. "Why don't I see if I can get some sort of cream? We need more beer anyway."

"We could just go home," Rosie said.

"And miss having a picnic supper?" Ray said. "Not on your life." He grabbed the wallet and car keys from his pants. "And don't eat all the chicken while I'm gone," he said.

Rosie lay back on her trouser-pillow. The shade, although slightly mottled, felt more restful than the afternoon sun, but this time she did not sleep. She thought of Ray standing in the sunshine, swimming far out, supporting her in the water. A troop of five teen-agers charged noisily down the little cliff and across her stretch of sand. They were carrying portable radios, blankets, frisbees, and three six-packs of beer. "Jeez," one said loudly, "people all over the place."

"That's okay, Pete," another one said, "you and Marlene can do it in the bushes." The others laughed.

Rosie felt self-conscious as they disappeared beyond the willow tree, as though she ought to be swimming, or hiking, or anything but sitting on a blanket alone. She moved again to the water and waded along the edge, ankle-deep, kicking up little sprays before her. The fisherman and fisherwife, as she liked to think of them, were gone; she wondered what their catch had been. She went a little deeper into the water and moved west into the shallows near the willow tree, lingering when she reached it, mesmerized by the patterns of light and shade. The water was clear here, stiller; she could see small pebbles on the sandy bottom, each distinct in its wet stone hue, each individual. She could see her own feet, white, shell-like in their distorted paleness. A breeze flicked through the tree and the pattern of leaves on water shifted, danced, moved everything above and below in a natural kaleidoscope.

She watched the slither of darker shade on blue-green water—slivers of blue, slices of green, moving black pebbles that were not really moving. The movement of the water slid, curved toward her feet, and she smiled, her eyes a little out of focus in this plenitude of light. Then she saw it. The lines of green and black came together: what curved over her feet, its head near her ankle, was a narrow snake. She did not think; she reacted from the spinal cord. Her arms went out first and then her feet. In a movement so frantic she might have been stamping the creature, she leaped from the water. Everything was out of focus now: her sense, her breathing, her heart. Ray, with a small grocery bag, was coming across the beach, was almost to the blanket. She ran toward him, flung herself on him, fingers digging into his back. She tried to speak, but only breath would come.

"Now that's the kind of greeting I like," Ray said, laughing.

"Snake," Rosie said. "Snake!"

Ray let the grocery bag slide down into the sand and took her by the shoulders so he could look at her. "What's the matter?" he said. "You saw a snake? Where? By the willow tree?"

"In the water," she said. "Right by my feet. It was green and black. It could have bit me."

"But it didn't bite you, did it?" Ray said. "Most of the water snakes around here are harmless—like garter snakes. Did it look like a garter snake?"

"I don't know," Rosie said. She was calmer now and a little ashamed. "I didn't stay to check."

"Hey, that's okay," Ray said, pulling her against his rib cage and stroking her head. She leaned into him and let the warmth of his body soothe her. "I yell when I see a snake too—it's like mice—they move so fast they scare you. That's why snakes get such bad press," he said. She did not reply; she simply let her body breathe against him.

That was how it started. When she thought about it sometime before dawn in her rocking chair, she was sure that that undulating flash in the water had started it all. "You're all right," Ray had said, giving her another hug. "Let's have a look at that sunburn," and "Let's get at this beer while it's cold." She hadn't drunk that much—two beers to calm whatever was still shaking inside her. And she had clung to Ray, wanting to be near him as though he could protect her from evil, wanting to be in the shadow of his arm. He had smoothed Noxema from the cool blue jar over her shoulders as she sipped the beer, and she had smoothed some on his shoulders though he confessed, when she was finished, that he had wanted a backrub more than he feared a burn.

The sun was lower then. The rays that slanted in on them were capable of little harm, and the shade of the willow slid out farther and farther onto the beach. "Your back is still hot," Ray said, laying a cool hand between her shoulder blades as he finished a beer. "Let's give it another dose." The Noxema made his hand cooler, and he rubbed more slowly now, kneeling behind her, smoothing and smoothing over her shoulders, down her arms, down deeper and deeper on her back. Then he put his arms around her, folding her arms beneath his, cradling his face in her neck. It was more soothing than any ointment could have been. They were motionless, looking out over the water, and all her earlier tremors calmed, ceased, smoothed out as ripples smooth when the wind dies. She could see inside herself peaceful water, a clear bottom, a shore where no sudden undulations could sweep across her feet. She wished to stay on that shore forever. She could not really have said when Ray's mouth and nose began, almost imperceptibly, to nuzzle her neck. When he made a noisy, gobbling motion at her ear lobe, she laughed. "That tickles," she said.

She could never understand how what happened so fast could happen in slow motion, or how their slow progression could have happened so suddenly. He was kissing her neck, slowly, making little nudging motions with his lips as a fish might make against the glass. She reached up and ran her fingers into his hair. It was soft and curly and very slightly damp. Her fingers began caressing his scalp. He made a humming sound of pleasure, and she continued the motion, ranging farther over his head. She was amazed that her fingers knew to do this, that it seemed so natural, so practiced. She felt very pleased with herself.

Perhaps that was why she did not really notice his lips opening wider and wider on her neck, sweeping her skin, softly devouring her flesh. Yet, afterwards, remembering, she knew that she had noticed it, that she could close her eyes and feel the exact sensation travel through her. Perhaps she had been a little drunk; perhaps she had wanted for so long to secure him, to keep him, to have him always with her; perhaps with a female instinct she did not know she possessed, she was fighting against a lonely future that until September had seemed so inexorably set. At the time, it seemed she did not notice that as her hand crept slowly through his hair, his hand had slid onto the bathing suit that covered her breast, but she must have noticed—else, how could she remember?

His kisses circled her, caught her under the chin, on the Adam's apple, on the open triangle at the base of her throat as he moved to the front of her. She had both her hands in his hair then, softly kissing the side of his head, as his mouth left her collarbone and traveled around and down. She knew she should tell him to stop, that this had gone far enough, but his hand was gone from her breast now; both arms were around her, his hands caressing her back. She knew she should speak, but her mind was busy with each new sensation, each new inch of skin that his lips covered, and she waited, somehow, for a pause in which she could tell him to stop. Even the next morning in her rocker, she did not know

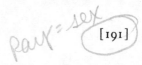

how he had so swiftly swept the strap from her shoulder, the cloth from her breast. She was too astonished to speak when she felt his mouth there, taking great gulps. It was like nothing she had felt before, except perhaps that kiss beside the frozen crystal creek. Currents in every part of her came alive, and the ripples traveled down. . . .

Ripples of shame traveled up and stained her face as she remembered it. "Ray," she had said, pushing his head away from her, "Ray, you can't do that!" He raised his head, and his eyes looked directly into hers with an expression that both frightened her and pulled at her—an immensity of longing that some old, unlearned impulse in her, some primordial remnant of the waters, wanted to envelop and embrace.

His head moved, not back toward her breast, but to her mouth, and he was kissing her as he had kissed her when the world was a fog-bound white. *Was it wrong?* she wondered, as she felt his mouth, his tongue. . . . Her head was clearer now. He had said she did nothing at the creek that she need ever feel guilty about. . . . And then another thought flicked through her: could she save him like this? Could she heal some dark wound within him? Would she still receive mysterious calls if she held him to her breast?

Ray was rising to his knees, pulling her with him. His hand on her lower back swept down under her buttock, pulling her body toward him, almost under him, pulling her against a hard protuberance that hit against her pelvic bone, her thigh. She began to struggle when she realized what it was.

The next day in her rocking chair, she was more frightened. The force of his body against hers, the force of the urge that seemed to have taken over his will, scared her more than it had on the beach when her fear had forced his body away from hers, and they had knelt there, staring at each other, until she heard the voices of the teen-agers and realized that her breast was still bare. Was that force, that urge, she wondered, normal? Was every man so possessed? She tried to think of a man like her father, like

Jack, like Father Griffin even, but she could call to mind no such images. All that floated before her now was the fat man in *Doctor Zhivago* forcing the blonde girl onto the bed.

She had covered herself there on the beach; she had grabbed her blouse and buttoned it, and was packing the picnic basket when the teen-agers, still lugging blankets and frisbees, but not so much beer, trooped through again from the opposite direction. Ray had knelt there helplessly, then began to hand her things for the basket, to put on his clothes, to stuff the empty beer cans into a paper sack. They had said nothing as they folded the blanket and followed the raucous sounds of the teen-agers back toward the dirt parking lot. She sat gingerly on the car seat, picking at a hangnail, waiting for Ray to turn the ignition key, waiting for the car to start. He turned to her when the motor was running. "I'm sorry, Rosie," he said. "I'm sorry . . . I know all the things I've said. . . ."

"Why?" she said. "Why did you let it happen? You were the one who wanted just to be friends. . . ."

"I know," he said. "I mean, I don't know. Too much beer, maybe. I lost my head. . . ." He was gripping the wheel as though he were in a race, as though he were about to round a tremendous curve, and he began shaking his head. "I want to make love to you, Rosie, I really do . . . but I want things to be right. . . ." He shook his head harder. "I'm sorry . . . you'll have to forgive me. I lost my head."

They drove home mostly in silence, the sun still flooding the prairie and making fields of sprouted winter wheat into flats of translucent green. There was so much pain in his face that at one point she reached out and touched his shoulder. "It's all right," she said. "It was my fault too. Don't blame yourself so much."

His left hand reached over and covered hers on his shoulder. "Thanks," he said. "Thanks, Rosie." But it wasn't all right—that much she knew clearly. How could she trust him to touch her again—though she wanted him to touch her, to comfort her for the distress his touches had brought—how could she trust herself? The fear she felt the next day in the rocking chair, the recognition of that surging force, had begun then, and she watched him as he drove, his face again set in that sternness which made him a stranger. She loved this man—her own behavior, her own yielding, was evidence of that—but she didn't know him. She didn't know what made him come and go, advance and retreat, rush out to declare his love and then run back to the safety of friendship. They were nearing St. Ives. "Are you hungry?" Ray said. "You didn't get any supper."

"Not really," she said.

He looked at his watch. "It's almost seven; we're due at Tom and Gina's in half an hour anyway."

She looked at him in amazement. She hadn't thought of the Pratts' party. "Just a few friends," Gina said when she called unexpectedly on Friday. "It's important to Tom—please come." Rosie had accepted on Friday, but she was different now, changed, as though some new coloration on her skin would let everyone know what had almost happened. It was not possible to do the usual things in usual clothes when you knew inside that you were not the same at all. She remembered going to the store for the first time after Mama's death, going to school as a young girl the morning Jack told her she had epileptic fits. It had not seemed possible to do those things, and yet she had done them. "Take it in stride," one of the voices inside her counseled, "other women have experienced more than this and have walked the streets after."

"Well, look at you two!" Tom said as they stood on the doorstep an hour later in clean summer clothes. "You can certainly tell where you spent Sunday." Rosie felt the flush of panic spreading until she remembered the sunburned brightness of her skin.

"Quite a crowd at Lake Shetek," Ray told him. "You should have been out there."

The others commented on her color also: Father Griffin, Carol Ann, and a couple from the public school staff who were sunburned too. No one else came. It was a strange party with a strange sense of expectation as they passed the usual small talk over cheese and crackers. Gina still entertained, as Ray said, "like a city girl," serving small snacks rather than the usual St. Ives fare of sandwiches, cake, and jello at ten or eleven o'clock. She brought in an apple torte at 10:30, and Tom seemed to take it as a sort of cue. He cleared his throat and adjusted the black frames of his glasses. "Gina and I have some good and some bad news," he said like a TV announcer. "The good news is that I've gotten the principal's job at a new school in Edina. The bad news is: we'll have to move. . . ."

"But you must come see us," Gina broke in. "You all go to the Cities sometime or other, and you must come stay."

"I wanted to wait till it was all settled," Tom said, smiling now, "but I signed the contract last week, and we just signed a guy from Le Sueur to take my place. His degree is from Mankato State, and he's been teaching in St. Peter. Name's Steve Bowen," he looked over at Ray. "Said he was your cousin, or cousin's son—I forget which—a really nice guy. He's already out of school, so they're moving into the old Prickett house next week." Tom sat back against the davenport.

Congratulations and regrets and promises to visit spilled on top of one another. Rosie said the usual things and turned to Ray. "Your cousin," she said. "How nice! I'll be anxious to meet him."

Ray smiled. "My cousin's kid," he said. He looked tired. Rosie watched Carol Ann whisper something to Gina, and Gina's eyes widen. She'll be in the Cities too, Rosie thought; they'll see each other . . . and then she realized with a pang that all three of them were moving from St. Ives.

The stars did not fade that night as she sat in the rocking chair in the sunroom, facing a dark and empty street. The sky lightened and absorbed them like liquid into dough. It was not possible to sleep, not possible to stay in bed. Her body ached from too much sun (her shoulders were covered with tiny blisters), and her mind ached from a sudden deluge of events after weeks and weeks that seemed static. She allowed herself bits and pieces of the scene at the lake: Ray's face as he declared a splashing war, his look as he questioned her about the snake, his jawline as he drove silently homeward.

She saw him at the party after Tom made his announcement, looking confused, befuddled, as though a door had opened somewhere that he hadn't known existed. He'd said almost nothing, she remembered. She had not realized the Pratts meant so much to him—that he would hold their loss so dear. Or perhaps it was his cousin—perhaps Tom's announcement opened memories he had intended to keep sealed. On the way home, he had been strange also, retreating into the stern and silent profile she had almost come to fear. "I'm sorry about this afternoon," he said as they walked to her door. His head was down; he seemed to say it to the sidewalk.

"It's okay," she said, without conviction. "It doesn't matter." There was an awkward pause when they reached the porch. Rosie started to turn her face up to be kissed, but checked herself. Ray's hands were in his pockets; he was toeing a loose edge on the Welcome mat.

"Ah . . . I need to talk to you sometime," he said. "There's something we need to talk about. . . ."

"Fine," Rosie said. She hadn't expected guilt to affect him so much, but it was something of a relief—maybe their friendship could continue after all. "Fine," she said again. "When?"

"Not tomorrow night," Ray said, "I promised Greg Berger I'd take a look at the transmission in his pickup. How about Tuesday?" He looked up for the first time, but didn't smile.

"Fine," Rosie said. "Oh—I go to that ceramics class with Gina at quarter to eight, but you could come for an early supper. About five or five-thirty?"

"Good," Ray said, toeing the mat again. "We'll talk. About five-thirty." He gave her a quick smile, a quick, perfunctory kiss, and turned down the walk, leaving her with the door still unopened.

She concentrated on his face in its sudden confusion, in its uneasy dejection, as the sky began to gray that morning. She was fighting off her own sense of loss, she realized, her recognition that Carol Ann would be absent too. She was fighting off her own shame, the memory of all those sermons on purity, fighting as she had fought off thoughts of confession the morning after the chivaree when she started to pack Jack's clothes. Somehow she must assimilate the afternoon's events: the guilt, the suspicions, the panic and the joy that kept breaking through. "I'll just confess it," she told herself as she waited for the dawn to come. "I won't go over and over it like I always do, I'll just go to Worthington this weekend and confess it like the time after Christmas; I'll just find some words to give him an idea of what happened and let the priest worry about it. . . . I'll just take it in stride," she told herself, "I'll take it all in stride." And as the robins in the old elm began to sing about the emerging light, she almost believed that she could.

independence

Chapter XIX

WHEN THE LIGHT FINALLY DAWNED ON THAT MONDAY MORNING, IT dawned in ordinariness. The splendor of the day before was gone. No amount of watching could dispel the clouds that had crept up from the southwest during the night and hung now on both horizons, threatening a day-long rain. Rosie didn't see the sun rise; she saw a gradual permutation of dark shapes into their daytime identities. She wondered if she was like that, a dark shape gradually being revealed by an indirect and unflattering light. Was Ray? Were they like the dark bulk of the grain elevators that even as their colors came clearer still hid their contents from sight?

She would have done better to sleep. Dora called promptly at six to say she had thrown up four times during the night, and would be out at least two days with the flu. Furthermore, Dora's circle of the Ladies' Aid was selling lunch at a farm auction that afternoon to raise money for new altar cloths. Would Rosie stand in?

Rosie stood most of the day, it seemed. She switched the menu to hot dogs, stirred up a great vat of beans, discovered ants in the latest shipment of sugar cookies, and explained to each and every first grader that there was no milk because the milkman was late. Ray arrived, all apologies, in the middle of the third grade, muttering something about the distributor on the truck. The high school girl who usually worked the serving line also had the flu, and the sub was slow, moody, and refused to wear a hairnet.

Through it all, Rosie's back radiated heat and soreness. She'd worn an old cotton blouse, but even that pulled at her skin with raspy fingers that never let her forget yesterday's events.

The auction ran much further into the evening than usual, and a sudden shower only prolonged it and added dampness to the heat. The lack of sleep had pulled like a weight on her muscles all day, and by 9:15 when the last box of assorted tools was sold, Rosie felt dizzy and a little nauseated. She wanted to sleep, but she was twelve miles from home. She wanted to clear her mind to a screen where only the road and the traffic would appear as she drove, but it was as useless as trying to fence out frogs. "I really want to make love to you, Rosie," Ray's voice came back. "Occasions of sin are all around us these days," said old Father McGraw. "Some sicko!" Carol Ann said, slamming down the phone. "Rosie, who do you think it is?" Dora wondered.

Her thoughts were so jumbled, so overpopulated with past and present, with longings and fears, that she almost missed the St. Ives cutoff. It was nearly ten now. She drove past the church, knowing something was amiss, but had parked in front of her own door before she was able to identify the problem: the kitchen light was burning in the church basement. "Drat!" she said. She had probably left it on when she went back to get the big coffee urn she took to the auction. Mrs. Geil would have called Dora by now, and Dora would tell her again about the electric bill. She sighed and heaved her body out of the car. She was at that point of weariness and tension where she would not sleep anyway—her legs would give a sudden jerk just as she was drifting off. She might as well walk in the night air and clear the nauseated feeling from her head.

She realized as she stepped in and out of the shaggy elm shadows that there could be another explanation: Carol Ann could be on the phone. It was all right, she told herself; if that were the case—perhaps they could talk awhile, perhaps she could get at least the obscene calls off her mind. . . .

She moved toward the soft glow that shone below the even softer colors of vigil candles shining through the stained glass windows. There was a comfort in the light, a consolation. When she reached the outside door, she closed it silently. She had a sudden fear of what the dark staircase might hold; but no, someone *was* talking on the phone. It was a low, amused murmur, a cozy sound of secrets that are not really secret at all. Rosie paused for a moment, warmed and intrigued by the private music of the sound. The murmur stopped with a slight humming sound. There was silence, but a silence somehow full of motion, and Rosie held her breath as she pushed the swinging door.

The light came from the kitchen, but it fell in an unimpeded line through the open doorway and gave sufficient illumination to the dark couple entwined beyond its reach on one of the old pews that lined the cafeteria wall. They sprang apart as the swinging door made a whispery scrape against the floor; but the time, too, was sufficient. She had already seen the half-supine posture, the straining arms, the hunger of the kiss. . . .

"Rosie!" Carol Ann whispered on an intake of breath.

"Oh my God!" the young priest said.

She wasted no time. She let the door swing back toward her face, turned on her heel and marched up the steps. "Rosie," the priest called after her, "wait!" but there was no waiting. She pushed through the heavy outside door, letting it slam—who cared who heard it?—and strode up the street toward home without looking back. "Rosie!" the young priest called after her from the doorway, but softly. It sounded like an urgent echo in the damp May air. She ignored him. He would not pursue her on the street, she knew. At least he had shame enough for that.

The phone was ringing when her own door closed behind her, but she didn't answer it. She stood in the doorway of the sunroom and tried to absorb the images that swirled around her, the thoughts that pulled in and out, making and severing connections in the brain. It was important to identify, to put a name on what she felt. Something burned in her chest like heartburn; but it wasn't heartburn, and it wasn't grief. It was all those sermons—all those years of whispered sins, and fear of hell, and nuns saying girls must be modest, must be careful, must not cause men to sin . . . all those years of squelching images that floated before the mind, of fearing the body, of wondering "how far you can go." All the guilt, the sense that something vital had passed her by, the shame rising like fluid in her throat. . . .

Why were they trying to call her? Were they going to apologize? Did they think she wouldn't recognize a passionate embrace when she saw one, that she didn't know what vows of celibacy meant? She stalked through the house to the kitchen, jerked the tea kettle from the sink and set it on the stove. The coils began to glow like a circular brand. She remembered standing in the living room, feeling the solid world shudder as the nun announced that she was leaving the convent, feeling the supports she had always clung to slipping fast. . . . *She owes me money too*, Rosie thought.

And that was the worst of it—it made you petty, and she didn't want to be petty. It made you small and clucking and eager to pick at bits of other people's sins. . . . There were only so many ways you could be: you could be free and easy and never make judgments and have no morals at all, or you could be tight and petty, picking at small sins, small wounds as chickens did, pecking any spot of blood until all was bloody and the injured chicken died. Or you could be solid yourself and trustworthy, but expansive—you could decide things on the basis of love, as Carol Ann had said. . . . "Said that, huh?" Jack had said. "She'll get a tit in the wringer yet."

A pale plume of steam was beginning to come from the kettle and its warning scream began to sound. Rosie reached for the knob, but there was another sound. It came from the back door where someone was knocking. "Rosie," the young priest was calling, but not so loudly the neighbors would hear, "Rosie, open up." He paused for a moment and then knocked again. "Rosie, I know you're upset—you have a right to be—but can't we talk?" Another vision of the young priest came back to her, and this time he was in the cafeteria weeping. "I can't be alone all the time," he was saying. "I can't be alone like this. . . ."

For a moment her anger vanished, and she moved the kettle off the coil and went to open the door. "But it's wrong, wrong," a voice within her said. "How can you be the only one expected to be pure?"

The priest looked gray, as though a subsiding flush had drained his face of its usual color. "I don't have any excuses to offer," he said, standing on the top step and gazing down at it. She did not move back to let him in. "What can I say, Rosie, except that I love her, and she's going away, and I'm a man."

"And that makes it all right?" she said.

He closed his eyes and looked downward again, shaking his head. "No," he said. "No, it doesn't—at least not in the usual terms—but someday priests might be able to marry . . . and then a few kisses wouldn't seem so bad. . . . And we weren't doing it out on the street. . . ."

"No," she said. "No, you were using the cafeteria."

"I'm sorry," he said, shaking his head again. "Look, we didn't plan this to happen—we didn't plan any of this. Things happen . . ."

He looked up at her. "You're really angry, aren't you?"

"No," Rosie said, "why should I be? It doesn't hurt me any." But she could hear the anger in her voice. "It's just . . ." she began in a softer tone.

"Just what?"

"It's just that I counted on you. . . . I'm mixed up about so many things, and you . . . well, you made it easier. You were free, but you still believed in something."

"And it's different now?" he said softly. She had a feeling he was scrutinizing her face, but she couldn't look at him. She thought she was going to cry.

"Yes," she said. "It's different now."

"Oh, Jeez . . ." he said as he dropped his head onto one hand and then put both hands into his pockets. "Rosie, I feel awful. What I've done to you is worse than anything. . . ." He tried to take her hand, but she put it behind her. "Don't ever go back from where you've come," he said, "not because of me or anybody else . . . Okay, Rosie?" She said nothing, and he breathed deeply in and out. "It's late," he said, "let's talk in a day or two, okay?"

She nodded. There was nothing to say.

He backed down the steps and started around the house.

"Rosie," he said from the sidewalk, "I still believe in something. . . ." Then he moved out of sight.

She wanted to cry more than ever as she closed the door and moved back through the silent house. *He'll go too*, she thought. Carol Ann was leaving, and the young priest would probably leave, and Sister Gaelynn would leave sooner or later. . . . They'd all go off somewhere and marry and love. They'd live in some happy land free from the mine-field of conscience, free from guilt pulling at the back of their throats. . . . And when they were gone, she would be left in St. Ives with the old nuns and the old priests. All the old feelings would come back—all the old fears— and she would sink deeper and deeper into the prairie . . . deeper and deeper into what she had always been. . . .

She did not expect to sleep that night; she was far too exhausted for sleep, but her tears seemed to loosen the strings that kept her muscles taut, and when she realized that the tears had stopped, it was morning.

Neither the priest nor the nun came through the lunch line that day. Father Griffin sometimes didn't eat, Rosie knew, and she overheard Mary McIvers saying that Carol Ann was leaving for Mankato with the debate team. She had worked in a somnolent manner all afternoon, her mind drifting, her eyes barely in focus. It was how she needed to work to preserve the calm, to keep herself anesthetized. When she had put the church kitchen back in order and checked the supplies for the next day, she drifted up the street as a blown leaf might drift, despite the fact that it was spring, that things were rooting and taking hold. She drifted through her door and into the kitchen where the meatloaf and baked potatoes were ready for the oven, and the jello was already in the mold. She found the envelope on the floor by the door when she came downstairs from changing clothes. It was sealed, but a message was written across the back: "I thought I ought to return this. I'll call you when I get back." The contents weighted one corner of the envelope, and she knew before she opened it that Carol Ann had returned the cafeteria key. Suddenly the house creaked around her, a repository of stale, leftover air. A key turned in an imaginary lock. She needed to get out, to escape into the open, to let her thoughts break free.

So Carol Ann needed a key to make phone calls, Rosie thought as she raked dead leaves from the flowerbeds, slashing at them with the teeth of an old bamboo rake. *So she needed a key so the other nuns wouldn't infringe on her privacy . . . wouldn't find out about her new job. . . .* The anger that had been Rosie's first response last night came back again: they had used her—they had made her an accomplice—and they didn't have the decency to tell her what was going on. "Deceit," she muttered to the small black ants that scurried over the peony buds as though they had a purpose. "Deceit," she said to the young delphinium she snapped off with her rake. But what had she expected? It was the way things worked: people deceived you for their own purposes—to keep you with them when you were growing up, or to leave you when you were grown. . . .

"You look like you're attacking the enemy with that thing," Ray said.

She turned and glared at him. He attempted a smile but with minimal success. "Did I scare you?" he said.

"No," she said. "I'm sorry. I was just thinking about . . . about some people. . . ."

"I hope it wasn't me," Ray said with a little laugh.

"No," she said. "It's just some people from school . . . some people I lent a key to. . . ." And then, because she was too tired to fight it any longer, the story came tumbling out. She told him about the drunken priest as they put the rake away and went back to the house; she told him the real purpose of the Sioux Falls shopping trips as he ate his meatloaf and hers got cold; she told him about the scene on the cafeteria bench as she poured him another cup of coffee and brought out some brownies for dessert.

"Funny," Ray said. "That's the part that really gets you, isn't it? The fact that you caught them making out? Since I was raised a Methodist, I'd be more shocked by the drunkenness."

"No," Rosie said, "what gets me is they lied to me—they used me. It's happened before. The one thing I can't abide is deceit."

"But they could hardly tell you they were . . ."

"They didn't have to tell me anything," Rosie said. "They didn't have to bring me into it. But they did." She put down her fork, went to the counter, and pretended to adjust the coffee pot. She could hear her voice take on an edge of tears. "I can understand getting drunk, and I can understand her wanting to leave . . . and I think I'm enough of a human being to understand falling in love . . . but I can't understand lying to somebody who trusts you—who's helped you—I can't understand letting a lie go on and on for months. . . ." She caught herself before the tears broke through, returned to the table, and took a deep swallow from her coffee cup. Ray said nothing. He was playing with his fork on the plate. "I guess it doesn't matter much," she said. "They'll all be gone soon."

"Yeah," Ray said. "I guess so." He was still playing with the fork. The silence became uncomfortable.

"You wanted to talk," Rosie said, "and I've done all the talking. . . ." When he didn't respond and didn't look up, she said, "What was it you wanted to talk about?"

"Oh, nothing much," he said. He looked at his watch. "You've got to meet Gina for that ceramics thing in ten minutes. We can talk some other time. . . . I'd better help you clean up."

"No," Rosie said. "Leave the dishes. What was it?" He had still not looked at her.

"Nothing to worry about," he said, getting up. He went to the cupboard and began carefully putting the leftover pickles back in the jar. "I just wanted to apologize again about Sunday," he said. "I know I say one thing and do another. I just wanted to tell you it won't happen again."

Rosie didn't believe him. He was, as Pa used to say, beating a dead horse, but there was a stubbornness about him that made her think he would say nothing else. He picked up his jacket, said he would call in a couple of days, and left by the back door.

What did he want? she thought as she finished the flowerbeds the next afternoon and broke dead canes from the raspberries along the fence. What had he wanted to tell her? She planted a few petunias in front of the porch. The rambling rose on the side looked thorny and feeble on its trellis. It had done poorly this winter, but the flowers had never been much. She could plant a different rose, she reasoned, something deep and lush from Burpee's catalog. Or she could fill the bed with another kind of flower. She examined the trellis: the bottom was stuck into the ground and the top fastened with wire to metal eyelets screwed into the porch. Pliers and a stepladder were all she would need to remove it.

"How come you're taking that down?" Ray's voice said behind her a few minutes later.

"I don't know," she said. "I just wanted to." They stood there awkwardly for a moment before he put out his hand to help her down. Ray looked different today. His facial muscles were tense, and his eyes had a flickering anxiety. She had not expected him. "Would you like a cup of coffee?" she said.

"Yeah," he said. "Yeah, that'd be good." He followed her into the house and stood by the counter while she measured grounds into her old percolator. "Your sunburn looks better," he said. That wasn't why he had come—to check on her sunburn—he hadn't even mentioned it yesterday.

"I wasn't expecting you so soon," she said. He didn't answer. She watched him walk to the table, brace his hands on the back of one of the chairs, and then turn to face her.

"Rosie, something's come up," he said. "I need to go away for a while—to go out west. I want you to come with me." She stared at him, not comprehending. There was determination in his face, as well as nervousness. Whatever he was anxious about, he had swallowed, as one swallows a necessary dose, and now he was determined to go forward. "I want you to come with me," he repeated, his eyes not leaving hers. "I got this job offer—in Billings, Montana. I got it a few weeks ago, but I just found out today that Mellomilk is planning layoffs. . . . Billings won't hold this job anymore—I have to go right away. . . ."

"What job?" Rosie said. It was the only question she could formulate. "At a dairy?"

He shook his head. "A soft-drink distributor. I'd be assistant manager." He seemed to see some of the confusion in her eyes. "We'll get married," he said. "I have a friend in Billings—a priest —we can go there and get married."

"Why?" she wanted to say, but it was the wrong question. Why so fast, so sudden? Why go away? Why are there things you don't tell me? Why is everything out of control? And yet, he was asking her to marry him . . . he was asking her to go with him—to be his wife. It was more than she had hoped for, more than she could grasp. "Now?" she heard herself say.

"Now," Ray said. "Tomorrow. I'd like to be on the road before the traffic starts. We'll head for the Black Hills and then on to Billings, and . . . and we'll get married as soon as we can. . . ."

Something in his last phrase slowed her, like a blinking warning sign. "As soon as we can?" she echoed.

"In a few days," Ray said. "As soon as we can get a license. I don't know how long it takes to get a license in Montana. . . ."

"But why Montana?" she said. "Why can't we get a license here?"

"Because I have to go," he said. "I can't pass this up. I'm not a wealthy man, Rosie, and I don't want to leave without you." He was pleading with her, but he was also impatient. His eyes shifted to the floor. "I love you, Rosie," he said. "I don't want to be without you."

She crossed the few feet that separated them and put her hand on his arm. A dozen voices, a dozen emotions were exploding within her, warning her, cajoling her, shouting their glee. . . . "I love you too," she said. "I just wasn't expecting this." He pulled her against him and buried his face in her neck. He seemed to need comfort, consolation, and she didn't understand. "I love you," she said again. "But aren't there other jobs here?"

He pulled out chairs from the kitchen table, seated her and then himself, keeping her close enough to touch. "Not very good jobs," he said. "This area is kind of depressed. And why not go, Rosie? St. Ives hasn't been that good to you—and you'd like the West—the air's not muggy, and there are mountains. . . ." She met his gaze without responding, trying to search his eyes. He lowered them to his hands again. "Things here just haven't gone that well for me," he said, "except for you. If I'm out of work for very long, I'll have trouble paying my debts."

"I have some money," Rosie said. "I have two thousand in traveler's checks right in the bureau."

"Good," Ray said. "Bring it. You can get what you need out there. That lawyer can rent your house, and in a couple years, when things are better, we can come back if we want, and live in it. . . . I need you, Rosie," he said. "I want you to go with me. I really want you. . . ."

It was what she had always wanted to hear, but it seemed old or unreal now that she was hearing it, as though she were in a late night movie. She wanted to go back to the business about debts, about things not going well. . . . She had a crazy vision of Ray in a poker game, of men in green eyeshades with half-smoked cigars and strange bulges in their pockets. . . .

"It will be an adventure," Ray was saying as he took her hand and began to stroke it. "We can pretend we're nineteen and have to elope. . . ." He was telling her she was beautiful, she was sweet. He was telling her he had not been happy for years and had never really expected to be happy again . . . and then suddenly, there she was! He promised that he would always take care of her, that he would get a priest to marry them, that he wouldn't touch her in the meantime—if she didn't want him to. . . . He respected her: if she wanted it that way, there were always motels with twin beds. . . .

"I don't know," she said. "I just can't believe that things can change so suddenly. . . ."

"I have to go," he said with a kind of desperateness. "I don't want to leave you here by yourself."

She started to say she would not be here by herself, but in that moment she saw herself rocking on an empty porch in an empty town, the years that sifted by so alike that she could not remember them. Carol Ann would be gone, the Pratts gone, the priest gone too, and Gaelynn. . . . She saw herself as an old woman, rocking on the porch with a rug on her lap. Once someone had loved her, but he had gone away . . . he was gone like the rich leaves of summer, and she could hardly remember his name. . . .

"Don't look so scared," Ray said. "It'll be all right. I promise you—it'll be all right." He stood up then and said he had to make some arrangements before the milk plant closed. And he wanted to give her some time to think—he knew he had dropped this on her all of a sudden—and whatever she did, his love wouldn't change.

"I'll call you at five-thirty in the morning," he said, standing and pulling her up with him. "All you have to do is say 'yes,' and we're on our way. I'll be here by quarter to six."

"I don't know," Rosie said. "I don't know what to say."

"Say 'yes,'" he said, looking at her, and for the first time, smiling. He brought his mouth down on hers and kissed her with great tenderness, though she felt little. When she opened her eyes, he was still smiling. He touched his forefinger gently to the end of her nose. "This is our secret, okay?" he said. "I can hardly wait."

"What now?" Rosie said to herself, standing in the middle of the kitchen floor. "What next?" She had the short-breathed feeling of having walked into her own dream—into the kind of tale she once used to weave. She wanted to call Ray back, to make him say it all again, or put it in writing, or give her something tangible—some concrete object—to verify the reality of what she had heard: Ray wanted to marry her; he wanted her to elope with him less than twelve hours from now. She gave a short laugh, but it wasn't funny, and it wasn't something from which she would wake; the proposal had been real.

Rosie unplugged the coffee they had never drunk, climbed the stairs to the little room that had been Pa's office, and sat in the rocker. The air was close, still weighted with a heaviness left from winter. She went to the window and raised the sash. It was evening now; the light was waning, and the fragrance of impending summer came to her from the west. West was where they would go if she left with Ray tomorrow—westward toward horizons that would never contract and press down upon her as these horizons did—westward as those covered wagons of her youthful dreams had done, into a new life, a new land, an opening meadow of morning and song. . . .

"But . . ." the voices within her said, "but . . ." She leaned on the window frame and tried to let them sort themselves out. She hadn't known Ray was hard up for money. She could have lent him money—or given him some. He never even mentioned financial matters except when he made those trips to Illinois. . . . The image of the poker table flashed before her again—of fedoras and muscles bulging beneath pinstripe suits. What was the name of the town Ray went to?

No . . . she shook her head to clear it. That was ridiculous. Ray had no more to do with that kind of setting than her mother did. His face, when it floated before her, was smiling, his forefinger caressing the end of her nose. "I can hardly wait," he said.

She couldn't wait either. She had waited long enough—she had waited almost forty-two years for someone to love her. If she didn't marry him, if she were not brave enough to run the risk, she might never have another chance. . . . "Well, they had their chances," Mama used to say of people who didn't amount to much. She saw an old woman rocking away the seasons with a rug on her lap. . . .

And yet . . . there was his uneasiness, his hurry, the slight misalignment of his face. The urgency of getting the job in Montana did not ring true. What if this were all a ploy to get her to some lonely motel in South Dakota? Or what if he did intend to marry her, but the license took time? She pictured a woman standing in a slip in a cheap motel room, her back to a man who stood in the shadows, her eyes full of fear. . . . But Ray had promised, had said he would not touch her until she was his wife. Ray had given his word.

Rosie lowered the window and went to her own room. She would decide later; it was impossible to decide now . . . but if she *were* to go. . . . She thought of the traveler's checks in the buffet drawer, of packing a lunch, of Mama's old leather suitcases in the dust of the attic. She would need plenty of clothes, a nightgown, something warm for evenings, and cool things for daytimes in the sun. She would need a good dress to be married in. She stood at the open closet door, trying to feel what it would be like to really leave here, to close the door and leave all this behind. She reached out to untangle the shoulder of a blouse that was caught in the long sleeve of another. She had stood at the open closet like this before, she remembered; she had stood here one night when the phone had rung, and . . . yes . . . yes—she had stood here the night she first feared that the obscene caller was Ray.

That was it. That explained his need to run away, his hurry, the embarrassment that had slightly altered his face. That explained why the story about the job didn't fit—because there *was* no job—or if there was, there was no hurry. There was only someone—man or woman—who knew the truth, who could expose him. . . . Rosie sat down on the bed, breathing hard. That was why Ray was running and wanted her to run with him—he was running from disgrace—and he was trying to insure that she could not reject him. Anger flared in her, and she closed the closet door hard. So he wanted to elope, did he? He wanted to drag her off to some godforsaken place where no one knew them, and he could start his telephone game all over again. He wanted to marry her so that any revelations would come too late—so that divorce would be her only recourse. . . . For better or for worse, that was the story. . . .

But maybe not. What if she didn't go with him, if he didn't run? What if his face appeared in the Worthington paper: "LUVERNE MAN CHARGED." She could see women talking over their shopping carts in tones the children couldn't hear—men saying, "Hey, d'ya hear about that guy that used to haul for Mellomilk?" She could feel Dora's searching eyes, could hear Edna Mueller say: "You poor thing, you . . ."

No. She couldn't let it happen. He had to go; he had to leave before word got out. Maybe if he left, the person he feared would just keep quiet; maybe the whole business would never come out. Maybe if she went with him, people would suspect nothing but an elopement; maybe they would laugh a little and say, "Well, still waters run deep, you know. . . ."

But to marry him—to live with a man who slunk into darkened

phone booths, pulled his cap low, changed his voice. . . . To wake up in the night and feel him watching her. But if she loved him . . . if she loved him and supplied his needs—made sure that his hungers were satisfied . . . if she bore him a child or two. . . . Maybe that was her mission in life; maybe that was what she was meant to do—to sacrifice herself for the sake of this man—to risk her own life for his salvation. She saw herself ministering to him, giving all that she had for his good, and she felt the same kind of nobility she had felt as a young girl when she dreamed of going to Africa as a nun.

She started down the stairs, relieved at the serenity she felt, but it was momentary. "You don't really think you can save him," one of the voices within her said, "you just can't face the thought of being alone." It was true. "I want him," she said as she sank into a chair in the sunroom. "I want him. Why is that wrong?"

She rocked for a long time in the light that turned from a translucent silvery glaze to a deeper and deeper blue, but nothing came clearer. There was no one to ask; there was no one to tell. The phone rang once, but she ignored it. She let it drift off into the haze of every other remembered sound. When it rang again, she thought of Carol Ann. "I'll call when I get back," the note had said. So the young nun was calling—the young nun who was going away not just to a job, but to life and love and marriage . . . to sharing her bed with a priest. . . .

Rosie stopped rocking. She walked past the door to the dining room, past the ringing phone. At the top of the stairs, she paused and entered Pa's old study. She took out a piece of plain white paper and wrote a note. "Dora," it said, "I am going away for a while. I don't know when I will be back. I know you can manage since there are only three days of school left. You can use my pay for this month to get some extra help." She started to fold the note, but added one more line. "You have always been kind to me," she said. "Rosie."

She put the note into an old business envelope, sealed it, and wrote Dora's name on the front. As soon as it was fully dark, she would slip down the street and put it under Dora's door. It would insure that she did not weaken; there would be no way then of turning back. She pulled the roll-top of the desk down and ran her hand over it fondly, feeling a little sad. If Pa hadn't died, if he had sat here for years and years, adding columns of figures and doing whatever business he did, things might have been different; Mama might not have hung on so hard. She might not be faced with this choice. . . . But he *had* died, Mama had died, Jack had died, and she, Rosie, was not going to die. Not yet, anyway. She was going to pack two suitcases and drive off blithely into the dawn and live the life that had somehow been pilfered away from her. She would go to the attic for the old leather cases. It would be dirty up there; the weather had been warm enough to bring all the spiders out, but it didn't matter. She was going to live in the world as it was now; she was prepared to face a little dust.

Chapter XX

WHEN SHE REMEMBERED THE NIGHT OF HER ELOPEMENT, SHE would remember it in a clash of bells. There was no sleep that night, no respite from the sense of speed, of motion, of blood that raced through her veins, of nerves that crawled within her limbs and would not allow her to be still. The phone rang off and on, a demanding, abrasive presence, but she did not allow herself to pick it up, to enter the room where its loud bell clanged. It might be an obscene call, and she would have to strain to recognize or not recognize the voice. It might be the priest or Carol Ann, and she had nothing to say to them now—nothing that would not come out sounding bitter and betrayed.

But what if the caller was Ray? What if he changed his mind or had something important to tell her? She went downstairs to the dining room, lit the little lamp beside the phone, and dialed Luverne.

"Ray," she said. "Ray, were you trying to call me?"

"No," Ray said. "No. . . . Have you decided?"

"I can't sleep," Rosie said, "and the phone was ringing. I thought it might be you." She looked at her watch. It was twelve-fifteen. "Did I wake you?"

"I can't sleep either," Ray said. "Maybe we ought to start. We could sleep later. Do you want to?"

Rosie looked around the room as though it could give her an answer. There were shadows along the back wall, and in the paucity of light from the small bulb, the house seemed mined, dangerous. The phone would ring again; the front door was not safe from messages; and worse: people would go away and leave her. . . .

"Yes," she said, knowing that by morning she might lack courage. "Yes, let's go."

She finished putting clothes in the old leather cases from the attic. She made sandwiches for the road. She put the traveler's checks and all the travel brochures in her purse. She went out with the flashlight, picked up the trellis that was still lying on its side, and dragged it to the basement. She locked the back door and checked the locks on all the windows, and she hardly thought at all. She was sitting in the dark in the sunroom, her bags around her, when Ray's car pulled up.

They were both strangely silent as they took their places in the car, both like children awed into silence by events of their own making, sitting uneasily on a suddenly stiff seat. The church tower slid past them; the stores of the main street were dark. The stop light at the highway blinked flashes of red over the closed Standard station, and the elevator reared up like the giant shadow of a finger and thumb.

They rolled slowly toward the South Dakota border past fields that floated in the darkness like a familiar dream. "I know every fence post," Rosie thought, "every farm, every tree. . . ."

The car lights that flashed through the back window were harsh, disturbing. There was a sudden jangle of speed and sound and high beams. "The police," Rosie thought, "the police coming to stop us. . . ."

"Damn it," Ray said, and stepped on the accelerator. The car swung past them at tremendous speed. It wasn't the police, it was a large sedan with a Worthington license. The patrol car was right behind, its flashing light stabbing the interior of their car. "Jesus Christ!" Ray said, and slowed the car again.

The patrol car disappeared over a slight rise, and the siren trailed off, leaving them with a graver silence. "Must've caught 'em," Ray said. They drove for a mile or two through darkness lit only by the security lights of occasional farmyards until red taillights appeared again, closer, closer. . . .

"They're stopped," Rosie said. "The police car's stopped."

"Probably pulled over that Pontiac," Ray said, but took his foot off the gas. A telephone pole was dangling at a crazy angle just beyond the patrol car, and the wire drooped dangerously close to the road.

"My God!" Rosie said. The Pontiac lay on its side in a field of winter wheat at the bottom of a slight embankment. There were no tracks, no sign of its leaving the road, but it had snapped one telephone pole and nearly toppled another. A state trooper was shining a flashlight through the shattered window, and another stood next to the patrol car, talking into a radio mike. A body in a green jacket was lying face down ten feet beyond the sheared pole.

"Holy cow!" Ray said. "They must have been doing at least a hundred." He pulled off the road just beyond the state patrol car and had the door open before he had the engine off. "Stay here," he ordered Rosie.

She rolled down her window and peered out. The state trooper who had been talking on the mike was moving his car so that its headlights shone directly on the wreck. Through the shattered windshield, Rosie could see a bloody arm, dark hair and a piece of blue jacket slumped together on the bottom side of the car—a jumble of limbs, of parts. It was impossible to tell how many were in the car. Ray had reached the trooper who was shaking his head, and Rosie started to get out of the car. She saw Ray peer in through the windshield and remain motionless for a moment; then he looked up at her. "Get back," he yelled. He said something to the trooper who said something back, and then Ray was running toward her. "They already called the ambulance," he said, talking fast, his face bloodless and rigid, "but they might be dead. Get back to the nearest phone. Get the priest. It's those kids." She looked at him blankly. "Those kids from school," he said. "The ratty ones. Go!"

Rosie put Ray's car in gear, aware that the seat ought to be moved up, aware that she was somehow angry at this disturbance when so much was at stake, aware that it was petty to think such thoughts. Lights were burning in the third farmhouse down the road, but she could rouse no one. She drove nearly to St. Ives and stopped again, leaving the car running. "An accident!" she said to the farmer with a two-day beard who answered the door. He was trying to button the overalls he had pulled on over his underwear. "I need to use the phone." A woman in a hairnet peered from a stairway door.

"St. Ives Rectory," Father Griffin said when the phone had rung twice.

Rosie wanted to hang up. She felt sick suddenly, as though the blood that was draining away in the wheat field were washing over her. She started to ask for Father Schwartz, but she choked it back. "An accident," she said, hoping her voice would be anonymous. "High school kids. They might be dead."

"Where?" the priest asked.

"The Lismore road. About a mile before you hit Highway 75."

"I'll be right there," he said. "Rosie?" he added tentatively. She hung up.

The scene seemed garishly lit when she returned. Mary Kay Mueller was standing next to an ambulance from Luverne, shivering like a little girl in a blue dress that stopped well above her knees. "It's that Runkle kid," she said. "And two others. They were at the dance in Worthington but they left before we did. That's not their car, either—they probably stole it. Jeez," she said, "Dumb."

Johnny Mueller moved from one spot to another with a crowbar that Rosie never saw him use. The ambulance driver was lowering himself carefully through the side window that was now on the top of the car, and Ray was handing him a backboard. No one seemed to talk, to breathe. A body was hoisted out, one arm dangling at a grotesque angle. The jacket was soaked with blood, and the jeans were completely torn from one leg. Another man from the ambulance shook out a blanket and tucked it around the body, but didn't cover the head. Rosie felt herself exhale with relief, then caught her breath again. The body with the green jacket had been covered with a sheet.

"I can't believe it!" Mary Kay kept saying. Rosie couldn't

believe it either. She could not believe a nun and priest tangled together in the dark. She could not believe that the old suitcases from the attic were in the trunk of Ray's car. She could not believe that Gil Simons' green jacket was on a corpse. He was just a kid. These things did not happen. They might happen in novels or in the movies or TV; they might happen in a place like Chicago or New York. But not in St. Ives. Not all at once. *Marion Runkle won't believe this either*, Rosie thought. Or maybe she will. Maybe that's why she's always so disconnected— so she can believe what happens to her. Her face, her floating blonde hair, were easily called up. "That priest was drunk again," Rosie could hear her say, looking at nothing. "Mickey seen it." Rosie saw Jack's face, Pa's, Carol Ann's looking up with guilty surprise. . . . Marion's face floated before her again, and this time it was an open pool of pain.

One of the voices within her began to panic, began to say that young men who stole cars, crashed them and died, would go to hell, unconfessed and unforgiven—that women who ran away with men, who gave themselves over to unholy lusts could also die—could end up unshriven in a ditch on some lonely road, unnoticed below an embankment. She began to realize that she must go back, that she must retrieve her bags, her old life, her security—that she must go back and confess her sins. She looked at Ray in the field just below her. He had blood on one sleeve, and he was stooping to pick up something. It was a piece of metal and he threw it down again. He moved a little closer to the pole and stooped again to retrieve some piece of debris. He was a stranger; she knew nothing about him. Why had she thought she could go away with him?

A car door slammed behind her. "Over here, Father," she heard a patrolman call. Father Griffin, wearing the same blue sweatshirt and clutching a box of holy oils, paused just on the edge of the ditch and looked at her—an intense look that was both pleading and sad. She looked away. His eyes were weary and bloodshot. *Drunk again*, she thought. Other voices inside her were suddenly louder than the voice that bade her to repent.

She had done nothing sinful yet, they told her; maybe she never would. She was in a world where one impossible shock was followed by another and yet another, these voices said—where everything was upside down, and even God would have trouble keeping track. She had made the decision. She had sealed it with Dora's note. To go or not to go, to sin or not to sin was already behind her. Whatever crime it was to love had already been committed.

The priest had climbed into the ambulance with the last of the three victims. The door had closed behind him and the siren was starting; the ambulance was moving into the road. Ray was coming across the field toward her. "Let's go," she said.

Rosie had never seen South Dakota beyond Sioux Falls. "More of the same," Jack had said once when he returned from a trip to Rapid City sponsored by the feed company. She didn't see much of South Dakota now. Her first impression was of vastness, of night air that stayed close to flat land—a thin layer of earth and air between the fire below and the emptiness beyond. She felt drugged again, as though her body and mind had drifted to sleep long ago, and only her will remained attentive. "Want me to pull over so we can sleep?" Ray said somewhere beyond Mitchell, but she declined. She peered at whatever the headlights illuminated and read Burma Shave and Wall Drug signs as though they were secret guides.

"You know, I feel rotten about those kids," Ray said at one point. "I thought they were such bastards—such a bunch of little punks—and now that Simons kid is dead. . . ."

"It's not your fault," Rosie said. "You couldn't have done anything," but she knew she would feel a similar guilt if she were capable of feeling at all.

"Yeah, I guess," Ray said. "But it makes you wish you had at least thought of them a little more kindly. . . ." He lapsed back into silence, and Rosie went on reading signs and concentrating on the names of towns that were only a small flash in the darkness: Reliance, Kennebec, Presho, Vivian. . . . "In a few hours, we will need to stop," her mind was saying. "In a few hours, we will check into a motel. . . ."

She must have slept, though she was not conscious of sleeping. She was in an eerie wasteland of layered red and brown dunes made redder by the horizontal rays of early sun. The sand curved away from the road like a fiendish labyrinth, and even the light could not be trusted. She had been there before, she thought. It was a hellish dream and the metallic light was making her ill. She turned her head: Ray was there, and beyond his shoulder she caught a glimpse of a sign that said "Badlands." It wasn't a dream.

"Morning." Ray smiled. "I was wondering if I should wake you. I took the alternate route so there'd be something to see."

She smiled back and turned to the window, but her stomach seemed to turn with her. The inside of her head was not as stable as the deeply creased dunes, coated and hardened with bronze morning light. She lowered her head carefully back against the top of the seat and closed her eyes, hoping the whirling would stop.

"What's the matter?" Ray said, and slowed the car.

"I feel a little sick," Rosie said, "a little queasy. I shouldn't have slept." Ray reached over and felt her forehead. "I'm okay," Rosie insisted, but didn't move her head. "I just felt dizzy. It's better now." She opened her eyes again and the light seemed less hard, less painful.

"Can you reach back and grab my jacket?" Ray said. "There are some Life-Savers in the pocket—peppermint, I think. Sometimes that helps."

She waited a moment, letting her stomach settle back to its proper place, then turned and caught the jacket by the sleeve, feeling sick again when she saw smears of dried blood. It was the tan poplin windbreaker with plaid lining that she had seen him wear often. One pocket was heavy, and she pulled out a wrinkled handkerchief, a small spiral notebook with a green cover, plastic-rimmed glasses with a broken lens, and the end of a roll of candy. The notebook was about three inches by five with a metal spiral on top; it was dog-eared, and someone had printed on it with a heavy ballpoint pen, going over the letters several times in an adolescent hand: "*Private. G. S.*" Rosie resisted an impulse to turn the cover.

"Try one of those and see if . . . Jeez, was that in my jacket?"

"What is it?" Rosie said.

"It's one of those kids'—I picked it up off the ground—the glasses too. I meant to give them to the cops."

Rosie turned back the cover. It must belong to Gil Simons who was dead—the initials were his—but she was looking for a name. The first page was printed neatly in pencil with one entry in ballpoint and one in red ink.

M. Mc.
274–6698

Sept 13			
Sept 30	*		
Oct 5	Man answered		
Oct 20	"	"	
Oct 24	"	"	Forget it!

"That's funny," Rosie said.

"What?" Ray said. Rosie turned the page.

L. S.
274–5519

Sept 13	*
Sept 25	*
Oct 5	
Oct 27	*
Nov 3	
Jan 7	*
Feb 14	** (twice!)
March 2	

"Well, it seems to be a record of some sort: initials, a phone number, and then a list of dates. Some have stars beside them."

"Maybe his girlfriends . . ." Ray said.

Rosie turned the notebook over. The next page was short.

Sept 10   * (old one answered)
Sept 16   *   "   "

"That's the convent number," Rosie said. "This page has the convent number." Something tightened in her intestine, and an unreasoned fear was rising in her stomach as the nausea had moments before.

Ray reached over and took a quick look. "He called the convent and an old one answered?" he said. "Doesn't make sense."

It was beginning to make sense to Rosie. She flipped the soiled page over, almost knowing that the next number would be hers.

R. D.
272–6964

Oct 5   *
Oct 22   *
Nov 5   *
Nov 11
Dec 9   *
Jan 18   *
Feb 9
Feb 14
March 9
March 30   *
May 17   *

October 5 was the night the first call had come; October 22 was the Oktoberfest; November 5 was the night she had played bingo with Ray. . . .

There were other pages, but Rosie didn't read them, other initials and numbers that leaped and fell and formed a record of sickness and sadness and fright. Suddenly, everything was before her: Gil Simons' watching eyes as she bent over a water fountain but didn't drink, his face as Cheryl Hinely snubbed him in the cafeteria, Ray's voice in the November night: "You're here all alone, you know. . . ." Gil Simons' eyes, his face . . . Mickey Runkle's curled lip—"Bitch!" The phone receiver was hitting the floor, lolling on the cord like an obscene fruit, creeping like a mouse toward her naked foot. . . .

And then shame moved in—the awful shame of her own suspicions: "None of it happened before I met Ray," she remembered saying to herself, wedged by her thoughts into the opening of a closet door . . . maybe if I give him my body . . . but there isn't any proof . . . the voice is too high to be his . . . Is it a sin to suspect? Is it a sin to trust? Is it worse than the thoughts I have of his body?

"What is it?" Ray said. "What's the matter?"

"It's a record," Rosie said. "A record of his calls. . . ."

"What? What do you mean?" Ray put out his hand for the notebook. He steadied it on the steering wheel and slowed the car, his eyes taking quick flicks down at the soiled pages. He let out a low whistle. "The St. Ives Caller?" he said.

"Yes," Rosie said. "I think so."

Ray's eyes were glancing swiftly down the page again. "November 5 is the first time we went out," Ray said softly. "I had no idea he called that night . . . you never told me. . . ."

"I told you," Rosie said, her voice sharper than she had intended.

"But not that it happened that night . . . not till a lot later."

"I told you . . ." Rosie could hear her voice rising.

"It's okay," Ray handed her the notebook and closed his hand tightly over hers. "Let's not argue. What could I have done anyway? How could I protect you from the phone?"

"I told you . . ." Rosie said. She was crying now. "I told you . . ." The tears were coming fast, and she raised the hand with the notebook to her eyes, then hurled the soiled paper at the floor.

Ray stepped on the accelerator until they reached the top of a rise where a bronze sign explained the vista below. He pulled in and had his arms around her almost before the car had stopped. "It's okay, it's okay . . ." he kept repeating.

"No, it's not," Rosie sobbed. "It's not okay." She struggled against him.

"Shhhh," he kept saying, "shhhh." He was stronger than she, and his arms stopped the struggle. Her body wanted to relax against him, but she fought that too, and she tried to fight the sobs that poured into the open collar of his shirt. He was kissing and kissing her hair.

". . . all you've been through . . ." She heard his voice like a soft flow of water: "You keep so much in, Rosie—you never want to trouble anybody. . . . Just let go, sweetheart, just let go . . ." He kissed her head again.

"That poor kid," he said when her sobs had begun to subside. ". . . but it can't hurt you anymore, Rosie. It's okay . . . it's okay." His hand had found her neck and was stroking it with the lightest of pressures.

Rosie knew there were other voices struggling in her head, swimming as in a turbulent sea, and reaching out for her attention. She knew she ought to attend to them—to pull them in one by one and listen to their messages—to line up all the pictures in her head into one coherent sequence . . . but she was too confused, too weary. Ray's voice floated on top, and she clung to it as though she were a tired swimmer. She let the muscles of her neck relax into his, the solid warmth of his chest carry her weight, and she slowed the ragged ends of her sobs until they were part of his even breathing.

When they were back on the road again, she rested her head on his shoulder, her left hand tucked under his arm. She was back in the cloud again, as she was on the day he first kissed her, but it was not a cloud of crystals. The brown land of Dakota rolled over and around and under the car as Ray drove westward—over and under the brown upholstery, the brown tweed of Ray's slacks, and the brown thoughts that his arms had covered over, at least for a time. She was aware, dimly, that clouds disperse, that landscapes change, that one cannot be hypnotized by endless brown forever, but she rode in the brown cloud now, not smug, not serene, but in the blessed relief of numbness.

Chapter XXI

ROSIE TURNED THE MOTEL ASHTRAY ROUND AND ROUND IN HER HANDS, putting her little finger first in one slot intended for the cigarette and then the next. She would have to tell him what she had suspected. She would have to confess.

They had driven from the vista point in the Badlands that morning not in the silence she might have expected, but in soft conversation. They talked about the scenery, and the difference acidity makes in certain crops, and how varying terrains can affect the way you feel. She had joined in the conversation; she had clung to it, but all the while voices within her were saying: "You judged him falsely. You are faithless. You were willing to believe terrible things." Her fear of what would happen when they got to a motel—if he would try to take her, or if she would give herself—was lost in the larger fear of rejection—of letting him know the awful truth. She should have told him in the Badlands when his arms were around her but she had been unable to speak. She should have told him when he pulled into a rest area near Rapid City and said, "Maybe we should rest a little, as long as we can put the car in the shade." Instead, she watched him sleep, and then somehow slept herself. She should have told him at Mount Rushmore where he insisted on putting dimes in the telescope not only for her, but for a group of traveling nuns.

She hadn't told him over their early dinner, nor when he pulled into the Willow Rest Motel and said, "I'll ask for twin beds. Okay?"

"Okay," she had said, the roof of her mouth suddenly gone dry. Even this was a reproach. Ray was honorable; he would keep his word. She was the one who was treacherous.

Perhaps she would never tell him. . . . But then the secret would be a dark pressure building up inside her, seeking to explode. Every word she spoke in all their years together would be like the little round weight on Mama's old pressure cooker—a skittery lid over a head of steam. She had to tell him. Even if he went away, she had to tell him. "I'll tell him when my finger has gone through three more slots," she said, turning the ashtray more slowly; but the slots passed, and her mouth wouldn't open, and her throat felt thick.

"You planning to smoke?" Ray said, amused. He was setting up some folding stands for the luggage.

Rosie put down the ashtray, embarrassed, and tried to study the paintings in the room: one was a fall scene and one was a covered bridge in winter. They were pretty, but they gave her nothing to do with her hands.

"Look, Rosie," Ray came over, took her arm, and seated both of them on the edge of the bed. "I know you're nervous. I know this is a big step, and I rushed you, and you may be having second thoughts. . . . But you're making *me* nervous, honey, standing there turning that ashtray, looking scared to death. You can still change your mind. We can just travel for a while and get married later. Maybe I won't want that job in Billings. We'll just be together for a while, okay?"

"That isn't it," Rosie said.

"I meant what I said about separate beds, Rosie." His arms were around her now, and he was nuzzling into her neck. "I want you—you know that—but not if it costs you too much. As long as we're here, and I can hold you, I can wait, sweetheart. . . . Don't you believe that?"

Rosie pulled herself free and went to the bureau. She picked up the *TV Guide* and held it upside down. "That's not it," she said. "You may not even want to hold me." Her throat felt as it had in the dust storm, but she swallowed the dry, bitter saliva and went on: "I shouldn't have come. I did a terrible thing—I doubted you

[226]

. . . and I don't deserve to be your wife, but . . ." it came out in a spurt: "but I love you. I never had anyone in my whole life, and I couldn't lose you—I couldn't! So I came, and I'm sorry. I shouldn't . . ."

"What are you talking about?" Ray's voice was gentle and his arms slid around her from the back. Her body didn't give way this time; her shoulders were stiff and expanded.

"Please," she said. "Please sit down. Please just let me say this."

He held her for a moment longer, and then she felt his arms slip away.

"About the phone calls—the obscene calls . . ." she started. There was no answer from anywhere in the room. She rolled the *TV Guide* tighter and turned it as she talked. "I thought it was just some crank, some bum the first time . . . and then Sister Grace said calls like that are usually from someone you know. . . . And I didn't think anything of it. But they kept coming. . . . The night we first went out—we went to bingo—you told me to lock the door because I was there all alone, and a call came. He said, 'I know you're there all alone,' and I didn't think anything about it. But it kept on—and I didn't know it kept on for those other women—Mary McIvers and the nuns—I thought it was just me. . . ."

"And you thought I was making the calls?" Ray's voice came from across the room in a neutral tone.

"Yes," Rosie nodded. "No!" she said. "No, I didn't really." The words came tumbling now, spilling like grain down a chute. "I thought that I should tell you, or give you up, but I couldn't. I couldn't do it. And then I thought that everybody has some faults, and maybe because you'd been married and all . . . I mean, after your wife was dead, you were used to it and couldn't have it. . . . I didn't even care, because maybe if I gave myself to you, that was all you needed. I didn't think you were insane or dangerous or anything, and I thought that maybe I could help you. . . ." She was sobbing now. She was surrounded by silence.

"I love you so much," she said as the *TV Guide* shredded in her hands. "It was wrong. I know it was wrong. You can't have a marriage when one person is full of lies and suspicions. . . . When

I saw that notebook in the car, I could have died. I was so ashamed. I should have told you then. . . . But I thought if we could just get married, it would be all right. You could have what you wanted, and I could have you. . . . I'm so sorry . . . I messed everything up. . . ."

For a long moment, she heard nothing but her own sobbing. Everything, her dreams, her plans, the Rosie who was part of a couple, all that was gone. She was alone again and empty. Then she felt Ray's arms around her. They were gentle, but they were not strong, and his voice seemed sad and older.

"No, my pretty one, no . . ." he was saying, his hand stroking her hair. "You're not the one who messed things up."

"I'm sorry, Ray," she said again. "I'm sorry."

"Rosie, listen!" he said. "Are you listening? It's okay. I don't care what you thought. You loved me anyway. That's incredible—it's incredible that anybody would do that. Do you understand?"

Rosie nodded, her cheek against his. The warmth of his body was beginning to seep through her layer of regret, and it lulled her sobs. She almost believed that Ray understood, that there might be happiness ahead after all, but there was a certain sadness in his voice, a slackness in his arms. She pulled back until she could see his face. It was gray and grim and sad and loving all at once. "It's not okay," she said. "It's not the same. I ruined it."

"No," he pulled her back against him and cradled her face in his neck. "No, you didn't ruin it, Rosie. Just let me hold you; just let me hold you for a while, okay?"

They stood in silent embrace for a long time. Rosie felt like someone who has been fished from a freezing stream and must ford yet another to be safe, but for the moment she was on land. For the moment, she was warm and dry. As long as he held her, nothing awful could happen.

Ray loosened his arms slowly. He took her face in his hands and looked at her. She had never seen such a sad face. He kissed her gently, then dropped his arms and walked across the room. He was facing the window that looked out over the parking lot.

"I'm sorry," she said again, but he shook his head.

"I can't do it, Rosie," his voice was very low. "I can't go on with this."

"I'm sorry," she pleaded.

"No!" he said sharply. "It isn't that at all." There was a long pause. "You did ruin it, Rosie, but not the way you think. Your goodness shames me. . . ."

"I'm not good," she protested. "I accused you of horrible things—I misjudged you. . . ."

He half turned and put up his hand to stop her.

"I'll fight to keep you," she said. "I won't let you go."

"No," he said softly. "No, you won't fight." She saw his hands become fists as he turned back to the window again. He brought them down hard on the window sill. "God!" he said. "Why does it have to be like this? You're not the one who's false—you're too good, Rosie. I can't pull this off." He raised his head like a stricken bird, and something like a laugh choked out. "I wish I'd made those calls," he said. "It would be so much easier."

"What?" Rosie said. "What?"

His head went down again, and his voice was very soft. "I can't marry you, Rosie," he said. "At least not now. I have a wife."

The rest was never clear when she tried to sort it out. She knew there was a night when neither of them slept, and a morning when they parted. She knew there was coffee in the all-night cafe next door, but whether it was once or twice she couldn't remember. Sometimes bits and pieces floated into the picture that didn't belong to that night at all. She knew he had explained it, but she could see him standing with clenched fists by the motel window, and she could see him say words with his hands around a coffee cup, shaking as he pulled open the little plastic container of cream, spilling half of it on the formica.

"She wasn't herself, Rosie," he was saying. "They said she'd be as good as new after the first operation, but she wasn't. At first, she'd cry over nothing, and then, as time went on, she'd fly into a rage. Sometimes in the morning—I worked in the office then—I was an assistant manager . . . sometimes in the morning, she wouldn't like the socks I was wearing—I mean, this was just to the milk plant—and she'd make me change them a couple of times, or she'd take food out and say it was spoiled, and throw it on the floor. One time she got mad and pushed over a whole stack of tomato cans in the grocery store."

He took a swallow of the coffee. "And she wouldn't have relations anymore. Or if she did, she was cold as ice, or she'd start to cry when I tried . . ."

"I don't need to hear all this," Rosie said.

"But I need to tell you," he said—or maybe he had said that earlier in the motel when he tried to make her sit on the bed and listen. "What I told you about the tumor was true, Rosie; it's all true. But she didn't die. She might as well have, but she didn't die."

Rosie heard the words with great clarity of mind but no feeling. Perhaps in the future she would never feel. She saw his face with incredible sharpness: the lines around the mouth that were suddenly deeper, the tiny triangle he had missed when shaving. She watched his Adam's apple bob.

"I got really scared when she couldn't remember anybody's name," the throat was saying. "Then she couldn't remember the words for ordinary objects. And when they opened up her head again, they just closed it. . . ."

"Then why doesn't she die?" Rosie heard her own voice ask. The tone was cool and clinical.

"I don't know. Nobody knows why she doesn't die. They said it's a remission of some sort, but they're never supposed to last this long. Her heart is really strong, I guess."

In the cafe, there was a plastic cream pitcher of Elsie the Cow with a big red heart around her neck; it was full of pancake syrup. Ray was drinking coffee and playing with it. "A month after the surgery," he said, "she didn't talk anymore, and then she didn't eat. I had to move her to a place where they could feed her by tube. I used to drive thirty miles every day and watch her muscles waste to nothing, and then the doctor said, 'Don't be so hard on yourself. She doesn't know anything anymore.' "

He drained the last of the coffee cup and wiped the napkin across his eyes. "I went every day for over a year. I watched her until I couldn't watch anymore, and one day I decided that the only way I could go on living was if I thought of her as dead—and she was in a way—the Marilyn I knew had been dead for a long time—and that's when I decided to move."

"Moo. Moo-oo," said a little boy in the next booth as he poured pancake syrup into the ashtray.

"Shut up," his mother said. "You're supposed to be in bed."

And then Rosie was sitting on the bed, and Ray was standing near the window pleading with her—or was it before they went to the cafe when he said, "I was going to tell you, Rosie, I tried. . . . When I first got to Luverne, Hinely asked about my wife, and I said, 'She developed a brain tumor two years ago. . . .' And next thing I knew, he had introduced me as a widower, and there were so many people there, I decided to just let it slide. . . ."

"There weren't always people there," she said.

"I know. . . . And I kept telling myself I'd tell you soon—or I'd tell you as soon as she died—but it got worse and worse, because all that time had gone by. . . . And then when I came to the house to tell you the other night, you were holding that key to the church. . . . You kept saying, 'They deceived me . . . it's the one thing I can't accept. . . .' "

"I know," Rosie said. "I know . . ."

And then it was later. It was after they had been in the cafe . . . or it may have been when he pulled back the curtain in the room because he said it was almost dawn. But it wasn't a good dawn, not the kind that come over the prairie. The air was muddy, and the last stars didn't twinkle; they sank; they were blotted out. There was no sunrise, only muddled light through strips of stringy cloud.

"That teacher," Ray said in the unclear light. "That Steve Bowen, my cousin's kid from Le Sueur—he'd know. There really *is* a job in Billings, but I've had the offer for a month. . . . I just had to get you away before that kid showed up. He'd know . . ."

And another time he said, "I don't suppose it would do any good if I divorced her?"

"You can't," Rosie said. "You already explained about the insurance. You've got to stay married to cover her." She felt no emotion again. Her mind was incredibly clear.

"But if we could somehow find a way to take care of her—if we could work it out . . ."

"No," Rosie said. "You'd be divorced. And you lied to me."

And then he said . . . but maybe it was later, when he was closing the suitcases, or maybe it was when he was still standing at the window with clenched fists and tears streaming down his face. . . . She wasn't sure what he'd said then; she hadn't listened for a while. But sometime his voice was saying: "I never meant to hurt you, Rosie. I never meant to do this. I never even meant to fall in love. I just wanted a different place and different people to think about . . . I just planned to keep myself occupied; I don't know if I thought I'd remarry when Marilyn died or not. And I just wanted to be friends with you—I know I told you that—what harm was there in having friends?"

Rosie hadn't answered. "Maybe that isn't even true," he said. "Maybe I loved you from the start. I remember the first time I saw you. It was in the cafeteria one time when I was late with the milk. You had squatted down to talk to a little, tiny girl who was crying, and you said 'Oh, who cares what they called you? I know a secret they don't know: you're going to grow up to be beautiful.' I thought you had the kindest face I ever saw."

Rosie wanted to run from all kind faces, all sad faces. She had wanted to run all night, except for those moments when she felt stunned like an ox under the butcher's mallet, or when her body seemed to have floated away and her mind was crisp and rational and clear. She had wanted to run when he said, "But if we waited, Rosie . . . please wait. She could die tomorrow. She can't go on living year after year. . . ."

But there were times when Rosie knew she would do anything rather than lose him—when the years of empty arms and longings she couldn't even identify rolled her up in them as she sometimes felt the prairie rolling up and smothering the town—when the thought of returning alone to St. Ives was something that could happen only in a nightmare. The street in front of the church became the Avenue of the Dead then, and the square brick house where she had always lived became a mocking tomb. She would look at Ray, his fists pressing into the window sill, and she would feel those hands unfolding on her body; she would feel his lips softly tracing the line of her neck below the ear. She would go with him—she would throw over St. Ives and the church and all hope of heaven and all that Mama and the nuns had said, and they would make their own heaven. For a moment she would rest in that thought, as Ray's voice droned beyond it, and then the enormity of it all would roll over her—this man who had betrayed her, who had lied, who had denied one wife and would have made an adulteress of another, who would have made her share the burden of his sins. . . . She hated him as he stood there at the window; how could she live with a man she hated? How could she trust him? But they had all betrayed her: Father Griffin and Carol Ann, Jack who shouldn't have died, and Mama. . . .

She remembered at one point (but maybe it was a dream) that she was running through a field of corn stubble, dodging a tornado, seeking a tunnel in which to hide. But she ran in spirals, always darting back; the field was pocked with deep, dank, and hidden wells.

She came back from that field to long hours of slow revelations, and silences, and now and then a rush of words as sudden as ice breaking up in the flood of spring. She had listened to Ray's every scruple, to all the times he had tried to tell her and couldn't, to every chance that had played into his hand. She listened to his pleas that they go to the rest home in Illinois—that she see his wife for herself. He confessed over and over that he was selfish, that he was a victim of passion: "My God, Rosie, do you know how long it's been? I thought I wasn't alive anymore. I thought I wasn't a man. . . ." He told her what he had planned for their life together, or maybe it was what she had planned, and *she* told *him*. It didn't matter. Sometime he had said, "You take the car. Leave it with Hinely. I'll get it somehow."

Sometime he had written an Illinois address and phone number on a piece of paper. "When I'm free, when everything's settled down, I'll write to you, Rosie." Had he said that? "You don't have to answer; you don't have to forgive me, but for the rest of my life, Rosie, I'll want you back."

"No!" she remembered screaming, or something inside her had screamed. "No! Don't ever, ever touch me! I never, ever want you back!" But the paper was in her billfold; maybe she hadn't screamed; maybe she had said quietly: "I don't think so. I'm not that young anymore. . . . I don't know if there are enough years to get over this."

"Cry!" he had said at one point. "Cry, scream, hit me! Rosie, do something! I can't stand to have you just sit there like that."

She had cried. She had sobbed until she had no more breath, and her entire rib cage screamed with pain, but that was after he left her, she thought. That was after he called the taxi, and put the car keys on the dresser, and lifted his suitcase, and gently closed the door.

Chapter XXII

IT WAS DAWN AGAIN. ROSIE DEANE SAT UP IN BED AND PULLED HER knees to her breasts; her back was aching. She had gone to sleep at dawn or soon after in the slip and nylons she was wearing now. She had, at any rate, pulled back the covers and climbed into bed. She didn't know if she had slept at all as she lay in the semi-darkened room where daylight had gradually sifted in through the closed curtain, and then grown low again, and then was gone. Perhaps she had slept a little during the night.

Or maybe she was sleeping now. Maybe the last days and last year were all a kind of sleep where images and nightmares chased one another through a sky that was like a vast pale sheet, and she had lain in the meadow below, watching, her head cushioned on her arms, her face cooled by a sweet breeze through long prairie grass. Maybe she was dead, she reasoned. Death would be a sweet meadow, and a body as numb as hers might well be an illusion.

Brakes squealed, a horn honked, and somewhere outside her room, a truck shifted gears. Rosie turned her face toward the window, and her eyes caught something on the dresser: the car keys sat in the ashtray where Ray had left them. Pain entered the room as light would have done if she had drawn the drape. She ducked her head to her knees to avoid it, and then slipped down beneath the covers again, as though there she might find safety. "Hunger," said her stomach which had not eaten for a day and two nights. "Pain. Pain," said her mind.

When at last Rosie pulled her legs from the covers and slid

them to the floor, it was only because the body, which was somehow still hers, needed to move. She limped across the floor to the bathroom, rubbed her back as she sat on the toilet, brushed her teeth, and decided against brushing her hair. She put on clean underwear, began to put on the dress she had worn two days ago, then jerked it off and flung it in a ball on the floor. She pulled her burgundy pants from the suitcase, and found a white blouse. She ought to eat breakfast, someone inside told her, though she knew her mouth might refuse. She took her purse off the television set and counted the contents: $2,017.34 in cash and traveler's checks, a compact, a half roll of Life Savers, a comb, two Kleenex, a tin of aspirin, two sanitary napkins in a plastic sack. This was what she had in the world.

She knew with an animal's instinct that if she returned to this room after eating, she would die here. She would curl in the bed as under a stone, and the great sheet of sky would darken, and she would hibernate into a winter that would never end. She found that idea rather pleasant—to join her numbness to the numbness of the snake, the lizard, the prairie that slept within its own white skin. But some old animal within her insisted, gnawed as the coon Jack once trapped gnawed off its own foot. It was almost summer; it was a time for waking, a time for shedding skins.

She took her toothbrush from the bathroom, packed her slippers and an unopened bar of soap. She closed and locked her suitcase, put her sweater over her shoulders, flicked out the bathroom light. She left the motel key on the dresser and her dress wadded in a ball in the middle of the room.

She could not go back to the all-night cafe on the corner, so she drove, taking random turns, until she found herself in the old downtown area of Rapid City, parking in front of a coffee shop. To her surprise, she could talk. When she opened her mouth to order, a voice came out that sounded familiar. She could stir her coffee as any woman sitting in any coffee shop; she could spread the jam onto the toast; she could taste and swallow the scrambled eggs.

When she returned to her car, there was a problem: she

couldn't stay parked in a one-hour zone; she couldn't go to a restaurant because she had just eaten; it was much too early to find a motel. "You could go home," someone said at the edge of her brain; but Rosie caught a flicker of light through the leaves of the sycamore on the street by the St. Ives church, of Dora's curious face, of Jim Hinely circling, circling. . . . No, it was impossible to think of that much pain. She didn't bother to argue with the voice, she simply ignored it. She started the car, backed out, and drove. "Dinosaur Park," a sign with an arrow pointed. It would do as well as any; it was a place to go.

The park was almost deserted. Immense concrete reconstructions of the great beasts peered at her from a path that wound to the top of the hill. Rosie read each information plaque carefully. Dinosaurs had inhabited this region forty million years ago during the Mesozoic era. Fossils and footprints had been found in both the Badlands and the Black Hills. *All gone*, she thought as she climbed the hill. *All disappeared . . . one day here and the next day gone. . . .*

The first grouping near the base of the hill showed two beasts lunging at one another in combat. One looked more like an elephant or rhinoceros than a dinosaur. It had giant horns above its eyes and a shorter one on its snout. Its name was "triceratops" and it was fighting a tyrannosaurus rex, an awful creature at least fifteen feet tall. Rosie stared upward into the mouth of the second animal. It was one of the few that ate flesh, the sign said, and its mouthful of teeth was enormous. Rosie backed away as though she were in danger. One of these two would kill the other—that's the way it worked—that's how you became extinct: you killed off whatever was weaker, and then someone killed you. . . .

Near the top of the hill a brontosaurus, the largest of the prehistoric reptiles, stood. It weighed fifteen tons and had a two-ounce brain. It was a peaceful animal, the sign said, and was preyed upon by beasts much smaller. Rosie imagined a friendly, clumsy brontosaurus nuzzling its long neck against a tree, and then a sudden bloody and undeserved attack. The statue was eighty feet long, twenty-eight feet high, and could be seen for thirty-five miles, the sign said, but the real brontosaurus was gone.

The path curved downward, and another sculpture came into view: a strange creature with a tiny head and two rows of spade-like fins down its back. It didn't look much taller than Rosie. "It's a baby," she said, "a baby dinosaur." She ran to it and began running her hand over the rough concrete of its back. "It's just a little baby," Rosie said to herself, though the creature's back fins were higher than her head. "It had little feet and a little horned tail, and somebody killed it, and now it's dead." She felt a wave of sorrow for the vanished baby dinosaur. It was very ugly, and it looked big enough to take care of itself, but it wasn't; the unfolding of life was unjust. She ran her hand over the concrete armor of a backplate, and down the smaller and smaller concrete fins of its tail. "It had a mother, and other dinosaurs to play with, and it ate only grass. But it wasn't pretty and it wasn't strong enough and now it's dead—it can never come back." Rosie wept for the extinction of the dinosaurs. She leaned her head against a concrete body in Rapid City, South Dakota and wept that the brontosaurus and the stegosaurus would be no more. Her tears made small, dark streaks on the concrete hide, and she wept for the extinction of the powerful and the meek, for the death of everything young, for a bright, imagined world that had ceased to be—she wept for everything that would never come again.

A family with children had come over the hilltop. "Oh, look at the little one," one of them squealed. Rosie pulled her head away from the dinosaur, digging in her purse for a Kleenex as she continued down the hill. She didn't stop to look at a duck-billed, almost comic creature that stood on her left. When she got to the car, she wept again. She headed south, because she must head somewhere, and all along the highway, signs intruded on her field of vision: Stay! Eat! Visit! Turn Here! Don't Miss! The signs were painted orange and yellow and green and shocking blue and red. Last Chance! a sign said, Last Chance! Five hundred yards later it said: You Missed It! Rosie felt that she had failed.

She tried to look not at the signs but at the highway, at the hills and trees that rose all around her—not trees as she was used to them with round, friendly shapes, and embracing shades, but spikes of evergreen, sharp conifers, twisted pines. These were the "black" hills, she remembered; the Indians called them that. Old rites had been performed here, old pagan rituals, old atrocities, perhaps. There were unspeakable secrets even now, even in late morning. . . . Somewhere in the hills there were forbidden shrines.

Last Chance! another sign said. Ride a Cable Car up the Mountain! See the National Monument! Chapel! Waterfall! Rock Garden! All for $2.75!

A floating, rational Rosie followed the arrows to the parking lot and bought her ticket. It was all easy now; the Rosie in pain was almost gone. A teen-ager with acne helped her into the little red cable car that hung like a yoyo at the bottom of a string. Rosie sat near the front and waited, but the car was not yet full. "My, I feel a little queasy," a lady behind her said. Rosie felt nothing. Through the front window, she could see the cable-run: a wire supported by poles up a path cleared on the mountain like a razor swipe. "When it starts, I will be afraid," she told herself.

The car moved off the platform with a jerk. *Now it's starting*, Rosie thought, but the fear didn't come. A cable car ought to put you in danger, she knew. It should dangle you over a precipice, or whip you down a glacier's edge. "I think I could walk up faster," the queasy woman's husband said.

The top was also disappointing. Little white paths made of rock that looked like the ground oyster shells Jack sold for chicken feed ran in several directions. "Monument View——>" one sign said. "Rock Garden——>" "Chapel——>" said another. Between the rocks on the mountain top, someone had planted purple and white petunias leading to a little waterfall that sprayed down from the top of a boulder hunched up against the sky. It emptied into a pool lined with blue vinyl and tarnished pennies. Rosie looked at the size of the stream and the drain in the pool. "I think they've got a garden hose up the back," she said, but no one heard.

The "chapel" had a roof, a back wall, and two posts holding up the front. It also had two benches. On the back wall was a shiny picture of Jesus, a large version of the grainy two-pictures-in-one that come in the cereal box.

"See how Jesus watches you," a young mother was saying to her little boy. "Now move over there. Is Jesus still looking?" She smiled at Rosie. "The eyes follow you wherever you go," she explained.

Rosie walked back and forth to check it out. The eyes followed her all right, but Jesus had a wall-eyed, suspicious look, and she didn't like him.

She turned away from the eyes and followed the signs toward the monument viewing point. The path led upward and around a bend to a lookout with a sturdy fence. Rosie expected any second that the great faces would loom before her, but they didn't. "Where is it?" she said to a teenage couple lolling on the fence.

"Over there," they laughed. "You can see the side view." She followed the pointing finger to a small group of profiles that distinguished one outcropping of rock from the many around it. "You can see it lots better at the National Park," the girl volunteered, "and it won't cost you nothin'."

"Thank you," Rosie said. She was ready to take the cable car down. She felt immensely weary and will-less, as though feeling nothing was wearing her down. She retraced her steps toward the platform, but rounding a curve, she saw a faint footpath veer off into the woods. She felt a mild urge to follow it, to know its secrets, and in her will-less state, that was urge enough. She stepped onto a floor of soft, brown needles, and the forest closed behind her like a door.

The path dropped down rapidly. There was no sunlight in the forest, but her eyes adjusted, and it wasn't dark. There was lichen on some of the stones now; they were not bare as before, and tangled roots protruded up through the needles of the path. Her foot caught on one of these, and she fell forward, grabbing a branch to stay herself. Just above the branch she was holding, another branch had been broken; pine pitch had seeped out, run down, and hardened into an amber bead. "Wounds," she heard someone say, and it was the other Rosie speaking, the one capable of pain. The tree was bleeding its own kind of blood, and the other Rosie had returned. She started to run, despite the roots, and it was that other Rosie running. She stumbled again, and this time fell, her face skidding against the dirt and a stand of spindly fern. "Damn," she said, not trying to get up. "Damn it." Her cheek and her knee were both smarting. It didn't matter, she knew. She could lie there in the dirt, alone and injured, and no one would care. Her eyes filled with tears of pity. It was true; no one on earth knew where she was, no one was concerned.

She sobbed quietly into the brown pine needles that picked at her face like straw. She wanted to cough forth her anguish, to let out the bitter screams, but the forest would not let her; it demanded silence; it offered only sleep. She lay in the path until her body stopped heaving, then she sat up and brushed the needles from her hair. She continued on the downward path, but this time slowly. There was no place to go; there was no hurry. Something rustled through the woods off to her left, and she stood still for a while, but then the silence resumed. She was very tired. She wanted to sleep. Sleep was all that seemed good to her.

Suddenly she stood in the light again. Not sunlight, for the sun had gone under, but a light that was strangely strong. She had come out of the woods into a narrow strip of meadow and scrubby juniper. A dead tree perched at its edge, silvery white against the sky. Far away were other mountains. She moved wearily, instinctively, toward the meadow's edge. "Be careful," the Rosie who had been cool and floating said. "There's a drop there," but the Rosie who was walking continued up to the edge.

The cliff dropped sharply for about ten feet, and then leveled out to a partially grassed slope that was steep but not sheer. It rolled downward for another hundred feet or so, and then there was another edge. Rosie could not see beyond it; there might be another meadow there, rolling down steeply, or the ground might simply end; hundreds of feet below would be a river or jagged rock. You could survive a fall from the point where she stood if you could stop yourself on the steep slope—if you could grab a bunch of grass that did not pull free, or a juniper sprig. Or you might roll; your legs would crumble from the ten-foot drop, and your body, like the tumbleweeds that blow across the prairie in a high wind, would simply turn over and over, picking up speed—would roll to that second edge and then over. Then you would not have a body anymore. You would float down that second slope, whether there was ground there or only air. You would be borne up by a mild mountain current.

She was very tired. She was tired of a weariness and ache that came from her very bones. She was tired of something—she could not remember what—that was clutching at her throat. She was tired of roads and paths and having to decide where she should go. Sleep would be better. It wouldn't matter if she slept here, because no one would know. No one would be worried. She would be causing no trouble. She would take all her old weariness and all her griefs, and she would go to sleep with them. She contemplated extinction the way she contemplated a bird, perhaps an eagle, that swooped from a neighboring mountain, spread his wings and simply coasted, stationary, on the great, buoyant mass of air. No one missed the eagle when he flew; all that he had ever lived for was that one long moment when he rode the air. She could ride with the eagle if she took one more step.

"She's going to do it," the rational Rosie said, but her voice was very small. "You've got to get her back from the edge—you've got to make her stop." She didn't pay much attention to that voice; it was a minor nuisance, but the voice continued, and she noticed that one of her feet had moved backward, and then the other, and then she was walking along the embankment, but several feet from the edge.

She was tired when she reached the parking lot. Her knees felt as if they had melted now, and her lungs were tired of such deep breathing. The sun had made the car warm, and the air inside it heavy; she wanted to curl into the upholstery and let the heaviness of her body seep into the cushions and slide away. If she slept, she could forget everything.

She drove by an act of the will, but stopped at the first filling station to ask about motels. "Half a mile back," the man said, "a whole bunch of 'em," but Rosie had stopped listening. Her eye had caught a partial profile and a husky shoulder as a man took his change from the attendant and pulled away. It wasn't Ray. Of course, it wasn't Ray. The car had Colorado plates, and there was a dog in the back seat. Of course, it wasn't Ray. She thought she saw him again in a Volkswagen van that passed her on the highway, and again in the corner booth of the Howard Johnson's coffee shop. Each time, a current of pain went through her like a shock from an electric fence. Each time, she was awake again.

"He's not here," she told herself. "He took a bus to Illinois. He's somewhere else, and you won't ever see him. He's gone." But the words were more of a wound than a consolation. "He's gone," seemed to echo in all her hollow spaces, and when the waitress brought her order, her eyes were full and she couldn't look up. She slept in a room at the Howard Johnson's. It was barely six o'clock, but she pulled back the sheets and crawled inside and let the great weights on her body overcome her.

Chapter XXIII

ROSIE COULD NOT REMEMBER WHAT HAPPENED IN HER DREAM THAT night, but it took place in her sunroom, and the windows that faced the street grew and grew until she was afraid she would fall. She woke groping for her quilt, her old walnut nightstand. When her fingers met motel formica, she felt a sudden longing for home. She sat up in bed and felt, above her pain, a need for the comfort of her rocker against her back, for the familiar contour of her flower beds, the smell of sweet clover mixed with the grass. She longed for the prairie where every road was straight and expected, where in dreams she never fell. She longed for home, but she couldn't go.

She couldn't face the questions, the curiosity, the stares at her face, and the ridicule behind her back. "No fool like an old fool," Mrs. Geil would say. "You said it," Edna Mueller would add; "still waters run deep." "Where did you stay?" Dora would ask and mean, "What happened once you got there?" She could never stand behind the steam table and face the nuns again, Rosie knew, never joke with Father Griffin. Most of all, she could never walk on any street she had walked with Ray without seeing again the anguish in his face, never enter any door without tasting the bitterness of her choice.

She could not go home, but she could not be still either. Without ever deciding to, she began to travel. She went to Custer National Park and to Sylvan Lake. She drove to Rapid City, bought a camera, and went back to the lake again. A man tried to pick her up in a restaurant in Keystone, and one night a man lurked in the shadows outside her motel. "In the dark, all men are the enemy," she'd once heard a woman say on TV, and Rosie decided it was so. She fled from them as she fled from the ghosts who followed her: the shape of Ray's head behind a dime-a-look telescope, the sound of his laughter in a dining room. . . . She went to Deadwood and tried to imagine the women of the old West; she went to Nazareth Caves and tried to pray. . . .

The Nazareth shrine was reached through a series of passage-ways that were enormous and damp and, like dream corridors, never-ending. The shrine itself was a large irregular room with a floor that had been leveled. Candles in stained-glass holders hung at various heights and cast moving fingers of green and rose and purple light on the dusty brown wall. She traced them, watching how the light darted across her hand. She had a sense that she had done this before, a sense of—what did Carol Ann call it—*déjà vu*? She had been in this place in another time, another body; she had once been covered with the same stroking light.

She remembered, then, the Rosie of September sitting on the porch, feeling lonesome and smoky, putting her finger into square after square of sun on her thighs. She could see that Rosie as she could see a photograph, and she realized that the figure looked strange and dumpy. The hair was cut wrong, the woman was heavier and slouching; she was allowing age and gravity to have too much pull.

"This is worse," she said, convinced. "That was numbness, but this is pain." She rocked herself away from the pain, from the edge of the endless pool. She was Rosie Deane, forty-one years old, sitting on a bench in a cave in the Black Hills, South Dakota, and most of her life was gone. She had known that in September, in the week of Jack's death, but then a new Rosie took over from somewhere inside her—a new Rosie who had somehow been there all along, who perhaps belonged to those adolescent mem-ories of sunshine and long grass. And that new Rosie had decided there was plenty to do. She had driven the car, bought the clothes, gone to the matinee. She had invited herself to a chivaree, made friends with the young priest, had accepted a date with the milkman. She was the one who kissed, who touched, who handled money, who said, when Rosie despaired of all standards except the most scrupulous, "but precisely how will you sin—who will you offend—if you go off together and marry him?" She was the one who had driven the car in the past few days when pain had blinded and choked her, and she was the one who had said, "You've got to stop her," at the edge of a mountain ridge where the sheer weight of hopelessness had invited her to step forth onto the air and float forever and forever down.

And then Rosie stopped. She backed up again to that mountain ridge and viewed it as on a little screen. The woman who stood on the cliff was weeping; her face was scraped and her hair hung with dead needles and leaves. She was not thinking of God or sin or old catechism questions; she did not choose to die—she was beyond choosing. She was a being so overcome with pain that her only instinct was to make it stop. She wanted only the anesthetic of sleep, the promise that there would be no more painful wakings.

But the other Rosie had *thought*. The other Rosie had said, "You've got to stop her"—had been capable of choice, and had made it. The Rosie who had sailed blithely into all the trouble was the Rosie who had saved her life.

Tears were splashing on her hand, and in the flicker of purple light they took on some of the iridescent splendor of oil on wet pavement. She imagined a range of colors, a range of light, a life in which fear of offending is less important than love, and she opened her arms to the other Rosie and embraced her. She had a sense of oil spreading over her pain, and though it did not go away, she was better able to endure it. She had been given the strength to choose life on that mountain, and she had chosen it. Perhaps this was what was meant by "grace."

Reptile World was a "must see" according to the travel book, but it was creepy. She had come only because she had nearly exhausted the Black Hills but still could not go home. The snakes stared with malicious, unblinking eyes from their little glass cages and curled and writhed around each other in a big open bin. When the afternoon show was announced, Rosie took her seat as though daring them to entertain her. A cowboy of sorts in a sequined shirt came on in front of a western backdrop and showed how to milk a rattlesnake. He held the snake under his arm, his thumb and forefinger on its jaw, and milked the venom into a little glass. Rosie didn't know why anyone would *want* to milk a rattlesnake. The cowboy said the venom was like the albumen of an egg. He said if you injected yourself with albumen, you'd probably die too, but Rosie doubted it. Everybody clapped. Another cowboy with a southern accent brought on a trained chicken which could count by making the right number of pecks on a little bell when asked to add and subtract. The answer was never higher than four. Then the program went back to snakes again, and Rosie left. A girl in a skimpy turquoise cowgirl suit had come on stage and was letting boas wind around her arms and legs.

"Snakes of North America," the sign on one side of the exhibit room said and, determined to get her money's worth, Rosie slid from case to case in a kind of fascinated revulsion: eastern diamond-back rattler, western diamond-back, copperhead, cottonmouth—all could kill you. Then the smaller or non-poisonous snakes: king snake, green snake, milk snake, hognose (who could roll over and play dead), garter snakes of various colors, bull snake. She slid past the garter snakes without looking —they were too close to a remembered willow and lake—but she watched the bull snake for a long time: "A native of various habitats in North America," the little placard said; "its diet consists chiefly of birds, birds' eggs, rodents, and other small mammals." She looked carefully at the snake's undulating body, at its lightly scaled roundness like a well-stuffed sausage, at the jaw with the detachable hinge. The snake raised its head and moved toward the glass. It flicked its forked tongue and opened its mouth as though to swallow. As it did, a hinge somewhere inside her opened and she stepped into the memory that had been hovering just outside her reach. She was screaming in horror, and the sharp edge of a rock was cutting her hand as she flung it, and it bounced off the snake's body, and she flung it, covered with weak reptile blood, again and again. . . .

She was twelve. It was the summer her legs were too long for all her skirts, and her slacks crept up well above her ankles. It was the summer she felt compelled to keep a diary and stole a half-used ledger from the bottom drawer of Pa's old desk. She would sneak it out under her shirt when she went for long walks, which were her only way of being alone, and she would move its hiding place from the bottom of her underwear drawer to the pile of feed sacks in the garage, to a small space behind the carrot box in the basement. It was the summer Mama's eyes were everywhere, noticing every pimple, every silence, every gesture of a high school girl or movie star that she tried on for size.

"He looked into my eyes, deep and soulful," she would write. That was the kind of thing they said in previews of movies with Cary Grant. Or she would record those emotions that usually floated at a distance from her, but sometimes banged against her like June bugs against a screen on a hot summer night. "I feel funny," she would write. "Not sick. Just funny. I feel like something is going to happen to me." Or she would make confessions: "Mary Lerner gave me an old lipstick her mother threw in the trash," she would confide; "she told me what comes out of the Kotex machine in the high school toilet." Or she would practice writing great novels like *Cherry Ames, Student Nurse* or *Girl of the Limberlost*. Rosie told no one about the novels. Mama didn't even like her reading them unless they came from the Catholic school.

She was looking for a shady place to write one day in early summer. She usually sat with her back against one of the older stones in the Protestant cemetery half a mile from town. There were wonderful old fir trees there where the wind would whistle just as she knew it did in Norway or the Canadian Rockies, and she didn't have to worry about its being consecrated ground, because Protestants didn't bless things. But today Protestant ladies were planting marigolds and petunias in the newer section, so she walked past the graveyard and then along the fence where a small slope of long grass leveled into a field of corn. It had been a wet spring and the lower ground was a little soggy.

She almost stepped on the eggs before she saw them. They were nestled in last season's grass which was twisted so cleverly into the new growth that it made only a dimple in the slope of slightly shifting green. Big eggs. A runaway pullet, perhaps? But the eggs were the wrong shape and too far from the nearest farm.

"Pheasants," she said, almost aloud. The most beautiful bird of the plains. Usually she saw them dead in the fall, dumped out from a hunter's sack, but sometimes one would flash up in a sudden flurry of color at the edge of the road and fly into the nearest tall corn. Once, when she was dreaming at the edge of Kanaranze Creek, two hens and a cock had come by, picking at various weeds, while she held her breath for what seemed like forever. And now she had found a nest, a secret dip in the grass, and she was the only one who knew.

After that, the nest became a shrine. She didn't visit it every day; she didn't want the hen to become nervous. It was a special thing, a time when she walked very quietly all the way from town, left the diary on a rock alongside the graveyard fence, took off her shoes and held her breath. She never saw the eggs again. She would tiptoe barefoot along the cemetery fence, and then, with excruciating slowness, move through the long grass toward the dimple on the slope. She would stop when she could see the pheasant's back. The hen was crouched low over the eggs, absolutely rigid, her instinct telling her to blend with the grass. Rosie never went closer. She knew she and the hen were both holding their breaths.

She was halfway out the door one day, her diary under her blouse, when Mama called. "Oh no, you don't," she said. "There's two dishpans of peas to shell."

"I'm just going for a walk," Rosie said. "I picked all morning."

"I picked all morning too," Mama said. "And I'm canning all afternoon. What's that on your face? Do you have lipstick on?"

"No," Rosie said. "And I have to go to the bathroom first."

"You'd better scrub your mouth while you're in there."

"You'd better scrub your mouth," Rosie mocked to her image in the bathroom mirror. Even her own face wasn't private. She took the diary from under her blouse and hid it in the stack of good towels Mama never used.

It was four-thirty when the peas were done. "Kin I go?" she asked.

"You have to set the table at five-thirty," Mama said with a warning look.

She had raced down the road to the cemetery, catching her breath in big gasps when she reached the gate. Then she moved more slowly, saving her breath, along the fence. When she reached the top of the slope, she hardly breathed at all.

Something was different. She could hear the sound of her own heart, but she could also hear the high-pitched peep-peep-peep of tiny birds. They had hatched! She stole closer, expecting the hen's mottled back, but she wasn't there. Rosie felt her heart go faster. She could see the nest now; she could see the little birds, fluffy brown chicks, their mouths open, their peeping strident with alarm. *I've scared them*, she thought. *They can already tell when someone's coming.* Then she saw the snake.

It was a big brown snake, the kind Lester Monk had chased her with on the school yard until the nun caught him and sent him home. "They don't bite!" Jack had said. "Jeez, you always get your pants in a bunch!" This one was half curled around the nest, his head on one side of it, his tail hidden in the grass. "They don't bite," Rosie said and took a step closer. Then she saw the snake's head: it was distended and the jaw was dislodged; the awful membrane of the mouth was stretched around a half-swallowed pheasant chick. Its soft backside and the ends of tiny wings protruded; the legs stuck out stiffly—like little stick fingers on something a child might draw.

"Damn you!" Rosie said. The snake raised its head, the chick still protruding, and fixed its eye on her. "Damn you," she took a step backward, and her bare foot scraped against something hard. The snake began to move as she bent for the rock, but her blind hurl into the grass caught and stunned him.

"Damn you!" She was crying now as she retrieved the rock, her foot only inches from the snake's head. "Goddam your filthy hide!" She hurled the stone again, this time accurately. The snake's tail twitched back against her leg. She didn't scream, but tears were running down her face. She pounded the rock down again and again until it was covered with reptile blood, and chick blood, and some of her own where the sharp edge cut her hand. Then she hurled it as far as she could throw into the soft rows of young green corn.

"Where do you think you're going?" Mama grabbed her arm as she raced through the door toward the stairs. "What's going on?"

"A snake was killing the chicks," she sobbed. "A big snake. It had one halfway in its mouth, and the legs were sticking out. . . ."

"What chick?" Mama said. "Where were you?"

"Pheasant chicks," she said. "By the cemetery. There was a nest in the grass and they were just hatched and a snake was eating them."

"Well, take it easy," Mama said. "Nobody's eating *you*." She let go of Rosie and went back to the stove. "Good thing, probably. Those pheasants are getting like weeds. They eat too much of everybody's corn."

"What?" Rosie said.

"I said; 'Good thing. They eat too much of everybody's corn.' Some of them ought to die. Now get the table set."

"*You* ought to die," Rosie said, but not aloud. "You never understand anything, and *you* ought to die." Something in her throat was screaming though her mouth didn't form a word. She had a quick vision of Mama dead, felled by a rock, of Mama gone, and herself confidently fixing the meals, wearing high heels, buying lipstick and movie magazines. In a blur, she saw an enormous snake strike and sink its fangs in her mother's leg. Then she bolted from the room.

She finished sobbing over the bathroom sink. Her face, when she raised it to the mirror, was puffy and tired. She took the washcloth and bathed it in cool water. Her whole body was damp and sweaty; she could feel a trickle start down the middle of her chest, and her crotch felt sticky. She removed first her blouse and then her skirt and began to run the cool cloth all over. She pulled off her underpants. The crotch was stained with a dark, thick smear of blood. In the first, frightened moment, she didn't know what it was. She was bleeding—perhaps dying. Then she thought, *It's the curse.* Mary Lerner had said that was why you needed the Kotex machine. "Give yourself another year," she said, "you'll see."

But this wasn't another year. This was this year. "I got the curse," Rosie said, almost aloud. But Mary had said, "You just bleed. It runs out your third hole. That's all. No big deal." This didn't look like "just bleeding." It had a funny smell. It looked slimy and cold and almost black. What came from inside her looked like blood smeared over a writhing black skin.

She felt her stomach rise in a great heave. She turned to the stool and reached to turn up the seat, but blackness came from the right side of her and spread to the region in front of her eyes. She had never fainted before, but she knew it was happening. Something buzzed on the side of her head, and she could feel herself fall.

Rosie did not eat dinner that night. She drove instead to Sylvan Lake and watched the light wane and the twilight intensify into a kind of preternatural quiet. She could look at it now—at the memory of the snake and the pheasant chick—at the little girl whose longings stretched across the border into womanhood. This was the Rosie who had been lost, the Rosie of long, brown legs and smuggled lipstick, the Rosie who asked questions and dreamed dreams, the Rosie with a diary full of fantasies. This was the Rosie who had wished her mother dead, who had killed that day one destroyer of secret beauty and called down death upon another.

Rosie saw Mama's face turn from the sink, and she stepped from the clarity into a pool of shame. It was a terrible thing to wish your mother dead, a terrible sin. There was nothing worse than to kill father, mother, to take the life of those who had given life to you. "Your mother entered the shadow of death to bring you into the world," Sister Ignacia said in fourth grade. Rosie hadn't known what that meant, but she pictured something towering and mysterious. This was what she had sinned against that summer afternoon; this was the life she had taken.

But she hadn't. Mama hadn't died, logic said. Mama hadn't died until twenty years later. She, Rosie, had been a child, with a child's untempered rage, and that rage had done Mama no real harm; Mama had gone on washing canning jars. And she, Rosie, had gone upstairs, had sobbed to the mirror in the bathroom. When the swoon came, she had believed it was death coming to claim her.

There were more swoons after that, but she half expected them —she half expected punishment for a sin she couldn't quite remember: she forgot the snake, forgot her own curses. School seemed harder that fall, and there were menstrual cramps. She had to study for Confirmation class, and gradually she forgot the diary. The stories wouldn't have come true anyway—not for a girl subject to fits—so it was all just as well—except that someone within her was gone now. Mama had chosen good crops over the promise of a pheasant's wing, and for that Rosie had never forgiven her—did not forgive her now. Mama had said beauty was irrelevant, but Mama didn't die; the only blood that mixed with the blood of the snake was her own.

There were no snakes in her dream that night, only the streets of St. Ives that became steeper and steeper, then gradually moved indoors. She remembered dimly that something was lost, gone, and she couldn't find it. "Oh, what could I have done with it?" she said as she wound down stairway after stairway. She didn't like this place; the light was sorrowful. When she reached the bottom she was in the school cafeteria, facing the stainless steel cooler. "Oh, there's no milk," she thought, "no milk for the Elsie Cow pitcher." She opened the door, which stretched to her feet, and stepped into a walk-in cooler. All around her were frosty racks, and all were empty. The light was brighter ahead, and she walked into a shining room that was bare except for a coffin set up on hay bales. Ray was in the coffin, but his name was Raymond. His curly hair was slicked back, and his fingers were wound with a black rosary. Raymond was white and stiff and dead.

Now I won't have to go alone, Rosie thought. *Now Raymond can go with me.*

"Do you love him?" Death asked.

Rosie was not surprised to hear him standing behind and to the left of her, just out of her sight. This was Death, she knew, and you could not lie to him. "Yes," she said. "Yes, I love him."

"Ha ha!" said Raymond. He sat up in the coffin and threw the rosary aside. His eyes gleamed in the white mask of his face. "Ha! I told you she would say it!"

He leaped out of the coffin and was gone. Death was still waiting at the corner of her eye. Rosie turned her head away from him. The room had become a corridor with a shining floor and stainless steel walls. It's so cold, Rosie thought, and now there's no one to meet me.

"Do you forgive him?" Death asked.

"No," Rosie said. "No, he's a liar."

"Then you can't go with him," Death said. "You come with me." He moved up beside her and reached for her hand. . . .

Rosie groped for the bed lamp, knocking the shade askew. The light blinded her for a moment, and then she was able to focus on her left hand which was unsinged, unblemished—which had not touched death after all. She sat huddled in the bed, still feeling the chill of the dream, and wondered what she ought to do. It was 4:00 A.M. It was too early to get up, but she did not want to sleep again—did not want to chance going back into the stainless cooler which was really a coffin, an entombment where only Death would take her hand.

"Do you forgive him?" Death asked.

"No," she said again. She wanted to forgive him, but how was it possible? How could she forgive a man who had betrayed not only her but his very own wife? A picture began to form of a female corpse that looked remarkably like Ray lying on a stark white bed. The corpse looked very sad. . . .

No. That wasn't right. . . . Ray's wife wasn't dead. She was alive somewhere in Illinois, breathing into the dark night of a nursing home. *If I knew what she looked like*, Rosie thought, *if I knew if she forgave him* . . .

She threw back the covers and went to the dresser where she had left the atlas. She remembered one detail from that last, awful night with Ray. It was all she would need to know: the nursing home was in a town called Normal. It was south of Chicago— two long days of driving. She got a pencil from her purse and traced a route that avoided St. Ives and dropped down through Iowa. She folded the atlas, put on her clothes, drew open the drapes, and waited for the light.

Chapter XXIV

THE TEA DID NOTHING FOR ROSIE'S HEADACHE. IT HAD BEEN POUNDing when she awoke sometime long before dawn. She had lain there for perhaps an hour; she did not want to turn on any lights. When the air had brightened enough to see bottles in the medicine chest, she took three aspirin; when it was lighter still, she pulled from the closet a checked housedress she had not worn for almost a year and went down to make some tea. She had hardly slept at all.

She had been all right on the long drive home from Illinois yesterday. The hazy numbness had come down and stayed there, and she drove with the kind of dumb endurance women have for menial tasks, mile after mile, hour after hour. It was not until Mason City late in the afternoon that she began to panic. How could she drive into St. Ives? How could she ever buy gas or groceries, walk down the street without averting her eyes? How could she live in a town where everything was electrified with memories? She pulled off the highway and ate chicken-in-the-basket at a Country Kitchen, coaxing the haze to come back again. When it didn't, she found an outdoor theatre, locked all the car doors, slunk low in the seat, and watched a grainy rerun of *North by Northwest*. By the time it was over, it was ten P.M.; she would not get to St. Ives until after midnight.

She thought of turning off her car lights once she pulled off the highway, but if anyone was still on the street, that would only attract more attention. She circled around the edge of the town where all the windows were dark and sleeping, turned off the car lights when she reached the alley, and concealed the car behind a closed garage door. She entered the house as she might enter a public building, feeling that it was not hers, but that she would not be thrown out.

She had awakened with a headache, and now she sat in the kitchen with uncombed hair, swirling cold tea in a cup. The curtains above the sink had faded, she noticed. She had made them from checked gingham during the years Mama was sick; maybe they had faded long ago. Everything was faded: her housedress, her skin, her sense of being the competent woman who had found the nursing home in Normal, who had told the staff she was a cousin of Mrs. Bowen and had come to see "how Marilyn is." The other Rosie was no longer with her, it seemed; she had blanched before forty years of accumulated memory, forty years of choosing the safe, the accepted thing. She had vanished in the haze overnight, and none of her color remained.

Rosie traced with her finger the pattern of the plastic tablecloth. What would she do today? What would she ever do? The tablecloth had cracked where Jack once set the teakettle on it; now it was drying out. The paint on the radiators was beginning to chip. The pounding in her head was like the pounding in a radiator that needs to be bled. She thought for a crazy moment that bleeding the pipes might help, but then the pounding shifted back to her head, and blended with pounding at the back door. She kept her eyes on the radiator. Between the pipes there were little cobwebs that were beginning to sag like mournful, elderly beards. She had never noticed them before. The pounding came louder.

"Rosie, open up." It was Father Griffin's voice. She started up out of long habit, then sank back into the chair. She couldn't face him. He would know where she'd been; he would think she'd been dumped, deserted . . . and that was as shameful as living in sin. What could she tell him? What could she tell anyone? Why had she come back here at all?

"Rosie, I've got to talk to you. Rosie?" The voice was sounding impatient. She would have to do something. She stepped over to the little mirror on the shelf above the sink and ran her fingers through her hair.

"Rosie, dammit, open the door!" The voice was lower but more emphatic. "I know what happened. Ray called me. You want me to keep yelling till the whole town hears?"

She opened the door. The priest looked the way he always looked in his light blue sweatshirt—only a little more concerned and annoyed. His freckles hadn't faded in the ages she'd been gone. "Ray called you?" she said.

"Yes," he said. "He was worried." The annoyance left the young man's face, and he reached for her hand. "Rosie, I'm sorry," he said. "What a rotten deal."

They stood for a moment balanced in the doorway. She had hated him, she remembered—he had deceived her—but she could feel no hatred now, only a sense that *he* did not hate *her*. "Can I come in?" the young priest said. She looked away and motioned to the kitchen table. When he was seated, she sat across from him but didn't look up. Her finger began tracing the pattern in the tablecloth again.

"He called from Illinois," the young priest said, "to see if you got back all right. He feels terrible, Rosie—and he *should*, I guess—but mostly he was worried. We all worried—you weren't here, and you'd checked out of the motel. . . ."

Rosie traced intricate loops in the yellow lace that was printed on the white plastic. She did not shift her gaze, but the pattern was beginning to blur.

"Do you want to talk about what happened?" the priest said very gently.

"No . . ." Rosie said. She could hear the quaver in her voice, and, in the silence that followed, tears were falling on the hand that now traced blindly over the surface beneath it. She felt a hand cover hers and stop its movement, and she brought her other hand up to brace her head. Why was she crying now when she had cried so little in all those days of pain? Why was she breaking down before the simple gentleness of someone she ought not even to trust? Mama would not have caused this torrent if she were here, or Dora. . . . "You make your bed, you lie on it," Mama would have said. "Listen, I knew there was something funny about that man," Dora would have told her. "Lucky you found out when you did. . . ."

After a time, Rosie pulled her hand away from the priest's and fumbled in her pocket for a handkerchief. "I'm sorry," she said.

The priest put his hands in his pockets and leaned back on the chair. "I wish there was something I could say," he said. "I wish I could tell you love doesn't hurt this much." There was an odd tone in his voice too, and Rosie looked at him over the handkerchief. Murmuring sounds from a dark cafeteria flashed through her memory—a tangle of black-clothed limbs. . . . She went to the sink to hide her discomposure, filled the teakettle, and put it on the stove. "Is . . ." she said, her back to him. "Is . . . does Carol Ann know too?"

"Yeah," he said softly. "You mean a lot to her, Rosie. She was really worried. She left this for you." When Rosie turned, he was holding a rumpled envelope.

"Left?"

"She's gone. To Minneapolis. For good." He put his hands back in his pockets and stared at his shoes.

Rosie turned over the envelope; her name was written in a confident, rather boyish hand. "Why didn't you go with her?" she said. "You love her."

She heard him sigh and looked up to see him rock the chair forward and clench his hands on the table. "I wanted to," he said, "but I couldn't. That's not my life, Rosie, I'm a priest. . . ." He looked up and smiled rather wryly. "A poor excuse for one, you're probably thinking, but there it is, nonetheless. . . ." He looked at his hands again, and talked more easily: "I don't want to live my life alone—you know that—but right now I had to make a choice. . . . Things will change—they have to—but that could take years and years . . . I couldn't ask her to wait. . . ." He looked up again. "I won't be seeing her anymore," he said quickly, "so you'll have to let her know you're all right."

Rosie nodded. "Why do things have to hurt so much?" she said.

The priest shook his head. "I don't know," he said, "I don't know." There was an awkward moment, and she reached for the teapot and the instant coffee.

"Those boys . . ." she said, "the ones in the accident?"

The priest took the cup she held out to him. "The Simons boy was killed," he said. "You knew that?" Rosie nodded. "Mickey Runkle is still in the hospital. They transferred him to Sioux Falls for more surgery on the leg. . . . He may have a permanent limp, his sister told me, but he won't lose it. And the Roekamp kid who was with them came out pretty good—a concussion and some broken bones."

"It's really too bad . . ." Rosie said, sitting down with her coffee.

"Yeah," he said, and they both fell silent. The priest took a long swallow of coffee. "Open it," he said; "open your letter." She slid her finger under the flap. There was a Minneapolis address at the top of the page and a date a week earlier.

Rosie—

Jim told me about Ray's call. I am so sorry—I had hoped you were off to a happy new life. I wish I knew some words that could soak up pain. We could all use them.

I just wanted to tell you that there are three openings for teachers' aides in the school where I'll be teaching. I don't mean to tell you how to run your life, but you said once that you wished you had a job with kids, and it might be good for you to get out of St. Ives for a while and start fresh someplace else. Please come. I'll be lonely at first. You can stay in my apartment until you find one of your own. I found one with oak woodwork and French doors.

We all love you.

Carol

"Did she tell you about the job in the Cities?" the priest asked. Rosie nodded. "Do it," he said. "Go. It's what you need."

Rosie shook her head. The other Rosie might have been able to manage Minneapolis, but the other Rosie was gone, and this one could not even manage St. Ives. "I can't," she said, and knew she needed a reason. "Look at me," she glanced down at the faded housedress, the bedroom slippers. "I'm not somebody who can move to the Cities. People are different there—they've been around. . . ."

The priest looked a little disgusted. "You own better clothes than that," he said bluntly. "What are you saving them for? And who says they're so different? Christ, Rosie, don't sell yourself short! Just because you're down right now, you don't need to . . ." he stopped. "Sorry," he said more quietly, "I should give you a chance to recover before I start yelling, shouldn't I? But I mean it, Rosie. The way out of St. Ives is the same road as the way in—you just go in the other direction. Look," he said, "if I were smart, I'd try to keep you here—most of my friends are gone, you know—and Dora *did* make sure to say your job is waiting, but . . ."

"Does she—?"

The priest put up his hand to stop her. "Yeah," he said. "She knows. Don't ask me how—I didn't tell her—but she knows."

Rosie laughed. "Well," she said, "that will save me the trouble of posting a sign. I can just sit tight and let the whole town say, 'Poor Rosie . . .' "

"That's why you should go," the priest said. "You don't need that."

"I know that, Father, but——"

"Jim," he said. "It's about time you called me Jim. And you *have* been around—you've been *somewhere* for the past two weeks. . . ."

"I was in the Black Hills," she said. "I just stayed there."

"The whole time?"

"Well, most of it. I saw everything in the guidebook. And then I went to Illinois. . . ."

"You went to see Ray?"

She shook her head rapidly. "No. No, I won't ever see him. I went to see his wife."

The priest looked at her with astonishment. "You . . . why? I mean, why did you do that?"

"I don't know," Rosie said. "I just needed to see her. I needed to see what she looked like, and well, I guess I thought it might help make some sense of it. . . ."

Father Griffin was shaking his head slowly from side to side and beginning to smile. "You're a wonder!" he said. "You just got in the car and went to see his wife?"

"Yeah," she said, smiling a little in spite of herself. "I told them I was her cousin."

"Did she . . . was she conscious?"

"No," Rosie said. "It was kind of awful. She was just lying there with all these tubes in her head, and tubes in her arm. She never moved—I don't know if she could. Her arms were all wasted away—no muscle at all. The bones looked like they belonged on a bird. . . ."

"Did they tell you anything—the nurses?"

"No. Just that she wasn't in pain. And that it might be any time. . . ."

"Rosie," the priest said, "I know you don't want to think about this now, but someday she *will* die, and Ray will be free. . . ."

She felt her eyes fill again, and put up her hand to stop him.

"Okay," the priest said, "okay. . . . But he does love you, Rosie, and I don't think you should say 'never.' He was wrong, and he knows it, but if you saw his wife, maybe it will help you understand. . . ."

"I *do* understand," she said, though the tears were contorting her voice. "That's the problem. I understand, but I still can't forgive him. I want to hurt him—I want to get back. I looked at that woman, and I thought, 'She isn't even a person anymore— why don't they just take the tubes out and let her die?' But I couldn't do it either—not if I'd loved her. And I thought, 'What if it was Ray? What if he were lying there?' I couldn't come every day and watch—I knew that—I'd have to do what he did and go away. . . ."

"But then you——"

She shook her head. "I can't forgive him . . . that's what's the matter with me. I can't forgive. . . ."

There was a silence, and she retrieved the handkerchief from her pocket and blew her nose.

"Have you forgiven me?" the priest said softly. She stopped crying but didn't answer. "I hurt you, Rosie. The shock on your face that night was pretty plain."

"Yes," she said. "Yes, I forgive you. There are worse things than love. . . ."

"And Ray was guilty of loving you. . . ." the priest said. She didn't answer. She looked hard at the pattern on the tablecloth. "When you were gone," he said across the quiet, "I had a long talk with Dora—or maybe I should say *she* had a long talk with *me*. She said a lot of things—about your being ill when you were young—about your mother. . . . Life has been a little rough on you, I guess."

Rosie blew her nose again and kept her eyes down.

"What about your mother?" he said. "Can you forgive her?"

She nodded. "Yes," she said. "She was just frightened, I guess, or greedy. . . . She didn't want to be alone."

"And you allowed all that to happen, Rosie. I don't mean when you were a child—you allowed it to go on when you were an adult. A lot of years . . ." he said. She could sense him shifting in his chair. "I have to try to forgive my own excesses, Rosie," he said, "and it's not always easy, as you know . . ."

"And you want to know if I forgive myself?" she said.

"Yes," he said. "Are you sure it's not Rosie you can't forgive?"

"I don't know," she said. She looked at her hand lying on the tablecloth where the morning sun was just beginning to catch it, and she saw the green and purple flickers of candlelight that had played across her hand in Nazareth Caves. She had forgiven herself then in that muted light—she had forgiven the Rosie who risked, and who ran after pheasant wings, and who got her into trouble. It had not occurred to her that she would need to forgive the Rosie who spent twenty years waiting for life, who had always chosen safety, who was always willing to submit. . . . "I don't know," she said again. "I don't know."

Father Griffin was smiling when she looked up. "You can think about it when you're packing," he said.

"I haven't *un*packed," she said.

She walked with the priest across the living room as he was leaving, across the carpet where she had tumbled blocks as a child, where she had steadied Jack when he was nineteen and came home late, lurching through the door—across the carpet where Ray had stood so many times. . . . She did not know if she would continue to walk here. The old walnut door opened easily, as it always had, and they stepped out into sunshine. She ran her hand over the warm top rail of the porch as she watched the priest walk to the end of the block, turn, and wave. But he didn't wave. He winked and joined thumb to middle finger in a sign the school kids made to signify "You did it!" or "Good show!"

She smiled as his broad back moved a little clumsily into the middle distance. She wished she could be as sure of things as he was; but then, perhaps he wasn't sure, perhaps he just kept moving. . . . The sun was a warm surprise on her back, hitting her directly, and when she turned to the east, she remembered that the trellis was gone. She had dragged it off one night centuries ago. She would need new flowers for that spot; she would need some shrubs to landscape the walk, and she ought to have someone paint the trim on the house.

Inside, she walked through rooms that had not changed, yet were charged with a difference, a newness, a kind of nostalgic sadness she could not even name. She walked up the stairs slowly. There was the desk Pa had used to record the comings and goings of their financial life; there was Jack's room, the closet empty now, the door open. She picked up the impatiens plant at the end of the hall. It had died for lack of watering, but this was a bad year for impatiens anyway. In her own room, she ran her hand over the quilt her grandmother had made, then flopped one of the suitcases up on her bed and began to unload the dirty laundry. Out came the burgundy pants, the blouses, the sweater she had snagged on a branch in the woods. One dress she had left wadded in a ball on a floor in Rapid City, but everything else was here. The priest was right: she had some decent clothes—why was she saving them? She kicked off her bedroom slippers and pulled the checked housedress over her head. She wanted to try the linen sheath to see how it fitted—to see if the weight she had lost made any difference.

When she came down the stairs to look at herself in the long walnut mirror, she was wearing hose and pumps. Her hair was combed back a little more sharply than usual, and though it needed trimming, the style gave more definition to her face. She wasn't beautiful. Even though she had applied makeup with a freer hand, she would turn no heads on the street. But the linen dress fitted well. It had classic lines, she decided, sleek and professional. It would be a good dress to wear in a city . . . a good dress for job interviews. . . .

But if she went to St. Paul, if she took that job at the school, no one would know where to find her. She saw herself sending her address to Dora, to Father Griffin, to Aunt Nellie. . . . She could see her pen moving across a sheet of thick white paper: "Ray," it would say, "I have taken a job as a teacher's aide in St. Paul and am living in an apartment at this address. . . ." But what would she say next: Please don't write? I need time to think? I don't know what the future holds? She would want to say: "Much of what you gave me was beautiful . . ." but that might imply too much. Perhaps she could say simply: "I just wanted you to know where I am."

Rosie looked at the face in the mirror and saw a smile begin to form. She might not go to St. Paul. She might take a long trip to Hawaii—she had over a thousand dollars left—or she might take a bookkeeping course and get a job in Worthington. She might even go back to the cafeteria and watch the children grow up. . . .

She brushed back a stray strand of hair, and fastened her gold earrings. The woman whose blue-gray eyes looked back at her from the mirror was not young, but she was attractive, pleasant. She had an air that was competent and mature. She looked like a woman you would hire, Rosie thought—like a friend you could trust. She tried to see herself as an employer might, a school superintendent, for instance, sitting in his big leather chair in an office cushioned with the quiet of a summer afternoon. Typewriters would hum in the distance like cicadas, and the air would carry the slight vibration of busy people doing significant things. There would be a smooth oak door on which she would knock, and the man's face when he looked up over his glasses would betray just a hint of pleasure at the dignity and poise of the woman before him. "Good afternoon," he would say.

"Good afternoon," she would respond, extending her hand. "My name is Rosemary Deane."